BRUSHING WITH DANGER

DANGER

The Awakening

KATHLEEN RENEE CONWAY

To everyone who believed in me, put up with my shenanigans, and listened to me cry. Especially Jazmine, who without your help this book would not be possible. To my husband, Brian who waited up till wee hours of the morning for me to quit typing to escort me and Jazzy from the Camper in the dark, as well as Ashton who was always telling me "You got this ma." Thank you and I love you.

To all my readers, thank you, truly you are all amazing and I love you all.

CHAPTER 1

It's 6:30 A.M. and my alarm is driving me up the wall again. Was it four or five when I got home this morning? Time seems to be running together for me. I can still smell the smoke from cigars, and cigarettes from the clients at the house last night. Shit, I need to get up, but I just want to sleep. Duty calls however, so I must get out of bed.

I will take a quick shower, then get dressed and do my make-up, because God knows I need to hide the dark circles that have mysteriously appeared over the last two hours. Haha, now I am laughing at myself, that's just great. I'm sounding like a few of my clients at the center. Oh well, off to the shower I go. The water is warm this morning, running down, soothing the sore muscles that were worked, mmmmm, that is good, it is always good. Coffee? Oh hell, I forgot to put it on, oh well, I will stop by the coffee shop on the way.

Heading out the door, I realize that I left all my clothes from the night before in the dining room, of all places. Shit, now I have to pick them up before Sarah comes home. Sarah is a nice girl that I leased a room to a couple of months back. She is young, full of life, and likes to party. I do not have to worry about her coming home usually till about noon. I turn back into the house and pick up my things, stash them in my room, and head out the door.

Slow traffic, great, I am already twenty minutes behind this morning, and this is not making it better. Oh well... What can you do, right? I hate traffic in the mornings, it takes me an hour to make a one-mile trip, which leaves me with too much time to reflect on things otherwise forgotten. Things like the new gentleman that visited the house last night. He was tall, slender, and very handsome. He seemed like such a timid thing, that I almost passed him on to someone else. I really did not think that he was my forte. Was I ever wrong....

Jeremy walked in and asked what our price was, Sereena told him, and he just smiled. He filled out his paperwork, which everyone is required to fill out and showed his credentials (which consist of H.I.V. and

Hepatitis test results.) Sereena, then asked him what his taste in pleasure was.

He laughed and said, "all of it ". That made me giggle a little when she told me. She buzzed my room and asked me to come down. She told Jeremy that she had a special lady for him that she thought would fit all his moods. I walked down the stairs and to my surprise there is a gentle looking man standing at the counter. I wondered as I walked toward them if he was new to this world of pain and pleasure. As I approached, I looked at his face trying to see some hardness of life, but there just was not anything to reveal what he had hidden inside. Sereena introduced us, and I asked him if he liked to be top or bottom?

He replied, "I enjoy both sides of the coin, however, I do like my woman to scream for me, loudly."

I smiled, a soft smile as the pressure gripped me low at the thought of him being able to make me scream.

He looked at me and asked, "That's not a problem for you, is it?" I had to laugh at that.

After a few moments of conversation, I thought about Ami, she likes screaming, just because she thinks it is fun.

Then Jeremy cocked his head, and said to me, "Yes, I think you will do nicely."

That grabbed my attention. Was there something inside of me waiting to hear him say that? Subconsciously, I mean? When he looked at me, it was like he reached all the way inside of me and caressed me deep down. I started feeling that warmth rising up my thighs, and the pressure in my most intimate parts began to tighten.

"Follow me," I said.

We walked up the stairs and as we did, I could feel his gaze upon my back. It was like a soft summer's warmth, everywhere his eyes touched. What is it about this man, which makes me so distracted? As we came to my door, I turned and looked into his eyes. What I saw there made the pressure tighter still and the heat stronger. It was readiness, and desire. This could be interesting, I thought to myself.

My room is one of the bigger rooms here. Basically, because I have the most stuff to fill it with. Me being into so many different things, a girl must have her toys. I have a king-size bed in the center of the room, and only one window on the east wall, covered with black curtains trimmed in red. On the north wall, I have a set of wall mounted shackles, one for each wrist and one for each ankle. I had them lined with leather, so they do not cut the skin during rough encounters. Besides these I have several toys hanging on the wall on both sides. Included in these are: whips, cat of nine tails, shoehorn, a couple of different shaped paddles, three floggers, a Cuban quirt, a small punishing rod, a large rod and four sets of nipple clamps. On the south wall, there is a very erotic picture hanging. Behind it is where I keep my cash, in a safe. I have handcuffs hanging on each side of the door. I have a canopy over my bed with four English style posts and handcuffs on each of them. The carpet is a deep burgundy with green print embedded in it.

I opened the door and stepped inside; Jeremy followed like a good little pet. He slammed the door behind him. It startled me, and I spun around to find him smiling yet again. Ok, I have my panic button, I thought, as I seen the look on his face. Quit overreacting. Just breathe Serraid, just breathe.

Why did this young man make me so damn nervous, and completely turned on at the same time? Was he doing it intentionally? Was he even aware of what he was doing?

He asked me my name, I told Him I was Serrie, that is what I always told my clients here. Makes it less personal if you know what I mean.

He said, "Serrie, that has such a ring to it, and it's incredibly sexy ". I told him thank you and walked over to the bed. I told him to put his wallet and coat on the shelf by the door. As he took his coat off, I could almost see the slight muscle tone under his shirt. Was this guy for real? I mean, does he expect me to hurt him, really? Could I? I mean he seems so tender.

"What was that?" I asked as I realized that he had said something, and I missed it. I felt embarrassed.

He said, "I want to chain you to the wall, and play hard tonight. I want to give you something that you have been wanting for a long time Serrie, yet no one has given to you." At those words he moved towards me with hasty steps, much faster than I pictured him moving.

Before I knew it, he had my hair wrapped in his hand and pulling my head back, kissing my throat. He said, "I want to hold you by this throat of yours, and shove myself deep inside of you, as hard as I can, until you scream for me to stop." My knees instantly became weak, and I could feel the moisture starting to build between my legs. Where the hell did this guy come from?!

I struggled as I tried to speak without letting him know that he had affected me so strongly. My voice was shaking when I said, "You were given the rules here, no sex, just play. That is why it is called tease and denial. So, your little plan of driving deep inside of me is not going to happen here." He laughed at me!

He looked at me with a solemn look on his face and said, "I know the rules, Mistress, but rules are made to be broken." His voice is so deep, and husky when he speaks. It touches me everywhere inside, like water does a vase when you fill it.

I struggled to breathe, part of me wanted this, yet a part of me remembered the little girl, cowering in the corner wanting the horror to stop. I stopped that memory before it could surface. It made me so angry that I would remember something like that right now. I decided right then, that yes, I would allow him to do as he pleased to me. I will not remember that memory of so long ago tonight. The pain of the memories trying to rise countering my better judgement and making me want to drown them away. Could he do it? Screw it I am going to drown these fucking memories before they get me.

He must have seen the change in my eyes. My mask covers my face completely. I have eye holes, nose holes, and a hole to speak out of. I like it that way because some of our clients would know me. I truly do not want anyone to recognize me on the street. My secrecy is very important to me; it always has been.

Jeremy grabbed my arms, hard enough to bruise, and shoved me against the wall. He cuffed one wrist and then the other. My heart was beating too fast now, as the reality of the situation set in. He ran his hands down my arms, and down my waist to my hips. He squeezed my hips sternly. He then moved his hands lower to my thighs, then my calves, to my ankles. He chained one, then the other, all the while he was breathing in the center of my core. His breath felt warm, and so good. I could feel pulsating between my legs, growing stronger with each moment. He was making me want him increasingly. I moved my hips out, just a little, to allow him to press into me. He moaned, as he did, it was like an explosion went off in my groins. I must calm down, I told myself. Losing myself in moments like these usually never end well. I have such a tight grip on my emotions, even the sexual ones, I normally do not find someone who can break through and take my emotions and play with them.

He looked up at me and smiled, as if he knew exactly what was going on right now. He stood up and pressed against me. I could feel the hardness pressed against my thigh. My body reacted and I pressed into him. He grabbed the whip off the wall and took three steps back. He looked at the whip, as if contemplating on what to do with it, waiting for me to protest. I said nothing; from the surprise of this man that I did not see coming. I am intrigued by what might happen. MMMM, this is going to be fun.

Then he looked at me and said, "This is going to hurt a little."

He drew back and the first sting was not so bad, it hit me right across the front of my left thigh. Then again, he drew back, this one hurt more, it struck me on my right ribs. The third strike landed on my left arm. He was hitting with such precision, that I knew he had planned this, and yes, he had done this before. With every strike, I became wetter, and my pulse was getting stronger. I wanted this to hurt, to drown out the noise. Shit, I did not even make a safe word. What the hell was I thinking? And with another strike that thought was lost to the quietness. This is when I feel whole, when I do not have to think, do not have to remember, this is what I was made for.

The want, the desire, the need to have him plunge deep and hard was becoming too much. I moaned, and he snapped to attention. He had been looking at the toys on the wall, but when I moaned it distracted him.

He walked over to me, and placed his mouth lightly across where my ear was and said, "Don't worry my lady, I'm going to hurt you till you beg me to stop, then I'm going to fuck you hard enough to make the pain stop as you are screaming your pleasure, washing away all that haunts you." "What!," I said, who is this guy? How could he possibly know about what haunts me? Fear grabbed me right then, did this man know me? I cannot place him anywhere. No groups, no sessions. Damn it! I cannot think while being this aroused. Heart pounding, trying to think. He is not anyone I know. Has someone found out about me and sent him here? I cannot reach my panic button, and I am starting to panic!!

He moved over and undid my shackles and replaced the shackles with my face against the wall. I contemplated on stopping him, but fuck I need this, I need to forget these memories that keep trying to haunt me. God, I am so fucked up. I heard him take something from off the wall, but I could not tell what it was. Suddenly, he hit me. He had chosen the small rod. I could feel it swelling up. It would leave a mark, and at the same time, a moan slipped past my lips as I became warmer and wetter. I could feel my own moisture building in my suit. My pussy twitched with desire. I wanted to feel something, anything, touch me there. Suddenly, he was there behind me, pressing me against the wall. Grabbing my throat, and pulling my hair, he pressed himself against me as hard as he could. I was pretty sure that he did not have his clothes on at this point. He slid his hardness between my legs and against my most sensitive spot, which is when I knew that he was naked. The feeling of him there, pressing against me, blocking my air, and yanking my head spilled me over the first edge.

My legs began to shake as I moaned my pleasure with what air I had left in me against the wall.

He paused, as if to stop and whispered, "You like that don't you? Yes, you do, you just came for me. But my sweet, that was a moan, I want a scream."

As quickly as he was there, he moved away and I heard a chain rattle. I do not remember having a chain anywhere in here. Oh shit! He brought one with him!

"You can't bring outside items into this house!," I yelled. Then it made contact with my ass. DAMN IT! I yelled.

He was behind me again, this time he said, "You are getting closer. Do not worry I bought this today, it is clean."

"You are not supposed to bring things in," I said again my voice shaking with fear mixed with pleasure. Damn my fucked feelings!

He giggled and replied, "I just did my lady, what are you going to do about it right now?"

I thought about that for a moment. It did feel good, so good in fact that the pulse between my thighs was screaming at me by now. The heat was spreading down my legs, making my toes want to move.

"I will allow you to keep it, for now. If I say enough, you must stop. You would do good to remember that rule, it is not to be broken." I stated.

He pressed closer against me, if that were possible, and said, "You would do good to remember, Madame that you are the one chained to the wall, and to remember your place here."

With those words said, he moved away again. He hit me, this time across the back of my thighs. This was harder than the last time, and I wanted to scream enough! Then the feeling spread through me so suddenly it took my breath away. I could not speak; I rode the waves of pleasure as they flooded my senses. My back arched, the need to be touched rode across my body. A wave of pleasure rode up my spine to my throat, until I could breathe again, and I yelled, AGAIN!"

He complied, he hit me again, except this time he hit my ass. It arched my back and my neck, it buckled my knees, until all my weight was being held by my wrists. I then stood back on my feet. The pleasure rode me low, and then high and then low again. I was writhing against the wall, pleading for something to touch my breasts, or my thighs, or even my clit. I needed to be touched, to be brought to release. But I would not give him that satisfaction just yet. My mind was quiet about the past for the first time in a long time. I needed to see what he had next.

As if he could hear my thoughts, Jeremy grabbed the cat of nine tails. He came up behind me and spoke low in my ear. "I'm going to make you want me; I'm going to make you hate me, but most of all I'm going to make you need me."

With that, he stepped back. My pulse was raging against my throat. What did he mean, he is going to make me want and hate and need him? I have had many excellent lovers, why was he so sure of himself? Or is it a front? But God knows I want him right now. I need him to hurt me. He seems to know what I need, and he gives it to me as if on command.

"Please don't stop." I said with a shaken voice, part pleasure, part pain.

He swung back and hit me across the back with the cat. The pleasure spread up and down simultaneously. I rode that wave, until the next strike connected. It hit me across my thighs. My knees buckled again, and I could feel the strong pulse between my legs. I was going to cum again. I welcomed the orgasm, as he hit me again and brought me screaming with my pleasure. Without thinking, I begged him to plunge into me. I begged for his touch. He hit me again across the legs. I wrenched and bucked, I needed him, right now, God, I needed him inside of me right now!

"Please take off my suit, please Jeremy strip me down, and let me feel it on my skin."

He walked over and unzipped the suit that was keeping me in one piece, or at least that is how it felt. He started pulling it off my arms. As my arms were released, he chained them back. When both arms were free of the suit, he pulled it down my back until just the top of my ass was bare. He stopped. I heard him move backwards. He hit me again on the bare skin, which was still raw from all the other blows. It was like riding an ocean of pleasure. I came and screamed my pleasure out. He walked over and pulled the suit down to my ankles. Then he hit my ass. I could feel my muscles flinch as he hit them. My orgasm came so fast that I could not breathe. There was no sound that I could make. He hit me again, and the orgasm gripped me harder. Then something happened.

His mood changed. I could feel it, like the air I was breathing. He hit me again, and this time there was no pleasure from it. I felt the sharp sting of the pain as it rose through my body, with the second hit, I could feel the tears starting to build in my eyes. How could this be happening? How could I be so warm and then hurt so much? Why was he doing this? I asked him to stop, told him that he was hurting me.

He said, "That's exactly what I want to do." His voice was different, colder somehow.

Panic started in my throat and tightened my chest. My button, I did not have the chance to get it before he chained me to the wall. Shit! How could I be so careless?! He could kill me, and no one would know it until they found me. Shit, shit, shit! My mind started running and I was scared as hell when the pain struck again. This time it was across my upper back. He hit me hard enough that it took the breath from me. I let out what scream I could manage. Another one hit me across the legs, my legs fell out from under the weight of the blow. I cried out, asking him to stop. Another blow hit my ass.

This time I screamed, "ENOUGH! Please stop!" He did not stop; he hit me again. This time I was crying, I could feel the tears running down my face. I pleaded and begged him to stop.

Nothing happened for a moment. Then I felt him press against me. I could feel the hardness of him, and I was glad that I was wet enough to accommodate him. He slid between my thighs and moaned as he found it moist. He grabbed my hips and squeezed them. The pain was receding, and pleasure was starting to replace it. He reached around and put a set of clamps on my nipples. The sensation went right to my lower parts. He pressed harder against me until I was completely trapped against the wall. His hand slid down my stomach, and past my navel. He found my opening and started playing gently at first, then he slid a finger inside. He grabbed me there, cradling my pussy in his hand. He moved his finger slowly in and out his thumb rubbing my clit. Then harder, he began to drive his finger inside. I could feel myself opening for him. The tension built so strong that I was certain that I was going to cum again. Then suddenly, he stopped.

I bucked my hips, begging him with my body to keep going. He knew what I wanted. He took himself, hard and throbbing and slammed it into me. The feeling of him sliding across my lips, and deep inside threw me over the edge. I started screaming my pleasure to him, bucking my hips. He grabbed my hips and pressed me solidly against the wall, so that I could not move. He said, "Not yet."

He slid out till just his head was inside, then he slammed himself deep inside again. He held it there, pressed as deep as he could go. I tried to move; I wanted to move and ride the waves of the pleasure that was building again. He then started moving in and out, faster harder until He just stopped.

He unfastened me from the wall and shoved me to the bed. He cuffed me to the bed posts, and said, "I want to look into your face when you cum again for me. I want to see the pleasure move across your eyes. I want you, to see mine when I release mine inside of you."

With that, he drove himself deep inside of me. My back arched with the pleasure of the feeling of him inside. He moved hard and fast until the edge was no more, and I was falling down the pleasure of it all. He held my head so that I could not turn it away and he made me look at him. He plunged deeper and harder until I screamed my pleasure to him, clasping my hands open and closed, needing to tear my pleasure into something with my nails. I felt him shudder, as he plunged one more time and he was lost inside of me. I could feel him spill over me, through me, all at once. His release drove me again, as we rode our pleasure together.

I lay there trying to slow my breathing before I passed out from a lack of oxygen. Right now, there was no pain, only pleasure. I knew that later all the marks on my body were going to hurt, but right now I do not care. All I could think about was how in one time He had become something I had never had.

When he rose and released me from my bonds, he smiled at me and said, "You, my lady, were wonderful."

Then he got dressed, walked to the shelf, got his wallet, and laid some cash on the table and left. Just like that, he was gone. I sat there trying to figure out what the hell had just happened. I mean, this was not part of the deal here. I never fucked my clients. I saved that for people I chose outside of this place, but never here.

I got up and got dressed and headed downstairs. Sereena looked at me and smiled. She asked me if he was as gentle as he appeared. I told her, hell no, he was amazing.

She walked over and whispered in my ear, "Did you fuck the client, Serraid?"

I looked at her and simply said, "Yes."

She smiled and patted my back, and said, "It's about fucking time girl."

With that I told her I was taking a break. I went to my room and cleaned up the place. I got lost in the memory of what just happened. I could feel the heat relight inside of me.

I unzipped my suit and started rubbing my breasts. I slid my hand down farther until I found my clit and I wanted to release again. Wasn't earlier enough? I guess not, I rubbed my fingers over the slippery top, until I could feel my orgasm coming. I rubbed faster and slid a finger inside, then I felt myself pulse around my finger until I was moaning my release to myself. I fell asleep. I woke with a tap on my door, when I realized that my suit was still undone. I quickly got it zipped back up and answered the door. It was Sereena, she asked if I was ever going to go home. I said yes and grabbed my purse and left.

CHAPTER 2

I would like a double chocolate latte please. Ok, it is seven forty-five, I have fifteen minutes to get my coffee and get the rest of the four blocks to work. The coffee is not bad here and it is convenient so, it will have to do.

"That will be six dollars please." said the cashier. Ok, got my coffee, now it is time to fly to work.

At the center, Cheryl was sitting at her desk looking at me with her beady eyes. She is sixty-three years old, and she dresses in clothes that were made for people in their forties. She always wears her hair in a bun, which contradicts her clothing, but she does not seem to be bothered by it or aware of that, I am not sure which. Sometimes, I do not like her much. She always checks on my time and is always sticking her nose where it really does not belong.

As I walked by her, she gave a, humph sound, right before she said, "Someone had a late-night last night, didn't she?"

I smiled and said, "That, Cheryl is my business and no one else 's."

I walked to my door and fumbled with my keys, because She had made me a bit nervous. I think sometimes that she is looking for a reason to get me out of here. Finally, I got the right key, unlocked my door, and went into my office. Whew! I set my stuff on my desk and slumped in my chair and just closed my eyes for a minute. I dislike people nosing around and asking questions. It always makes me feel like I am being interrogated.

My first client is due at eight-thirty, so I started trying to get files updated, and filed away. Who is my first client today? I wondered as I looked at my schedule. Oh, yes, it is Pamela. Pamela is a 22-year-old female, she is five foot ten, very tall for a woman. She has black hair long enough to sit on, and she has deep green, almost emerald eyes. I see her for a cutting habit. She used to work as a prostitute, and now she cuts herself to mark herself so no one will want her. She does this when she gets angry or upset. She now works at Penny Price; it is a little thrift store on the other side of town. She has worked there for the last three years. She got off the streets when a man named Anthony met her on a corner, walking his way home from work. He had missed the bus that night and just so happened to walk Pamela's way. She offered him her services, which he declined, and in return offered her free room and board, to help clean her off the drugs and help her obtain employment at a legal profession. She was tired of feeling like a used-up piece of paper, so she accepted his offer. She has been at Anthony's house ever since.

"Come in," I said, when I heard someone tap on my door.

It was Donald. Donald is one of the other counselors here at You Are New Center. He is 57 years old, married with three children. Don is six foot two, there is grey hair where his black hair used to be at one time when he was younger. It makes for the perfect salt and pepper look.

"Yes, Donald?," I asked as he opened the door.

"Uh-hum, excuse me Serraid for interrupting your morning paperwork, but do you have a moment to speak with me?"

"Why sure, Don, what's on your mind this morning?" I replied as he sat down. Funny he would sit before hearing my reply. Usually, Don was not this eager to speak with me, something had to be important.

"Serraid, over the last couple of weeks you have seemed like you are, how do I say this, pre-occupied mentally. I just want to make sure that you are doing all right. How are you doing? Are you feeling ill? I mean, I am sorry I am rambling. Just, are you doing all right?"

I stared at him, wondering where the hell this had come from. Had Cheryl been talking again? If I find out she has I will have a talk with her myself. "I am doing fine Don. I have been a little tired over the last week or so, but other than that, yes, I am fine."

He looked at me with those professional, I am looking deep inside your head, eyes and said, "Good, I am glad that you are ok. It is just I heard you are showing up later than your usual times, and you are looking a little rough around the edges, so I thought I would stop in and see for myself, if you were all right or not."

I smiled at his newly found concern for me and instantly thinking that me and Cheryl were certainly having a serious talk about this later. I reached over my desk and placed my hand on his and said, "I am all right Don, I promise. Just having some trouble sleeping, that is all. It happens to me from time to time, no biggie. I will be back on track in a couple of days."

With that he stood up and came around my desk and hugged me. He told me he was relieved that I am ok and he was sorry he bothered me. My phone buzzed, and Cheryl announced my client was there for her appointment. I told her I would be up in a minute. I turned to Don, smiled while walking him to the door. I told him that I had to get busy helping troubled people now.

He looked at me and said, "I am glad to have you here Serraid, you do a lot of good with your clients. I have witnessed strong headway with most of them. You are doing a great job. If you ever need anything, even just to talk, you let me know, ok?"

"Ok, I will do that, I promise." He smiled at that, turned, and headed to his office.

I shut my office door and leaned against the door. What the hell is going on this morning! Just who in the hell does Cheryl think she is by going to Donald and telling him this shit! If I did not need my job, I would kick her ass! No, I will speak with her about this between my morning and afternoon clients today. I am going to tell her to keep her damn nose where it belongs! With that, I walked toward the lobby to call Pamela.

Pamela was sitting in the chair, Indian style. She had short cut off shorts on, with a red shirt, and grey sneakers. She had her hair in a ponytail, and her make-up, as always, was too dark. I smiled at her and asked her if she was ready to come talk to me.

She giggled and said, "No, but I have to anyways, if I want to get any better, right?"

"Right," I said smiling. That made her giggle even more.

As we reached my office, Pamela looked at me and frowned. She said, "You don't look like you've had any sleep."

I looked at her with punishing eyes, and said, "I have not slept well for the last two days, but be assured, I'm fine."

She walked in hesitantly, as if debating on whether to go in or run in the other direction. Did I really look that bad today? I caught a glance of myself in the mirror on my way to my desk. Shit! The dark circles are horrible today! I am going to have to take a night off and get some sleep, or people are going to start wondering if I can do my job. I cannot have people wondering, and asking too many questions, which I will just refuse to answer anyways.

The truth of the matter is I have not been able to sleep without having dreams that somehow leave me feeling sad and lonely. The other night when I slept, I dreamed of a woman in a very old dress, like they wore in the Victorian age. She was in labor with a child, and I was the midwife. She gave birth to triplets. I remember telling her that she had two boys and a girl. They were so beautiful. When the mother died from blood loss. There was nothing I could do. I felt so helpless. I woke that night drenched in sweat and feeling as if I had lost something. I could feel the grief as if I were there. I have been having a lot of dreams that seem completely real lately.

CLAP! The sound spun me around looking for the source, when I saw Pamela looking at me with cautious eyes. "Are you sure you are all right? I was just talking to you, and you seemed like you were on a different planet!"

"Yes, I am fine, was just looking at the dark circles under my eyes. I think allergies are messing with me early this year." With that said, we sat down in our chairs. I grabbed her file and a notepad. I would have to take notes today if I wanted to keep up with the conversation. Shit, here we go…where we stop no one knows.

"Well, Shawn asked me out again yesterday. I told him I would not go out with him. I feel like every time he asks; he is one of the guys I do not remember, and when he does ask and if I say yes, he is going to try to get me on the streets as his. I know this is probably just fear, but it scares the shit out of me."

"I understand why you are afraid. It is a big step, trying to get serious with someone."

"Yeah, and if I do go out with him, and I really like him, and he finds out what I used to be, what will he think of me then?"

I looked at her and said, "Well you could tell him before hand, that way he knows up front. Or you can wait, but you must tell him before you two get intimate."

She smiled at me then. "I know I will have to tell him. That is one of the reasons I keep telling him no. Also, I thought about telling him in hopes of it running him off. But I do not want anyone to know at my workplace either. I have not told anyone there yet. I just do not want them to look at me different, you know?"

Oh, I knew about not wanting people to know things about me. I live that life myself. I wish I could tell her that, but I cannot. Sometimes, I wish I could tell someone, anyone. But I have no one I trust to tell.

The rest of the session went by in a blur of my own thoughts. I was remembering a young woman about her mid twenty's long blonde hair. She was dressed in a Roman dress. She was chained in a dungeon to the wall. She was crying and begging for her life. She had been tried and convicted for having an affair on her husband. I was not sure where this memory came from though. Maybe I saw it in a movie once. Weird, I was somehow able to follow Pamela's conversation, with "yeses and no's" here and there.

It seemed to work, because when our time was up, she smiled and said, "I feel better now. Thank you, Dr., for listening to me."

"Serraid, please just call me Serraid."

She smiled and said, OK. Then she turned and we walked to the front desk so she could schedule her next appointment. I went back to my office so I could work on Pamela's file and put it away and take a five-minute breather before my next session. I updated her file and clipped my notes from today's session inside. I could not concentrate today. Shit, if I do not get my head together, I am going to have to go home sick today. Damn it! Do I really need a night off? Yeah, maybe I do. Ugh! Well, I could just tell them I am not feeling well, I mean by the looks of my face, they would believe me.

No, I must stay and act like everything is normal. Last night, keeps running through my head though and I am so frustrated today. I have not had anyone affect me that way in a very long time. What the hell is wrong with me? I really need to find someone I can talk to before I lose myself completely.

"Yes, Cheryl I will be right there, thank you." Great my next client is early. No wait, shiiittt, I have been sitting here for 20 minutes! I am losing time too, great that is not a good time to be losing it. I got out my timer, so I did not accidentally allow a session to go over and so I was not late getting another patient to my office.

Florence is my next client. He is 29 years old and has a problem with physically abusing women. He wants to stop, and that is why he is seeking professional help. That thought made me giggle. (professional, who me?) He beat his last girlfriend Julie, when she was pregnant with their child, she miscarried; She then left him. He has been single for almost a year now. He has had girlfriends, but he ends up hitting them eventually. Now he is trying to stay single for a little while, until he gets some treatment to help him. Well, I certainly could do that. With that thought I got up off my chair and headed toward the lobby.

Florence was sitting in a chair reading an old issue of National Geographic. He smiled when he noticed me at the entrance way. I smiled back and asked him if he was ready to get started. We went to my office quietly. I let him go in before me and I shut the door behind us.

I sat down in my chair and set the timer. Florence gave me a, what is that for look ', and I explained to him I was not feeling well and I was going to set it, so our session did not go over our allotted time. I turned the timer on and picked up his file.

I asked him how his day was going. He said, "Well today I met this beautiful woman at the store, and we got to talking over the veggies and she asked me for my number. I gave it to her. I know that I should not have done that, but I just keep thinking, maybe, this time I will not be that way."

I stopped him right there. I asked him, "Florence, do you know how it feels to be hit, like you hit these women?"

"No, but I think that I do not want to know how they feel. I know how I feel when I hit them. I do not even know what makes me do it, just I get mad, and I snap and before I know it, I have already hit them. It is like I do not even have time to think about what I am doing."

I told him I thought he needed to understand how he makes them feel. "I think you need to understand why you do these things. Do you know how you feel when you hit them, I mean really know?"

He answered, "Well, I know I get mad, and I keep thinking I won't be told what to do by no woman."

"So, you think that these women are telling you what to do?"

He said his mother used to treat his dad like shit, and she was always nagging on him and his father, that nothing either one of them did was ever good enough. And when he gets mad, he thinks of his mother yelling and screaming to the point he cannot even hear what his girlfriend is saying.

"Florence, how would you like some real therapeutic treatment?"

"Sure ", he said, "what do you have in mind, and will it actually help me?"

I told him about the Cat house and what they did there, that I knew a woman who works with me sometimes to help both men and women with this sort of problem. He agreed to go tonight.

I called the Cat house and set him up and appointment with Sereena. I told her I wanted to book this young man with Serrie. She set up the appointment and then lowered her voice and said, "you know you were supposed to take the night off."

I told her I knew that, but this takes top priority because this man is trying to stop doing this to women.

She giggled and said, "If anyone can make him want to stop it's you Serrie."

I laughed at that, then said goodbye and hung up.

"Ok, Florence you are scheduled to see a Madam by the name of Serrie at 10pm tonight. Make sure you do not tell anyone about this place; it is only for top clients. I know you have had all the blood tests that are required already done for your physical. Just bring those results with you to that appointment, they will not allow you to participate if you do not."

He said OK and then the timer went buzzing. Florence got up with the address in his hand, smiled and said, "Thank you for helping me. I really do not know what I am in for, but whatever it is, I hope that it helps."

I smiled back and told him no problem, opened the door, and walked him back to the lobby.

I went back to my office and checked my schedule. It is 10:30 by this time. I sat there dictating Florence's file, I left out the part of the referral though.

My eyes started feeling heavy, I may need to go home and get some rest. I was supposed to sleep tonight, but duty calls. I love to play dominant. I started thinking about what I would do to Florence. I think maybe a good spanking for him, and then if he does not like that I may whip him a little. I will certainly hit him at least once. I started feeling things tighten as I thought of what I was going to do.

My mind kept wondering back to the night before. Why was this man, bothering me so much. Who is he, and how did he know what to do that I liked? Ugh! I will think about this later.

I picked up my phone, called Cheryl, and told her I thought I was going to go home for the day and asked her if she could reschedule my last three appointments. She said my next client was already there. I told her I did not have another appointment until 11:30. She said this gentleman had an appointment at 10:30. I did not have anything written down in my book. Great, now I was forgetting to write shit down. Fuck!

Ok, I will be there in a minute. Who is my next client? She said, "Mr. Cook."

"Is he new?," I asked. She said yes, he had signed up almost a month ago.

I walked to the lobby and when I got to the entrance I froze. I saw the blonde hair, and the shoulders. This cannot be who I think it is…. Oh God, please do not let it be him.

The man turned around. When he did, I had to force myself not to run. I could not believe it; David was standing there just looking at me with a sparkle in those perfectly blue eyes!

"Are you ready Mr. Cook?"

He said yes, and I pointed the way to my office and told him I would be right there. He walked to my office, and I went to talk to Cheryl.

"When did he sign up for therapy, and what did he say he needed treatment for?"

Cheryl said, "Here is his file, I think you may want to read it before you go in there."

I smiled and said thank you. I sat in a chair by her window, opened his file, and started reading. It said he was suffering from post-traumatic stress syndrome. That his ex-girlfriend had beat him almost to death and now he has nightmares. He has insomnia and is starting to daydream.

I closed the file, smiled at Cheryl, said thank you, and headed to my office. I did not know what he was up to, but I did know David was always dominant and there was no way He allowed a woman to top him. I just cannot believe he is there in my office. What the hell does he want with me? When I left him, I never thought I would see him again! That was a chapter in my life I wanted closed!

With my heart in my throat and nerves on end, I walked in and shut the door.

"David, what the hell are you doing here?," I asked.

He smiled and said, "What, are you not glad to see me even a little bit?"

"David, I know what you put in your file is a lie, I also know you did not come here for therapy. So, I ask again, what the hell are you doing here?"

He looked at me with a not so friendly look that made my heart skip a beat and said, "Well I was in town and thought I would stop in and see how you were. I never expected to find you in this profession. You were always so good at being bottom. I have missed you Serraid. I wanted to see if we could have dinner and catch up."

"Oh, hell no!," I said. I told him I did not want to have dinner with him ever, and I wanted him to leave! I told him I did not live that life anymore. I told him to get up, and I would escort him out, and if he ever showed up around me again, I would press charges!

He stood up and flew over to me; I must be tired because I did not even see him move. He pushed me up against the door and kissed me.

"I said that I have missed you and this is the welcome I get in return. Let me tell you Serraid, I know what you are, and I know how you like things, and you will never be satisfied with the average joe doing you. I want to fuck you until you beg for me to stop. I want to feel you cum all over me as I draw your blood and whip you till you cry out. What do you think about that?"

I looked at him, and said, "David I will give you to the count of 3 to let go of me and then I am going to yell at the top of my lungs and believe me you will be escorted out of here and charges will be pressed!" I put my knee in his groin as I told him that. He doubled over and I opened the door, hollered at Cheryl, and told her that Mr. Cook is leaving now.

He stood up and said he would not bother me again, and he was sorry he ever took the time to look me up. I did not smile or anything, I kept my face as blank as I could and told him that he better not ever contact me again, I would have him thrown in jail if he did. Then I went and sat at my desk.

He left and slammed my door behind him. I called Cheryl and told her I was taking the rest of the day and to make sure to cancel all my appointments, then I hung up. I sat there and shook as I cried. My mind was all over the place, my nerves were screaming, the mental and physical pain re-surfaced.

I cannot believe he just showed up like that. What the hell was he thinking? Did he think I would want anything to do with him? I left in the middle of the night with nothing but my purse. I left my clothes and everything. I wanted my life; I wanted to not be a whipping post for someone to keep beating until my body did what he wanted it to do. I had enough of that when I was little. Fuck!

I waited until I knew he was gone before I left for my house, I did not want him to follow me home. Now I am really on edge. I left the office and headed for the house. The whole way home, I could not stop shaking. I needed to calm down, I cannot believe he re-surfaced expecting me to be the same weak pathetic person that he met years ago.

CHAPTER 3

I got into my car and headed home. My eyes were heavy, but my mind was racing something fierce. How could David know where to find me? How could he just show up like that thinking I would by some chance go back to that! I hit the steering wheel and screamed because I was so frustrated. I have too much to deal with without having to deal with this!

I pulled up to the house and got myself under control. I did not need Sarah to see me this way. She is very perceptive sometimes, and I really do not want her to ask questions if she is home. Sometimes I wish I had not rented out that room, yet sometimes I am glad for the company. And the thought of her body, and to feel it. Oh hell, who am I kidding, I still have not beat my sex addiction. I just hide behind a degree and call myself cured. But I cannot bring myself to tell Sarah because she seems so docile. Oh well, that is a thought to put on the back burner for now. I got out of my car and headed for the door.

I unlocked the door when I heard voices in the house. My heart jumped into my throat because of the male's voice, 'there's no way he could have found out where I lived.' I thought. I straightened my shoulders and put on my best blank face and walked into the house. Sarah was sitting at the kitchen table talking with a young gentleman, he was handsome and vibrant looking. I released a breath I did not realize I was holding. Paranoid, who me? I snickered to myself as I walked into the kitchen. Sarah stood up and asked me what I was doing home so early, then she looked at my face.

"Oh…My…. God…., you do not look well Serraid, come here and sit down and let me get you something to eat."

"Thank you, Sarah. It is good to see you too." I said as I sat down in the chair, she gave me.

I reached across the table to the young man that was sitting there and shook his hand and said, "Hi, I'm Serraid."

"I'm John.," he said.

He had black hair with red highlights and blue eyes. It seems like a weird combo, but I think he has in contacts.

I would have asked but some things are just plain rude to be asked right after meeting a person. So, I settled on a weak smile, I know did not reach my eyes, but he smiled back. I looked away. I thought to myself he looked vaguely familiar; I took another look at him. His jaw line and his voice sound so familiar, but for the life of me I cannot figure out why. I decided to push the thought away. Maybe I am just too tired, and everything is starting to sound alike. Hell, now I am really starting to sound like a couple of my clients. I looked to see what Sarah was doing, and she was making me some chicken noodle soup. I am not sure what she does to the canned soup, but she always makes it so yummy…

"Thank you, Sarah, for making that for me.," I said as she handed me the hot bowl.

Sarah smiled at me, placed the back of her hand on my head, and felt for a fever. (She always plays mother when she thinks I have exhausted myself.) and said, "Serraid, when you're done eating, why don't you go and lay down and sleep for a while?"

"I will," I said and smiled back at her.

She went and sat down with John and gave me a look of disbelief.

"What? Why are you looking at me like that?" I asked her.

She giggled, and said, "Serraid, you never give up that easy, so you must be ill."

"I am just tired; I have not been sleeping well lately. And I think it is catching up with me."

"Well then, it is settled, when you get finished eating, you are going to go lay down. I will give you something to help you sleep, and then you are going to sleep. I have the house, so do not even think about producing reasons to why you cannot go to bed right now."

I smiled at that because she knew me so well. I said, "Ok, Sarah, I will get some sleep. But I must be awake by 8pm because I have a client that has invited me to a therapy group to give my opinion on what I feel about it."

She gave me a seriously suspicious look and said, "O.K. I will wake you up by eight but tomorrow night you are not scheduling anything because I'm going to stay at home, and we are going to have a girls night here."

I smiled and it reached my eyes, "Ok, sounds great Sarah. Thank you for always having my back."

"Don't mention it, someone has to take care of you, or you would be a mess." She said as she laughed.

John stood up and said he was going to get going, because he had some things to do. We told him thank you for stopping by and to visit anytime he wanted.

I finished my soup and took a sleeping pill that Sarah gave me and headed for bed. I laid down around 1:30. Man I hope to get some good sleep.

I woke up at seven thirty, sweating. I had a dream about the man from the cat house last night. He was making love to me like no one ever has before. In my dream we were in a meadow. It was beautiful and green. He had stripped off my petticoats and stockings. He had me laying on an old wool jacket. He looked a little different his hair was a different color, yet I knew this was the same man. His eyes were the same, and his voice was just as sexy. He was very gentle with me; I remember feeling the breeze running through my bright black hair. He was riding me like a mare in heat, kissing me taking me inside his mouth. I felt as if I was worried about getting caught. I felt as if I needed to keep watch, yet I could not hold my eyes open due to the pleasure building between my thighs. I woke wondering why I would dream of this man in that context. I sat up and felt heat rise to my cheeks when I realized the dream was better than I originally thought it was, because I was so wet there was a spot on the sheet.

I went to stand up, but I felt a little dizzy, so I sat back down on the bed. 'What did Sarah give me,' I thought to myself. After a couple of minutes, I stood and went to take a shower. I had to get my clothes and everything ready for my appointment with Florence. I thought to myself as I got ready, how I was going to make him understand why he should not do this to women. A part of me was afraid he was going to learn to like it, and he would become worse. I began second guessing myself, because I certainly did not want to do to him what David had done to me. I mean Florence is so young, and I do not need that shit on my conscience. I pushed that thought away, I knew what I was doing and I am nothing like David!

At 9 O'clock I headed for the cat house. I wanted to get there in enough time to set up my room and decide what the best course of action was. Florence was my only client for the night, so this should go very smoothly. 30 minutes later I arrived at the cat house. I walked in and Sereena sat in her chair. She looked up and smiled at me when I came in.

"Well hello Serrie, are you ready to teach your bad boy a little lesson?," she giggles when she says it.

I walked over to her, and smiled and said, "Oh, I think that after a few sessions, I don't think our Florence will want to hit another woman again."

She laughed out loud, and it made her eyes sparkle when she laughed like that. "I am heading to my room to get things ready. Page me when He arrives."

She said OK and I headed upstairs to get prepared. I stepped into my room and looked around. I wanted to make this experience something that Florence would not forget and would never want to repeat on either side. I picked up a blindfold and decided I would not use it. I wanted him to see me hit him; I wanted him to see it coming. I would chain him to the wall and make him beg for me to stop. I picked up my mask and put it on. I laid a paddle on the table by the wall. I will spank him and make him cry out. I would tell him what to do and he will do it! I will make him face the anger he has against his mother and make him see that I am not her.

My phone went off and I answered it. It was Sereena, she said that my client was here and ready for his session. I told her that I would be right down. I ran my hands down my dress and took a deep breath. I said to myself, "You are doing this for his good Serrie, you will not turn him into a monster." Then I walked out the door and headed downstairs to get my client.

As I came down the stairs, I saw Florence sitting there in the chair next to Sereena. I smiled even though he could not really see it through my mask. I walked over to him and offered him my hand. I could see the sweat on his forehead. I could see his nervousness like a robe wrapped around him.

He reluctantly took my hand and I introduced myself. "I'm Serrie, and I understand you were sent here by my friend for some therapy."

He shook his head a little too fast and said, "Y, yes, she said you could help me with a problem of hitting women."

I nodded and said, "I will try my dear, I will try. Follow me uhm, what is your name again?"

"Florence, m, my name is Florence."

"Ok, follow me Florence and we shall see what we can do."

I began walking toward the stairs. I peered behind me and realized Florence was hesitating. I turned and said, "Don't be afraid Florence, you are safe here, I give you my word." He smiled a small smile and started slowly walking with me.

As we reached my room Florence peeked in and went pale as he seen all my toys in there. I turned and said with a very demanding tone, "Florence, go inside and we will begin." He looked at me, and I saw anger flash across his face at the tone I used with him. Then he settled his face and walked into the room. I followed him. I told him to stand over by the wall. He walked over and stood where I had told him too. I grabbed my whip and told him to take off his clothes except for his underwear.

He paled and said, "Why do I have to take off my clothes? I am not here to have sex with you."

I laughed a very empty laugh, and looked him right in the eye and told him with a deep demanding tone, "I will not tell you again Florence, you either take off your clothes or I will give you one stripe with my whip, do you understand?"

He stood there for a second with a look on his face that said that he was contemplating on leaving the room, and then he shook his head quickly and started unbuttoning his shirt. I felt a little tension release that I was not aware was there. I stood there and watched this man strip down to his boxers.

"Hmmmm thin boxers, I am going to enjoy this very much Florence. I want you to turn around and face the wall."

He looked at me and said, "I won't face the wall, I won't turn my back to you."

SLAP! The whip hit his chest just as he finished his sentence.

"Now, turn around and face the wall Florence, I will Not tell you again!"

I saw the anger flare up his face and saw his eyes go black. I was preparing to hit him again; in case he had an idea of hitting me back. Then He turned and faced the wall. I saw his shoulders move a little, as if he were trying to hold back tears that he was hiding. I walked up to him and took his left arm and chained it to the wall. He tugged at it and said with his voice shaky, "Why are you chaining me up? I did what you asked me to do."

I told him, "I'm chaining you so that you don't move and so I don't hit you somewhere I don't want to hit."

I took his right arm and went to chain it, when he pulled it out of my hand and said, "I did not sign up for this shit! I will not let you chain both of my hands up to the wall."

My heart sped up, as fear started to grip him, excitement gripped me. I hit him again this time across the back. He let out a cry, and at the sound of the cry, things tightened low in my body. I told him to put his other hand on the wall. I said, "We can do this as easy as you want or as hard as you want, it's your choice Florence." he put his hand on the wall, I saw tears flowing down his face.

I laughed and asked, "Awe, did I hurt you, Florence? Did you not like the whip?"

He hung his head as far down as he could and replied, "I didn't realize that it hurt so bad."

I walked up behind him and grabbed his hair, and pulled his head back as far as I could without breaking it and said, "I will make you hurt Florence, I will make you beg for me to stop, and I will make you never, ever, ever want to hit another woman ever!" He cried out from fear. I could smell it all over him. I could feel it run over my skin like water in the shower. The feel of his fear and my arousal mixed strengthened me giving me the energy to finish what I had started.

I walked over to the table and picked up my paddle and slapped it against my hand. Florence flinched and let out a whimper. I laughed at that.

"What is so fucking funny?!"

"Oh…. this" I hit him with the paddle right across the ass. It was a good hit too. He screamed from the pain and the sound. He was crying harder now.

He said, "please, please don't hit me again."

I looked at him and laughed, "What? What are you asking me? I have hit you three times, and you are asking me not to hit you again? What about the women you hit, how many times did you hit them, Florence?"

"I.I do not know, I do not know, OK! Just please do not"

I hit him again in mid-sentence, he screamed a high-pitched scream like a woman. I laughed loudly! I could feel his fear, taste it like the lingering flavor or candy. There was no anger there only humiliation and realization of the things that he had been inflicting on his women.

He cried, "Please, I didn't mean to hit those women, I don't know why I did it, just please don't hit me again."

I thought to myself, Man, I really thought he would be tougher than this. Do not break him Serrie. I could feel things tightening in my body, and I was getting wetter with each cry he made. I was getting turned on by his pleas for me to stop. I hit him again in the same spot on the ass with the paddle as I did, I said, "You do not like that do you Florence? You do not like the pain, but you like giving it. You will not give pain again without being willing to take a little pain too."

I hit him again and again. I could feel myself tightening as he stood there crying for me to stop. I could feel the moist smoothness. I walked over to him and told him his crying was getting me wet; I was enjoying his pain. That I was going to fuck myself thinking about him crying for me to stop.

He jerked at the chains, "Please just let me go, I want to stop now! I want to go home. I will not hit anyone else ever, I promise, just please do not hit me again."

I giggled at his futile pleas. A part of me felt sorry for him for I remember a time when I had been in his place. When I first met David. I thought he hung the world. He seemed like he was a genuine therapist with my best interest at heart. He taught me the things men did to me were not my fault. And he said he could help me beat the addiction to sex I struggled with. He took me home one night and chained me down and whipped me and made me scream and beg for him to stop. But he did not stop. After a while I began to like the pain and welcome it as it brought me harder and faster than ever. But the other part of me wanted to bring myself to orgasm while beating Florence. I was really beginning to fear that I was becoming David. Is this how he started out? Is this what happened to him? Oh hell, I did not know. But I did know that I am not David, and I will teach Florence not to hit women ever again. I turned away from him, so I could re-gather my thoughts. I wanted him to cry out; I wanted him to feel how those women felt when he beat on them.

I turned back around and yelled, "SHUT UP!!!!! Quit being a pussy! You will stay here until I tell you that you can go, and not a minute sooner! Do you understand me?!"

He shook his head yes, and I hit him again. I could feel the rage inside of me. I wanted to make him pay. I grabbed my whip, and I hit him across the shoulders hard enough to leave a nice whelp on them. I hit him again lower this time. He flinched and he cried and begged me to stop. I came back to myself and saw the whelps on his back beginning to bleed. Shit! I had lost control of myself. Florence half stood kneeling there against the wall, crying. I dropped the whip and walked over to him.

I hugged him, and asked, "Are you alright Florence? I did not hurt you too bad, did I?"

He raised his head, and he looked at me with a tear-stained face, and his eyes were blood shot and puffy and said, "I just want to go home. Can I please go home now? Please!"

I stood up and released his hands and told him to get dressed and go. I told him to make sure not to tell anyone about this except for his counselor who sent him here. He agreed and got his clothes on. When he went to put on his shirt he winced from pain. I helped him get his shirt on and told him I was sorry I hurt him. I told him I did not know what came over me and I am sorry I lost control.

He said, "It is ok, now I know. Now I know how it feels to have someone lose control on me. Does it feel this way to the women?"

I told him he would have to ask his counselor that question; I was not able to give advice. He shook his head and said he understood and walked out the door. When the door shut, I went to the bed and sat down and put my head between my knees, I was feeling very lightheaded and thought I was going to pass out. "What have I done?" I asked myself aloud. Why did I lose control? I never lose control. Never.

I was sitting there with my head between my knees when I felt a hand on my shoulder. I jumped and squealed because I had not heard anyone enter the room. When my eyes focused, Jeremy was standing there in front of me. My heart jumped and suddenly my body remembered everything he had done the night before.

"Good evening, are you well?"

"Yes, I am ok, but what are you doing here? I only had one client tonight." I was so going to have to talk to Sereena when He left. I sat there wishing I had just taken the night off when He grabbed me around the throat and pushed me back on the bed.

"I am going to give you what you are wanting, what I see in your eyes right now. I am going to hurt you Serrie and then I am going to fuck you and make you release all your tension on me." With that said, he kissed me hard enough, that I had to open and let him in my mouth, or my lips would bruise and break under the pressure. I felt my body tense, and I started getting wetter than before. He squeezed my throat harder until I could not breathe. I grabbed his hand and tried to pull them off my throat, but he squeezed harder, grabbed my hand, and held it to the bed. He pressed himself on top of me. My mind screamed no, and my body screamed yes! I could feel tears beginning in my eyes from not being able to breathe. I could feel my face turn blue. Fear began to well up inside. I struggled against his hand. He released me a little and I took a gasp of air just before he tightened his grip. Everything was beginning to go grey with spots in my vision. I started kicking and hitting trying to get him to release me! I tried saying something, but nothing could make it out of my restricted air way. I could feel the bruising starting. Terror took over and I panicked; he was going to kill me! Oh, God he was going to kill me! Then everything went numb, and blank. I sank into that silence that is nothing and yet everything. I knew there was something I should remember but could not think of what it was. Twenty minutes later I woke up. I opened my eyes and went to roll over, but I could not move. I was tied to the bed, and my clothes were off. I yelled "hello!"

Jeremy walked over to the bed with a wicked smile on his face. He told me that he was glad that I was awake. I struggled against the ropes and could not get them loose.

He looked at me and said, "I have tied you well, and you won't get loose until I decide it is time."

Another wave of fear collided over me. I started screaming for Sereena because I could not reach my panic button.

Jeremy walked over to me and gagged me. I tried screaming but it was too muffled for anyone to hear. I started crying as I spotted a knife in his hand. I shook my head no, and he smiled at me and said, "Oh, yes, my dear, tonight you get the knife, I will do what I please and there is nothing you can to do stop me. I will use whatever I want to, and there is nothing you can do about it."

I shook my head faster as he got closer to me. I did not want him near me with the knife. I screamed and cried and begged with the gag in my mouth. I thought to myself: I must calm down, or I will not be able to breathe at all through my nose. Funny thing about crying, it swells your sinus cavities so no air will pass through and in turn it creates pressure for the tear ducts to release their tears. I had to calm down. Sereena knew I did not have another client, so if I do not go down soon, she will come and check on me. I knew she would because she had done it before.

Ok, just breath Serrie, it is going to be ok. You will be ok. I opened my eyes, and Jeremy was leaning over me with the knife. He pressed it to my throat, and I could feel my pulse speed up as fear set in again. Oh, God She is not going to make it in time! He is really going to kill me! My eyes went wide, and I started crying again. He leaned in and kissed the tears off my face and pressed the knife harder on my throat.

He whispered in my ear, "Do not worry Serrie, I am not going to kill you. But you will like what I do."

He reached down with his other hand and ran his finger across my stomach and farther down between my legs. "Oh Serrie, your body is liking what I'm doing." He slid his finger inside slowly and brought it back out and brought it up to my lips. He glazed my lips with my own moisture, and I moaned from the pleasure of the feeling of him doing it. He took his hand back down all the while tracing the knife down my chest, over my stomach. Fear welled up again. 'Is he going to cut me or…. oh God no, please do not let him put the knife inside of me.'

He stopped the knife just above my opening. He laid it there. And then he shoved two fingers inside of me hard and fast. My hips came up just a little to help the angle of him inside of me. I could feel the pressure building between my legs. He was going to make me cum soon. I tried saying, "soon" but the gag was in the way.

Then he sat up quickly and pulled his fingers out of me. He walked over to the table and got the blind fold. I was shaking my head, fearful that if he put that on me, he was going to kill me. I tried fighting him, trying to keep him from putting it on. He grabbed my hair and pulled my head against the bed. He held it there so tight that either I could allow him to put it on, or he would rip the hair out of my head. I laid still. Knowing this may be my last moment on earth. I wished I would just wake up from this nightmare but also feeling his arousal, and mine mixing like a fine wine that made it even more tempting. The World went dark from the blind folded. I could hear him moving around the room and trying to place the sounds with memory of what was there. But my mind was not working well because I was a little in shock. A hand touched me, a gloved hand. I could not tell if it was him or someone else. The hand grabbed my thigh and squeezed hard enough to leave a bruise. I screamed behind the gag. Tears began to flow again. I tried shaking my head hoping to get the blindfold to give me a peek of who was touching me. Another hand grabbed my other thigh and squeezed it hard enough to bruise. I tried to move my thighs back where they were, but my feet were tied down now. I fought against the ropes and tried to shake free. Nothing happened; No sounds that I could hear. I could only hear my pulse in my ears. I felt the knife move beside me, and a sharp burning feeling on my thigh. I could feel the warm trickle of blood beginning.

"NO! No! Please stop, please do not kill me!" I screamed behind the gag.

Again, my body was responding, with moisture between my legs. I could feel things tightening and my pussy swelling from the need of release. I tried to will my body to quit, to not encourage this or these people to go any farther. I tried calming myself, but I was not doing a good job. I was too panicked to calm down I was enjoying this too much to calm down. I was breathing too fast and could feel myself hyperventilating.

I felt the knife again against my other thigh. A sharp pain and again blood. I tried to concentrate on the blood flow and tried to feel how bad I was bleeding. It did not feel like a lot of blood. Just a cutting. Ok, Serrie, you have had cuts worse than this before, just calm down. There is still a chance to make it out. Sereena will come; she will check and find you here! You will be fine. That is what I told myself. My body on the other hand wanted more, it yearned for another touch, another pain, to bring me screaming. I felt something slide inside of me hard and deep. I could feel the vibration. He had put a vibrator inside of me.

'Ok that's better than a knife, you will be ok' then the first wave of my orgasm hit me. It bowed my back and made me press my head into the bed. The Orgasm hit me so fast with no warning. He rammed the vibrator in and out hard and fast. I could feel it hitting that sweet, sweet spot inside, going over my cervix, tightening my body around it as another orgasm was building. Then suddenly, he stopped. I felt a mouth over my clit, sucking, biting, and shaking back and forth. The feeling of it was too much and it brought me screaming around the gag from pleasure. I could feel my body spasming as he kept sucking and shaking me. I could feel the pleasure going from me to him and back again like an electrical current.

A hand squeezed my nipple hard enough to make me cry out, then I felt another hand around my throat again. I could feel a body pressed against mine. Laying on top of me. I could feel the hardness of him; I tried bringing my hips up so he could slide inside. But he kept just out of reach. He would just rub against my opening teasing, bringing the tightness back in a rush of pleasure. I moved my hips, silently begging for him to enter me, when I felt the knife at my throat. I stopped moving, not wanting to give him a reason to hurt me. He pressed the knife harder on my throat and then thrust himself inside of me at the same time. He shoved his way inside, not being gentle. He hit the very bottom of me. I moved my hips up to help the angle, but he pressed the knife down again harder and felt it cut just a little. Then he started working his way in and out of me. Pressing and pushing, pulling, and rubbing. I could feel the tension getting tighter. I was going to cum again soon and hard. I wanted to scream from the pleasure of the feeling. His free hand took off the blindfold, grabbed my hair, and made me look him in the eyes. He slammed himself hard and deep inside of me. Working my spot like he knew exactly where it was. He kept rubbing against it and pushing harder inside of me. The feeling of him rubbing that spot and the pain of him hitting the bottom of me brought me screaming. I reached with my hands to find something, anything to scratch my pleasure into, my eyes wide, wanting to look into his eyes. To see the pleasure building in his eyes. I could tell he was close. I tried moving my hips again and he said, "Stop moving, or I'm not going to last." I stopped because I wanted to ride this wave of pleasure as long as I could. He said, "soon, so close," then he thrust himself inside deep one more time and I felt his body spasm inside of me, releasing his tension there. The feel of his pulsing brought me again, I screamed my pleasure around the gag, clawing the blankets trying to draw blood from something that did not bleed. Then with one last push, he collapsed on top of me.

After a few minutes, our breathing became somewhat normal. He rolled over, removed the blindfold from my forehead, and giggled. He looked at me in a way that no man has ever looked at me and one he had not earned yet and said, "sorry if I scared you too much. I wanted to you be completely satisfied when I was done."

He reached over and pulled the gag off my mouth. I smiled. I wanted to yell and scream at him, but I smiled. I could not be mad when my body was still having small spasms of pleasure going through me.

"Thank you.," I said. "It is like you know exactly what I need and what I want. How do you do that?"

He looked at me and said, "I am not sure what to say to that. I just read your body and give it what it wants. You are so lovely and strong, and yet so fragile. Sometimes you need to remember that part."

I did not know how to respond to that, so I said nothing.

(Jeremy thought to himself he knew he was playing a dangerous game here with her. But he needed her touch. He longed for her. He desired her, like a drink of water on a hot day. He knew time was short, and for him that meant starting over again. He wanted this all to end, to tell her who and what he was. He needed to go before he confessed all to this one woman that he has ever loved. He got up and got dressed.)

He then released me and allowed me to get dressed. He went for the door. As I watched him head to the door, I had this urge to run to him and hug him and kiss him. My body wanted to touch him. It wanted him to hold it. (What the hell is wrong with me?) I thought. This was not like me. I did not want to keep my clients. I always wanted them to be gone.

When I realized that I had gotten carried away in my thoughts, I looked up and he was gone. Just like that with no word, no goodbye, just gone. Why does this man bother me so much? I asked myself. A little voice inside of my head, said it is love. I said that part to shut the hell up, I was not going to do that again. And I headed for the door. When I got downstairs, Sereena was peering into me with her eyes.

She giggled and said, "Did you enjoy the little surprise?"

"You knew he was coming up and you didn't tell me about it?!" I was shocked at the thought that she knew! "How could you do that to me Sereena? I mean, He scared the shit out of me! I thought he was going to kill me at first!"

She giggled and that pissed me off even more. She said, "Well did you enjoy it or not?"

I felt the heat rush to my face as I blushed, I lowered my head and said "yes."

She came over to me and said, "Honey, you have to learn to enjoy what you enjoy. And this man, seems to know what you need, and he seems to really like you a lot. He really is a nice guy, and he has a completely clean record. Before you ask, I checked for you. Because he has been inquiring about you a lot. If I did not know better, I would say that he is infatuated with you, or maybe it is something else. But I know that look, and you have had it both times he has visited you. And I am telling you, there is something special about that one."

I looked at her with a burning look that made most people back away, but she knew me too well to let it affect her that way. I said, "Sereena, please do not tell me you think he is a good match for me. Please do not play match maker with me, ok? Oh, and do not ever let him in my room again without telling me he is coming up first. Is that clear?"

"Serrie, I am sorry, I thought you would like the surprise after getting so worked up on that kid. I saw how Florence ran out of here. Serrie, you hurt him and you needed someone to take that out on. Or someone to release you from it."

I sighed and said nothing for a few minutes because she was right. I could not argue with the truth; could I? I told her I was taking the next night off and I was not coming in for any reason. Because I needed a break. And I said, "Oh, and do not be thinking more on the idea of me and Jeremy because I do not make a habit of fucking my clients! He is the only one I will do that with." I said the last part with a smile because I knew I meant it. I loved how he felt inside of me, how he scared me into an orgasm.

Oh hell, I like him ok...

I went for the door and started to my car. I reached my car and saw a note on my windshield.

It read: *Serrie, thank you for the wonderful time you allowed me to show you tonight. I hope I didn't frighten you too much. I promise I won't ever sneak up on you like that again. I hope to see you again soon. Until then, Jeremy.*

I stood there staring at the note. He knew what car I drove, Oh shit! That means he could have my plates ran and find out where I lived. Oh hell, even the thought of that excited me. What the hell is it about this man that turns me on and makes me want to touch him. I smelled the note, and it smelled like his skin. Not his soap or cologne but his skin. It was like returning home from a long vacation. My body was drawn to his like a magnet. I was not even sure if I decided I did not want him if I could stop my body from needing. I must get hold of myself with him. I tucked the note into my pocket and got in my car and headed home.

I arrived home and there was a light on. I thought how weird that was because Sarah is usually out partying. Wonder if she is all right. I reached the front door, and Sarah opened it for me. "Serraid, I am so glad that you are home! There was this weird guy that came by for you, he said he knew you in Oklahoma, and he was a friend of yours."

My heart leaped in my throat as fear gripped me, it had to David. How the hell did he find out where I lived? "Did he leave a name or number?"

"No, she said, but he did leave this ", she held her hand up and I saw the bruises started on her wrist.

I hugged her and took her inside. I asked her to describe him to me. She did and I knew it was David.

"Sarah, if he ever shows up here again, do not answer the door for him and call the police. I am going to go down and get a restraining order in the morning. He is bad news Sarah; he is a bad man from my past who I ran from a long time ago. Sarah listens to me, do not ever answer the door to him again. And start keeping the door locked even when you are home." She looked at me with tears in her eyes and hugged me tight.

"Did he hurt you, Sarah?"

"No, he just scared me a little. He really did not hurt me Serraid. I promise. And I will keep the doors locked." She looked up at me and her face softened, and touched my face and said, "Serraid, if you ever need to talk to someone, I want you to know that I am here for you. I mean, I look at you like a sister, so…If you need me to, I will listen."

"Thank you, Sarah, I really appreciate that. And you are too. Ok?" She smiled and said OK.

I took Sarah to her room and got her settled in for the night. I went through the house and made sure all the windows and doors were closed and locked. I checked all the closets to make sure they were empty. I know it is silly because there are no monsters in the closet, but it made me feel better to know for myself he was not hiding somewhere in the house waiting for me to fall asleep to jump me in the middle of the night.

I went up to my room and laid down on the bed. As I drifted off to sleep, I thought of Jeremy and what he had done to me tonight. My eyes grew heavy, and sleep washed over me, and I slept.

CHAPTER 4

I was sitting at the table drinking my coffee when a knock at the door broke the silence and my concentration. I jumped at the sudden sound. "it's just the door silly," I told myself. Sarah was still sleeping. I got up and went to the door to see who it was. I looked out the little peep hole and did not see anyone, but there was a package on the doorstep. I opened the door and picked up the package. It was not too heavy, but there was something in it, and a smell I could not quite figure out. I took the package, went into the kitchen, and sat it on the table. I got my box opener and started opening the box. There was a note on the top, and a bunch of that pink Styrofoam packing stuff inside.

I read the note, *Serraid, I hope that you enjoy my little present for you. It's not much, and it didn't cost anything. Have a great day, and remember this, some things just are not replaceable.* I stood there staring at the note wondering what the last part meant. There was no signature, so I did not know who it was from.

I started rummaging through the stuffing when my hand hit something furry. I stopped and looked down carefully. My cat Patches was laying there with his throat slit! I screamed at the sight of my precious little cat, who could have done this? I woke up sweating and screaming.

Sarah crashed through the bedroom door with a ball bat in her hand. "What is it? What is wrong?!"

I sat there trying to catch my breath, and said, "A nightmare, just a bad dream, I am ok. Have you seen Patches?"

She came over to the bed and sat down. "Yeah, he's asleep in the hallway on his bed, why?"

I told her about the dream that I had. She said, "Jesus, Serraid! What do you think that it means?"

I told her I thought I was just dreaming because of David showing up here last night while I was out. "I will be all right, just let me calm down. Shit, I am shaking. The dream seemed so real Sarah, it was like it was happening."

"I will go down and make some coffee, and you go take a shower and then come down and we will eat something. What time do you have to go into the office today?"

I told her that I was supposed to be there by eight, but I did not know if I wanted to go in today or just take a personal day. Then I thought about my clients I had today. I only had three scheduled today. Surely, I could make it through that. It was Friday and this is always my short day.

I got up and told her I would go in, but I would be back by lunch. "Thank you, Sarah, for being here with me. And thank you for offering to make coffee and breakfast. I will be down in a little while."

"You're welcome, and do not forget, tonight we are having a girl's night here. I mean it Serraid, do not forget."

I smiled at her and said, "I won't forget, I think I actually need the night off."

I went to my closet and picked out my light grey skirt suit, and a white sleeveless shirt to go under the jacket, with my grey garter and the dark tan thigh highs. I wanted to be somewhat comfortable today. I grabbed my smoky grey high heels and headed for the shower. I laid the clothes on the bed on my way. I never could get dressed in the bathroom right after taking a shower.

The shower felt so good. I turned it as hot as it would go and just let it hit my shoulders where all the tension seemed to be grouping for the day. As I stood there letting the water hit me, Jeremy flashed through my mind. My body grew tight instantly energized at the memory. Ugh! What is wrong with me! I leaned against the shower wall and thought about my clients for the day and how much they did not want to change, or at least that is how it seems. But my body just would not give up on the memory of Jeremy. I stood there with need rising in me, I leaned back just enough for the water to hit just above my clit. The sensation sent a shiver up my spine; I moved just a little to let it spray over me. My body tensed as the need grew stronger, I slid a finger down and found myself wet, and not from the water. I played over that spot in slow circular motions, giving in to the feel of the pleasure building. The orgasm took me quickly; I pressed up against the shower wall and tried not to make any noise that would alert Sarah again. That is all I need for her to walk in on me like this. As the wave settled, I started washing my hair and finishing my shower. Some of the tension was gone, and I felt a little better. Sarah came through the door and said the coffee was ready. She scared the crap out of me, and I almost ripped the shower curtain off the wall.

"You scared the shit out of me! How long have you been there? I am sorry, thank you for letting me know, I will be down in a bit."

She smiled and said, "You're welcome. I have not been here too long." With that she winked, turned, and went downstairs.

I stood there with my pulse in my throat. Shit, how long had she been there? I was trying to think, but I was too caught up in the orgasm to remember if she was there or not. I hope she did not see that. With that thought I turned off the water and got out. I dried off and dried my hair quickly. Then I slapped on some make up. I went out to my room and put on my clothes, took a quick look in the mirror, satisfied that I could pass as being ok, I turned for the door.

When I arrived downstairs, Sarah was sitting at the table with her back to me. I had a thought of paying her back for the scare upstairs. I crept up behind her and grabbed her shoulders and yelled, "Hey!"

She jumped and spilled her coffee on the floor. And then she started crying. I grabbed her and told her I was sorry.

"It's ok, I had it coming, I guess. Your breakfast is done and there is fresh coffee in your cup."

I smiled and said, "Thank you Sarah, I am sorry for scaring you."

She laughed and said it was ok and then cleaned up the coffee she had spilled. She went and poured herself another cup. I had an industrial size coffee pot I inherited from a friend.

We sat there in silence for about ten minutes, me eating my breakfast. The coffee was hot and black, just the way I liked it. I drank it and savored the feel of it on my pallet. It was always good to wake up with coffee in the mornings. It made a gloomy day seem a little brighter.

"Ah, the wonders of caffeine."

She giggled and said, "I know what you mean. Sometimes it feels that is all that is running in my veins these days."

I finished my breakfast, told her thank you again. She reminded me not to forget tonight. I assured her I would not forget and headed out the door. I stopped in the living room where Patches was lying on the couch. I walked over to him; he gave me a soft meow and raised his head as I petted him. Sometimes just petting him made me feel a little calmer. It was like he had natural Xanax in his fur and when I petted him, it secreted through him to me. I giggled at the thought. Told him to be a good boy today and headed out the door.

I drove the whole commute to work with no instances. I sat in front of the center and took a couple of deep breaths. I only had three clients today, and then it would be over. I just really wanted to go back home and go to sleep. But duty calls and I had to help people. Yeah, I help people; funny I know.

I walked in and Cheryl sat at her desk as normal. Today she had a bright blue shirt on with a dark blue Minnie skirt with 5-inch heels. I smiled, even though it did not reach my eyes, and said, "good morning, Cheryl."

"Well good morning to you too Serraid, I'm glad to see you looking better this morning." She smiled when she said it.

"I got some sleep finally last night. Do I have any messages?"

"Yes, in fact you do. Cynthia would like to see you before you leave today. And There was a note taped to the door when I got here today, it was addressed to you, so I did not open it. I thought it was strange that someone would leave a note like that. Now where did I put that? Ah, here it is."

She handed me the note and I said, "Thank you."

I headed for my office. I turned around at the entrance of the hallway and asked, "Cheryl did Cynthia say what she wanted to see me about?"

"No, she just asked me to tell you that she would like to see you before you left today. I told her that I would tell you as soon as you got here."

"Ok, thank you, I will go and see her before my first client then."

I turned and headed down the hallway to my office. I had to put my briefcase on my desk and then I would go see Cynthia and find out what she wanted. Then, I would come back and read the note that was left for me, and then it would be me off to help clients.

I walked to Cynthia's door and knocked softly. "Come in!"

I opened the door and stepped inside. She smiled and it reached her eyes and made them sparkle. "Thank you for coming to see me, Serraid. Please have a seat."

"You're welcome, I was surprised when Cheryl told me that you wanted to see me. Is everything all right?"

She shuffled some papers around her desk, as if she were looking for something. I could tell that she was a little nervous, and that made me a little nervous. Because Cynthia never wanted to see me. In fact, I could count on one hand how many times she had wanted to see me since she started here.

Cynthia is beautiful. She has shoulder length fire red hair, bright green eyes and she is petite. She is 5'2", and her facial features are very soft. She looks like she just came out of a package. She has a smile that will make you smile, whether you are in a good mood or a bad one. You cannot help but reply with one back. I have wondered a few times if her lips are as soft as they appear. They are full lips and always perfectly smooth. I have always wondered how she kept them from chapping.

"I wanted to get your advice on something. I have this client that is a recovering addict. She wants to stay clean, or at least that has been her story for the last year. But the last couple of times that she has been here she seems to be, not herself. I had a feeling that she was using again, and so the last time that she came in, I done a U.A. on her. Serraid, I had to know if she was clean or not. Because I am not going to sit here and let her lie to me."

"I understand that. What did the test show?"

"She tested positive for methamphetamines. I just do not know what to do. If I turn her away and she does something to hurt herself then I will feel responsible. But if I keep seeing her, then she will have to quit the drugs, or I cannot help her. In fact, I feel like I have failed her. I mean if I were helping her, I feel that she would not have started back on the drugs."

"Cynthia, you know that we cannot control what people do outside of the center. And she chose to use again. That is not your fault."

"I know, but why did she start using again? Did I say something wrong, or did I not say enough?"

"Listen, I have known you for a few years now, you are a great counselor. Do not let this beat you up. You know that you did all that you could do for her, and you could only go by what she told you. It is not like we follow our clients around all day long. Did you speak with her about this?"

"I would not tell her the results of the test until the next time that she came in. She is supposed to see me today. I just do not know what to say to her. I feel like I have failed her somehow."

"First, you need to realize that you did not fail her, you cannot keep her from making choices. Second, you need to speak with her about this and find out what made her start using again. And find out how she feels about using again. Third, you need to sit down with her and speak to her about possibly going to a treatment center for at least 6 months, that way they can help her kick the habit and stay clean. And you let her know that you are here for her, and that she can tell you anything. That she does not have to hold anything back from you."

"Thank you Serraid, please do not tell anyone that I asked you for advice, I do not want certain people, like Cheryl, thinking that I cannot do my job. I just know that you are good at this and that you have helped some people that the rest of us could not reach. I really appreciate you speaking with me. I will talk with her when she comes in today. I will let you know how it goes."

She smiled and stood up; I stood up with her. I went to go to the door, when she grabbed my arm, I slowly turned around because I felt my pulse speed up at her touch. I really wanted to kiss her right then, especially when I turned and saw the look on her face. Such relief and so much passion. Maybe I was seeing it wrong, maybe that is what I wanted to see. She looked at me, drew me in, and hugged me hard and said, "I really mean it, thank you." I could feel how much she appreciated the advice.

I pulled back enough to see her face and told her that it was not a problem and that I was there for her anytime that she needed it. A smile slipped across her face, which did not fit the situation. I felt things low go tight and I released a breath that I did not know I was holding.

She giggled and said, "I guess that I should let you get to your clients for the day. Have a good day Serraid and hope that you have a great weekend."

I squeezed her shoulder and said thank you and turned to leave. As I closed the door behind me, I sort of leaned back against it. 'What the hell was that all about? She has never touched me before. And why did I feel that attracted to her? Ugh, I just could not figure it out, nor did I have time to.' I stuck that thought to the back burner and headed for my office. I had three clients today and then I could go home. That is if nothing went wrong or no unscheduled person showed up. Just the thought of that made me nervous.

I walked into my office and decided to wait on the note; I would have to look at it later. My first client should be arriving at any moment now.

My first client for the day is Terry; she is a 26-year-old female. She came to see me because her boyfriend is abusive to her. She is bi-sexual, and she brings women home for her and her boyfriend to have sex with. Her boyfriend loves it when it is happening but after the fact, he tends to get violent with Terry and punishes her for liking women. He calls her a whore and a slut. He beats her sometimes. She wants to leave him, but she loves him so much. She wants me to help her to not like women anymore. I have told her that I cannot do that, that is something that she must decide for herself. There is no magic cure for this sort of thing. I have also advised her to get out of the abusive relationship that she is in, and that maybe if she accepted who she was, then she could truly be happy. That she needed to find someone that likes the same things as she does.

My phone rang and it was Cheryl telling me that Terry was here for her session. "She looks pretty bad, Serraid. She looks as if someone used her for a punching bag. Do you want me to call the police and file a report?"

"Thank you, Cheryl, I will get her, and I will handle the reporting. I will talk with her about it." With that said, I braced myself for what I would see. It must have been bad if Cheryl was warning me first. I started for the lobby.

Terry sat in her chair, with her head leaning down. I could see that her upper lip was swollen, and her cheek was bruised on the left side. She still had her sunglasses on, so I could not see her eyes. She had a green shirt on that looked as if it spent way too much time in a drawer somewhere. She had on dark blue jeans and a pair of green sandals. She had a peace sign necklace on, with matching earrings. She had her brown hair pulled around her face to help hide the damage that her boyfriend had done. Her shoulders were slumped as if her back was hurting, and she was trying to find a spot that did not hurt quite as much. I felt sad, seeing her look like that. She was such a nice girl, and I could not understand why her boyfriend or anyone for that matter would do this to her. She has a strong will too, and I cannot figure out why she would let anyone do this to her.

I tried to smile a comforting smile as I said, "Terry, are you ready?"

She jumped at the sound of her name. She looked up and smiled a little, "y yes I'm as ready as I'm ever going to be."

She stood up and followed me to my office. I turned when we got to my door and let her go in first. She sat down slowly in her chair, using the arms and her hands to slowly lower her down in the seat as if it hurt to sit down. My stomach was clenched as I watched her do this. It brought back memories of my past when I had hurt that bad. I could feel tears well up in my eyes. I would not cry damnit!

I closed the door and used that as an opportunity to clear my eyes before Terry saw them. I turned and walked to my desk and sat down in my chair. I opened her file and made a quick note on her appearance today and noted that I would make an official report to the police department after she left.

She sat there and looked at me as I was noting her file. "I know it looks awful, and it feels worse than it looks. I think he hurt me this time."

I looked up at her and felt sorrow at the look on her face. "Terry, what happened?"

"Tom wanted to go to the bar last night. He said that he needed something different. I tried talking him out of it, but he got mad saying, 'you just don't want me to have any fun!' I tried telling him that was not it, that I just did not want to fight anymore. I told him that if we went to the bar, I was not going to bring anyone home with us when we came back. He said, 'you will do it, and you will like it. I need someone new; it has been a while since we shared a woman. I know I got mad before, but I promise Terry, I will not get mad this time!' I believed him because he looked and sounded so sincere. We went to the bar and while we were there, Tom pointed out this pretty girl that was there. I went and invited her to come back to our table and have drinks with us. She agreed and told me that her name was Regina. Well, the night went on, and I could tell that Tom was hot for her. So, we took her back to our place. We had a great time. We all had sex together and we all loved it. Tom told me while we were having sex, that he loved how tight she was and how sweet she tasted. I sat back and watched them have sex, and he had a great time, she loved the feel of him inside of her. She said that she loved how big he was and that he knew how to hit the right spots. I went down on her while he had sex with her from behind. She had so many orgasms and was moaning and scratching us. She went down on me while tom fucked her and I ate her. Oh my gosh, she was so good at it. And I slid a finger inside of her while he was inside of her, and she loved it. I thought that we all had a great time. After we were finished, she got dressed and I walked her downstairs to leave. Tom was sleeping on the bed. When we got to the front door, she turned and kissed me and asked if we could do this again sometime. Then she slid a hand down my shirt and played with my nipple. I grabbed her, kissed her, and slid my hand up her skirt. We had sex right there in front of the door. I laid her down and took her clothes off and then took mine off. I went down on her until she was about ready to have an orgasm then I sat on her and rubbed myself on hers. And we orgasmed together. It was wonderful. She told me that I was the first woman that she had been with and that she had never done anything like this before, but that she wanted to be with us again, and that if not both she at least wanted to be with me again. I told her to remember where we lived, and she gave me her number so that we could keep in touch. I gave her my number and told her to call me. Then she left. I went upstairs to take a shower, and while in the shower, Tom woke up. He came into the shower and said that he had a wonderful time. I was nervous because he always gets pissed after the fact because he says that I make him cheat on me. But this time he climbed in the shower, and we made love in the shower, and it was wonderful. He seemed happy and satisfied. I silently said thank you God and then turned off the shower and went to get a towel. Tom stood there in the shower and watched me dry off, and he was already getting hard again. I asked him if he wanted to make love in the bedroom again and he said yes. We went to the bedroom, and he pushed me down on the bed, then he grabbed my vibrator and slid inside of me. He said that he wanted to pretend it was another man fucking me. That made me nervous because he never says anything like that. He has never wanted to share me with another man. He brought me hard and fast. Then he slid the vibrator in my ass, and he slid in behind me. He fucked me in both holes. He came fast, and hard. He laid there for a few minutes, and I honestly thought that everything was going to be all right with us. He turned and looked at me, and I knew that look. He was mad, just like that, with no warning, no reason, he was pissed!

He hit me and said that I was a cheating whore! And that I made him cheat on me with that other woman. I cried and told him that he promised that he would not get mad because he was the one that wanted another woman for the night. He screamed at me and hit me again and said that I was a cheater and that I wanted other men, that he could see it when he told me that he was going to pretend the vibrator was another man. I shook my head and cried, no, I do not cheat! I do not want another man, just you Tom, please! He hit me again, this time with a closed fist. He said that this would be the last time I ever made him cheat on me, and it would be the last time that I wanted any other man ever! He grabbed my vibrator and rammed it inside of me and then pulled it out and rammed it in my ass, he was screaming the whole time, 'whore, you fucking whore, there will never be another man here or here. You will never bring another woman here to tempt me with. You are a fucking whore and a cheat!' He kept ramming it inside of me and hitting me with his fist. His rage was too strong, no matter what I said, nothing helped, it just seemed to make him more pissed off!"

She sat there catching her breath and crying. I took a deep breath and whipped the tears from my eyes. I hated Tom, and I could not figure out why she stayed with him. I know that she loves him but enough has to be enough! I let her calm down for a few minutes before I said anything.

"Terry, you cannot blame yourself. Tom is the one that wanted to go, not you. You did what he asked you to do, and he still punished you for what he wanted. Terry, you have to put a stop to this. You either must stop giving in to his requests or you will have to leave him. His temper is progressing, and the beatings are getting worse, you cannot allow this to continue. You really need to leave him. I am going to have to report this to the police this time. Because I can tell that he has hurt you badly. Have you been to a doctor?"

"No, please do not contact the police, I promise that I am all right, I'm just a little sore. I don't want him to go to jail. Please, please don't call the police!"

"I have to, you are hurt too bad for me to just let this go this time. Look at yourself, he has hurt you for something that he wanted."

She sat there and cried, and after a few minutes she agreed to press charges. I told her that while he was in jail that she could get a protection order against him so that he could not come near her. And that she could take time to heal physically and emotionally.

"This is not a healthy relationship, Terry. He is getting worse, and one time he could kill you in one of his rages. He will not mean to, but he will before he calms down enough to realize what he has done. I am advising you as your therapist to walk away from this. I know that you love him, but he does not love you. You are a wonderful person, and you deserve better than this. This is how someone treats their dog when it has bitten someone, not how you are to treat another person."

"I know that I just have been with him for so long, I am scared of being by myself. I know that I need to leave him, because deep in my heart I know that one day he is going to seriously hurt me. And I do not want to live like that."

I picked up the phone and called the local police department and requested an officer to come to the center. I explained to the officer on the phone what had happened. They said that they had an officer in route. I said thank you and hung up the phone. I called up Cheryl and told her that an officer was on his way and to bring him to my office when he got here. She said that she would do that. I told her thank you and hung up.

"Terry, I know that this seems to be a bad thing to do to you. But I promise this is the right thing for you to do."

She sat there and cried, and I let her. I knew what it felt like to fear what would happen to you if you stayed and on the other hand what would happen to you if you left. I knew that fear all too well. I wanted to go over and hold her but that may have made her distrust me and I did not want that.

She looked up and asked me, "Can I have a hug please?"

I got up and walked around to her and wrapped my arms around her and held her while she wept. She shook as she cried. I just held her and patted her back lightly like a mother would a child. There was a knock on the door.

I walked over and opened the door. The officer was a woman; she had long black hair and dark brown almost black eyes. She stood a good five inches taller than me. She smiled and said that she was here to take a report of an assault.

I said, "of course, please come in. My client, Terry, is the one that needs to press charges against her boyfriend. He assaulted her pretty bad. Terry, this is officer…Gerard, (I read her badge as I talked) she is here to take a statement from you. Do you want me to stay in here while she does this, or would you like me to get you something to drink?"

She looked at me with her puffy, bloodshot eyes, and said, "I want you to stay, but I could use something to drink."

I told her that I would get her something to drink and that I would be right back. "I promise" I said. (I needed some time to process all of this. It brought back too many things too fast. And I could feel the heat building up behind my eyes. With David showing up and the dream and now this, my past was slapping me in the face right now and I started to feel as if I could not breathe.)

She smiled and said thank you and I walked out the door and headed for the vending area.

I reached the vending area; it was empty thank goodness. I leaned against the wall and just let myself go. I stood there and cried silently with my face away from the door so if someone came in, they would not see my face.

I stood there and prayed, 'please God help me out here. I do not know how much more I can take. I ran from my problems and now they are all following me again. Help me to know how to help Terry.'

Praying always made me feel a little better. I do not go to church because most of those people judge me for what I am. And I do not need any other judge but God. I just wanted to go home; I was tired of this day already. I decided that I had taken enough time for myself, and I had promised Terry that I would come right back. I wanted to make sure that she filed the charges. I was afraid that Tom was going to kill her. I had not lied to her about that when I told her. Statistics say that it is more common in this kind of situation. I was betting that Tom's parents were always punishing him for something that they did and then put the blame on little Tommy. It pissed me off enough that I stopped crying. Anger was a great thing to chase away the pain, and I was a professional at it. I straightened up and walked over to the Fridge and grabbed a Pepsi out and started walking back to my office. My step had force to it now, I was pissed. Pissed at Tom for what he had done to Terry, pissed about David showing up, oh hell, I was pissed at myself for sending Florence to the Cat house. Damn, I was just pissed.

I stepped back into my office; Terry was crying, and the officer was writing as fast as Terry was talking. Officer Gerrard looked up at me when I came in. She told Terry that she had enough information to file charges and that they would arrest Tom. Terry said thank you.

The officer asked her if she needed to be seen by a doctor, and she thought that she should.

Terry said, "No thank you, I am fine. I do not think I am seriously hurt."

The officer nodded and took one of her cards out of her shirt pocket and handed it to Terry and then handed me one as well. She said if anything happens, call the number on the back of my card. I will come personally. Point for her, she was taking this seriously.

I said thank you and walked the officer to the door. She shook my hand and said that she could find her way out. I told her thank you again for coming so quickly.

She said, "It is my job. Please do not hesitate to call if she needs anything. She really needs to be seen by a doctor, but she will not listen to me. Maybe you can convince her to get herself checked over by a doctor?"

"I will try and let you know if she does."

She turned and headed down the hallway.

I turned back to Terry, and she said, "The officer said that they were on their way to arrest Tom right now, and that I cannot go back home for at least an hour. She said that she would call me as soon as they had him in custody, that way I knew it was safe to go home. Do you mind if I stay here until she calls?"

I smiled and said, "Terry you can stay here, that will not be a problem. We have a lounge area in the back, come with me and I will take you there and help you get comfortable. You can lay down and rest until you can go home. I really wish that you would go to the hospital and let a doctor check you over, though. You may have a concussion or something of which you are not aware."

She smiled, "Thank you, but I am fine really, I don't think that I'm hurt too bad. It just looks bad. I will lie down and rest for a while. Thank you for being here for me and helping me to be strong enough to do this."

She walked over to me as she spoke and wrapped her arms around me. She then leaned up and kissed me. I froze and tensed up.

"Terry, what are you doing? I do not think this is a good idea."

She leaned away from me and said, "Please, I need this. I need to feel the closeness of someone when I'm hurting. Please, I'm sorry if I crossed any lines, I just thought maybe you liked me too."

"Terry, you are my client, I cannot be this way with you. I do like you; I just cannot do this with you because I would be violating my code of conduct. Do you understand?"

She reached up and kissed me again, pinching my nipple as she did. I felt things go tight. She was beautiful and very sexy, but she was my client, and I just could not do this…What the hell am I going to do, I thought. She bit my neck and squeezed my nipple harder. That brought a small noise from my throat. I could feel myself going wet. I wanted her.

"You are not violating anything, I'm starting this. I want to feel you, all of you, I want us to explore each other, and please each other. Please, it will make everything better. You know it will."

I did not know what to say to that, so I said nothing.

She pressed me up against the desk and kissed me deeply, that is when I saw that the door was open. I stopped her and said, "I have to close the door."

I walked over to the door and closed and locked it. I went back to my desk and called up Cheryl and told her that I was going to have Terry in my office until the police called her and told her that she could return home. I told her that we were not to be disturbed, because we were going to be talking in detail about what happened. Cheryl said OK and hung up. What the hell am I doing? I did not even get to think the next thought that would have been because Terry pulled up my shirt. It caught my breath, because I wanted this, yet the professional part of me knew this was wrong.

Terry kissed my stomach and licked a line between my breasts. She pulled them out of my bra and flicked my nipple with her tongue. It felt so good, and tightened things low in my stomach. She flicked it again and it made me moan. She giggled, and looked up at me, when she took my nipple in her mouth and sucked as much of my breast as she could into her mouth. My eyes rolled up, from the feeling of being in her mouth. It made me wonder what it would feel like to have her over things farther down. This made the moisture flow faster. As if she sensed it, she slid a hand under my skirt and slid my panties to the side. She rubbed across the outside of me; I moaned and moved my hips just a little. She slid one finger inside and then pulled it out and rubbed my clit with the moistened fingers.

"MMM You are so wet. You like this, don't you? You want to feel me inside of you?"

I shook my head a little too fast, and I grabbed her and kissed her, as she shoved three fingers inside as deep as she could get them. I felt my body contract around her, hugging and growing tighter. She moved in and out slowly, rubbing my clit with her thumb. I could feel the pressure building, shit! She was going to bring me too fast.

"You have to stop, or you are going to make me cum"

She smiled and said, "I want you to cum all over my fingers. Then I'm going to lick it off you."

Just the thought of this threw me over. My head went back, and my back arched and I felt the contractions of the orgasm fighting against her fingers, she slid down and started licking me, this made my eyes roll back and a deep moan from my lips. I moved my hips up just a little so that she could get a better angle. She sucked on the outside of me, and this brought another orgasm that undid me. My knees buckled and I could feel myself losing control.

She giggled, and said, "Damn girl, you taste so good."

She took her fingers out of me, and slid them down her pants, and put them inside of her. She pulled them out and ran them over my lips. She tasted like plums. I undid her pants and pulled off her panties. I licked between her lips, her hips bucked and moved wanting more. I pulled back and rubbed my fingers over her wet lips. She moaned, I leaned back in and kissed her there like I would kiss her mouth, deep, exploring every inch that I could reach. I could feel her tightening about ready to have an orgasm, I suck her clit into my mouth and shook it a little while I shoved two fingers inside of her, she gasped and then the orgasm hit her. She became so wet so fast, her hips bucked. I wanted to feel my clit slide over hers. I straddled her and placed mine on her, I started moving slowly letting the pressure build, letting her feel my wetness mixing with her. The feeling was amazing. I moved faster now, rubbing, pressing back and forth. The orgasm hit me with no warning. It threw my head and arched my back and brought a moan from my throat and arched her back as the orgasm hit her at the same time. We came together. And it was wonderful.

I slid to the side and laid there looking at her. She appeared calm. She looked at me, and said, "You don't know how long I have wanted to do that. I have wanted to feel you since the first time I came to see you. You were wonderful, and so good. Can we do this again sometime?"

I smiled at her and told her that yes that would be lovely, and that next time I do not want it to be here. I heard footsteps coming down the hall. I jumped up and helped her get her clothes on. Her face appeared a little better somehow.

We had just got dressed when there was a knock on the door. I took a quick peek into the mirror to make sure that I was presentable, then I opened the door. Cynthia stood there. She said that her client had agreed to the treatment. And that she was relieved. She looked so peaceful. She hugged me and brushed my neck with her lips. What the hell is going on with her today? She has never been this way.

I pulled back and asked her if she was alright.

She said, "yes, just feeling a little pressure and no way to release it."

"What do you mean?"

"Well, I have not had sex in about six months, I 'm sorry Serraid, I guess it is just pouring through, I did not mean anything."

I assured her that it was fine. But inside I wanted to pull her into the office and kiss her and make her feel wonderful. She was so damn sexy, and those lips...I wanted to kiss her lips. Cynthia turned and went back to her office.

Terry's phone rang, the police picked Tom up and arrested him. She could go home now. She said thank you and headed for home.

I sat there in my chair and took a couple of deep breaths, I felt exhausted, drained somehow. I usually did not feel this way after sex, but this time was different, Terry seemed to feel better, and some of her bruises even looked a little better. I had to figure out what was going on today. I mean do I have a sign that says, I am frustrated please rub here, posted somewhere? I giggled at that thought. Cheryl called and said that Stephen was here for his session. Ugh! I did not know if I had the patience to help him today.

Stephen is 30 years old and suffers from schizophrenia, he hears voices that tell him to do things. He has a severe case of this.

I walked to the lobby and told Stephen that I was ready. He walked behind me because he had a phobia of people following him. He sat down on the couch. And looked at me suspiciously. I asked him how he was doing today. He smiled and said that he had not heard any voices today, and that he thought that he was getting better. I smiled back at him and told him that it was good.

"Are you taking your medicine again?"

"Yes, I started it after I left here last week. You said it would make the voices go away, and today it has."

"Stephen, you need to take it every day. The medicine that you are on takes time to build up into your system. Once you quit taking it, it stops working. You must keep taking it even though you feel better. Do you understand?"

"Yes, I promise doc, I will keep taking it this time. I do not like the voices at all. Some of them are angry. They want me to fly out of my window at night. They tell me that I was born to fly. But I am too scared to try it. What if I hit the ground hard and never wake up?"

I smiled at him softly, trying not to laugh. Stephen would take his medicine until he started feeling better and then he would quit. He thought that if the voices were not there, that he could stop because he was cured. Sometimes, he got bad and had to be restrained in the hospital ward for a few days to get his meds back into his system. Sometimes, I got so frustrated with him that I wanted to throw him out the window just to see if he could fly. I know that does not sound like anything a counselor would say, but let me tell you, we think things like that all the time about our clients, it is either that or go crazy with them! I mean, if we cannot joke about things like that, then what are we doing here? Right? Psychopath, who me?

"Did you hear me?"

"Oh, I am sorry Stephen, I was thinking about something. What did you say?"

He smiled and said that it was ok and then repeated what he said. "I have had a voice telling me that I was supposed to be a woman. It wants me to get women skin and wear it."

"Women's clothing, you mean?"

"No, their skin. Like it wants me to take their skin and wear it."

"Stephen, does this voice tell you why you should do this? What it wants to gain from it?"

"No, it just says that I would be happier if I was a woman, that I would not have to struggle as much as I do now. That I could change my name and everything and be a completely different person."

"Well, you know that is not how that works, right? I mean just because you wear the person does not make you that person. This is not a natural thought. How many times has this voice told you to do this?"

"Only a few times, maybe three or four times. I argue with it. I tell it that is nasty and I do not want to wear a woman. And that I was happy being me. The voice tells me that I am not happy, that I see all these women walking down the street and they are smiling and dressed so nice, and that I could be them."

"Stephen, this is not a healthy thought. You know that you should not do something like that. That would require taking their lives. And you cannot do that. That is against the law." You have not done anything to any woman have you? I asked.

"No, I would not do that, it is gross and nasty thought. I do not like that voice much, it scares me."

"You know that I will have to report this, just in case anything happens and that voice comes back and too strong, don't you?"

"I know that, and I am not going to listen to that voice. I am glad that the voices are not talking to me anymore. I think I can stop my sessions with you now that they are gone."

"Stephen, no, you cannot. You must come here and see me even when the voices do not talk to you. We have discussed this before. And you know that there is no guarantee that the voices will not return."

"Yeah, but this time it is different, I feel better than I ever have. I really feel like this time, I am cured. I do not see the people in the T.V. anymore or the people outside of my window anymore either."

I sat there knowing this would be a downhill battle, because we have danced this dance so many times before. Ugh! He frustrated me. I would have to call his overseer and make sure that they made sure that he made his future appointments, and to let them know about the women's skin issues as well. I will be calling his doctor and letting them know that information as well, that way they can adjust his meds if needed. Stephen stood up and said that he was going to go.

"But you still have 30 minutes left in our session."

I noticed a tick that he had developed with his head, I do not remember that being there last week. I will tell his doctor about that as well.

"I am leaving, I do not need to be here today, I have nothing to talk about, there are no voices, and I am feeling great. So, I will see you next week." With that he walked out the door.

I sat there astonished that he had just got up and left. What the hell was he thinking?! Oh hell, I do not want to know what he is thinking. I picked up the phone and started calling his overseer and his doctor. There was certainly something going on with Stephen. I am going to recommend that they hold him for 72 hours and do some tests. I believe that he has progressed even farther than we thought that he had. The comment about women's skin stuck with me. Had he already hurt a woman or women? Shit! I would call the local police department and see about recent missing females. Maybe if I hear that there have not been any in the last couple of days, then I will feel a little better.

I spoke with his doctor and told him what Stephen had told me about the women and about the tick that I noticed today. He said that he would call him today. He said that he agreed that he would put him on a hold for three days, just to make sure that he does not hurt anyone. I am hoping he has not already hurt someone.

Cheryl buzzed and I picked up the phone, she said that my next client was early and wanted to let me know, since Stephen had left early. I told her thank you and that I would be up as soon as I finished with the paperwork I was doing.

My next client is Ebb. She is suffering from the loss of her brown Boston Terrier. His name was snuggles and Ebb is having a hard time letting go. She misses her thirteen-year-old friend. She took his death extremely hard and even had to go on Prozac for a while. She seems to be doing better now. I walked up to get her.

Ebb stood at the counter talking to Cheryl. She seemed happy today. I was glad to see her smile, which meant that she would be in a good mood for our session today. I needed good moods, after the morning that I have had.

Whew! It has been a rough day, just one more and you are out of here Serrie, just one more…

Ebb smiled and followed me to my office. I commented on how lovely her sundress was, she said thank you.

We got to my office and sat down.

She looked at me and said, "I think that I have decided to get another baby. I have found a breeder that has a new litter that is almost ready to be taken home. What do you think?"

I smiled at her and said, "I think that if you feel that you are ready to take that step, then I support you all the way. You will make one of those little guys a good mommy."

She smiled wide, flashing teeth. Her happiness spread across her face. I saw her eyes light up. "Thank you so much for all your help. I still miss my snuggles, but I know that I must let go, because he is in a happy place now."

I looked at her and hoped that she would not turn for the teary side now. "I think that you have coped very well through all of this. And all I did was listen; you did all this yourself Ebb. I was just here to help guide you, that is all."

She smiled again and said, "I know, but you have helped me so much. I want to bring the new little girl in and let you meet her when I pick her up. Would that be all right?"

I nodded and realized that she may not see it, and said, "yes, that would be lovely."

She stood up and said "well that is all I wanted to talk about today. I think that I am going to go pick out my baby."

"You still have fifty minutes left of your session, for which you have paid."

"I know, and do not worry about refunding the rest of the money, I want you to keep it. That way if I need to come back, I am paid in advance for some of the sessions."

I did not know what to say to that. "Thank you so much Ebb, I am so glad that you are feeling better, and I am glad that you have come to this decision on your own. I am sure that you will be a great mommy to this little girl that you pick out, and she will love you."

She walked out the door and went to pick out her little new puppy.

I sat there and decided to wrap up my paperwork and then head home. This turned out to be an all right day. Now if it would just stay that way it would be great. I finished my dictations and still left the office thirty minutes early. I stepped outside and felt the sunshine on my face; Its rays warming my skin. I blinked at the brightness of it. I should have brought my sunglasses. I could smell the peonies that were in bloom by the center doors. They always smell so good. I loved the colors. Maybe I would have to plant some of them at the house. That was another task to put on my to-do list. I had a lot of things on that list as of now. I giggled at that, thinking that I probably would not get any of them completed. I procrastinated too much.

With that thought I got into my car, sat my briefcase on the passenger seat, and started the engine. I headed home. I had called Sarah before leaving the office to see if she needed anything on my way home. She said for me to stop by the liquor store and grab some alcohol; she had picked the movies.

I stopped by the Stop and Shop Liquor and picked up a twelve pack of Budweiser and a pint of vodka and a gallon of orange juice. Yeah, it was going to be a good night. I got back to the car and headed for home…

CHAPTER 5

(Friday night to Saturday night.)

I arrived home, and the house looked a little dark. I wondered to myself, what is Sarah doing? I parked the car and got the bags from the Stop and Shop Liquor store and my briefcase, locked the car doors, and headed into the house.

When I got up to the porch, I tried getting my keys in place so that I could unlock the door. Sarah opened the door with a huge smile.

"Hey, you, let me help you with those. You get comfortable so we can get this night started."

"Sure, I am going to jump in the shower quickly and get some pj's on. I will be down in a bit. Oh, and Sarah make sure the door is locked, ok?"

"I will. You just go and shower and get comfy. I got this down here. I will make our drinks while you are getting relaxed."

"Thanks, You're the greatest ever." I said as I started up the stairs.

"No problem, I've been looking forward to this night for a long time." She said as she headed into the kitchen with the alcohol.

Once upstairs, I placed my briefcase by my dresser and got into my pajama drawer. Should I wear something conservative, sexy, or old? I decided on my cat flannel set, they were so comfortable, and soft. They always made me feel safe.

I headed to the shower. I turned on the hot water and started taking my clothes off. I wanted to feel the hot water hitting my shoulders, draining the tension away. I stepped into the shower, and man did the water feel so good. I needed to wash the day away.

After washing my hair, and scrubbing all the tension away, I turned off the water and grabbed the towel and wrapped my hair in it. I then grabbed my other towel and started drying off. I looked at myself in the mirror and realized how bad I looked. I looked like I had not slept in days; I felt that way too. I got dressed, unwrapped my hair, and combed it out. Then headed downstairs.

Sarah was in the front room, with drinks on the table as promised.

"I got two movies for us to watch. Robin Hood and P.S. I love you. I was not sure if you would want an action movie or a romance movie, so I got one of each."

"We can watch both. I love action and romance. Is this my drink?" I asked, pointing to the green glass on the table.

"Yes, that is yours. I made this one kind of strong. Figured by the way that you looked when you came through the door that you would need a good stiff drink to help relax you a little." She replied with a smile upon her lips that I could not decipher.

"I do need a good stiff one. Thank you, Sarah."

Sarah walked over and put Robin hood in the DVD player. She then came back to the couch, grabbed her drink, and sat down beside me. I giggled because it reminded me how young she was.

"What are you laughing at? I know you are not laughing at me…" She giggled as she sipped on her drink.

"Actually, I am laughing at you. I was just thinking about how young you are. You always seem so carefree. I wish that I could be like you more often."

"Girl, you just have to learn to let loose and relax a little, that is all. You have to learn to leave work at work. Do not bring it home with you."

"I know, I just worry so much about things. But enough shop talk. Let us start this night off right." I said. I raised my glass and said, "here's to friendship, love, laughter and just two girls hanging with each other."

"Here here," Sarah said as she tapped my glass with hers.

We both laughed as the movie started. We sat and drank our drinks and watched intensely as the movie played on. Sarah stretched out her legs.

I looked at her sitting there and thought, she is gorgeous. I wondered what it would feel like to kiss her lips. Then I thought, what am I thinking! I cannot think this way about her. She is young and I cannot take advantage of her like that.

I settled back on the couch and finished watching the movie. We laughed at some scenes. Then Sarah got up.

"I'm going to get another drink; you want one to?"

"I will pause the movie and go with you. I need to get something to eat anyway."

We went into the kitchen, and I grabbed a loaf of bread and some sandwich meat out of the refrigerator. I grabbed the Mayonnaise and some lettuce. I made a sandwich.

"Do you want one, Sarah?"

"No thanks, I ate before you got here."

"Ok, but don't say that I didn't offer." I said laughing.

Sarah made our drinks, and we went back to the front room. We sat down and re-started the movie. I settled back and enjoyed the taste of my sandwich. I always have loved the way lettuce crunches in my mouth. It always reminds me of when I was a little girl, my mother would make me lunch, and I would complain about the lettuce. She would say, "Serraid, just try it, you will like it." She was always right too. I giggled at the thought.

"What are you giggling about? You are not getting drunk already, are you?" She said with a puzzling look on her face.

"No, I was just remembering how, when I was a little girl, my mother would put lettuce on my lunches, and I would complain about it. She would always tell me to try it, and I would like it. I would try it and she was right; I did like it." I said with a smile on my face.

"You are so weird. But I love it. I never know what you are thinking about." She said with a warm laugh.

I could tell that the alcohol was kicking in on her. I could feel the warmness flowing through me too. Sarah then reached over and brushed my hair with her fingers. I felt dizzy, as if something were wrong, and there was a weird smell in the air.

"The next thing I remember is waking up in the chair and all the blood everywhere. I called the police because Sarah was nowhere to be found. They did not seem to be listening when they got to my place, so I started yelling at them. Please, you guys need to be doing something to find my friend!"

"Ma'am you need to calm down, we are doing everything that we can do right now. We have cars out looking and the rest of the officers are going door to door to see if any of the neighbors have heard anything."

I sat there and looked in disbelief as officer Juan told me this. I wanted to find my friend. I could not bring myself to think about what could have happened to her. The last thing I remember is sitting here and watching a movie. How the hell could this happen? I told her to make sure the door was locked. That is, it!

"Officer? Can you tell me if my front door was locked or if someone busted in?"

"We didn't find any evidence of forced entry."

I thought to myself, ok, so no one forced their way in, so what happened? Think Serraid, think! A loud voice caught my attention; I heard someone saying that they needed to come in because he was a friend. Every cell in my body tensed, because surely David would not be that bold. John came around the entry way. I sighed in relief at the sight of my neighbor.

"John! It is Sarah, she is missing and there is all this blood, and I do not know what happened. The cops do not seem to be doing anything, and I do not seem to be able to remember anything."

"Serraid, just calm down. The officers are combing the entire six-block radius right now for clues. They will find her."

"I hope you are right, and I hope they find her alive. Why would anyone want Sarah? She is young and nice and does not deserve this. Why didn't they take me?" I said as I started to cry. Why was this happening!

John pulled me in for a hug, and as soon as his arms wrapped around me, I felt at ease. I looked up at him and the look of serenity on his face made me warm all over. He felt so familiar, but that was silly because I had just met him a few days ago. I pulled back away from his embrace and said thank you.

"Are you calmer now?"

"Yes, thank you so much for being here. I know that Sarah would be very appreciative."

"If you need me to, I can stay for a while. I will make sure that we are doing everything that we can do to find her."

"Thank you, I would like that. I really do not want to be alone right now."

We sat on the couch as the police finished taking their pictures and their samples and were packing up and getting ready to leave. One of the female officers came over to me and asked me if I was holding up ok. I told her yes and that I really needed to know what if anything they had discovered.

"Well right now we are collecting evidence. We will take it back to the lab and run some tests and see if we can get a match on anything. I promise, Serraid, we will let you know when we find something."

"Thank you, Officer, Mallard. You have been the nicest officer here. I just want to let you know that I appreciate you treating me like a person and not just a victim or a suspect."

With that she smiled, turned, and walked out of the house, taking the last officer with her. They did not seem to think that there would be a ransom request, due to all the blood, they were really expecting to find Sarah's body somewhere. That was the hardest thing that I had to think about. I could not imagine her laying somewhere lifeless. Ugh! What am I going to do? Everything was quiet, John had gone to the kitchen to make some soup for me to eat, even though I had told him that I did not feel hungry. I heard a scratch and called out to my cat.

"Patches, here baby! Come to momma! Kitty kitty!"

After a few minutes he did not come, I stood up and wandered through the living room. I looked under the sofa and under the chair, nothing. Where the hell could he be? I kept calling out to him with no luck. I felt my heart jump up in my throat as I walked over by the stairs. I could hear the scratching sound coming from under the stairs. It appeared that some of the boards had been removed and replaced.

"John! Come quickly!"

"What is it Serraid? Are you hur...." His words trailing off when he saw me there with a hammer in my hand. "What are you doing Serraid?"

"Shh and listen."

There was another scratching sound and a soft meow this time.

"See!! My cat is in there!" I began prying the boards off one by one. "Hurry go to the kitchen and get my flashlight out of the top drawer."

As I got the last of the board off the wall John handed me the flashlight and We looked in. What we saw made my heart jump through my throat. I could feel the bile settling in my throat. I jerked my head away before I threw up. I thought to myself. Please do not let her be dead. Please God do not let her be dead.

"Help me!" I said as I started frantically yanking the wood off the wall. "Please, Sarah, can you hear us?" What seemed like an hour later, we were pulling her from the cubby under the stairs. I checked for a pulse, and it was faint. She was bruised up and bleeding.

"Call 911, John! John! Snap out of it! Call 911 right now!"

As He fumbled for his cell phone from his pocket, I held my best friend in my arms and rocked her slightly. Praying for a miracle and wondering how this could have happened.

A scene flashed through my mind.

I was sitting in the middle of a cold room. The floor was made of marble. There was a fire in the hearth. I sat cross legged and rocked slowly as I held my tattered clothes to my breast. Wishing for death and not finding it. Hating the man that had done this to me. Wanting revenge, yet to scared to try.

"Serraid! Earth to Serraid!" John was standing there snapping his fingers in front of my face. "Are you all right? I mean you seemed like you were on another planet, your stare was blank."

"Yes, I am just exhausted and worried. How long till the ambulance arrives?" I could hear the sirens then and knew that Sarah Would be all right. But where did that flash of memory come from? And what did it mean? I was beginning to think that I needed to take some time off from everything and just concentrate on me before I lose it.

"In here! Hurry please!" The paramedics came in quickly and started taking care of Sarah. I sat against the wall crying and praying for a miracle. Patches walked over to me and sat on my lap. He was covered in blood. I looked toward the cubby again and that is when I saw it. I quickly reached over and grabbed the piece of paper from where Sarah had been laying.

I unfolded it and read what it said: *Serraid, remember how I have been most patient, and forgiving. I have spared your friend, all though, I didn't want to. But remember my compassion toward her when you think of me. Serraid, do not push the envelope of my mercy too far, as my patience is running thin these days. Love, D~*

My eyes filled with tears and my hands were shaking when I read that note. What does he mean do not push my mercy? I do not know why He did this! What did David want with me? What!!! I got pissed and stood up too quickly. My eyes went blank, and I felt as if someone stuffed a cotton ball in my head.

I leaned against the wall and calmed down a bit. I looked up and John was staring at me.

"Are you alright? What is that?"

"I am fine, I just got up to quickly. This is a note from whoever put Sarah in there."

"Let me see that." John said as he grabbed it out of my hand. "It looks like very old paper."

When John opened it up and read it, his face went red, and his pupils blew up to almost the size of his eyes.

"I must go right now! I am sorry Serraid, give Sarah my best, but I must go home now."

"Are you all right John? Do you know this signature?"

"Listen! I do not have time to answer your silly questions; I must go right now!" With that he ran out the door.

What the hell was that about? I wondered? Why had John acted like that? Did He know D? That is impossible, Serraid you are just being paranoid. I told myself.

I followed the ambulance to the hospital, praying the whole way that Sarah would be ok. When we arrived at the hospital the doctor was waiting for her arrival.

After thirty minutes a nice nurse came out and told me that I could go to Sarah's room.

"Is she going to be ok?"

"Your friend is going to be fine physically, emotionally she may be a wreck for a while. The assault kit confirmed that she has been raped, and she has a few cuts and bruises too." She said as she grabbed my arm comforting me.

Anger filled my whole mind. I wanted to kill him. He could have done this to me, and I would have understood, but why my friend? Why her? Ugh!! I began stomping toward Sarah's room. Just outside of the door, I stopped and recollected myself. I decided that Sarah was going to need me to be strong, not weak and pissed.

I smiled as I came into the room and saw her sitting up.

"Hey, you, how are you feeling?" I asked Sarah as I walked up to her bed.

"I have been better. What happened? The Nurses are not telling me much of anything right now." Sarah said with an emptiness in her eyes that should not ever have been there.

"Tell me what they have told you and I will tell you what else I know, which is not much of anything. Sarah, I am so sorry sweetie." I began to cry as I hugged her. Thinking that all of this was my fault.

"Serraid, you did not do this to me. You cannot blame yourself for this. Whoever did this, chose to do what they did. You did not cause this." She said with sincerity in her voice.

I hugged her tightly as we cried together. Knowing that she would not be the same young, carefree person that she once was, that she was just last night. I screamed inside of my head, I cried, and I got pissed. My heart started beating faster and faster. I began to feel as if my skin was on fire.

Sarah broke the silence as she began telling me what she knew. "The nurse said that you found me in a closet under your stairs, there was blood all over the place, but that it was not mine. She also said that…." She trailed off, beginning to cry. I held her closer. I knew that the nurse had told her about the rape. Ugh! I am going to kill him I thought to myself. "That I was raped. She asked me if I wanted the emergency morning after pill. I do not know what to do Serraid. I have never had to worry about this. Should I take it? I mean do you think there could be a chance that I am pregnant? Please Serraid tell me what to do!"

"Shhh, Sarah, it will all be ok I promise. I know that it is hard right now, it will get better. You worry about every minute by minute. Do not think past that right now. I think that it would be safe to take the pill just in case. I promise Sarah, whoever did this to you will pay. That is a promise that I make to you today!"

"Thank you Serraid. I will tell the nurse that I want the pill. She said that I could go home after a few hours. They want to watch me for a few hours to make sure that there is not something internally that they have missed. I just do not know if I want to go home just yet."

"Sarah, that is so understandable right now. If you do not want to go home, we can get a hotel room. I will not leave you alone for a while. John came by today when the police were there. He was worried about you. He said to tell you that he hopes that you get better soon."

She smiled at me when I told her that, for one second, she looked like the old Sarah. I wondered how much she actually remembered, but I was too afraid to bring up pains that were better left unsaid for now. Like she read my mind she began speaking.

"I remember having drinks with you. I also remember you making that sandwich and laughing about the lettuce. I remember that I pushed your hair out of your face as I thought…Well anyway, I remember hearing a noise behind me and then there was a blur of something. You passed out and then I was slammed against the wall…."

"It is ok Sarah; you do not have to talk about this right now Hun. Just rest and take your time babe."

"Yes, I do! There is something that I am supposed to remember to tell you!" She slapped her head.

I grabbed her hand.

"Sarah do not do that sweetie. It is ok, your safe now, I am here. He will not hurt you here."

"Shut up!!!! He has already hurt me Serraid! Can't you see that?! Look at me! I am hurt!" She broke down and released her anguish. Tears streamed down her face, and she looked so broken. I wanted to tear something up. My heart sank looking at my best friend, knowing that someone from my past did this to her.

"I am sorry Serraid, I did not mean it. I promise, please do not be mad at me. I do not know what got into me. I am sorry, I did not mean to yell at you like that."

"Sarah, it is perfectly normal to react that way. You are doing great Hun." I said as I ran my fingers through her hair and hugged her. I wanted to cuddle her like a mother or sister would. I wanted her to feel safe.

"I remember him telling me that I was going to like being with him. His breath smelled bad too. His face was blurry, and I could not see it really well. I tried to focus but it was like my eyes just did not want to see what was in front of me. He whispered in my ear as he...."

"It is ok Sarah, take your time sweetie. I am sorry that you are having to go through this."

"Raped me. He told me that I reminded Him of you. That he could not wait to get back inside of you. But I would have to do for now. He told me to tell you that you had till midnight tomorrow, which would be tonight. He said that you would know from the note he left at your office what it was that he wanted."

Just then I remembered the note that was taped on the office door that Cheryl had given me. I never took the time to read it. I had forgotten about it with everything that happened that day. Shit! That means I have to go to the office and get it. "Sarah, I have to go to my office and get this note. I will make sure that there are officers right outside before I leave."

"Please Serraid, do not go, do not give this man what he wants. Do not do anything for him!"

"Sarah, I won't. But I will make him pay for what he has done! I promise it will all be ok. I will be back in a few hours." With that said I kissed her forehead and walked out of the hospital room. I looked for an officer and told them that I wanted them to watch her room as if it were their mother. They agreed and said that they had orders to protect her from Officer Mallard. Point for her. She was smarter than she looked.

I got to the Center and went into my office. I turned on the light and jumped when my coat rack scared me. I got mad at myself for being so jumpy. I began remembering what Sarah had said in the hospital. Why would he rape her when I was right there if that is what he wanted? None of it made any sense.

I found the note; I opened it and started shaking at what it said.

'Serraid, I hope that this note finds you doing well. I must admit that you have me intrigued and reminiscing about how times were in the past. I see how fast the world moves today and wonder to myself how we ever managed in the past without all the amenities that there are today. I remember petty coats and hoop dresses, suits, and ties. Whatever has the world come to? Anyhow, down to real matters. I have missed you love; I wanted another chance. I know that I shouldn't deserve it, but I just cannot simply walk without you by my side. I have decided to meet at the pier at one a.m. on the morrow. Until then my love, stay safe. Love ~D.

My heart was in my throat. Now I know why he came to the house last night and what he meant by patience. I was supposed to meet him last night! Damn it! But that still does not explain why he would rape Sarah with me there! If it was me that he wanted, I was right there. Why not simply take me? I screamed out my frustration, turned and left the Center. I was going to get answers. I had to go back to the house and make sure all the blood was cleaned up and make sure that I did not miss something that could cost another friend's safety. If the blood was not Sarah's, then whose was it? I will be calling police and find out if they know.

I saw the police car as soon as I turned the corner by my house. I knew that they were going to be hanging around for a few days just to keep an eye out. I waved as I passed them. I pulled up in front of the house and went inside. The smell hit my nose as soon as I opened the door, and the bile immediately rushed to my throat. I would not throw up, I told myself.

"Hey there, you need some help cleaning up?"

I jumped at the suddenness of the voice. I turned slowly and saw John standing in the doorway. I released a breath that I did not realize that I was holding. And tried to smile.

"John do not sneak up on me like that! You scared the crap out of me!" I said with my finger pointed at him and walking toward him.

"I am sorry, I just thought that you might want some company and some help cleaning up the mess. How is Sarah doing?" He said with a smile that somehow seemed so familiar, but I could not place it.

"She is doing as good as expected. She is pretty shaken up. She was raped, John. Whoever did this raped her, and I was here and could not do anything to stop it. He left me a message, with Sarah too. I must meet him at the pier at one am. He had left that in a note at my office the other day. I just read it today. That is why he came here because I did not meet him. He told Sarah that I am to meet him tonight at one am."

"Have you told the police about the notes yet? Serraid you will, need some help with this." John said with a peculiar look on his face.

"I have not told the police about the notes, and I do not plan on it either. I know who this is that is doing these things. I should have killed him when he put me through all the bad stuff, he did to me. But I was too weak then, all I did was run. I am done running John, I am going to pay him back for all that he has done to me, and Sarah. Do not try to stop me because you will not succeed. I will get my vengeance." I was steaming by this point. I had to slow my breathing before I passed out from hyperventilating.

"Ok, Serraid. I understand. If you want, I will help you. Would you like to sit and talk with me and fill me in on who this is and why he wants you?"

"Let's get this house cleaned up and then I will make some coffee and will tell you what I can remember." I said as I started for the kitchen.

I reached the kitchen, got under the sink, and grabbed the bleach and some old rags. I handed them to John. Then I went out back and grabbed some wood that I had planned on using for the back deck, but it would have to do for the stairs. An hour and a half later we had all the blood cleaned and the wall fixed under the stairs. It smelled better in there too. I sprayed some air freshener and went to kitchen to put everything away when the phone rang.

"Hello, yes this is Serraid. Uh-huh. Ok. Yes, I have one, his name is Patches. Why? What? Really? No, I only have one cat, no others and he is fine. As far as I know, He is the only one on the block. No, her shirt was still intact. Why? What? That is weird. Ok, thank you. Bye." I hung up the phone. What the hell?

"Who was that?" John asked.

"It was officer Mallard. She asked me if I had any cats. I told her Patches and that I do not have any others. She said that the blood all over the house was feline blood. She asked me if there were any other cats in the neighborhood. I told her that I did not think that there were. It is weird, why would someone spread cats' blood all over my house? Was he trying to make me think that Sarah was dead? Maybe trying to throw off the cops?"

"Could be." John said. "Maybe, he wanted to scare you. And if that was his mission, he accomplished it because you were scared when I got here Serraid. I know that you saw the blood and automatically thought that she was dead. So, in a sense he got what he wanted. A moment of pure fear from you." John walked over as he talked and placed his hand on my shoulder.

"She also said that the blood had traces of cotton in it. Like it contained fabric. What the hell does that even mean? How can blood contain fabric? The only thing that I can think of is that he used a towel or something to strain the blood before he spread it all over, or he used a cloth to spread it." I was starting to get a headache from all of this. I could not think of why so many things did not make any sense with this. I went to the cabinet to get some Motrin.

John watched me as I took something for my headache. He smiled and quickly looked away. "There could be other reasons for the blood to contain cloth. I am not a blood expert but don't drug addicts use cotton to filter their drugs? Maybe he had drugged the cat before killing it. Serraid, we need to go through the house and make sure that there are no other notes or evidence or no one hiding in here at all."

"I agree. I will take the upstairs; you take the downstairs and the basement." I said as I headed up the stairs.

"Why do I get the downstairs AND the basement?" He asked with a smirk on his face.

"Because you are a man, and you are stronger than me. And you are not as good looking, so they will not take you." I said with a laugh.

John threw a book from my shelf at me as he laughed. "Gee thanks. That was a superb compliment…"

I turned and headed up stairs. I checked all my drawers and closets. I looked in my tub, under the bed, in the linen closet. There was nothing. Then I went to the attic door. And I saw it. A smudge of blood on the handle. My heart started racing. Suddenly John was right next to me.

"What is wrong? I heard; I mean thought that I heard you scream." He said, scratching his head.

"What? I mean, there is a smudge of blood on the attic door handle. I just saw it, and my heart started racing and then there you were. How did you do that?"

"I was already heading up the stairs; I thought that I heard you scream. So, I ran up the rest of the stairs. Are you ok Serraid? You look a little pale." He said with a concerned look on his face.

"I am fine, I think that all this excitement is taking its toll though. I feel exhausted, drained but I will be fine. I am going to open the door, if anything jumps out, I expect you to kill it…" I said staring at his eyes. He knew that I meant it.

"Ok, open it. I am the man after all so I will kill whatever comes out." He said as he laughed.

I opened the door, and nothing happened. We both went in and headed up the stairs. The light switch is just at the top of the stairs. I almost reached it when John grabbed my hand and put a finger to his mouth.

"Shh, don't make a sound." He whispered in my ear. He then went around me and sniffed the air. What the hell is he doing? I thought to myself. I thought that he smelled cologne or something. He lunged around the stairs in one leap, and I heard this horrible growl! I ducked down thinking that there was a huge dog hiding in my attic. A moment later, John came around the corner.

"Well, what was that all about?" I asked, letting the anger bleed through my voice.

"What? Well, I thought I smelled something. But it was just patches. I am not sure how he got up here but here he is." As if on cue, patches came around the corner and meowed at me.

We went back downstairs, and I started coffee. I packed a bag for me and Sarah for a couple of days while I waited for the coffee to brew. There were a lot of things that we needed to talk about. And the more I am around John, the more I am wondering if there is something wrong with him. Something just is not quite right. I just cannot put my finger on it. All I know is that I must go through everything with John and then get back to the hospital to Sarah.

Two hours later, I had told John everything. John told me that he would help me in any way that he could. He said that me and Sarah could stay at his place for a while if we wanted to. Now, I was sitting in the hospital watching my best friend try to act like nothing was wrong. She was trying to be so strong. But I could see the anxiety and the fear. Oh, yes, they are quite different.

The nurse came in, and Sarah signed her release papers. "Where are we going to go, Serraid?" Sarah asked as we walked out of her room.

"Where would you like to go, Sarah? Oh, John says hello and he offered his place if we wanted it. He said that we could stay if we liked." I said with a wink.

"No, I really do not want to go that close to home yet. Can we just stay in a hotel for the night? Maybe tomorrow we could go home. "

"How about we go to hotel six. We will stay there for the night. It is closed in, and you must have a key just to get into the building. You can take a hot shower and get some comfy clothes on, and I will order pizza, and we can just hang out and relax for the evening." I smiled and tried to erase the shadow from her face that was clouding her normal perky attitude.

We got to the hotel, and I rented our room for the night. I made sure that they put us on the second floor and that we were in the middle of the building. That way it made it harder to sneak up on our room. Paranoid, who me? I just wanted Sarah to be safe. I phoned the police and told them where we were, and they said that they would send a car over to keep a look out.

Sarah took a shower; she stayed in there for an hour and a half. I finally went to the door and knocked on it because I was getting worried.

"Sarah, are you alright in there?" I asked with fear, trembling my voice. I kept having this image of her hanging herself. It is common you know, for rape victims to try to kill themselves...

"I'm ok, just soaking and trying to scrub this off of me." She was crying and sounded like she was in pain.

"Sarah, I'm going to come in., ok?"

"Ok, just don't laugh at me or anything."

"I won't laugh Sarah, I promise." I said as I opened the bathroom door. "Oh my God! Sarah, honey what did you do to yourself?!" I rushed over and grabbed the towel and rushed to get her out of the tub.

"It will not come off. I have scrubbed and scrubbed but it will not come off me! Get it off me Serraid, please! Just get it off me!!!!"

I looked to see what she was talking about. There was nothing there except the deep scratch marks that she had made with her fingernails trying to get whatever it was that only she could see off her. This is completely normal behavior. A lot of victims feel dirty, and they feel like their assailant is still on them hours sometimes years after an assault has occurred. I looked at this sweet girl, and tears filled my eyes, my heart broke. I helped her out of the shower and got her to bed. I knew there was nothing that I could do to fix this. But I would most certainly deal with the person that has done this to her.

~ Unknown pov~

He stood there looking at himself in the mirror, thinking to himself how life has many faces. Some of them are good, some are bad and some just have no meaning at all. He thought of her, remembering the smell of her skin, the touch of her hand as it slapped his face. Oh, she was a great woman, and in time he knew that he would have her.

He was excited about the meeting that they had arranged for this night. He stood at attention as his face wavered at the thought of having her to himself. And she would do what she was told if she wanted to continue to have her friends near and dear to her.

His thoughts ran together, some from the past, some from the future. He could remember her when she was young and naive. How easily she was convinced of who he was. How easily he took her and broke her. He was getting aroused just thinking of the things that he did to her all of them years ago.

He found her sitting outside on a warm summer's day. She was magnificent, in her yellow dress, her hair flowing in the wind. Those sexy eyes, pouting lips, and full breasts. He knew then that he had to have her. He approached her and became all that she wanted with her heart. He knew when she kissed him that he had succeeded. How easy it was to take her. The nights that she willingly gave him her love. The weakness that entailed her when she loved him. He yearned for that time again. His heart ached for her love. His breath was shallow and shaky, and his heart thumped as he thought of her. He could feel his erection beginning.

He got mad at the power that she had over him. How she made him do things that he never wanted to do. How could one woman hold one man in her power the way that she did?

Her friend was nice; she was so sweet and innocent. She was like new strawberries in a strawberry field, so tender and juicy. She was the first woman he has been with since he was with Her all those years ago. And the only reason he could be with this woman now was because she had Her scent on her so strong that it was so easy to pretend. The fear and pain radiating off her friend was intoxicating, strengthening him.

Why didn't he just take Her? She was right there. No, she must suffer, she must know that nothing that she can do can change this outcome. That he will have what he wants. She will give it to him!

He slammed his fist into the glass as he thought about Her stubbornness. How she fled from him after one night of passion that overtook him. He could not control himself. He went to her with his own guard down, when she did not accept him, he took her and made her look at him while he violated her. She had had him on more than one occasion, but not as he was. He wanted her to have him as he was born, natural with no additives. She could not handle it. Because of her love for Him! Slam!!! His fist hit the rest of the glass on the wall. As he shouted. "That stupid, conceited woman! Does she think that she is too good for me?! That I am below her?! Does she find me so appalling that she cannot love me for who I am?! I will have you woman! Whether you like or want it or not!"

He stormed out the door and headed for the pier. He had some things to prepare before their rendezvous.

CHAPTER 6

Serraid's POV

(Saturday to the following Sunday. 8 days.)

At 12:30 I decided to start getting ready to go and meet David. I was not sure what I was going to do when I got there, but I had to think of something. Maybe I could reason with him and see why he has done this. Then I could kill him. Yeah, that would be sweet.

I got in my car and headed for the pier. I called John and told him I was heading there to meet David. He said that He would meet me there. I asked him if he wanted me to pick him up, he said no he would take his bike, that way we could arrive at different times and hopefully go undetected. I said OK and hung up the phone.

I had decided I would take the gun I bought at the pawn shop last week. I have never shot a gun before, but it can't be that hard, could it? I packed it in the waist of my jeans and headed out the door. I knew that Sarah would be ok because the police were watching the hotel room and besides, it is me, he wants, well it is me he is going to get. David will learn I am not the lonely, scared girl that he once met. I still had a hard time believing that a man who was so loving could turn into someone so evil.

I began thinking about when I first met David. I was standing at the corner shop waiting for the cashier to ring up my items. I dropped the basket I was carrying. He offered to help me pick them up, I agreed. He gave me a card and told me that he was a counselor and if I ever needed anyone to talk to that I should come see him. I had a lot of problems at that point in my life. I was scared, hurting and I wanted to die most days, I felt as if I deserved to die. I decided to see David. He was wonderful. I spoke to him about things I had never spoken to anyone about. I told him of the abuse I went through as a child. At my second session, I began telling him about a friend of my mother's that was supposed to be a Christian man, we used to go over there all the time. This man would get me in another room and touch me. He would make me touch him too. He would tell me how good it would feel for me to touch him, and I could make him feel like no one could. This man had two sons; they would make me run from one side of the room to the other while they would take turns touching me. I used to have nightmares about it. Once when I spent the night there, this man took me in his bathroom and made me perform oral sex on him. He said that I was really good at it. I was only 9 years old at the time. David explained to me that I was the victim, and they were adults and they should have known better. But I still felt dirty, because at the time when these men would touch me, I liked the attention, and it felt good. A part of me thought it was ok for this to happen, yet I was scared all at the same time.

David assured me this was normal and that all victims would go through this. I had a hard time believing him though. That is when he took me to a group where victims met, and I found out that in fact this was normal, just most people would not talk about it.

David kept seeing me as my counselor. After a couple of years, he became my lover; I fell in love with him. I know that people will say it was not right of him and he broke every oath he ever took. But I know what we had at the beginning was real. Even after he turned to and allowed the evil out of himself.

A few years after we moved in together, David changed after one night when he had to go out. He said he had a meeting with a guy that knew of a client that was in desperate need of help and wanted to know if David would help. I always supported him because he was so good at counseling. It was so easy to talk to him, it was like things just poured out of you even if you did not want them to. That night when David came back, he was different. His eyes seemed hardened somehow. I asked him, "Did everything go ok? Did you meet this new client?"

He said, "Yes, I did, and I will not be seeing that client ever again. I declined them because there is nothing that I can do to help. She is beyond my expertise."

That was weird for David, He never gave up on things that easy; but then again there is a first time for everything. I thought maybe he finally met someone that he could not help.

As the days and weeks passed, he became more agitated, and very short tempered. I asked him if he was feeling ok. He would always tell me he was fine, and I should not be asking him all the time. Then one night he came home from the office, and he walked over to me, I knew by the look on his face something was wrong with him. I just did not realize how wrong until it was too late.

SMACK!!!! His hand landed on the right side of my face. He did not say anything, he just looked at me. I ran toward him, to hit him back. He grabbed my wrists and turned me around and slammed my face first into the wall.

He ripped my panties off and bit the back of my neck and shoved himself deep inside of me.

My wrists hurt, and my neck hurt where he had bitten me and the dry entry hurt as well, yet I could feel the excitement build between my thighs. He whispered in my ear, "you like that don't you? I can feel you getting wet around me, and I can feel your excitement building. I want you to come for me right now." As he was talking, I could feel my release on its way. He bit me one more time and brought me. I screamed with my pleasure and my anger against the wall. I could not understand how he could force me to such pleasure like this. It was the first time that he had ever done anything like this with me. I hated it, I did not want this to happen ever again. Yet when I think about it, my body would respond with the memory of the forced pleasure. I would get to pissed off at myself.

As time went by, he brought home toys, contraptions, whips, clips, belts, and the like. Then he began bringing home other women and other men. He made them beat me while he had his way and brought pleasure to me in the roughest ways. As time went on, I began to love his roughness and began to accept it as his love.

Then one night, he beat me almost unconscious. I had come home from a card night with the woman. There was a man in our home, and David was not there. I asked the man where David was. He said that he had stepped out, that he told him to have a great time with me while he was gone. I told this man I did not want any part of what he had in mind. The man did not take that news too well. He grabbed me by the throat; I slapped and scratched him. But he would not let go of me, he squeezed tighter still. When I thought I would pass out, he let go a little, and then he ripped my dress off and entered me. He held my face, so I was looking at him the whole time. If I closed my eyes, he squeezed my throat until I opened them again. He kept telling me how long he had waited to do this to me, as himself. How I had excited him for so long. He finally finished as his orgasm was over and he released me. I ran to mine and David's room. About an hour later, David came home, and the other man was gone. David came in and seen me on the bed. I told him about what the guy had done and how horrible it was. How I hated that man and how I would kill him the next time I saw him.

David got furious. He stood up screaming and yelling and throwing things around the room. He kept yelling about how I did not appreciate anything he did for me, and how I was a useless whore like all the rest. How I would never amount to anything but someone to spread my legs wide and let all the paying boys play. Then he began to hit me, telling me that it was my fault that this man had his way with me. He said I had wanted to cheat on him, and I waited until he had left to bring another man to our bed. Tears filled my eyes as this man that I loved was turning into someone I did not know. He was turning into all the men that hurt me in the past. I began to hate him that day. He kept beating me until I lost consciousness.

That night, after I woke up and David fell asleep, I decided to leave. I left everything that I had. I only took the clothes I had on. The only other thing I took was the cash I had been saving for a rainy day. Guess that was my rainy day, because I used the cash to get me a new identity. I decided to move completely away and go to school. That is when I decided I would become a counselor and help people.

So tonight, I would finally get my revenge on the man that hurt me the most. I dressed in a black shirt and black pants with black boots. I did not want to be seen unless I wanted them to see me. I sat at the end of the pier, wondering if he was already there.

"Awe, you decided to finally grace me with your presence." A familiar voice spoke from the dark.

I could feel the anger creeping up my spine. I did not want to flinch and reach for my gun too early, because I wanted to have the element of surprise.

"Yes, I showed just as you asked David. What do you want? I am tired of these games." I said while trying to control the tremble in my voice.

"Ah, dear, dear, do not be so cumbersome. I only wanted to be in your presence again after so long. I have missed you precious lady. I have missed your touch and your smell. Please, love do not be hostile with me tonight, not after all we have been through to get here." There was a smirk on his face, taunting me...

"David, I do not know what fantasy you have produced in your head, but you and I have been over for a long time now! Remember you are the one that got mad when a man forced himself on me! I still try to get his stench off me! And you expect me to forgive you! I loved you, you bastard! I loved you and you used me! You hurt me and loved every minute of it!" I screamed at him.

Suddenly, like a quick wind, he was there in front of me! Was I losing time? Did I space off from anger? Where the hell is John?

David reached up and pushed the hair out of my face that had fallen while I screamed at him. His face was distorted with anger, I knew he planned on hurting me. I knew he was very angry; I knew this look and I braced for the reactions.

He reached up, grabbed the back of my head, and pulled me into him. He kissed me hard enough to bruise my lips. I could taste my blood when he busted one of my lips open. He groaned as he tasted me. I felt the bile climb into my throat. I did nothing to stop it; I vomited on him. I could not help it, but I laughed.

"You bitch! You will pay for that! All I have done for you; All I have given to you, and this is how you repay me!" he screamed in my face.

I could feel fear trying to creep up my spine, and the look on his face. I knew that I had made a mistake. I remembered my gun. I reached around and pulled it out of my waistband of my jeans; I put it to his head and was trying to pull the trigger when he grabbed my wrist and broke it! I cried out with the pain. I tried not to scream, but it hurt so bad.

He looked at me with a smile on his face and said, "Awe, what is the matter love, did you finally figure out that you will never kill me? That I am just too strong for you. You love me dear, just admit it and this will all be over; deny it and this will take all night. It is your choice love."

I spit in his face. I would not give him the satisfaction of telling him that I missed or loved him. I hated this man! I wanted him dead and somehow some way I would kill him if it was the last thing I did in my life. "I fucking hate you, and I will kill you David, this I swear to you!"

He squeezed my throat, the air was cut off, and I began to feel weak and lightheaded. Where the hell was John? David is going to kill me, and John was supposed to be here to help. I tried to scream with what strength I had left, but no sound would come out. Darkness fell over me.

When I woke up, I was in an old Victorian sized bed. I did not recognize the room. There was an aroma coming from somewhere in the house. It smelled delicious. I then remembered last night, panic set in. I could feel the weak feeling taking over my legs. I looked down and that is when I saw the bruises. Oh my! I leaned over the bed and threw up as I realized that he had his way with me while I was out. Anger rose up through me.

I got up and headed for the door. It was locked. I started beating on the door and screaming, "Let me out! Open this door right now! Right fucking now! HELP!!! Someone help me!"

I stopped as I heard heels on the hardwood floor on the outside of the room. Then a key in the keyhole. I went to the side of the door with a book in my hand to hit whoever it was over the head as they came through the door. Hey, do not laugh about the book, it is all I had. A woman taller than I was walked through the door with a tray of food. I stood there in disbelief. There were other women being hurt in this house. This changed things. I could not leave them behind.

I asked her what her name was. She said that she was not allowed to talk to me and if He found out he would make her pay. I told her I would not tell anyone; I swore to her. She sat the tray of food down and turned and went out the door locking it from the other side.

I sat there smelling all that yummy food, my stomach growled, begging me to eat something. I walked over and smelled the food, wondering if it was poisoned. It looked and smelled so good. Then a thought hit me. I would rather be dead than to be trapped here, so I took a bite of the food and waited. When nothing bad happened, I sat and ate all the food. Whoever cooked this was a superb cook, and a wonderful juice maker. I lay there with a full belly and was almost in a dazed sleep when I heard familiar footsteps coming.

My heart jumped up in my throat as they approached the door. I did not want to see him right now, or ever for that matter. "Go away! I hate you! I do not want to see you, you stupid, insolate man!"

I heard him grunt and then the door slammed open. He rushed over with almost more than human speed, and he grabbed me by the arms. That made my broken arm throb with pain. A scream escaped my throat. "You will be hospitable while you are in my home Serraid! Do you understand me, you ungrateful wench? You will speak a tone that is fitting a woman, and you will not speak unless you are spoken to, and you will obey my every command, or I will make sure you are tortured daily! Am I clear?" he finished his speech with spittle flying from his mouth to my nose.

"I would rather die than to listen to anything that you say, you jackass! So, either kill me or let me go because you will never get what you want on my own free will. You will have to take what you want. I loved you once, but I hate you now! I want to see you rot in hell you bastard! Do you hear me? Rot in hell!" I spit the venomous words at him hoping that he would just kill me and get it over with.

He dropped me on the floor and went out the door and locked it. I sat there wondering what the hell just happened. I knew I had pissed him off and he wanted to kill me; I saw it in his eyes. Why had he just walked away? Why? I got up and started looking around. I decided I would begin to look for a way out of here.

There was a window, but it was boarded up. There was a little hole, I peeked out of it and all I saw was water. Where were we? A boat? I stood still trying to feel any wave movements. There was none. So, we are not on the water. Then where were we? I peeked out this hole again and I noticed that we were by a pond.

Think Serraid, where is there a pond around here? Ok. I had to stop and think. I went over to the bed and thought and thought about where there might be a pond around here, wherever here was. My head started to hurt. I lay back on the pillows and fell asleep.

I tried to turn over but there was something holding me in place. I opened my eyes and screamed when I saw the restraints on my ankles and wrists. I pulled at them and screamed at the top of my lungs. Suddenly, the door opened with a bang! David walked over and ripped my dress open. He had a pot of water with him. I could see the steam coming off of it. I began to struggle against the ropes. He looked at me and said, "You have such nice tits, I almost hate to do this to them, but they will heal." With that said, he began pouring the hot water on my chest.

The hot searing pain hit me immediately. My whole chest felt like it was on fire. I could feel the swelling and the blistering beginning as soon as the hot water hit it. I screamed from the pain. I begged him to stop! Nothing I said would stop him, I knew. I could tell by the blank, evil look in his eyes he would not stop until he was good and ready.

When all the water was gone, he simply turned around and left the room. I heard the door lock behind him. I lay there and cried and cursed him under my breath. I was in so much pain that it did not take long for the shock to set in. I could feel it is cold breath, settling over my skin. I sank into it, welcoming the numbness and the black void that it offered with it. Shock, it is a wonderful thing when it is really needed.

I sat in the middle of the night along the riverbank. Waiting for him to show. When I heard horse hooves, I excitedly turned to see my lover. But it wasn't my lover that was there. It was a man I didn't know. "What is a beautiful lass like yourself doing out this late with no escort?" he asked as I could feel his eyes going from my head to my toes.

"My Bo will be here any minute. He rode ahead to clear a branch from the road." my voice trembled as I tried to lie to this stranger.

He hopped off of his horse and smirked at me. He circled me like a hawk does its prey. My heart was beating and in my throat. I would not lose control this time. I could not tear this man apart. I would defend myself but not kill him. I looked at him, and my skin began to burn, I then shoved him into his horse, I screamed at him and ran. He followed me, shoved me down on the ground and ripped my petty coats and took me right there. He left me torn and crying as he rode off into the night. My chest felt like it was ripped apart. That's when I woke up!

My heart was pounding from the dream I had. What the hell was that all about I thought to myself. Man, this is getting to much.

I tried to move, but the pain was too much. I wanted to get out of here, because I was really feeling like he was going to kill me. I heard a boat in the distance. I was hoping that the police were on their way to rescue me. But I doubted they even knew I was missing. Sarah! I thought of my friend that I promised I would not leave alone. Would she ever forgive me? Where had John gone? Why had he not shown up? Was I doomed to die here? Because I would die before I gave in to him and gave him what he wanted. I fell back into the darkness of shock. I did not dream this time though. There was nothing but darkness in this room. I fell deeper, until all my senses were shut down and there was simply nothing, no pain, no sound, no temperature, nothingness. It was sweet, sweet bliss. I embraced nothingness like a long-lost lover. My old friend, which has never failed me, even when I was little. I embraced the darkness.

I could hear them talking and I knew those voices. I tried opening my eyes but could not get them open. I lay there and tried to say something, but my lips would not open. I started to panic as I realized I was paralyzed. I thought to myself, oh my God, what is going on, why am I paralyzed and what is he going to do to me while I cannot protect myself! I could feel my heart racing, but I could not do anything about it.

I heard a familiar voice speaking in my ear, "Serraid, calm down sweetie, it is ok. We have you at the hospital. You are going to be fine. I love you."

The voice was so familiar, it was so calming. I could not help but relax. If he said that all was going to be fine, then all was going to be fine. I could hear Sarah's voice too. I must be dreaming, I thought to myself. Because I am nowhere near Sarah. And what was Jeremy doing here? He did not even know me outside of the Cat House. Yep, I was dreaming. My mind was finally breaking down and trying to make my pain less by putting good things in my head. Now I knew I was hurt worse than I originally thought.

I woke up and tried to speak but there were tubes in my throat, and I.V.'s in my arm. I started panicking and trying to rip the tubes out. Sarah reached over and stopped me while yelling for a nurse. I knew there was no way I could be here. I knew whatever he was doing to me was really bad for my mind to be playing these tricks on me. I passed out again from exhaustion.

I was walking by a lake; there was this gorgeous man walking with me. I didn't recognize his face. But I felt as if I loved him. We walked arm in arm. He turned and looked at me and kissed me. I felt his love all through my body.

When I woke, there was only one light on above the hospital bed. I looked around the room. John and Sarah leaned against the window talking quietly with each other. I tried to tell them I was awake; my voice was raspy and came out as a creak.

Sarah ran over and called for the nurse. Sarah started crying and hugging me, telling me she thought they had lost me. She kept me from moving too much, I asked for a drink of water, but she said I could not have that yet. My throat felt like sandpaper though.

"What happened Sarah? What am I doing here and how did I get here?"

"John found you Serraid at a lake house. He brought you to the hospital and told them he found you in your car by the pier. They do not know anything else. You were burned pretty bad. Oh Serraid, I love you, and I am sorry this happened." She sobbed as she spoke.

"Sarah, it is ok. I will be ok. It probably looks worse than it actually is. And I love you too silly girl."

John walked over and smiled at me. "Look who decided to join us again."

"It took you long enough to find me" I said with half a smile on my face and letting my anger seep through for him to see. I still felt a little groggy.

"What did they give me and how long have I been out?" I asked as I tried to test each limb to see if it was going to cooperate.

"They gave you morphine for pain, once they extubated you; you were out for a week." Sarah said with soft compassion in her eyes. "Don't worry, I have called your work and told them what happened and let them know you would be out for a while."

I smiled, "Thank you Sarah for everything. How are you feeling honey? Are you ok?"

"Serraid, I will be fine. You have helped me through this. By having to sit and take care of you it has kept my mind off things; I will be fine. You just worry about getting better."

"Thank you, and I will. Would you mind if I speak to John by himself for a minute, please?" I asked gently, trying not to hurt her feelings.

"Sure, let me get him" she said as she kissed my forehead.

John came back into the room from talking to the nurses. "I hear that you want to speak with me."

"Did you kill him? Did you get him John?" I asked with anger and heat in my voice.

"He was not there Serraid, and my main goal was to get you out of there and to get you to the hospital. I was trying to save your life." He said with regret, showing on his face.

"Where were you the night on the pier? What happened that night? I thought you were supposed to have my back and help protect me?" The anger is more prominent now.

"I got caught in traffic. There was a bad wreck, and I had to go around. By the time I got there you were already taken. I am sorry Serraid, I have failed you." He looked down and started crying.

"John, I know you tried. I am not mad at you. This was not your fault and I forgive you. Thank you for finding me and saving my life. I will never forget that." I could feel my anger toward him dissipating as we spoke. The look on his face showed me that he was truly sorry.

"I will always save the ones I l…" The nurse came in and cut off his sentence. I wondered what he was going to say. I thought I had a pretty good idea.

After the nurse was done taking my vitals. I was tired and needed more sleep. I fell into a deep sleep. Where I had more old dreams of times not present. When I woke up, I wondered what was causing me to have these dreams. And why did I keep thinking I heard Jeremy in this room? Was I falling in love with that man?

"Sarah, has there been anyone here named Jeremy?"

"Not that I'm aware of why?" Sarah asked with a confused look on her face.

I saw John stiffen up. I looked over at him and wondered what his problem was. But I was too drugged up to really focus on it.

"I just keep thinking I hear his voice in this room when I am waking up. There is something about that man that has attracted me. I cannot get him out of my head. And I guess I am missing him a little." I said with a blush.

Sarah smiled at me. I asked her for a phone. I called the Cat house and asked if Jeremy had been by for a while. Sereena said no, and I told her if he did come by, to have him call my cell. She was shocked I was allowing a client to call my personal cell. I told her to make sure she gave him the message. She told me she heard what had happened and that she would make sure I had all the time I needed to recoup. She also told me she hoped I catch the bastard and rip his balls off and keep them as a souvenir. I giggled as I told her I would and hung up the phone.

John had walked out of the room by the time I hung up the phone. I wondered if I had said something wrong. I mean no one knew who I had called. I told Sarah I had called a friend that owns a pub. So, it is not like she could have told him. I would ask him about it when he got back from wherever he went.

I was feeling tired again and decided that I was going to try to sleep again. The nurse had come in and changed my bandages and to their surprise I was healing faster than I should have been. They did not understand it, but they did not say anything either. Some people just heal faster than others.

I woke up and to my surprise John was still gone. I asked Sarah if she had heard from him. She said that she had not. I was starting to worry about him. About where he was and what could have happened to him. When Jeremy walked into the room. My jaw dropped to the floor. How did he know where I was and who I was. Had Sereena told him everything? I would have a talk with her.

A smile came across my face involuntarily as I looked at him. He smiled back at me and walked toward the bed. I could feel my body respond as if he were electricity and the closer, he got to me the stronger it became. I could feel energy returning back to my body, and warmth across my chest. I cursed it under my breath while keeping a smile on my face.

"Hey there. How are you feeling? I spoke with Sereena, and she told me that you were here. It is nice to see you just not under these circumstances. And to think you are just as beautiful without your mask as you are with it."

I blushed and could not help it. It made me mad when my face did that. "Thank you, Jeremy. I am glad you came. Somehow you make me feel better and safer. I wanted to see you. I have missed you a lot." What the hell was I doing telling him these things. The words just came out of my mouth without me wanting them too. It must be the damned morphine they were giving me here. Ugh!

A smile spread across his face. He kissed my head and said, "The feeling is very mutual, I have missed you too Serrie."

"Uh-hum, Sorry to interrupt but I am going to get something to eat. It looks like you are in good hands here for right now." Sarah said with a smile and blush.

"I am sorry Sarah, this is Jeremy. Jeremy this is my best friend, Sarah."

"Good to meet you, Sarah. I am sure you are as lovely as your friend."

"Thank you, Jeremy. I am sure you are lovely to." Sarah said with a blush, crossing her face. "Ok, well I am going to get something to eat. I will be back in a little while. Jeremy, you will be here for a little while right?"

"Yes, I will be here for a while. Go and eat, Serraid will be fine, I promise."

With that said, Sarah went to eat. I knew she was just trying to give me some space. And I must admit, I wanted some time with Jeremy. I could not figure it out, but I felt so warm and safe with him. I wanted him to lay on the bed with me. I felt as if my body would heal itself if he just lay with me.

I smiled at him as he sat down on my bed. He brushed his knuckles along my arm, leaned over, and whispered in my ear. "I want you just as much now as I do at the house. You are magnificent, my lady. How your body beckons me."

I felt the heat rise through my body. It felt like my whole body was on fire. Yet rejuvenated and healing if that were possible. "Jeremy, what is it about you that makes me want you close to me?"

"We are meant to be Serrie. I was made for you, and you were made for me. I feel it, I feel you are my mate. You are the one that I have been searching for." He said with a seductive tone to his voice.

"Jeremy, I am not sure I believe that. But I do know when you are near me, I feel empowered, warm, safe, and good."

"I know what you mean. I feel the same way to Serrie. Just lay here and sleep my lady. I will watch over you and I will protect you." He spoke as he was laying down beside me.

The warmth of his face, on my skin as he lay down. His breath smelled sweet and the energy from him was very exciting. I lay there and tried to sleep as he slowly rubbed my back. It felt so good to be held. I lay there relaxing, and soon I was in dream world.

I slept hard for three hours curled up to Jeremy. I woke up and there was no one else in my room. I looked for Sarah, John, or Jeremy. Maybe they all went to rest or shower or something. I lay there trying to remember the touch of Jeremy's hands. I got up and stretched out as far as my healing body would allow me to. I knew that my stomach would leave a scar. I just wish that I could get the cast off my arm. It was itching.

Just then, Sarah walked through the door. "Hey, you, did you get a good meal?"

Sarah looked at me as if I were speaking a foreign language. "What do you mean meal? I was talking with the nurses."

"Well, when Jeremy showed up, you said that you were going to go and eat. So, I figured you actually got a decent meal."

Sarah came and sat next to me touching me on the shoulder. "Serraid, are you sure that you are, ok? There has not been anyone here, hun. You have been sleeping for the last eight hours."

I thought to myself. Oh shit, I was dreaming about him. This is not good Serraid, you never dream of anyone. Ugh, I have been through too much lately and it is taking its toll on my mind. Why am I dreaming of Jeremy though? This is so frustrating. I should have known it was a dream when he was so gentle and loving and when he told me what he told me.

"I am sorry Sarah, I must have been dreaming. Man, the medicine that this place is giving me is really messing with my head. I think I need to talk to the doctor and make them stop giving me anything."

Sarah laughed and looked at me seriously. "I know this probably is not a great time to tell you, but John has not been back since he left earlier. Do you think that He is ok? I mean He is probably just resting."

"He is probably ok, why do not you call his house and see if he answers. If he does not then we can worry. If he does answer, then we know that he is ok."

Sarah reached over and grabbed the phone, dialed John's phone. It rang five times. When finally, he answered. "Where the hell have you been?" Sarah asked.

"Well, we were worried about you. Make sure to call us the next time that way we do not worry. Uh-huh, ok. We will see you in a little bit. Ok, be careful bye."

"Well, where has he been?"

"He said that he took a shower, grabbed something to eat, and grabbed some much-needed sleep. Something in the way he said it though, I am not sure I believe him Serraid. I think he has been up to something."

I laughed at that. "Probably so Sarah. But what are we going to do? I say that you call him back and tell him to bring us ice cream."

Sarah called him back and requested that he bring us ice cream back with him. He agreed to bring us some. The nurse came in and changed my bandages. She gasped when she pulled my bandages off. "Oh my gosh, I have never seen anything like this! I must get the doctor and have him look at this, I am also going to call radiology and have them re-do your x-rays on your arm."

I looked down, and to my surprise, my chest was almost completely healed. There were only a couple of spots that were going to be scarred. I would not have believed it if I had not seen it with my own eyes. About ten minutes later I was in radiology, and they took more x-rays of my arm. The radiologist looked shocked when she looked at them. "I cannot believe this! I mean I know that it is real because I did the original x-rays. It is just that I have never seen anyone heal this fast."

My arm was completely healed and there were very little shows of it ever being broken. They took my cast off finally, and man that felt amazing!

The doctor came in and looked at my chest and decided that he would keep me for 24 more hours just to make sure that there were no secondary infections of any kind. He said that he had never seen anything like it before in his career, and he had no explanation for it. He left and me and Sarah just sat there and stared at each other.

Sarah was the one that broke the silence. "How is it that you are healing so fast Serraid. What have you been doing?"

"I, I do not know, I mean I have been sleeping a lot. Other than that, you know because you have been here all along. I do not know how I am healing so fast." I was starting to feel tired again and decided I might as well rest until John got there. I slept and did not dream at all. When I woke up, I decided that I wanted to take a shower.

I showered with the hottest water I could get. When I was done, I put on some clean clothes. I thought to myself, Man it feels so good to be clean. "Sarah, Has John made it with the ice cream yet?"

"I have just now. Here is your ice cream little lady. I am glad that you are up and feeling better. I heard about your wounds healing as fast as they are. It is amazing! I am glad for it though, because that means we can get out of here faster and look for the scum bag that put you here in the first place."

I smiled at the thought of killing that man. I wanted revenge like no other. I sat back, enjoyed eating my ice cream and reveled in the thought of killing the only man that hurt me the most. I would kill him for all the men that had ever hurt me and for all the women that he had and will ever hurt.

CHAPTER 7

The next morning the doctor came in and gave me one last look over. He said that I looked like I had never been assaulted, and I had a clean bill of health. With that said, he would release me from the hospital. I was so glad to get out of there. I was tired of being in one room. I wanted my own bed, and my shower. I wanted to go home.

Sarah and John were happy that they could go home too. They have been so great through this whole ordeal. They both stayed with me the entire time.

On the ride home, I sat and wondered what the dream about Jeremy meant.

"Sarah, are you sure that there was never anyone that came and visited me in the hospital that you didn't know?"

"No, believe me I had my eyes open for strangers. If someone had, I would have known it."

"Ok, it is just that I had a dream. It seemed so real, but if you say no one was there, then no one was there I guess."

I was starting to believe the medicine had given me a good hallucination. Either way, I knew that somehow Jeremy had been there, and him laying with me is what made me heal so fast. I could not explain it, but I just knew inside of me that is what happened.

We pulled up to the house. I went in and grabbed all the mail from in front of the door. Patches came running toward me as soon as he heard my voice. I missed him, and his purr. I told Sarah, I was going upstairs and taking a shower and getting some comfy clothes on. I just wanted to relax for a bit. I had to call work and check in with them. I also had some investigating to do…I asked John when he wanted to get started, He said he already had, and he would fill me in when I got out of the shower.

I stood in the shower and absorbed the hot water into my skin. It felt so good to just be home. I wanted to relax, but the thought of David coming back scared the hell out of me. He was good at being so bad, it is like he knows my schedule, and he knows how to get to me. I thought about what all happened when David had me at the lake house. Whose lake house, was it? Who were the servants that were there? Ugh! It was all so frustrating.

Then a thought of Jeremy lying next to me crossed my mind. My body remembered how good he felt lying beside me. The warmth, the security, why was this happening with him? I do not go all warm and googly over anyone. I am an adult, and I am past that. But just the thought of his body laying cuddled around mine, woke things low in me up. I could feel the desire rising in me. I wish that he were here. Suddenly, the shower curtain opened. I squealed from the sudden change in the bathroom. I looked up and Sarah was standing there looking pale.

"Sarah, hun, what's wrong?" I asked her while turning off the water.

"There was a package delivered while you were up here, and I opened it. I am sorry Serraid, I should not have opened it. I wish I had not opened it!" She said with a shaky voice.

"Well, what was it and who sent it? I am not mad about you opening my package, Sarah. You should know that."

She went even whiter and then she leaned over the toilet and threw up. I knew there was something wrong when she could not even tell me what was in it. I picked up my cell phone from the sink and called John. I told him that a package had been delivered and that he needed to come over right away. I did not even get the last out and he was at the door. How did he do that? I wondered if there was more to John than met the eye, but I was too busy worrying about Sarah to think any farther than that.

"Sarah, come with me and lay down for a bit, John and I are going to look at the package, and we are going to figure this out." At the mention of the package, Sarah leaned over and began throwing up again. I decided to leave here there and get some clothes on.

After I got dressed, I ran downstairs. John was standing by the box; his face was white, and his eyes were wide. He was sweating. Something was terribly wrong. I slowly walked the last four steps to the box and got a grip on myself then I investigated the box. What I saw was horrible. It was the woman's head that delivered me my food when David had me as his prisoner. I fell to my knees. This was my fault. I had talked to her. I had made her talk to me. She said that he would kill her, and I did not listen. "Oh god! I killed her!"

"Serraid, you did not do this. He did! This is not your fault; do you hear me?" John hugged me from behind, rocking me back and forth.

"She told me she could not talk to me, that if she did, he would kill her! I made her talk to me! I wanted her to talk to me so I could figure out how to get out of there!

John, I got her killed! This is all my fault!" I could feel the rage building up inside! I wanted him to die! I wanted to kill him slowly with my own bare hands. I wanted to make him pay! I wanted to feel his life slowly draining from his lifeless body! I promised myself that I would kill this man. Suddenly, my ribs began to burn, my whole body began to burn and feel as if I were breaking everywhere. What the hell was happening to me?

"Serraid, calm down sweetie, just calm down and listen to the sound of my voice. You are safe, Sarah is safe, there is no threat to you right now. I am here and you are safe. Hear my voice Serraid, listen to the tone and let it relax you. I am here, Sarah and you and I are all safe. Just calm down hun. That is, it, just breathe."

John was rocking me and talking to me. As he was doing so, I could feel the heat dissipating and the pain was going away. What the hell? I do not understand what is going on.

"What is going on with me John? You know, don't you? Why won't you tell me?" I asked as tears began streaming down my face.

"Serraid, I am not for sure, but I know that something is going on. I promise we will get to the bottom of this together. But you must keep a handle on your rage. I could feel the difference in you when you got mad just then. I promise as soon as I know something I will tell you."

I could not help but feel that John was holding out on me. He knew something that he was not telling me. I could not prove it right now, but I knew. And when I did find out, then I would set him straight too. Was he working with David? Was John a part of this? I looked at him to see if I could spot any deception there. Even though I knew he was holding out information from me about myself, I did not feel as if he could be so evil to be like David either. But then again, I never would have thought David could have been that bad. I pushed Johns arms away from me.

"Stay away from me! Are you working with Him?! It makes so much sense now, you were "conveniently" not there when I was taken, now you were so close that you were here before I could finish my sentence on the phone! Did you deliver this package?!" I screamed this as I was backing him against the wall. I could feel my anger taking over me again. The heat was getting painful again! But I did not stop.

"You knew about all of this didn't you? You did not think that I would figure this out, did you?! I will kill David and anyone who has had a hand in this do you understand me?! That means if you helped him, I will fucking kill you too!"

"Serraid, calm down! I am not helping anyone but you and Sarah! I would not help that crazy psychopath if I had to, I would die first! But you must calm down right now!" His voice sounded panicked.

"Calm down? Calm down!!!! I do not want to calm down! I want to kill something and eat it! I want to make him pay!" What was I saying? I do not want to eat anyone. The pain in my hands was so painful I thought someone was cutting them. I looked down and there my fingers were distorted and out of place.

"What the hell?!"

I woke up and I could see the living room ceiling. John and Sarah were bending over me. They were saying something, but I could not make it out because of the loud ringing in my ears. I tried telling them that I could not hear them, but I was not sure there was any sound coming from my mouth either. My tongue felt swollen or something.

That is when I remembered the box with the head of the dead servant in it. I looked around and there was no box. Had I fainted or something? Were the meds from the hospital kicking in again? Was I seeing things that were not there? Oh God, please do not let me be going crazy. I saw patients like this. I know the signs of schizophrenia. I could feel the tears running down my face.

"Serraid, are you all right? You fainted; you scared the shit out of me!" Sarah had this look of fear on her face.

"I'm fine," I said with a hoarse voice. "What happened?"

John looked at Sarah and then at me and answered me in a shaky tone. "You fainted when you realized the servant that gave you food at the lake house was dead and her head was in the box that was delivered here. How are you feeling now? Better?"

I remember the box, and I remember coming down and seeing you looking at it and being pale. I remember thinking about how much I wanted to kill David I remember getting angry. Then, I woke up looking at the ceiling. Maybe I am still not up to par on my body yet. I am not one to faint. Are we sure there was not some kind of poison or drug in the box?"

"There was nothing but a note in the box. I read it and believe me I hate this guy too! I want him dead as much as you do." John said with a tone I did not understand. He sounded as if he were trying to convince me, but he, of all people, should know that I trust him.

"Let's go to the kitchen, I will make some coffee and some sandwiches, and we will all figure this out." Sarah, said as she headed to the kitchen. She looked like she was feeling better.

I stood up and it felt as if my body had been run over by a Mac truck. What the hell? It must have been the fall when I fainted. I had this sinking feeling in my stomach that told me something about this event was just not right. I just could not remember it though. Surely if anything else had happened, Sarah and John would have told me though. I dismissed the thought and headed for the kitchen. John stood by the door watching me with suspicion. I turned around and looked at him with my counselor look and said, "Is there something that you are not telling me, that I need to know?"

John smiled a soft smile and said, "Nope, I was just wondering how Sarah could eat after all of this. Does she really expect us to eat anything?"

I laughed at the thought because knowing Sarah, yes, she did. I looked at him with a smile still on my face, "yes, she probably does. It seems to comfort her. Honestly, I do not know how she eats like that and stays in shape."

We laughed together and walked into the kitchen. Sarah had the coffee started already, and she was making sandwiches when we walked in. John and I sat at the table.

I just wanted this day over with already. I cannot believe it went from relaxing to hell on earth in a matter of minutes. Maybe I should leave, disappear that way my two friends would not be put on the spot and in danger. I decided to call work.

Cheryl answered the phone. "Hey this is Serraid. I wanted to let you guys know that I am home. I plan on coming to work next Monday. I am fine really; I need to get back into the swing of my normal life and its activities."

"I am so glad that you called Serraid. Earnald has been here for the last few days. He wants to talk to you. Hold on and I will put you through to his office."

Shit what could He want? I know he is concerned for all of us. He is a genuine person, and he tends to be overprotective like a father would be a daughter. I was waiting with my heart in my throat because I was afraid, he was going to ask me a lot of questions that I was not going to want to answer. I heard the phone click.

"Serraid, I am so glad you called. How are you feeling sweetie?" Earnald's voice was cheerful as always.

"Earnald, how are you today? I am doing all right, I feel ok. I was planning on coming back to work next Monday. I really need to get back into the swing of things."

"Uh-hum. Well, there is a problem. We have all had a meeting here at the office and considering what you have been through, Serraid, we all feel it would be best if you take some time off work here. We do not mean just a week either. You of all people know what these kinds of things can do to a person. And from what I understand you were having a rough time before this happened. Why didn't you come and talk to me? You know I am here to help in any way I can?"

"Earnald, really, I am fine. I have been off work for over a week now. In another week I will be even better. I know most people could not and should not return this soon, but I would not say I was ready unless I honestly thought I was. Please do not do this to me, I need my job."

"Whoa Serraid, I am not saying I am getting rid of you. You are one of the best damn counselors I have! I am just saying we all feel you need some substantial time off and it is going to be paid as well. You will not lose any income, and you can work on getting yourself back together. You know we are all here so if you need to talk, you can come to any of us free of charge. We are your friends Serraid, and we care about you." he said with a smile I could hear over the phone. He sounded tired too though.

"Earnald, I appreciate you guys I really do; I really do not need any extra time off from work. I am not that bad; I have dealt with most of the things that have happened to me over the last few weeks. But seeing how you guys have all decided without me, there probably is no changing your mind is there?" I asked with hope, spilling through my voice. I would be having a talk with Cheryl when I get back because I know she is the one that told him I was not in top shape before this happened. Ugh, sometimes I hated that woman.

"No there is not any changing this. We have decided as a majority. Your paid time off started last week. And all your hospital bills have been paid for as well. In a couple of months if we feel you are ready to return then we will allow you to come back. We all care about you here Serraid and we want to see you get back together inside. Now you go and do what you need to do to help yourself and use us if you need to. Call anytime. But do not think you are coming back to work for a while. Do not worry about your clients, we have them all taken care of. We will talk soon Serraid."

With that he hung up. I knew he did it so I would not argue, and he probably felt guilty for having to do this in the first place. Earnald was a great guy and a fatherly figure to all of us.

"Damn it! You will not believe what they did at the center?!" I yelled from frustration.

John tried to hide a smirk and Sarah giggled…. These two knew something that I was not catching.

"Ok, come clean the both of you right now!" I put all the sternness in my voice that I could.

"We went and spoke with Earnald while you were in the hospital. Serraid, I am so sorry but everyone, but you know you need some time off. You will be busy trying to catch David and you do not need to let your clients down by being sidetracked all the time. You will not be doing anyone a service by doing that. You know it and we know it. Just think of it this way, this is like a vacation and a paid one at that. Now you can exert all your energy finding David and we can deal with one thing at a time!" Sarah said all of this while trying to look innocent and caring.

I could not help but smile and know that she did it because she cares about me and loves me like a sister and if it had been her, I would have done the same thing. Hell, I would have told any of my clients that, so I knew what everyone was saying was true. Damn it! I just hate it when people do things without my consent or even without at least asking me. (Me controlling? Nope.) After a few minutes of making Sarah and John squirm, I laughed and said, "Ok, now we can catch this bastard! Thank you, guys, for doing this for me, because you know I would not have done this myself. I love you guys and thank you for being here for me. I really do appreciate you so much."

Sarah and John came over and hugged me from both sides. The heat was intense and quick. I gasped at the force it hit me with. I knew this feeling. This is the feeling I got when Jeremy came and laid with me in the hospital or in my dream or whatever it was. Why was I having this feeling now? Was it Sarah or was it John? I did not really care either way, I just knew I did not want this feeling to end any time soon. Without thinking, I reached up and stroked Sarah's face. I looked into her eyes and knew that she needed to know everything was going to be ok. I saw the doubt there in her eyes. I saw the need for security. I squeezed John's waist and pulled him closer to me and Sarah.

John tensed under my touch. I briefly wondered why, but my thought got cut short when Sarah kissed me. Her lips were soft and plump. Her touch was like silk on my skin. I grabbed her and kissed her back. I turned her so that her back was pressed against John. He looked at us with fear and excitement in his eyes. I grabbed his hands and placed them on Sarah while I kissed her again. That was all the encouragement He needed.

We explored each other's bodies with our hands and our tongues and lips. Sarah tasted like a sweet honey melon. Her skin was so soft and silky. We were on the kitchen floor, our naked bodies roaming and exploring. Sarah's face was swept over with pleasure. I kissed my way down from her bellybutton to just above her slit. I breathed and kissed and teased her. She moved her hips up, silently asking for more. I kissed her back up to her belly button. She moaned as she lowered her hips. I reached down and rubbed my fingers across the outside of her. She moaned deeply from the satisfaction of finally getting touched. I slid a finger inside, feeling her wet, smooth skin there. I worked my fingers in and out of her. She moved her hips in rhythm with my fingers. I could feel her tightening and loosening as the orgasm was building inside of her. John was kissing her and playing with her nipples. She bucked and moaned into his mouth. He ate her pleasure as I gave it. The sight of both enjoying themselves excited me. I could feel myself tightening from apprehension of the pleasure I would feel. I flicked my thumb over the outside of Sarah's clit while thrusting my fingers inside when she bucked and moaned toward John, while the orgasm finally took her over the edge. She writhed and scratched her pleasure into John's arms. I stayed with her and kept her riding the wave until I felt another wave building. I leaned down and sucked on her and threw her over the cliff of pleasure. Her hips came off the floor as she screamed her pleasure into John's mouth. She slumped down from intense pleasure. The energy of her orgasm slamming into me like a sweet warm blanket that made every cell of my body feel alive.

As Sarah recovered from the orgasm that left her breathless, John leaned over and grabbed my shoulder and kissed me. He sucked Sarah off my lips. Kissing me deeply and passionately. I could feel need rising in me. I felt the heat from the hospital. I wanted this man inside of me, I needed him. I started playing with his nipple. I bent down and licked his nipple with just a flick of my tongue when I heard a groan come from deep within him. I flicked it again then took it into my mouth and sucked on it hard. He moaned deep. I reached down and found him ready; I wanted to feel him inside of my mouth. I bent down and licked a wet line from his head to the base of him. He grabbed me by the hair and pulled me up and kissed me very deeply, he crushed my lips with his mouth and brought on an instant need. I felt hands on my back as well. Sarah had sat up and started caressing my back, she reached around and pinched my nipples as she pressed herself against my back. John kissed me and slid his fingers down and began to work me loose for him to enter. I felt him slide one finger in as Sarah pinched my nipple, the pleasure was intense. I moaned around John's mouth. I raised my hips just a little so he could get a better angle when Sarah reached under me and slid one of her fingers inside with John's. I moaned as I felt the orgasm building inside. They worked me together, hard, and long and fast. Sarah wrapped her arm around my neck and grabbed my chin and turned my head to kiss her, that pushed me over the edge, the orgasm took me wave by wave of pleasure. I screamed my pleasure into her mouth. She bit my lip and sucked on it. That pushed me over again and again. Suddenly John grabbed me and pulled me over to him. He bent me over, so my face was in Sarah's lap, and said, "It's my turn." he then shoved himself inside, he pressed all of himself inside of me. Just the feel of his entry pushed me over the edge. I bent farther down and began licking Sarah's sweet pussy that was wet and ready, she moaned and moved her hips so I could touch the nicest part. I slid two fingers inside of her and met John's rhythm. John pushed inside of me at the same time I pushed inside of Sarah.

"Oh God, I'm going to…" I was cut off by Sarah pushing up against my mouth.

"Close, I'm so close…" Sarah said…

"Not yet not yet… Wait for me." John said… He pushed harder and faster…pushing me farther into Sarah. I could feel her tightening and I could feel me grabbing

John inside. I knew we were not going to last much longer. I angled my hip up just a little, allowing him to hit that sweet spot inside, when the orgasm took all of us at the same time. We rode the waves together. Moaning and screaming our pleasure out into each other.

We laid there recouping from our orgy. We lay in a puppy pile wrapped around each other. Laying there I felt safe and secure. I felt energized and something inside of me mended. The emotional pain lessened somehow. I knew we were going to catch David and we would make him pay for all the things he has done. I was so sure of it.

I could feel the heat from earlier. I sat up and asked John and Sarah if they could feel it too. They said that they could not feel anything at the moment. We laughed together knowing we were safe and just from the sheer pleasure of us cuming together. I looked at them and knew I loved them and I would do anything in my power to protect them.

An hour later we decided to get up and clean up and eat something. We were all starving. I volunteered to make something while Sarah and John cleaned up. I had cleaned up first, so it was only fair. There seemed to be a tension among John and Sarah. I could not quite place it. Was it because of what just happened between all of us? I wondered if we would ever do that again as I cooked some shrimp noodles. I wanted to be with them. I wanted to feel that safe heat again. As Sarah came into the room, I hugged her and said thank you for being so amazing. She smiled and nervously said, "you were amazing." I kissed her lightly on the lips just to taste her one more time.

John came into the room, and I hugged him. Instantly that feeling washed over me again. I gasped and stepped back.

"What's wrong Serraid? Are you ok?" He asked while holding me.

I kept backing up and said I was fine. All of a sudden, I did not want him to touch me. I had to figure this out. I needed to know what this was. "Do you feel anything when we touch? I know that sounds like a stupid question. I am not saying I am in love with you or anything like that. Just do you feel anything?"

John looked at me suspiciously. "What do you mean? I feel joy and peace when we touch each other. I feel love for a friend. Can you be a little more exact about what you feel?"

"Forget it, I think I am just tired. I think I need to go lay down for a bit." I walked upstairs. I had to figure this out. I felt it when Jeremy came into the hospital. Or had it been John and I thought it was Jeremy? Damn it! I hate not knowing shit like this! There was only one way to find out…. that would be to go to the Cat House. I will go tonight and hope that he shows up.

I laid down and tried to go to sleep when I remembered the note that was in the box. I got up, washed my face, and ran downstairs. John and Sarah were asleep on the couch. They looked so cute sleeping. I started looking for the note John said he had found.

"What are you doing Serraid?"

I jumped at the sudden sound of someone's voice. I turned to the couch and said,

"Sarah, you scared the shit out of me!"

"Sorry, but what are you doing? It looks like you are looking for something." Sarah stood up as she talked.

"John said there was a note in the package, and I just now remembered it. Do you know where it is? I want to read it."

"No, He must have put it somewhere. Maybe he did not want you to read it alone or something." She shrugged her shoulders.

"John, John wake up…" I shook him gently as I tried to wake him up. He groaned as he turned away from me. I shook him again and said his name louder this time. He roused up.

"Sorry I fell asleep; did I miss something? Has something happened again?" He looked confused from sleeping.

"Nothing has happened, I just remembered you saying there was a note in the package earlier. I want to read it. What did you do with it?"

He looked at me with fear in his eyes. "You do not want to read the note Serraid, you will only blame yourself more than you do already and you he is trying to scare you more. Please just take my word for it. Please..."

Anger filled me from within. I looked at him and did not try to hide how mad I was.

"Give me the note John. I will not ask again."

John stood up and grabbed the note out of his back pocket. I recognized the signature on the back of it. It was from David. Instant anger and rage built up inside of me. I felt the heat and the pain beginning again. What the hell was going on?!

John came over and hugged me from behind, I felt cooler and calmer. How did he do that?

I opened the letter with shaky hands.

The note read: *Serraid, you have escaped me yet again. This time, however, you have made a fatal mistake. I bet, by now you can guess the mistake in which you made. Know her blood is on your hands; she died because of you. She was my best servant, and it took me a long time to train her the way I wanted her to be. I guess now I will have to find another to fill her place, and that too is on your hands.*

I know that you hate me love, but I love you and I will not let you go so easily. Your treacherous actions will not go unpunished. This is just the beginning. Maybe I will take your little roommate as a replacement for Helga here. What do you think? Hmmm, I think she would do quite nicely. Yes? Oh, and for the fellow you have helping you, just know I will kill him. Do not be foolish girl, thinking you can save them both. I have taken from you many times and I will continue to do so until you give me what I want. All I have ever wanted was you to let me be myself. But I was not good enough for you. You wanted something different all the time. So, I had to pretend and hide behind a mask. Then when I do show myself, you are disgusted. How does it feel now? Are you disgusted? Do you even remember? You have one week to make your decision. Either you will come to me willingly or I will take you by force. Your decision love, make it wisely.

Until then. Kisses and know you are always on my mind.

Love D~

I stood there in disbelief, even though I knew the note was real, I was hoping to wake up. I could feel the tears stream down my face as I thought about Helga. She had been nice to me. I knew she was scared yet I had filled her with false hope. And now he was threatening Sarah too? What did he want from me?! What does he mean to be himself? Ugh I screamed as loud as I could! I was sick to my stomach as I realized what I needed to do. I had to go to him and let him do whatever he wanted to do to me. I had to let him have his way. I would not lose my friends or anyone else because I was too scared to face him myself.

John looked at me with scrutiny in his eyes. "Serraid, do not even think about it. You are not going to go to him. I can see it in your eyes. You know he will only imprison you for your life. He wants to own you. He is just trying to scare you into giving him what he wants. Do not listen to him, please!"

I got so mad I shoved John completely across the room as I screamed, "I did not listen to Helga and look what happened John, she is dead because I did not listen! How can you stand there and tell me not to listen when you know as well as I do what he plans on doing! I cannot and will not stand here and pretend everything is ok when it is not. I will not wait around for him to take someone I care about and make this his own personal servant. I will not do it! And you are not big enough to stop me! So shut the hell up and either help me figure out a way to deal with this or get the hell out of my house!"

In the blink of an eye John had me up against the wall. I did not even see him move. I thought, how is that possible? He squeezed my arms, and I could feel the heat radiating from him. It calmed my insides. Which in turn pissed me off. I did not want to be calm and how the hell did he do that? I tried to get away when I realized he was much stronger than me and he was not letting go. I tried to slam my knee into his groin, but he anticipated my move and blocked it. My knee hit his knee head on, and the pain was horrible. I cried out from the pain. John just held me there. I screamed at him to let me go! But he wouldn't.

"I AM strong enough to keep you from doing anything that you should not do Serraid. I do not want to be that person, but I can be, to save your life. And I will do it if it is necessary. I want you to know this. I am going to let you go if you calm down. We will figure out a way to handle this. All right?"

I sighed and knew that he could hold me there all day if he wanted to. "Alright. I will calm down. But we are not going to just sit here and pretend that everything is ok. We are going to find him and kill him."

John let go of me, as soon as he did, I drew back and slammed my fist against the side of his face. My knuckles met his jaw perfectly. Instant sharp pains shot up my arm, and that pissed me off even more. He laughed at me and slammed me up against the wall. Then he whispered in my ear, "So that is how you want it? Do you want to wrestle around the room? I know you Serraid, and I know that he messed you up. But I swear you will learn that is not the only way! I am going to let you go and then I 'm going home. When I come back, we will figure out a way to deal with David. And we will kill him. But even after we kill him, you will have to work on you and your demons Serraid, because if you do not, he will win the war even if it is within yourself." With that he let go of me and left.

I slumped to the floor and cried from frustration and fear and anger. Sarah came over and sat by me. She held me while I cried. I tried pushing her away, but she was not allowing it. She held on tight while whispering soothing words into my ear. "It is going to be ok Serraid, I promise. I know what the note said and he is not taking me. John will not allow it; you will not allow it. Together we will make sure this bastard will not hurt anyone ever again. I promise. Just promise me you crazy bitch that you will not go off and do something heroic trying to save everyone. Work with us this time please."

I hugged her back because I knew she honestly believed all of us were going to be able to catch and kill David. But they did not know him like I did. He would stop at nothing to get what he wanted. I missed the David

I fell in love with. Why did he have to change into someone so horrible? What happened that made him change like that. I cried even harder at the loss that I felt. I wanted Jeremy. That is when I decided I was going to the Cat house. I stood up, wiped the tears from my face, and told Sarah I was going to see my friend Sereena and I would be back in a couple of hours. I promised her I was not doing anything stupid. Then I grabbed my jacket and keys and headed for the Cat House.

I arrived at the Cat house and walked in feeling safer already. I am not sure what it was about this place that made me feel secure. Sereena was at her desk as usual. Her face lit up when she seen me come through the door.

"Serrie! How are you honey? Whoa, you look like hell! Have you been crying?" she rushed over and hugged me.

"Hey Sereena, yes I've been going through some things, and I'm stressed out so bad that the Center even gave me a couple months paid leave." I smiled as I said the last hoping to make light of it.

"What is going on girl? You know that you can talk to me. It was not Jeremy the other day, was it? I told him where you were, and he rushed out of here without getting your number. He said that he would go and see you instead of calling. He did not hurt you, did he? I did not mean to tell him where you were at, but I figured if you were giving him your cell number that it was ok."

"It's ok Sereena, and wait what did you just say?" I looked at her with a confused look. I thought to myself, that would mean he did come to the hospital, but why had Sarah told me that he had not? Maybe she did not know? No, because she went to get something to eat. What the hell? I would have to talk to her about this when I got home.

"Jeremy came in the other day after you called me telling me to give him your cell."

I cut her off. "You mean to tell me he did come to the hospital?"

With a worried look on her face Sereena said, "Serrie what is going on? Yes, he rushed right out of here to go see you. Do not tell him I said this, but I think that he is kind of sweet on you and by the way you are acting I think it is mutual." She laughed while she said that.

"Oh, well…. I just uh thought that I was uh dreaming from the drugs the hospital gave to me. That is cool he came though. I am not sweet on him; I am not sure what it is but sometimes it is like I need him."

Sereena nudged her head to the left and said, "uh-hem well look what the cat dragged in."

I turned and to my surprise Jeremy was standing there with a satisfied look on his face. He was so yummy looking I could feel the tightening starting and he had done nothing but stand there.

"Hello Jeremy, how are you this evening? I am not working tonight just here chatting it up with the girls." I hoped he did not hear the quiver in my voice…how did he make me want him so fast.

"Hello Serrie, hope all Is well with you. I just came by to see if you were feeling better than you were the other day at the hospital. I came by to see you, but you were out of it. They said you were kidnapped and held hostage. Did he hurt you?" and by hurt I knew he meant rape; he just did not want to use that term.

"No, I am all right. The damage healed. How are you doing? And thank you for coming to see me in the hospital. Did you meet my roommate Sarah?" I wanted answers and maybe, just maybe I could get some from him without him knowing I wanted them.

"No, they said she had gone to eat right before I got there. I bet she is nice though. I am glad you are doing better. Well, I am going to go, I just saw your car here and wanted to stop and see how you were feeling. I am glad that you are doing better." He turned to go.

I felt my heart sink to my feet as I watched him turn to leave. "Wait, you want to come up and talk for a bit? I mean I could use some company while I redecorate a little."

"I don't know if that is a good idea, I might be tempted to take advantage of your condition….and…" he said with a sly smile.

I laughed at the thought, at the same time my groin got warmer. "Come up I will take the risk. And who knows maybe that is just what I need right now." I turned and headed up the stairs. I just wanted to lay down with him and sleep for a while. Maybe if I asked him, he would do just that. But how do I ask him that? Man, I am so out of practice for the whole normal thing.

When we got upstairs, I opened my door and stepped inside. I turned and saw Jeremy's eyes scanning the room. I walked over to the bed and sat down.

"Explain to me why I feel the way I do when you are around. And I know that when you laid with me at the hospital, I knew that it was going to heal me and when I woke up and was healed, I was not that surprised. Can you explain that to me?"

"Serrie, I told you I believe you are my mate. And that is what mates do for each other. We only have one true mate that makes us whole and completes us. That is what heals our pains and troubles. It is very rare to find that."

"Jeremy listen, I do not know if I believe that. I believe there is something more to this and I am not seeing it. Please, if there is, please tell me the truth. I need a lot of honesty right now. I am tired of guessing. I am starting to feel I do not even know who I am anymore." I could feel the tears building behind my eyes. Why was I telling him these things?

Jeremy walked over and sat down beside me, taking me into his arms. "Serrie, I promise when I have the answers, I will give them to you. When the time is right, I promise I will tell you everything I know. Just know I am here and nowhere else. I am yours." He laid me down on the bed and curled around me. Instantly I could feel the heat rushing over me.

How is it possible I have this experience with two people? I lay there in Jeremy's arms and thought about John. There was something I was missing, and I knew it, but I could not for the life of me figure it out. I felt sleep overtaking me. Falling deeper and deeper into the dark pit of slumber land.

When I woke, I could feel the cold, empty space where Jeremy had been. I stood and stretched and walked downstairs.

"When did Jeremy leave?" I asked Sereena, as a blush ran up my face.

"About an hour ago. He said you were sleeping. Sounds like someone got a little cozy with handsome." she said teasingly.

"Haha.Sereena, we only talked and he held me and I fell asleep, end of story. I was really tired from all the excitement over the last few weeks." I tried to sound convincing.

Sereena smiled a smirky smile and said, "Sure, whatever you say. But I know this, Serrie, does not cuddle with her clients. You can say what you want to say but I think that there is more to this then you are letting yourself see." She then held out a little white box. "Here I got you something special for a special moment in your life. To commemorate your time with little Mr. Handsome, who you never let in." She said with a wink and a smile.

"Oh, Sereena, you didn't have to get me anything." I opened the box and there lay a beautiful necklace, it was black gold chain, with a cradle holding an opal and pink tourmaline stone that looked as if the two stones were melded into a perfect circle. The swirls in the colors were beautiful. I looked up with tears teasing my eyes. "Sereena, it is beautiful! I cannot take this it is too much!."

"Do not be silly Serrie, I want you to have it. It is both of your birthstones into one. I want you to have it and think of this silly old woman when you wear it." She smiled and took the necklace and placed it around my neck. "Here, turn around and let me put this on." She placed it on and closed the clasp. It felt warm and so nice.

"I love it! Thank you so much. I will always wear it." She hugged me and whispered something in my ear, that I did not quite hear. "What was that?" I asked. "Oh, it is nothing, just me being silly. Now, go home girl."

With that I said goodbye and headed for home. While at a red stop light I saw a man I thought was Jeremy I rolled down my window and hollered at him, when He turned around it was John. It surprised me because I was fairly sure it was Jeremy! Was I going crazy?

John walked over to the car and the warmth hit me immediately. "Hey John, you want a ride? Where are you headed?"

"Sure, I was headed home. I had to take care of some business a little way from here. I took a cab here but then I lost my wallet and could not get a cab back. What are you doing on this side of town?"

"Oh, I went and seen a friend for a while, and I ended up falling asleep. I just feel so tired, you know?" I tried for a sheepish grin.

"Yeah, I know what you mean." he hopped in the car and said thanks for the ride.

While he was in the car, I could feel the heat radiating off of him. What the hell is this? I had to find out. I mustered all of my courage, "John, I want to ask you something. Every time you are around me, I feel this heat coming from you. And when you touched me earlier, I could feel the heat and desire and safety from you. I feel that from someone else too. Do you know what that is? I know I asked you this before when we were arguing, but please will you tell me."

He looked at me for a long time. And then I heard him sigh a long sigh. "If I tell you, please promise me you will not hate me. Because it is not what you think it is. I have waited for this moment for a long, long time and now that it is here, I am scared shitless it will cost me you."

I began shaking, not knowing if I wanted the truth or not. I decided I might as well, I mean it cannot be worse than me going crazy right?

"Just tell me. I need to know. Because it makes me want to touch you, to lie with you. It is like you complete me and so does he and I am getting confused, and I feel like I am going crazy."

John laughed, "you are not going crazy. I promise." with that said he took off his wig and glasses. To my surprise, it was Jeremy.

"Jeremy! What the hell?" I slowed my car and pulled over to the side of the road.

"Wha what is this? Is this some kind of joke? I mean you pretend to be my neighbor. Why? WHY!"

Jeremy threw his hands up in defense of my yelling. "Calm down Serraid. I have wanted to tell you for a long time now. I have not liked lying to you. I wanted to show you something you forgot a long time ago. I wanted to show you that you can have gentle love and not need the rough all the time. I wanted you to feel safety. I did not want to tell you this way. I wanted to tell you the way I had planned on. But you caught on faster than I thought you would. I am in love with you, and I have been for a long time. I have watched you, push people away, I have watched you cut yourself and hurt yourself. I have watched you close yourself off from love because you were scared. I wanted to show you love is a good thing! That it is not always bad."

"And you thought lying to me was the way to show me that?! Are you fucking stupid?! I mean you do not lie to someone like that and then go, oh by the way I love you, but I have been lying to you'! I cannot believe this! I just slept with you, you make me feel so good and safe and warm! I was starting to fall in love with you, and here we are with truth shredding that love apart! Why? Why could not you have been yourself…."

I lost it, I leaned over the center console and started hitting him as hard as I could, the heat was back, and the pain ripped through my body like a jolt of electricity. "What the hell was that?!" I said as I looked down at my body. I thought he had stabbed me. I was looking to see how bad it was. "Oh…. My…. God… What the hell is wrong with me? Oh god help me please help me!" The pain tore my head backwards. My hands were not hands, they were deformed. Something was seriously wrong with me.

Jeremy wrapped his arms around me and rocked me and soothed me. My anger calmed and I could feel the pain going away. What the hell is going on? What is wrong with me? I am 35 I should not be going crazy at 35…. Darkness starting to take over………gone…

I woke up in my bed. It was morning, I could tell by where the light was hitting my room. My head was pounding, confused about how I got home.

I went downstairs and Sarah was sitting at the kitchen table.

"Coffee is done if you want some. Someone had a great night." she said with a giggle.

"John brought you home after you passed out last night. Must had been a good time." She said with a huge smile.

"What? That was not John, which was Jeremy pretending to be John!" I snapped.

"What the hell are you talking about Serraid, that was John?" She said with confusion on her face.

"Well Jeremy admitted to me that he was John, and professing his love to me last night, we got into a huge fight and I passed out. That must be when he brought me home." I said and knowing that I sound crazy.

"Are you serious? Jeremy is John? Is he crazy? Did he say why he pretended to be John?" Sarah said.

"No, just that he loved me." I said.

A knock on the door startled us, we both look and as if on cue there was Jeremy! Sarah went and answered the door.

"Why did you lie to me? I ask.

"I want to explain, will you please let me come inside and explain, please." He pleaded

"Yes, Jeremy, or John, what the hell do I call you?"

"Jeremy, call me Jeremy. Serraid, I do love you. I have for a long time. I have wanted to tell you the truth for a while. I hated lying to you guys and pretending to be someone else. But I wanted to be able to see you outside of here and show you some things. Please forgive me..."

I walked over to him and slapped him across the face and then kissed him as deep as I could. "I forgive you, and I love you too."

"I am sorry to cut in here. But I have a question. What are we going to do about David? We have to kill him." Sarah said with surety.

"Yes, we do." I said

"I agree." Jeremy said.

We all sat down and drank coffee. I decided I needed something to eat. I offered to make breakfast for us all. I wanted an omelet and bacon. I cooked breakfast and we all sat down at the table to eat. It was nice to have some of this puzzle figured out. I knew Jeremy was hiding something else from me though. I could not help but feel that Sarah was hiding something too.

I would figure all of this out, ... eventually. But I know that I want these two in my life. I love them, I would kill for them.

CHAPTER 8

After breakfast I decided to do some digging. I began checking billing records on David. I went to the Center and talked with Cheryl I kept her busy looking for something that I knew did not exist so I could snag David's billing information from when he came in under the name Mr. Cook. When I found what I needed, I told Cheryl to call me when she found what I had her looking for and I would come back and pick it up. I went to leave when I remembered the note that I was going to pick up. The one that was taped to the door of the center. I got to my office and stepped inside; I found the note lying under some files I had laid on my desk the last day I was here.

I opened the note. I did not recognize the handwriting though. It said: *Serraid, I will give you until the end of today to meet with me. I will meet you at the peer at midnight. Be there or I will make sure you get my message loud and clear the next time. Do not be late and come alone. We have some unfinished business, you, and me. Until then love.*

D~

It all came flooding back to me now. The night that Sarah was attacked. This is why He did it! And this is what he meant by, "he had been most patient." Holy shit! Reading this made me more determined to kill this psychopath more than anything else. And believe me I was going to kill him. I felt heat rise from my ribs and the pain seared through me. What the hell is going on, I thought to myself while trying to breathe. I looked over his billing info. There was an address, but I was betting it was a fake. There was a billing number, and He had paid in cash. Shit! Well, that was a dead end.

I decided to drive by the address and see where it was and see if it looked familiar. I was surprised when I started getting close, there was a lake here. And holy shit! There was a cabin on the lake! I picked up my cell phone and called Jeremy. "Yeah, listen I found the cabin. The address was on a billing paper from the Center when he came there. I will explain that later. Anyways, I am parked outside. No there is no one home, so I am going to snoop around. I will be fine, do not worry about me. You know where I am so if I come up missing again you will know where to find me." I hung up before he could protest any farther.

I got out of my car and headed to the front door when without a warning it flew open!

"How nice of you to make an appearance love! Did you come to give me your answer?" he said with a crooked smile.

I turned to run back to the car. I made it to the door but before I could get it opened, I was slammed up against it. He grabbed my hair and pulled my neck back and kissed me fiercely. I screamed against his mouth and tried to bring the heel of my foot into his groin, but he had me pinned too well for that. He shoved me farther into the side of the car.

He pulled my hair back more and said, "You will like what I am going to do to you right now. I am going to hurt you, and I am going to make you like it. I remember how you used to like me to make you bleed. You would get so excited. I am going to make you want me again, like you did back then."

I tried shaking my head no, but he held it in place. I screamed at him. "I fucking hate you! I want you to die! You will not have me; I will not let you! I would rather die than to have you again!"

"Now that is no way to talk to the man who was your lover for years. You are a naughty girl Serraid, and I shall have to teach you some manners yet again."

He ripped my pants off me in one aggressive yank. I am still not sure how he did it. I felt the force of it cut the front of my legs when the fabric gave way to the pressure being pulled on it. Then, he ripped my panties off me. I felt them cut me between my legs; I could feel a trickle of blood running down my leg. I tried not to think about it. I thought to myself, oh god, he is going to rape me!

"Please do not do this, David, can't we just talk? I want to talk this out. Please don't! Nooooo!!"

He shoved himself deep inside of me. I could feel my body ripping and tearing from the uninvited entry. My body was not ready for it, yet he gave it anyway. He slammed my head against the car, all the while he was driving deep and deeper inside of me. He found his rhythm and my body jerked against my car with each stroke of his rhythm. I could feel his breath on the back of my neck. He bit my shoulder hard enough to make me cry out. I could feel my body starting to respond tightening and lubricating trying to protect itself from the assault.

"I will kill you for this! This makes me hate you even more than I do right now! I fucking hate you!!! You hear me?!" I screamed all of this with tears running down my face. I truly hated him. I did not want this I tried pushing against the car to get a better angle in which hopefully I could kick him or knock him off balance. He must have felt me shift my weight because he shoved me harder against the car. I could feel the metal threatening to break my ribs, I cried as I realized that I was not strong enough to stop him from hurting me again.

He pulled out of me and turned me around, so I was facing him. I tried to struggle, but my legs did not want to move. They were in too deep of shock from the trauma of the assault being brought against my body. He looked me in the eyes, and he shoved himself back into me then He bit my nipple and shook it with his teeth. I could feel him slapping against me every time he went in. My body grew tighter. And I could feel my breath coming raggedly. I was trying not to think of what was going on. I did not want my body to respond to this treatment, yet it was. It was beginning to like it without my consent. This made me cry harder, even my body was against me right now. At that moment I felt so nasty, was he really raping me if my body liked it? I hated myself right then. I decided that I deserved this, because he had won, he had made my body like this even when my mind and heart screamed no!

He grabbed me around the throat and held me there. "I will snap your neck if you try to do anything to hurt me right now. Do you understand me, Serraid?"

"Yes" I said weakly. The look in his eye told me that he meant every word he said. I hoped by cooperating it would buy me some time and hopefully Jeremy would show up looking for me.

He kissed my neck and played with my breasts, and he picked me up and wrapped my legs around him. "Wrap your arms around me right now, but don't try anything stupid.," he said with a smirk. I wrapped my arms around his neck without any fight, and he began working in and out of me making my ass hit the car. I could feel him running over the sweet spot deep inside; when he noticed it, he began to thrust harder and faster. I could feel the orgasm building. I did not want this! Why was my body doing this to me?! Why was it giving him what he wanted?! I tried to fight it, but on a deep hard stroke, he bit my chest and thrust deep inside and that threw me over the edge with pleasure. He felt it, he let go of my chest and he kissed me hard on the lips. I screamed my frustration mixed with my pleasure into his mouth.

My eyes were wide open, and his face blurred a bit. I closed my eyes and opened them again and I was terrified of what I saw. The man inside of me was not David! This, this man, I knew this man from my nightmares. "Oh God! It cannot be you! Get off me, let me down you asshole!" I could feel the bile rushing up to my throat and I did nothing to stop it. I threw up on him.

He slapped me across the face as he said, "You BITCH! I am going to rip your throat out!" He slammed my head against the car; on the third hit of the car everything began to go black. I could feel myself slipping into unconsciousness. I tried to fight back the blackness, because I was afraid if I passed out, He really would kill me. He was screaming something, but it sounded miles away. I felt something hit me in the back and then nothing.

I woke up and I could feel the mask over my face. I panicked and jumped up too quickly. I felt the room tilt and my head spun a little. I could smell the clean smell around me, and I realized I was in the hospital. My body felt bruised, and I started taking inventory of the damage. I lifted the sheet and what I saw made me cry and gasp. My thighs were severely bruised. I had some stitches on my arm, and it was swollen and bruised. My head ached like someone hit me with a tree. I reached up and found it was bandaged up, which meant I had staples or stitches or both. My face felt swollen, and my right eye would not open all the way. My body literally felt like it had been someone's punching bag.

I looked around the room trying to find someone. My heart stopped when my eyes reached the door. He was standing there crying. I could not make out what he was saying to the doctor. My pulse was in my throat, and everything began to go fuzzy again. I fought to stay awake. I pressed my nurse's button. The doctor and David looked up and smiled at me.

"How are you feeling Serraid? I am Dr. Joseph; I have been treating you since you arrived here yesterday. Your friend found you and brought you here. You are a very lucky woman. If he had been a few minutes later, you would have bled to death."

"Who else is here besides him?" I wanted to know if Sarah or Jeremy were here.

"No one else. Is there someone that I can call for you?" he asked with sincerity in his voice.

"Yes, please call Sarah, her number should be on my hospital record. Please call her and let her know that I am here. She is probably worried sick about me. Did you say I could have bled to death?" I asked him suddenly, realizing what he had said. I must have been hurt worse than I thought I was.

"Yes, you cut an artery in your arm when it went through the window. Do you remember anything about yesterday at all?"

I shook my head, trying to think about yesterday. I do not remember every detail clearly. Tears began to sting the back of my eyes. I choked down a sob that began to clump up in my throat. 'Hold yourself together Serraid' I thought to myself. "No, the last thing I remember was driving my car. It is all blank until I woke up here. What happened to me Doctor?"

"Well as far as we can tell you must have stopped somewhere for directions, at a gas station and shortly after you had an accident. I have informed our in-house counselors, and they will be sending someone up to talk to you now that you are awake. Your friend here, David was the one that found you and called 911 when you did not show up at the cabin."

"There will be no need for that, I am a counselor, and I will be fine. I assure you I have a great support staff, and I will make it through this just fine.." I smiled a reassuring smile at the doctor.

"Ok, but only if, you are sure. You know once this all settles into your mind about what happened and you start remembering it will take you back and make you feel weakened and possibly scattered. It is no problem for them to come up and talk to you. I will go and make this call for you and let your friend know you are here." With that, he turned and headed out of my room. Which left me with David.

"If you think this is going to buy you points to save your life, you are dead wrong." I looked him straight in the eyes. I hated him, and I decided He would pay for what he had done, no matter how much he tried to make up for it. One thing that did not make sense though, is why would he almost kill me and then save me?

"Serraid, please listen. I saved your life yesterday. We were just supposed to meet at the cabin and when you didn't show, I went to look for you and found your car wrecked and you were injured so, I called EMS and this proves I still love you."

DON'T! Do not tell me that you love me! After everything you have done to me, after every way you have hurt me and ripped my heart out. Do NOT tell me you love me! You lost that right a long time ago!"

David goes to say something else, but I cut him off saying: "Do not try telling me more lies! You are more stupid than I believed you were!" I looked into his eyes, and that is when I noticed something. These eyes are empty and darkened with more hatred than I have ever seen before. A memory tries to come from my nightmares with the same eyes and his face blurred and everything went dark.

Hours later I wake up and Jeremy and Sarah are now here. David is nowhere to be seen.

"What the hell happened? Where were you going Serraid?" Sarah asks.

"I was going to meet David and got into a car accident and almost died." I tell her weakly. "David found me and called an ambulance, and he saved my life. I woke up here and he was here the doctor, and we got into and fight and I passed out, now you are here." I said bracing for lecture going to get.

"What the hell were you thinking, Serraid, going off by yourself to meet a lunatic after everything he did to you, to all of us?" Jeremy was angry.

"I just wanted to put an end to this without anyone else getting hurt fighting my battles." I said.

Sarah came and set down on the bed, she took my hand and said, "Serraid. We know you are trying to protect us, but damnit, you have to trust that we can help protect you too. You almost died. Do you hear me? You almost died. Please can you just see we are just as worried for you as you are for us?"

I went to answer her when the hospital room door opens. What I saw made my heart stand still and my blood run cold. David in the flesh standing there, with coffee. I start to panic because why is he here?

"Finally, we thought you had gotten lost with our caffeine." Jeremy said. I sit there with my jaw on the floor; my blood is boiling at this point. I lose my shit. I sit up and frantically say as I point, "That's David!!!"

Jeremy looks confused and looks between me and David, "You must be mistaken, this is Dayvan. My friend."

David or Dayvan whoever he is has a guilty look on his face, Jeremy notices this look and narrows his eyes as he asks, "What is that look for? I know you, and I know that look."

Dayvan sat down the coffees on the table, and took a deep breath and said, "Remember when I told you that I had checked on Nal…I mean Serraid."

Jeremy slowly stands shaking his head yes and says, "I do, go on." In a very cold tone. I am looking between them trying to figure out what the hell is going on. Why is Jeremy so angry, I can feel his anger right now.

Dayvan says, "So I seen her, and I couldn't' leave. I love her so much man, I could not leave. I wanted to get closer to her. So, I used a fake name to get close, and one thing led to another." He trailed off looking like a kicked puppy.

Jeremy swiftly goes across the room and pins Dayvan against wall by his throat and says, "You really did all that horrible stuff to the woman we love!?" Jeremy is yelling and Dayvan's face is beginning to change colors.

"What. Are. You. Talking. About? I would never hurt Serraid, you of all people should know that!" Dayvan manages to say with hurt in his voice.

"Really, then why is Serraid saying that you left her and beat her, you raped her and kidnapped her, and you even beat and raped her friend Sarah!! I mean, are you calling her a liar? Fucking say she is a liar and I will rip your fucking throat out right here!" Jeremy growls.

Dayvan answers, "What are you talking about? That is not what happened, I would never hurt Serraid, and I did not even know who Sarah was until today! So, what the fuck man? What are you playing at?" confused and angry.

I look at Davids's or Dayvans eyes, and they were kind, soft like I remember before He changed. "Jeremy, stop, please. I want to hear what he has to say."

Jeremy lets go of Dayvan's throat and Dayvans take a gasping breath. "Thank you, I swear I would never do any of those things."

"Explain yourself, please Dayvan. I need to know what happened." I say softly, tears threatening to spill from my eyes.

The room goes silent as the nurse comes in to check my vitals, and bandages to make sure they were soaking through. I winced when she touched my arm. She gave me a sympathetic look, and said, "You have a PCA pump for the pain, there is no reason for you to hurt, dear." I heard a soft beeping as she pressed the button before I could protest. Then the nurse smiles softly and leaves the room as she says, "You all make sure to let her rest."

I told Dayvan to make his explanation quick because of the pain medication.

"So, you remember when I went to meet that client to help them late that one night?" He asked with hope in his eyes.

"Yes, I remember, you were reluctant to go and I encouraged you to because you were always so good at helping people." I notice Jeremy shifting his weight again, clearly pissed off, but I do not have time right now to deal with his bullshit.

"Ok, so you remember I left, I met the client and helped them, it did take a little longer than I anticipated, which is why I left the voicemail for you so you would not worry. As I was leaving the client's house, I got a phone call from the police saying there was a house fire, and the entire house was lost along with you in it."

Jeremy softened a little and said, "I remember you telling me this. You showed up on my doorstep wanting to die. I remember the funeral and everything. It took all I had to keep you from following her to the grave."

I was so confused, I looked at him and coldly said, "You came home that night, and you were hard, and cold and rough. You were different."

"I planned your service and everything. I mourned you for years, I could not understand why that had happened to you." Tears streamed down Dayvan's face as he remembered the events as if they happened. I believed what he was saying. The tears were real, and I remembered the night he went to help his client.

"I remember you came home that night and you said that you could not help them. I thought it was weird because you never gave up on people that easily. You always loved a challenge."

I lay there and wondered how this could happen. I wanted to believe him, yet my heart was torn in two. I remembered the man I fell in love with and I remembered who he had become. I remembered all the horrible things that He had done to me and people cared about. Half of me wanted to believe what he was saying was truth, yet the part of me that wanted revenge kept telling me that he was a lying sack of shit.

"Tell me something that only you and I would know. I want to believe you, I do, but I am having a tough time because in my memory you changed into a horrible person that night. Please if you are truly the real David or Dayvan, make me believe you."

"Serraid" he said taking my hand. "Do you remember the time we were walking down the alley behind our home, we walked by this little parlor, and you smelled the food coming from the shop. You begged me to take you in and get you something to eat. When we got home that day, you were so ill, you had to lay down for the rest of the day. I remember you woke me up in the middle of the night when you miscarried on our bed. I held you while you cried, I cried with you. We mourned the loss of our child together. I told you everything was going to be all right, that we could try again" Tears were rolling down his face as he kissed my hand.

I began to cry because I had not told anyone that story and there was no one else there that night. So, no one could have known about it. I wrapped my arms around his neck and hugged him; I pulled him close to me. I could feel his heart connect with me. I realized right then how much I had missed David, I mean Dayvan and how much I still loved him.

Jeremy stood there with a puzzling look on his face, and he was thinking.

The look in his eyes told me he was just as uncertain as I was about all of this. My heart sank as I saw the hurt and fear in his eyes. I wanted to erase that.

"I am so sorry about all of this. How can this be happening?"

"I do not know my lady, but we will figure this out, I promise. I have heard of these things happening before. It has been an exceedingly long time since the last time I heard of this. But I do know that we must kill this mystery man, more now than ever."

"I just do not understand. I am scared, please hold me, and kiss me and make me feel safe again. Please tell me I will not lose you. I cannot lose you Jeremy. I just got you and I do not want to be without you. I know you are right for me; I can feel it. My heart tells me so. Yet I have this longing for Dayvan too. I know you do not want to hear this, but it is how I feel." I cried onto his shoulder.

"I understand, you loved him very deeply. I know that you have been away from him for a long time now. It will be hard, but you do not need him like you need me. I love you Serraid, I want you to know that. But I am not going to lie, it will hurt me, seeing you two together especially if any feelings you have for him come to the surface and begin to show. I am not sure I can handle that right now. I need you too, and I know that you are my mate. I know this deep within my heart." He kissed the top of my head as he spoke to me.

I knew that Jeremy loved me. Feeling him close to me I could feel the heat coming from him and it steadied me. I did not understand this feeling with him and I, but I do know that whatever it was, it was certainly good.

I grabbed him and pulled him down so I could kiss him. His lips were soft and pliable. I loved it when he kept them soft and suckable. I could feel the need rising in me. I felt things low grow tight with want. It also reminded me of how bruised I was, that did not matter though. I needed to feel his lips on mine to help wash away the bad. I moaned as he kissed me deeper. He must have sensed my desire because he raised up and smelled the air.

"You smell like me, mmmmm I want to make love to you right now. Is that, ok? I know that you have been through a lot but damn, I want you. I want to take all of the last couple of days from you. I want to reclaim you. I want to help you heal and erase the traces of this from you."

I kissed him and wrapped my arms around him and that is when it hit me full force in the face, a flash back of trauma. I froze, and I began to cry, and then sob! Jeremy held me there and rocked us back and forth and rubbed my head. He let me cry out my pain and my hurt as if he knew exactly what I needed.

I raised my head up and I wanted to tell him all that happened, but I could not remember clearly. I wanted to unload all my worries upon him. How did he do that to me? How did he make me want to tell him everything?

Jeremy noticed that I was starting to get sleepy from the pain medication, he helps me get comfortable and holds me as I drift off to that wonderful darkness I have called my friend.

Next thing I know, it was dark and wet and there was a lot of screaming in the air. I wondered what was going on. I looked around and saw a waging war. There was a village attacking another village. It was a blood bath. It was over someone taking another man's bride. He was angry and he was going to pay the whole clan back for it. And there were children lying dead in the trenches, women weeping for their children. Husbands fight to protect them. It was horrible. That is when I saw him. He was riding a wild black horse. He reared up in front of where I was standing, he looked at me and grabbed me and took off with me. I kicked and screamed for him to let me go back to my people. He would not listen, and all of his people were behind us. They were leaving my village as well. I could do this to protect my people, I told myself.

Once at his clan's village, they bathed me and wrapped me in linens. They put me in a long house made of trees wrapped in pelts, where they washed my feet and rubbed them with oil. Then, they left me there. That is when He entered. He bowed to me and me said, "I know this is not what you wanted, but you are owed to me for the loss of our women. I will have you and you will bear me children, or I will kill your whole village." I knew this man was speaking the truth. I had all intentions of staying there and doing as I was told to do. He took me right there that night.

Three nights passed and there was a commotion outside while the men were hunting. Suddenly Dayvan came into the tent and picked me up and took off with me. "What are you doing? He will kill our village. Please let me go back! Do not do this to our people. Please, he will kill them all because you took me."

"He will not be able to kill them because I have hidden them. They are safe now. I know that you are hurt and I will take care of you. I have promised your father you will survive and I intend on keeping that promise."

I woke up with my heart pounding. Not making sense of the dream. It had to be because of the memory flashback or something to do with what has happened to me.

"You look like you had a bad dream."

I looked over to see Dayvan sitting there calmly. He approached me slowly, uncertain of his boundaries. I knew he wanted to reach out and touch me and hold and comfort me, but he was too afraid to get too close. I began shaking as I started crying. That is when he closed the distance with a few steps and held me. I could feel the heat from him instantly, that warm, safe, calm feeling. I froze in his arms. How could this be happening? I did not understand how I could feel this way about two guys at the same time. I could feel his heartbeat. And I knew he loved me. I could feel it radiating from him. Something about it rubbed something inside of me awakening something that was lying dormant. I wanted him to hold me closer still. I snuggled against him and

He pulled me completely against him. I could feel us melting together and I loved the feeling. Suddenly, pain ripped through me from my spine to my feet. I looked up in fear from the suddenness of it. "What was that?"

"I think I better step back a few steps for a moment and let you calm down. Are you upset about something right now? I did not make you mad, did I?"

He looked as if he had been beaten down. I did not understand what the hell was going on with me anymore. "Do you know what that was?"

"Well not exactly, no. I wish that I did though. Maybe I held you too tightly, and I hurt your ribs or some other injury they missed. Maybe I should call for the Doctor."

I pulled him closer to me and snuggled in closer. I wanted to feel his body against mine. I wanted to take off his clothes and feel his skin against mine. I did not care about the injuries, about the pain. I wanted to heal and I knew this was the way for that. Before I knew it, that is exactly what I was doing. I had his shirt off and he was pressed against me. The feel of his skin was so nice and somehow it just felt right. I had no worries at that moment. All I knew was I was beginning to feel whole again, and I did not want to lose that feeling.

"Please make love to me. I need you too. I need to feel you; I need you to help me."

"I am not sure if that is such a good idea right now. You are still injured." He tried to pull away but I had a tight hold on him.

I took off his remaining clothes with one yank, and I pulled him to the bed with me. I found him hard and ready. I wanted him right then. I pulled him down to me and I kissed him deeply. I wanted to taste him. I wanted to feel him. I needed him right then and I could not even explain why.

He slowly slid inside of me, and the pain was sharp and quick. I hissed as the pain hit me. He stopped for a second and looked at me asking me with his eyes if I was all right. I pulled him down farther, wanting him to finish the decent inside. He took the hint. He pushed and slid out all the way to the tip, just teasing me with just enough to make me squirm for more. I moaned, "please." I needed him. I wanted him to go faster. I began moving my hips in my own rhythm, forcing him to match mine. I could feel the first wave of pleasure hit me. It was like slow, warm rain. It did not take over me; it just simply washed me. Then he started pumping in and out faster, harder, deeper the length of him was amazing, and I could feel the orgasm building. I knew I was going to go. The pain was there, and it helped the orgasm build with each burn of movement.

"Almost, please don't stop." I pleaded with him. I wanted this, I needed this so badly. I did not want to lose it. I pushed and pulled with him until he brought me. I scratched my pleasure out into his chest, feeling my nails tearing his skin. That excited me even more when I felt the warm trickle of blood that I had created. I raised my mouth to where I had bled him and slowly licked the blood from his chest. The taste of his blood was like sugar, sweet with a hint of something bitter. It made me hunger for more, I opened my mouth and bit into him, holding as much of his skin in my mouth as it could hold. I wanted to feel my teeth grind together I wanted to bleed him more. I began to buck against him. He moaned and I knew he was close. I played my tongue over the skin that I held in my mouth. I wanted him to feel everything that I was doing to him. I bit harder and I heard a grunt come from deep within him. Then I heard this deep growl. The vibrations from his growl pushed me over the edge one more time. I writhed under him in pleasure. I melted with his body. He lost his, and I could feel him spilling into me. That brought me screaming. I could feel our bodies melting together. I had not felt that in an exceptionally long time. I could feel my body healing, the energy renewing.

"I have missed you so much Dayvan." With that I rolled over and he held me while I slept.

I woke up to arguing. Two men. It was Dayvan and Jeremy.

"How could you do this? How could you sleep with my woman?!" Jeremy yelled out.

"She was my woman before she was yours! I was just doing what she wanted me to do. I did nothing against her will. Ask her and she will tell you the same thing.!"

"Could you guys please keep it down, I am trying to sleep. Man, my arm itches." I looked down and most of my bruises were gone. It was amazing. I pulled the bandages off and was amazed at what I saw. The incision was healed, and the stitches were laying there. I called the nurse to come and check my head, to her surprise the staples had fallen out, and it was all healed. She called Dr. Joseph, and he confirmed I was good to go. I got to go home! Home, I have missed it so…

I thought about it. Could the sex with Dayvan have healed me just like laying with Jeremy had? And if so, why was that and what did it mean? There were so many things I did not understand, and yet I knew someone had the answers and they just were not telling me about it.

"Hey, can someone tell me how I am healing so fast when you guys are around? I do not understand it at all. I know there is something going on, so why don't you guys just tell me already? Please."

They looked at each other and spoke at the same time. "I do not know. If I figure it out, I will let you know. For now, let us just get you home." They glared at each other as if they were going to fight again.

"Guys, could you not fight over me right now, please. We are not in high school anymore and I think we are a little old for this shit. We all must get along for now. You hear me boys?"

They both nodded their heads yes and we headed toward the house. Sarah had gone home yesterday to get the house cleaned and ready for when I came home. She was waiting at the door for us when we pulled up in the car. She shook her head as I walked up to the door. I grabbed her and hugged her tight. I love Sarah and I have missed her so much.

"I love you bitch. I have missed you and welcome home."

I smiled because she had a way of doing that to me. "I love you too hooker and I am glad to be home. I love you Sarah, and I am sorry I have not been able to be here with you lately."

"Hey, I understand. I know how you have the hots for the doctors at the hospital, so you keep finding reasons to go stay in their presence." We both laughed.

Yep, that was Sarah, funny till the end. She was awesome and she was my best friend. She looked at Jeremy and then at Dayvan and asked, "So how are things between the boys? Is it getting any better? Or are they still fighting?"

"They are having a pissing contest, and they are treating me like the fire hydrant. It is really getting on my last nerve. I mean, I have a history with Dayvan and just began to have something with Jeremy. I do not know what

I am going to do, Sarah. I just do not know." I hung my head trying to thwart off the headache that was starting to set in.

"Babe, I know this must be hard. I have to admit; I am having a hard time with all this too. I mean you were in love with this guy, then another guy that looks like him comes along and pretends to be the guy you are in love with, but he is not him and he hurts you. All the while you believe it is the same man, so you run to escape him. You come here and are hell bent on not getting close to anyone and along comes Jeremy, which turns out is also John. Things heat up and you begin to fall in love with Jeremy, then out of nowhere here comes the bad guy. And then comes the real guy you loved. It IS confusing and I am glad it is not me in your shoes. But I am here for you. I will be here for you every step of the way." She reached over and patted my shoulder and moved my hair away from my face.

"Thank you, Sarah. I know it is all a mess and I just cannot make any decisions right now. I want Day... I mean this guy dead! I want him to pay for what he has done to all of us."

Just then the doorbell rang, I jumped at the sudden sound of it. I stood up and headed for the door. But would not you know, Dayvan and Jeremy were already there, like good little watch dogs, nothing escaped them by no means. I grunted out of frustration. I just wish these two would chill the hell out for a little bit.

"Look guys, I appreciate the fact that you two feel you have to out-piss the other male here. But let me tell you, I will out-piss you both if you do not calm the hell down. This testosterone challenge you have going on is getting on my last nerve. I can answer my own damned door. I do not need you two to go around taking care of everything. I am not helpless, and I refuse to be treated like I am. Just because I was taken, I will not be treated like a broken vessel. Am I clear?!"

Dayvan looked at me and smiled, "Perfectly, my dear."

Jeremy got mad, I could see the heat rising, his neck and his vein in his head began to pulse. He gritted his teeth and said, "As you wish, my lady."

"Thank you. Now, if you will excuse me, I would like to see who is at the door." I pushed the aside and opened the door. The postman was standing there with a package, and my heart felt like it hit the floor. What could this possibly be now? Everyone was accounted for, and as far as I know patches was still here. As if on cue of my thoughts, patches came around the corner and rubbed against my legs and purred softly with a soft meow. I signed for the package, told the postman thank you and closed the door.

We all stood around the box not moving to open it. I think we were all afraid of what we would find. Finally, after a few minutes I decided to open the box.

I broke out in a laugh of relief when I saw the contents inside.

"Man, we really have to work on our paranoia ". I lifted the basket out of the box. It was from Earnald and the clan at the center. It was a bottle of nice wine 1928 to be exact. And some fruit and cheese and crackers. "Are they trying to tell me something?" I was laughing so hard I could hardly talk. Sarah started laughing with me.

Dayvan and Jeremy were looking at me and Sarah laughing, they were so serious when they both said at the same time. "I don't get it."

That made me and Sarah laugh even harder. I looked at them and between laughs I said, "Haven't you ever heard the expression, 'would you like some cheese with that wine?' It means to stop whining because people are tired of hearing it!"

You could literally see the light flash on in both of their minds. A smile crossed their faces and then they broke out in a full-blown laugh. A roaring laugh. I wiped the tears from my face from laughing so hard, and my ribs hurt. I decided to go upstairs and take a shower; I needed some relaxing time.

"I'm going to take a shower guys, I will be back down in a bit." I looked over and seen Jeremy and Dayvan looking hopefully at me. They were both hoping that I would invite one of them to go with me. My heart sank when I realized eventually, I was going to have to make a choice between the two. That hurt me, I did not know how I was going to come to that decision. I knew Jeremy was still sore about me and Dayvan sleeping together. I did not know how I was going to make it right with Jeremy. I did not want to hurt either one, but let's face it, a person cannot have two people they love in their lives without hurting someone eventually.

"Guys, I know this is hard. I am sorry and I really do not know what to do. Dayvan, we have such a long history, some of it is not even really with the real you. But I love you." I could see Jeremy flinch at those words. "Jeremy, I fell in love with you, because you taught me something I had forgotten something that Dayvan worked hard to teach me. You showed me what it was like to be loved. And I am so grateful. And I know me sleeping with Dayvan in the hospital really hurt you and you are doing a great job at hiding it. But I do not want to hurt either one of you." I began to cry as I spoke. "I do not know what the right thing to do is. It will take me some time to figure this out and I will need your help to do it. What I need right now is a shower and some time to think. If you two want to help, try to get along. I know this is asking a lot and I do not have any right to ask you guys to get along, but I need this right now." After saying that, I turned and walked up the stairs to take a shower.

Once I got to the bathroom I sat on the floor and cried. I was crying for Dayvan and what we had lost. I was crying for all the times that I wanted him dead. I cried for all the times he must have thought about me and mourned my death. I cried for Jeremy and what we have, and at the thought of losing it all. How did my life come to this? What did I ever do to make this happen? I knew there were no answers here on the floor, but I needed to cry. At times like these I wish I had my father here to comfort me. I needed someone to tell me it was going to be all right. Someone to hold me and make me feel safe. Someone other than one of the two men downstairs.

I must have fallen asleep because next thing I remember was being a child, but not a child I knew. I was sitting on a man's lap; he was smiling at me. He told me he loved me and he was so proud of me. The joy that welled up inside of me seeing my father's face, but I did not know this man. Who was he? I felt so safe in his arms. I knew he would protect me. A woman I did not know walked into the room, and I knew that she was my mother and she was beautiful. I have always longed for parents like this. One's that love their children and showed them that they loved them. A home that was not dysfunctional.

Out of nowhere, my dream changed. I was about 5 years old laying in my bed when a man crawled in behind me. He began fondling me. I remember my heart pounding in my ears from fear. I wanted out of my bed. I got up and ran to bathroom. I remember being so sore that I could not use the bathroom without it hurting to the point where it made me cry. Why had my dream changed to this? I do not want to remember this! I went looking for my mother, she was wrapped around a strange man passed out from too much alcohol. I cried because I did not want to go back to my room. Because the man was waiting for me. So, I decided that I was going to run away the next day. I did not want to be here anymore. I wanted a new life. Somewhere I would be safe.

I woke up sweating and crying. What the hell made me dream that? It started off good, then ended badly, like so many of my dreams do. Sometimes I feel like someone is playing a nasty game of chess with my life. They give me enough good just to rip it away and laugh at the disaster it leaves behind. Sometimes I feel like I am nothing but a pawn in a twisted game.

I stood up and turned the water on. I wanted to wash this dream away. I needed to get the nasty feel of the man off of me. I could almost smell him on me. My stomach lurched at the memory. I climbed into the shower, the hot water felt so good on my skin. I grabbed my scrubber and poured some soap on it, I began scrubbing my arms, neck, and chest. I scrubbed so hard I could feel the burning. I could feel the blood coming to the surface. I could still feel him touching me. I wanted it to stop! I scrubbed harder and harder, but it did not make it go away. I cried and cursed and threw my scrubber. I was tired of the same old fight within myself. I sat down in the tub and thought how good death would actually feel. I mean, I would not feel this anymore. I would not have to remember this shit anymore. I slapped myself; I would not let them beat me. I stood and rinsed off the soap, lathered my hair, and turned off the water. After drying off, I stood there and looked at the nasty red marks that were left. I will need a high-necked shirt to cover this. Because I certainly did not need to answer any questions right now.

A noise coming from my bedroom made me jump. I turned to see what it was. Sarah stood there. She looked embarrassed. "I am sorry, I just wanted to come and check on you. You have been up here for two hours. Are you all right?"

"I am fine, I fell asleep for a bit and then I took a shower. I guess I still need more rest. I am sorry, I did not mean to scare you. I am fine, really. I will be down in a bit." I smiled, knowing it did not reach my eyes but hoped that she would believe me. I did not need anyone asking questions right now. I was holding the towel high to hide all the scratch marks on my chest. I really did not need her to see them and start wondering what the hell happened, and I did not need her telling the guys and them going all macho on me. Ugh, would this ever end? How was I ever going to choose between two people that I loved that made me feel the same way?

"Ok, I have made some coffee and Jeremy left to get some donuts. He said he needed sugar. I will see you when you come down." She turned to head down the stairs. She made it a couple of stairs down when she turned back toward me and said, "Serraid, Dayvan wants to know if he can come" I cut her off.

"No! I will be down in a bit. Tell him I am sorry, but I do not want him or Jeremy around me up here right now." I sighed because it was the farthest thing from the truth. The truth was, I wanted both to hold me. Because they both made me feel safe and warm. I knew that if they were with me, nothing would happen to me. "I'll be down in a minute."

Sarah turned and headed down the stairs. I did not want to hurt anyone, but I was damned if that is not what was going to happen. I had to choose and no matter what way I decided to go, someone was going to get hurt. Fuck! What was I going to do? This was going to eat at me until I came to a decision. I really needed to talk to both and see what they expected of me, what they desired and if they could put some perspective on this.

I had just put my shirt on when I heard the front door slam! I turned and ran downstairs to find out what was going on. I saw Jeremy fly across the front room in a hurry, looking excited. He spotted me coming down the stairs. He turned and hugged me, picking me off my feet, spinning me around.

I laughed and asked, "What? What is going on?"

"Serraid, I may have found where the imposter is staying. I know where and when he goes. I met someone today who knows this man. And he told me everything he knew about him." There was a tone that made me think that this man had not given the information up willingly.

"Jeremy, we must be incredibly careful here. What if it is this guy, pretending to be another person and he is setting a trap for us? We must take that in as a possibility." I really wanted him to think this through before jumping on this. "I mean look at what happened at the cabin." My skin crawled cold at the thought of the cabin. I could feel my face going white from the memory.

I felt Jeremy's body stiffen and the anger rising off him. It hit me full force and I could feel the pain starting to roam through my body. "Jeremy, you must calm down. Really, we will get this guy. Let us just be smart about this, ok. Let us do some investigating into this place, we will keep watch on it and make sure that it is legit and not a trap. I do not want anyone else getting hurt or killed because we were naïve and decided to go on impulse here."

I could feel him calming down, he was swallowing his anger. His face softened and he said, "You are right. I guess I am just ready to kill this man, and I am not thinking straight. I want him to pay for what he has done to all of us. It is time he is ended."

I felt my heart break as I knew what he was saying. I could feel the hurt from him. He was hurting and I could do nothing to fix this, except keep my mind about me and make sure that we kill this man. "We will get him, and he will pay for what he has done, Jeremy, I promise. We must be smart about it. I do not want to lose any more people that I care about." I kissed him deeply, trying to drink the pain from his eyes.

Sarah and Dayvan walked into the room and asked what all the commotion was about. They stopped short in the doorway when they saw us there together. I felt my face blush, and I pulled away, I could not look at Jeremy because I did not want to see the pain back in his eyes, knowing I was the one that put it there. We filled them in, and we all formed a plan. We were going to survey this place and take pictures of everyone who came and went. We would note anything that was off or felt wrong about each person that we saw. We would compile a list of times when the place was empty. We would place surveillance there so we could listen to conversations and hopefully we would get something we could use. Now that we had a plan started, we had to get the equipment and items we were going to need.

I could feel the hope beginning to build inside of me. I wanted this over, and I knew that together we could do this. Together, that sounded so good and yet so impossible.

CHAPTER 9

Jeremy and Dayvan agreed they would work together on getting all the equipment that we would need. Once they had all of it, we could put all the equipment in place. They left to go round it all up and bring it back here. Meanwhile, Sarah and I decided to clean the place up a little and get some food. I was starving as if I had not eaten in weeks.

After cleaning the house, we went to the local food mart, and bought some lunch meat, bread, mayo, lettuce, tomatoes, and pickles. I also got some ice cream and chocolate syrup with some cookies. I had a sweet tooth going on. Sarah decided to get some potato chips and dip. After getting everything we could think of that we would need on a stake out, we went to the checkout counter and paid for it all.

We arrived home and surprisingly the men were back. "Wow, that was fast. I figured they would be out all day trying to get all that stuff." I told Sarah. "I will go and take these bags in, and I'll be right back to help you get the rest of them."

I grabbed a couple of bags and headed into the house. I walked toward the kitchen to place the bags on the table when I heard Dayvan say, "We really need to tell her all the truth, Jeremy. She deserves to know all of it."

"Not yet she does not. We will tell her when she needs to know. But right now, we have to protect her. Because if she knows the truth it will put her in more danger. We must wait Dayvan, even you know that."

I knew they were hiding something from me! I thought to myself. Well, I am not letting them off the hook that damned easy. I walked into the kitchen threw the bags on the table and said, "Tell who what truth? What the hell are you guys hiding and from whom?"

They turned surprised by my sudden arrival, their faces went white, and they glanced at each other. I could almost hear their wheels turning in their heads. That was good for me, because now they knew they were caught and would have to confess whatever it was that they were hiding from me.

Dayvan and Jeremy looked at each other with fear plain on their faces. "Hey Serraid, we uh, we were just talking about a lady who is hanging with this guy. She needs to know what he is. But Jeremy thinks that telling her would only put her in more danger." Dayvan smiled a weak smile trying hard to be convincing.

I was not going to let them convince me that I had not just caught them. I would get to the bottom of this. Then I thought about what they had said before realizing I was here. I guess they could have been talking about someone else. I just could not help but feel they were hiding something. I looked at their faces and could see the concern on their faces. After a few minutes of thinking about it, I said, "I agree with Jeremy, I too think if she knows it will put her in more danger than she is already in. I vote we do not tell her until she needs to know."

I could see them let out the breath they were holding. What the hell were they hiding? "What are you guys not telling me?"

They both sighed and Jeremy answered, "We have all the equipment, but they are all short range, which means that someone will always have to be in close proximity to the place at all times in order for us to continually monitor the place."

Sarah walked in with the rest of the groceries. "Oh, I'm fine, don't worry about me, I can handle all these bags on my own." she said with a puff as she put the bags on the table.

"I'm sorry Sarah, I got into a conversation and forgot to come back and help you with the rest of it." I sounded apologetic but I was stifling a laugh at the pitiful look she was trying to pull off.

"It is fine, really. I mean if I had to put up with these two, I would probably forget about me too." She said with a giggle.

The men looked at each other with an awkward face. They were not sure how Sarah meant that. I decided not to tell them. I giggled at the loss of thought they had. Oh, so they are not the smartest ones in the house, I thought.

"We got enough groceries to make sandwiches for the stake out. We got drinks and chips too. I think that whichever one of us are there, we should be fine." Sarah said as she winked at me.

I could not help but smile back at her knowing that she was teasing them, and they did not even know it.

"Me and Dayvan have decided that since we must be so close, we do not want you women anywhere near there alone without one of us with you. We have decided to take rotating 12-hour shifts. That way it's covered 24 hours a day and we are not switching so soon as to draw attention. Jeremy said. As he talked, I could see him stealing glances in Dayvan's direction hoping that he would back him if needed.

I could feel the anger welling up inside of me. Who did they think that they were, making these decisions on their own?! "Listen, I do not know who the hell you think you guys are, telling us what you want and what you do not want, but I am part of this. You have NO right to tell me that I cannot help with this. It was ME that he did this to! Did you forget that? And who died and made you the leader of this operation?!" I was so mad I was shaking and I could feel the burn in my eyes.

In an instant Jeremy was across the room holding me by the shoulders, then Dayvan was just there somehow. I could hear a low growl, and I could feel that warmth again rippling over my body. A low pain started through my body.

"Let go of her right now Jeremy! You have no right to put your hands on her. I will not allow you to harm her as long as I live!" Dayvan was very mad, I could sense it. It was like electricity all through the air.

"You have NO right to tell me what I can and cannot do to my woman! Back off Dayvan!" Jeremy said this between clenched teeth and with a deep growl at the end.

I felt the warmth spread through me at the sound of the growl. It sounded like a big animal, but it was Jeremy. What the hell is going on? Am I hearing things?

"Listen guys, let's all just calm down, ok? I mean we are not going to win any battle if we keep fighting amongst ourselves. We are letting him win if we tear ourselves apart from the inside." I was hoping they would listen to me, because I really did not want this to turn into a fist fight. I am not sure who would win and I did not want to find out.

"He will not hurt you; I will not allow it. Jeremy, let go of her right now! I will not tell you again!"

A smirk crossed Jeremy's face, and I was afraid of the words that were about to come out of his mouth. I tried to think of how I could stop him from saying something that would break this out into a full-blown fight. I did the only thing that I could think of doing. I leaned forward and kissed Jeremy. I kissed him thoroughly and deeply; I tried kissing him enough to make him forget what he was about to say. Dayvan growled and grabbed me away from Jeremy. I looked at him, and I could see it in his eyes. He was not going to forgive that one so easily. I did the next thing that came to mind. I raised my face up and I kissed him, hard and fast.

I heard more than felt Jeremy's argument of this. Next thing I knew we were all on the floor. I was stuck in the middle of Jeremy and Dayvan and they were trying to fight, but I was keeping myself in between them to keep them from making contact.

"Sarah! Help me!" I yelled, hoping that she would hurry before the situation got out of control entirely.

"STOP! RIGHT NOW!" Sarah shouted and then blew a loud horn! We all held our ears; man, it felt like someone shot me through the head. It must have felt that way to the guys too because they were holding their heads and wincing with the pain.

"Now, if you all are quite finished, maybe, just maybe we can all sit like adults and talk this through." Sarah said like a good nanny. She seemed to be aged 10 years right then.

We all looked at each other and started laughing so hard that we were crying. Sarah looked at us all with a bewildered look. "What? What the hell is so damned funny?"

"We are usually the mature ones and now we are acting childish, and you are playing the adult." Jeremy said as he was laughing.

A snow globe flew over his head and crashed into the wall behind him. "Are you calling me a child? I could rip your throat out for that!" Sarah said with anger that I had not known existed within her.

"Calm down Sarah, I did not mean anything bad or insulting about it. I was just stating a fact." Jeremy said, his laughter fading as he realized that she was not finding this funny.

We got ourselves under control, made some lunch and sat down at the table to eat. I ate three sandwiches and ice cream, and cookies and I still felt starved. Why was I so hungry? Did it have something to do with my fast healing? I pondered all this secretly.

"Ok, so we need to decide which one of us girls go with which one of you guys. I say we draw straws to decide, that way we can all have an equal chance here." I spoke low toned so not to make the guys go into "macho" mode again.

Jeremy looked at me with anger in his eyes and said, "We do not want you girls there with us. We are going to do this ourselves. We do not want you girls that close to the place, because if something happens to one of you, we are not going to forgive ourselves."

I was instantly hot! Anger crept over my whole body. Sarah noticed it and placed her hand on mine. "Guys you know we are not going to agree with that. We will be with you, or we will take our own shift. But we will not stay out of it." Sarah said with anger creeping into her voice, making it tremble.

"You girls just do not understand, do you? Or maybe it is that you do not want to understand." Jeremy was beginning to get angry. "We cannot protect you and watch everything at the same time. For the love of God, can't you just quit playing tough for a fucking minute and let us be the men?!"

I did not even have time to think; I had grabbed Jeremy and had shoved him into the wall. I could feel the anger getting the best of me. "We are letting you be men! But you do NOT have to protect us! WE can handle ourselves! So shut the fuck up and just do what we say! He has hurt both me and Sarah, and you need to quit being a misogynist and let us help you!"

The pain began to set in me again. I knew I was probably hurting things that were still healing, like say, my ribs. But I just did not care at that moment. I wanted something, I felt like I was starving again, but I could not be. I have just eaten. I bent forward and smelled Jeremy; He smelled so good. He smelled like, like fear and, and food? What? With that thought I let go of him and I took a couple of steps back. I felt the pain rip through my spine! I dropped to my knees and screamed with the pain that was overtaking my body.

"Serraid, listen to me, please. You must calm down, right now! Please remember that time we were on the beach, and we were walking and we seen that crab trying to crawl over that twig and we laughed because it seemed so much smaller than the twig on the ground, remember? You told me that you loved the way the sun hit my face when I laughed and the way it made my eyes sparkle." Dayvan was coaxing me. He was trying to calm me down and it was working.

I could feel my anger seeping away, as the memory of that day came flooding back. I was so happy then. We had just made love, and we had decided to go for a walk on the beach and watch the sun set. I remember seeing the light on His face and thinking to myself how perfect he looked in the orangish purple haze of the sun's setting. My anger was gone and all that was left was a feeling of contentment.

I looked up at Dayvan and began to cry. He wrapped his arms around me and held me while I cried. I knew he loved me, and I loved him, but I also loved Jeremy and that is where it got complicated. Jeremy! I remembered slamming him against the wall. I turned to see him standing there, looking lost and hurt with a hint of confusion.

I walked over to him. I placed my hands on each side of his face and looked into his eyes. "I love you, Jeremy." I said, and I meant it. "I am sorry, I did not mean to get that mad. I am not sure what the hell is wrong with me.

And when I get mad, I am seeing things." I began to cry again, Jeremy wrapped his arms around me, and I let him partly because I wanted him to and partly because I needed him to. I needed to feel the warmth and the security that his embrace would give to me.

I felt someone come up from behind me and hug the back side of me. I felt Jeremy go completely still. I knew it was Dayvan without even looking. I could feel his energy wrapping around me as well. Between the two of them I felt completely safe. Then I felt Sarah come up and hug us from the side. Yes, we were a family and together, nothing would harm us again.

After I had calmed down, I decided to allow the men to do the surveying. I figured that they were right, and they could not do two things at the same time. So, Sarah and I would go through all the notes and organize them as the guys gave them to us. We would be the ones who decided when and where to catch this piece of shit. I could settle for that.

"We need to make a safe word so that we all know we are who we are." That sounded so stupid when it was said that way. But it was the truth. I did not want this guy to portray any of us again. "We will write the word we want to use down and not say it out loud, that way if we are being listened to, then no one will know but us."

I gave all of them a piece of paper, and we wrote our words down. We showed each other and we remembered them. Then I took the pieces of paper and burnt them in the kitchen sink. I made sure that they burned completely and then I washed them down the drain.

Jeremy and Dayvan left to start setting up surveillance and to pick a place where they could stay for 12 hours at a time no matter if it were sunny or rainy. Sarah and I went to the department store and purchased a chalkboard. We would organize everything on it and then write it in a notebook. We bought all the supplies that us girls were going to need, and we picked up a couple of thermoses for the guys and a couple of lunch boxes. We made sure to get some freeze packs, I mean after all, we did not want the men to get sick from poorly stored food. We had purchased everything that we needed. We left the store and headed home.

We were sitting at a red light, and Sarah was looking out her window. "You are being awfully quiet, Sarah. Is everything all right with you?"

"I was just thinking about this jackass and what ARE we going to do with him when we do get him. I mean are we really going to kill him?" She looked at me and her eyes said that she certainly needed answers.

"Yes, Sarah, we are going to kill him. He is going to pay for everything that he has done to all of us. Because he has hurt us all. He raped and beat me and you, and he stole me from Dayvan and now he has come between me and Jeremy. I think that death is the least that we should do to him." My voice was cold as ice when I said it, and I knew it was, but I meant every word that I said to her. I was going to see him dead.

"It is just that what happens if one of us die? What happens if he catches onto us and he gets us before we get him?" Tears were starting to form in her eyes. He would pay for that too, I thought to myself.

"Sarah, do not waste another tear on his ass. We are going to kill him and none of us are going to die doing it. I promise." I reached over and wiped the tear from her cheek. I smiled a real smile because I smiled at the thought of him dying slowly. I could not help it, but he had hurt the people that I love, and he would pay for each and every thing that he did to us.

A horn honked behind me. I looked in my rearview mirror and saw some guy waving his hands impatiently at me, while honking his horn. The light had turned green, and He wanted me to move my damn car, I read his lips as he yelled at me. My rage was instant! I could feel the pain rip through me, and I opened my car door.

"What are you doing Serraid?! Get back here! You are going to get hit by a car!" I turned back and growled at her for her to let me go. At the sound that came from my voice, I jumped. What the hell was that?! I sank back into the car and sped off running the yellow light. I wanted to get home. I had a pounding headache, and I was starting to ache all over. Maybe I was coming down with the flu.

Sarah looked at me when we pulled up to the house, "Are you alright Serraid?" The concern in her voice let me know just how much I had scared her at the stop light.

I frowned at the thought that I had scared her. I looked at her and reached over and hugged her. "I am all right. I just feel so crazy. I think that I am beginning to have a breakdown or something. I am seeing and hearing things that cannot possibly be there. I think that I really need to talk to someone. I never thought I would hear myself say that, but I have never seen things like this before, and I am afraid that I am schizophrenic."

Sarah tightened her grip on me and with a soft sad voice she said, "You are not schizophrenic Serraid. I promise. Maybe it is just from all the trauma that you have been through lately." She smiled a smile that warmed my heart. I knew that she was trying to make me feel better. I gently grabbed her face on both sides and slowly kissed her. Her soft lips tasted like strawberries. Her body relaxed into the kiss. She reached over and grabbed my waist. Desire took me right there, before I knew it, we had gone inside of the house. I had laid Sarah on the stairs and pulled her panties off. I raised her skirt and kissed her thighs. She let out a low moan, and raised her hips, asking me to touch more. I lightly brushed over her and kissed the other thigh. I squeezed her ass as I kissed her. Then I found her with my tongue, she moaned from the touch of my mouth. I felt a shiver go through her whole body. I touched her with my fingers as I explored the outside with my tongue.

"Please, Serraid, I want you inside." I could hear the heaviness of the desire in her voice. I teased her a little more and right when she was about to ask again, I shoved my fingers inside her. They glided along her smooth, moistened trail. I reached the end of her and found her spot. I played on that spot with my fingers as I licked her clit. She gasped and moaned. Her hands found the handrail of the stairs. She pulled at it out of need for something to take her desire out on. Her hips bucked under my mouth. Suddenly she sat up, I looked at her with a puzzling look.

Sarah unbuttoned my pants and slid her hand inside. "MMMMmm, you are so wet" She pulled her hand out and tasted me on her fingers. I want to taste you. I traded her spots. I felt her breath on thighs as she breathed across it. It sent a wave of chills through my spine. I felt the heat building between my legs and my stomach tight from desire. I wanted to feel her mouth upon me and her fingers inside. I wanted to kiss her lips too though. She placed her lips upon my clit and shoved her fingers inside all at the same time. I felt the desire build instantly. I almost went right then. "Not yet" she said. I held it back. She found a rhythm. I could feel her reaching for that sweet smooth spot inside. She found it and flicked it gently a couple of times I felt the orgasm grip me I was so close.

As if she knew, she came up and kissed me. She placed herself on me and started moving as if she were a man. The feel of her rubbing against me sent hot desire and need all through me. "You're going to make me cum." I said in a shaky voice. Then just a quickly as I said that an orgasm took both of us. We rode the wave together on the same boat, we rode it until it subsided. The orgasm left me feeling calmer, and the flu feeling had dissipated, I felt spent as well. We laid there trying to learn how to breathe again.

"I love you Serraid, I really do."

I smiled down at her and simply said, "I love you to Sarah."

After a few minutes we got up and decided to carry all the supplies in from the car. My legs still felt a little wobbly. I giggled and told Sarah she had pleased me better than I had been in a while. There was just something about a woman making you feel that desire met. She looked at me and smiled. She was content too.

We opened the front door to get the stuff out of the car. We stopped dead in our tracks. The guys were sitting on the front porch. They both looked up as we opened the door, and they both had a shit eating grin on their faces.

"How long have you guys been here? And what are you doing back so soon?" I asked demandingly.

"Well, we needed a few things that we forgot in the box in the kitchen. But when we got here and saw you two through the open door, we decided to close the house and stand guard. You girls really need to be more careful. What if it would not have been us that came up today?"

He had a point. What if it had been the ass hole that we were trying to catch. And if he really was the man that I had lived with after Dayvan went to that meeting, then he would have enjoyed the show. These men however looked as if they had interrupted something.

"Well, us girls are going to get all the stuff out of the car. Feel free to help or you can get what you need and get back to what you were doing." I said with a giggle, thinking how they looked like a kid with his hand caught in the cookie jar.

"Jeremy why don't you and Sarah get what we need out of the box, and I will help Serraid get the rest of the stuff from the car. I need to talk with her for a minute if you do not mind" Dayvan asked politely.

"Yeah, come on Jeremy, I would rather deal with the technical stuff than the stuff in the car. Besides, I like your company better." Sarah said with a hint of sarcasm. I could see something in her eyes, but I could not quite place it.

I turned toward the car when Dayvan grabbed my hand and held it. I let him know what he was thinking.

"You seem to have relied on some of the old ways to deal with things. Are you doing it all again? And do not act like you do not know what I mean, because I do remember everything that you have ever told me." He said, looking deep within me. It was like he was going to spot the lie if I told it.

"Yes, I have. I don't do everything all the time, but I do still rely on the pain of things to get over the emotional things that happen. I am sorry that you guys walked up on me and Sarah. I like her a lot and she makes me feel good."

"I am not mad. It was…. interesting to see you so loose with yourself. It has been a long time since I have seen you that comfortable. I liked seeing you that way. And you know (he grabbed me around the waist and turned me to him) that if you need to talk and you need help dealing with something, that I am here for you. You can talk to me about anything. You know this." he lightly kissed my forehead.

"I know I can talk to you about anything, and I know you are here for me. I am sorry, it is still all so weird. I hated who I thought was you for a very long time. It is kind of creepy seeing you and trying to not want to kill you." I sighed at how that sounded. "What I mean is, it's going to take me some time to deal with all of this and to learn how to handle this."

Dayvan looked at me with a knowing in his eyes. I could tell what I had said hurt, yet he understood. He was a patient man. I just hoped that after all this time, oh hell I do not know what I hoped.

"Serraid, will you sleep with me tonight when before I go to my shift?" He put his fingers across my lips, knowing I was about to say something. "What I mean is, sleep, not sex, unless you want to, but sleep. I want to hold you and feel you near."

"Why does Jeremy have the first shift?" I wondered if he had volunteered for that to play macho.

"We drew straws for it. He drew first shift and believe me He was not happy about it." he said with a silly grin. He leaned down and began to kiss me. I felt my lips touching his right before I heard Sarah's voice.

"Hey you guys! Are you bringing stuff in or making out on the car?!" She giggled when she said it.

"I bet he had her do that! He is beginning to piss me off. And I feel outnumbered. Two to one. Him and her are a team you know?" He said with a smile. I knew he was trying to make light of it, but I knew this was all taking its toll on his patience.

"Yes, I will sleep with you tonight. I love feeling your arms around me. But know that if Jeremy asks me tomorrow to lay with him, I will do it. I will not give either one of you an advantage over the other one right now. I am not sure what all of this is, but I know I love all three of you."

"All three of us? You have another man on the side?"

"I mean Sarah too. I love her too, not like I love you and Jeremy but something to that affect. I just wanted to be honest with you. I want you to know what you are facing here. It is not a contest; I am not a prize. It took me a long time to love anyone after you, and now that I finally have, here you are again but you are not the you I ran from. It is all so damn confusing." I felt the tears starting to form in my eyes. I would not cry right now.

I grabbed some bags out of the car. I told Dayvan to get the board out and the rest of the bags. I quickly went into the house. As soon as I set the bags down Jeremy was there. He grabbed me and spun me into him and kissed me.

"Jeremy! What are you doing?"

"I wanted to get a kiss too! If he gets to kiss you so, can I! I am not letting you go without a fight; Serraid I love you! Can't you see that? This is tearing me apart seeing another man touch you!

"Jeremy, I know you are hurting right now. I am hurting too. I have a big decision to make and believe me," I touched his face with my hands. "I am not going to make this decision lightly. I promise you this, I will not choose either one of you until I am sure which one I need. To find that out I have to spend time with both of you. I am going to sleep in the same bed as Dayvan tonight. And tomorrow if you want me to, I will sleep with you in your bed. Just as I told him, I am not giving either one of you an advantage over the other one right now." I saw the red go to his forehead, and I knew that he was mad. I could feel his anger streaming from him.

"So, you want to have your cake and eat it too?!! I cannot believe that you would want to put us both through all of this! You are being selfish Serraid, and you damn well know it! I do not want to share you with another man, and I certainly do not want another man's hands on you! You do not know how long I have waited for you to love me! Damn it woman! Are you out to rip both of our hearts out at the same time or is it that you wish to see us fight to the death?!

I gasped at the thought of them killing each other. I pulled away from Jeremy.

"I cannot believe you would say that, you selfish, childish little pompous asshole! How dare you say that to me! After everything that I have been through here lately and you are going to stand there and tell me this now?! Here is a newsflash for you Jeremy! It is hard for all of us! I do not want to hurt either one of you, but I love both of you and do not want to lose either one of you either! I must make this choice and in order to do that I have to know which one I need, so I will do it my way! If you cannot handle that then tell me right now and I will make sure you will not share me with anyone because you will not have me at all! So, what do you want? What are you going to do?" I was so mad I was shaking all over! My hands hurt so bad, I went to look down, and Jeremy tilted my face up to his.

"I love you Serraid, I know this is hard for you. I am sorry, I was not thinking of anyone but myself. I did not realize how hard this must be for you." he kissed my lips softly and I kissed him back. "Please forgive me, my lady. I am truly sorry."

I sighed and relaxed against him. The pain was gone. I looked at my hands, and they were red. I was glad this argument was over. I did not want to fight anymore tonight.

It would be so much easier if these men would play together and share well. I laughed at the thought because I knew it would never ever happen.

"What is so funny?" Jeremy asked me.

"I was just thinking how much easier it would be if I could get you and him to share nicely. We could puppy pile in the bed." I felt his body go still. He felt like he had quit breathing. "Don't worry, silly, I'm not asking you to do that." I looked up and smiled at him. "But you have to admit, it would make it easier."

With that, I turned and to my surprise, Sarah and Dayvan were standing there with their mouths open. "Hey!" I snapped my fingers loudly. They looked at me as if they had been in a trance.

"I can't believe you two just argued like that and made up that easy." Sarah said, "You are going to so have to teach me that trick." She giggled. Then she went quiet, afraid that she would start another argument.

"Well let's get this finished so that we can eat dinner before our first shift." Jeremy said, handing Dayvan the wires and what looked like a little black box. Dayvan and Jeremy left me and Sarah to set up our things for our part of the project. We decided to set up our operations in the Fourier that way it was not visible from any outside source. We put up the chalk board on the wall. We decided to cut it into four distinct parts. One for times, two for people, three for places, four for anything else… We had never done anything like this, so it was a learning experience. I mean what do you put for this kind of shit anyways.

After we got everything set up, we decided to cook dinner. We made Spaghetti and meatballs some asparagus and garlic bread. We had just set the dinner on the table when the guys walked through the door. Something about the way they looked, we decided to test the safe words. When they had both given us their words, we gave them ours. When all was satisfied, we told them that we had cooked dinner, and we were ready to eat.

"We got everything set up and we found a vacant apartment right by his. We rented it to make it the base of our operations. We have full access to the building so we can see him no matter what level of the house he is on. We also met some of our neighbors today and made friends with them. That way if we need to, we can use their apartments." Dayvan stated all of this with a crooked smile on his face.

"That is good. The sooner we get something on this guy the better. We only have till the end of this week before his deadline and let's face it. I don't want to be at the receiving end of his wrath. I really think he meant what he said about he would make me pay."

Both Jeremy and Dayvan went completely still when I said this. "The time has passed by so quickly. We will make sure that if we must go past his deadline there is no one left alone."

Even as he said it, I knew the four of us would be safe, but what about everyone else I cared about. Friends and clients at the Center, friends at the Cat house. We could not protect all of them at the same time. I knew that but I just had to trust the guys and believe we would have this man caught and killed before I could find out what he had in mind next.

CHAPTER 10

After getting everything set up Jeremy took the first shift. He left to go to the apartment that he and Dayvan had found. He wore a disguise that fooled even me when I looked at him. It was made of a grey wig, a sticky kind of skin that looked wrinkled and he had fake skin to slide on his hands as well. He looked like he was in his sixties. I would not have known it was him if I had not watched him put it all on. Dayvan and Jeremy had decided to go in disguise to the apartment. That way the bad man wouldn't recognize any of us. Because if he did, then the whole operation would be washed out.

When Jeremy arrived at the apartment, he was supposed to call us and let us know that he had made it. We had all our parts rehearsed. Now it was just a matter of waiting for this guy to make a mistake. He would, and when he did, we would be there to take his life from him. About thirty minutes after Jeremy left the phone rang, I picked it up and Jeremy said he had made it to the club, and he met a woman and not to wait up. Without answering, I hung up. This way if anyone was listening, it sounded like me and Jeremy were fighting and that possibly were splitting up.

Sarah and Dayvan were watching a movie, but I could not sit still. I had to do something. I decided to go to my room and clean a bit and take some much-needed alone time. I wanted to just get all this over so I could move forward, whatever that meant. Dread began to set in, because the sooner this was over, the sooner I had to decide on what to do about the men. I went upstairs and walked to my bedroom door. I looked in and man it was messier than I had originally thought. We had all gone through my clothes looking for items for different costumes. I had told them I would clean it all up myself. They had taken me at my word and here I was. I can't blame them, looking at this mess, I didn't want to clean it either. I giggled at my lack of enthusiasm and began cleaning.

I picked up all my clothes off the floor and laid them on the bed. I decided I would start there; I had to fold every piece of clothing and either hang them up or put them in a drawer. I spotted something in the corner that looked out of place. I walked over to pick it up and my heart jumped into my throat when I saw a ripped pair of my panties. The sight of the torn panties thew me into a flashback of the cabin and the man who wasn't David. My head felt like it was trying to explode, like something was pressing inward. This is the exact pair that this motherfucker had ripped off me the day at the cabin! I quickly looked around and checked the window; it was locked and there was no one in the house. I know these were not there earlier, I closed my eyes and tried thinking back to earlier when we were all in here trying on clothes. Shit! I said to myself because I couldn't remember them being there. If he had been in the house, then he knew that something wasn't right. Could he have been on to our little plan all along? I thought about it and there was no way because there was no evidence of what we were doing here except for the chalk board on the wall. There was nothing written on it however so I doubted he could have known.

I ran down the stairs and at the sound of me running Dayvan and Sarah jumped up and turned.

"Tell me your safe words right now!" My voice squealed as I demanded this.

"Serraid, what is going on? Are you alright?" Sarah looked concerned.

"Please, don't ask questions, just tell me your damned safe words, both of you right now!" I was trying to be patient, but we had all made this deal, that if anyone asked, we would give them our safe words.

"Teether," Sarah said.

"Pancake" Dayvan said.

I let out a breath I hadn't realized I was holding. It was them; it was really them. "Sherlock" I said.

"You want to tell us what this is about, Serraid?" Dayvan asked.

"Well, I went up to my room to clean, and I saw these in the corner on the floor. These are the panties that psycho ripped off me the day he…. the day I went to the cabin." I could feel the tears well up in my eyes and the shaking at the memory of that day and the adrenaline wearing off from finding these. "I had a flashback of the man who wasn't David or I mean Dayvan, and him tearing these off me." I held the ripped panties up for them to see.

Dayvan and Sarah came over to me and hugged me. "We will search every room of the house and check every window and make sure they are all locked." Sarah said to me. I could hear the fear in her voice as well. I knew he had hurt her too, the night he came in here and raped her. I wanted him dead for all the things he had done. I wrapped my arms around Sarah and hugged her tight. I wanted her to feel safe, but how could she when he had gotten into our house without us knowing he had.

"I'm going to call Jeremy and let him know what has happened. I think he should be on higher alert there by himself. I have a sick feeling about this guy; he is more cunning than we originally planned him to be." With that Dayvan turned and went into the kitchen.

Sarah and I walked through the house and checked all the windows. The one in the downstairs bathroom was unlocked and had been recently opened. We could tell because the shells that I had on the ledge had been moved. We locked it and finished checking all the windows, they were all locked. We went into the kitchen and Dayvan was not there. Where had he gone?

"Dayvan, where are you?!" Sarah and I hollered at the same time. I felt my heart start to speed up. I had to stay calm. We heard nothing in return. We began looking through the house even though we had been all through the house already. We got to the back door and Dayvan was standing there still on the phone. He did not seem to notice us.

"I haven't felt anyone in the house, and I did not sense or smell anyone in here since you have been gone. Yes, it is weird, I agree. Ok, be careful. See you when I get there. If you have any problems, call me, I will come right there. Ok, bye."

He turned and I could see the worry lines around his eyes. "Is he ok? What did he say about this? Sarah and I found the bathroom window unlocked and someone had used the window today." I said.

"Jeremy said there has not been too much activity there, he also said that he is going to get a security system put into this house. He does not want anyone unprotected right now. He called a friend of his and they will be out here tomorrow to install the system."

"That is too expensive, I cannot allow him to do this. I just can't." My pride was welling up in me. I did not want anyone to spend that much money on me. I did not feel it was worth the effort, the money. And I hated it when someone spent money on me because they usually always threw it in my face, what they had done.

"Yes, you can and yes you will. You must be safe Serraid. If not for yourself, think of Sarah, she needs to be safe too." He said with an embarrassed look on his face. I could tell by the look he had not wanted to go that low, but sometimes you must throw low shots to get through my pride.

"I cannot believe you just said that! But you are right. I want Sarah to be safe. I want all of us safe, and I want this son of a bitch dead!" I yelled out my anger, and I meant every word of what I had said. The thought of everything made a hunger well up in me that I didn't know I could have, yet there it was, the need to protect what was mine.

Then I thought about the conversation he was having on the phone. "Oh, what did you mean by you didn't feel, sense or smell anyone here?"

Dayvan looked shocked at my words. He stuttered a little, and said, "I just meant that, uh that I couldn't smell any cologne or anything. You know how you can walk into a room right after someone and you can still feel them there a little?"

I nodded yes because I seem to do that a lot too.

"Well, that's what I meant. I just didn't feel anyone had been here. I guess I had convinced myself that since we had locked the doors and stuff that we were safe here." He finished with a shy smile.

I didn't really believe him fully, but what was I going to do? I had no other choice but to drop it because I just didn't have the energy to argue or debate anything tonight.

"I'm going to go back upstairs and finish cleaning my room, I'm tired and I really need some sleep." I turned and headed upstairs. I knew I had sounded rude I was just too tired to care.

Once in my room, I felt as if my space had been invaded. I was wishing I had not told Dayvan he could sleep with me tonight. I just wanted to be alone and soak in a hot tub of water and scrub this nasty film off me which was starting to slide over my skin. I could feel its cold fingers sliding smoothly over the well-worn path of my skin in which it had taken so many times throughout my life. I closed my eyes and tried pushing it away, I didn't like this feeling, I wanted all of this to go away. It kept creeping over my skin. It settled there like it belonged, and maybe it did. It had been familiar with me since I was little. Sometimes the feeling of this cold made me feel better, it let me know that I was still alive. Then the tears started.

I walked to my bed and threw myself face down on top of my comforter, I cried silently onto my pillow. I didn't want anyone to hear me, now that the film had settled, I just wanted to drown in this disgusting feeling I was having. I wanted to bathe in it until it left me. I knew this would work because I had done it before. I rolled my head over to get some clean air; my hair fell off my face and that's when I saw the knife on the side table. I kept it there so I would feel safer. I knew it was stupid, but it helped sometimes.

I grabbed the blade and felt the soothing cold steel of its point. It felt so good against the hot film on my skin, my legs ached so badly, I could almost feel the blade cutting my skin. It would feel so good, I thought to myself. I didn't want to do this. I started crying because my body wanted something my mind did not want. It was this way all the time! My body craving things that my mind detested! Would it ever end? Would it stop when I died?

Before I realized it, the legs of my shorts had been raised and the blade of the knife was pressed against it. As the cold blade set into the skin, I could feel the warm rush of energy, the soothing fingers of the pain start to settle over me, scraping the thick nasty film away. 'Deeper' I thought. Then, I pressed harder, feeling my blood trickle down in a slow slick line. I raised the blade and watched the blood run down over it and drop off the tip of it. Inside I felt the warm resolve that always came with doing this. I replaced the blade against my leg and pulled it down again, feeling the sweet song, it sang to my skin, the warm inviting pain that held me like a parent welcoming a child home. I felt the warm rush of blood over my hand, suddenly I came to and realized I had cut too deep. Panic washed over me, I grabbed the shirt that was lying next to me and pressed it against my leg. "Dayvan! Sarah! Please help me!" I yelled weakly, part of me hoping they would hear me and part of me hoping they wouldn't. Did I really want to be saved? I was not sure right now, the peace of death sounded so inviting.

"Oh my God! Dayvan come quickly! Hurry, she is bleeding badly!" Sarah yelled as she grabbed another shirt off the bed and tied it around my thigh. "What have you done babe? Oh God, what have you done to yourself? Please, please be ok!"

"What hap…" Dayvan was talking but everything went black, and I didn't hear anything else. I heard the ocean, but that was impossible because I wasn't near the ocean. I must be dreaming but the peace was so outstanding. No worries, no pains, could this be my death? Could this be what it is like when you die? My thoughts trailed off to nothing……

I woke up with the sun shining upon my face. I tried rolling over to cover my eyes so I could sleep a little longer, I was exceptionally tired but for the life of me couldn't remember why. I tried moving but nothing would move. Was I paralyzed? No, I shouldn't be. I tried moving again and the pain in my leg was horrible.

It all came flooding back to me, I remember sitting there and cutting my thigh. I hadn't meant to cut that deep, it had been an accident. I was afraid no one would believe that story, but it was the only one I had. I opened my eyes, looked around, and tried to speak but my mouth was so dry, and nothing came out. I looked around and I could feel the panic starting to set in. Why couldn't I move my body and why was nothing working for me? Was I dead and this was my punishment for taking my own life? Oh god please let someone be here. I don't want to be alone.

Jeremy set up and smiled at me for a split second and then he looked angry. "What the hell were you trying to do, Serraid?!"

I tried to answer him, but nothing would come out, my mouth was just too dry. Jeremy must have realized it because he handed me a cup of water, but I couldn't get my hand to work. I could feel it, but it wouldn't move.

"Oh, for the love of God! Here," he held my head up and gave me a drink. The water was so cold, and wet. My throat absorbed the water as soon as it touched it. The water tasted so good. It was like running an ice cube over your skin in the summer, the cool refreshing, reviving of it. He kept letting me drink until I spit it out.

"Fuck! You almost drowned me you asshole!" I was mad and wet. "Why won't my body move for me? What's wrong with me?"

"You are worried about me trying to drown you! When just last night you tried to kill yourself by cutting the artery in your leg? And you are worried about drowning?! I can't believe this, Serraid. What were you thinking?! Huh? Tell me what!?"

"I didn't mean to cut that deeply. I was just cutting and somehow it happened. I swear I didn't mean to cut that deep. Please, please believe me!" I should have been crying but my eyes wouldn't make tears. I could feel the sensation of crying without tears. What the hell was wrong with me? "What is wrong with me?" I asked hoping he had an answer.

"We had to restrain you last night after Sarah and Dayvan came up." He lowered his face, clearly ashamed of what news he had to share with me. "You put up a fight when they tried to save you. You threatened to kill Dayvan, and you cut Sarah."

"OH MY GOD is she alright? Did I hurt her? Please take me to see her. I didn't mean, I don't know what…shit I don't remember anything after Dayvan walked into the room."

"Sarah is fine. A little shaken up, but alright. She is going to be ok. You, on the other hand, almost weren't. You almost succeeded in taking your own life and we have decided to restrain you until we know for certain that you are alright."

"You can't keep me tied up like an animal! You can't do this to me! Please let me up, please I have to get out of here!" I began to feel that film sliding into place over my skin. I could feel the bile rushing up to my throat. Jeremy must have noticed it because he brought me a bucket.

"Here throw up in this, I will get you a cold washcloth. You will be ok Serraid, you won't be harmed here. I'm not going to hurt you, and neither is anyone else." He walked into my bathroom, and I heard the water running.

I looked around my bedroom and tried to see what the hell was holding me down. I could see the chains wrapped in cotton around the headboard and foot of the bed. I wiggled my wrists and sure enough the chains moved. That's when I saw my legs and my waist. There were cuts everywhere. But, how? I had only made two cuts before I passed out.

"Jeremy, I only made two cuts, how did I get all these cuts?" My voice trembled. I wondered, had I made more cuts and lost track of reality while doing so?

"You did that to yourself. Even though for some reason you are healing faster than usual, you still have a lot to heal. You should have seen your injuries when I first arrived home." He said, while he gently placed the cold rag on my head.

I threw up everything I didn't have, dry heaving sucks! When I was done, I asked Jeremy for another drink of water, I needed to wash this taste out of my mouth.

He gave me a drink, and I rinsed my mouth out and spit it in the bucket. "Can you bring me some mouthwash please? And how do I use the bathroom?" I asked.

"Here is your mouthwash. And about the bathroom, when you need to go Either I or Dayvan will escort you there and back. Now we are having to pull double duty. Why won't you tell me why you did this?" He looked at me pleading for honesty, which he believed I was depriving him of.

"I swear, Jeremy, I didn't do this. I had two cuts on me when I passed out. I really didn't mean to cut that deep. I swear it! Please believe me!" I could see the disbelief in his eyes. I tried to turn away from him, but the restraints wouldn't let me. My heart began to beat faster. I could feel it; the panic was well on its way.

Jeremy rushed over to me and straddled me, and in a tone that clearly stated he was mad, hungry and full of desire and disgust all at the same time he said, "If this is how you want to do things, then so be it Serraid. I thought you had got past all this shit! But if my lady wants it, then she will get it the way that she wants." With that he pulled my panties down to my ankles and began to unbutton his shirt.

"Jeremy, what are you doing? No, I don't want this." but I could feel my body tightening up. I could feel the hunger to have him building.

He took the knife from the nightstand and held it to my throat. I could feel the coldness of the blade threatening to cut me. "I will do this, and you will like it. You have refused to listen to anything I have said, so now I will show you, maybe then you will understand." He began kissing my thigh just above where I had cut. He moved upward raising the shirt I had on up with his nose as his tongue licked a wet line up my stomach. I felt my stomach tighten and the warmth began to build between my legs. He made my body want him, but my mind was still in panic mode. He was going to hurt me and there was nothing I could do about it! Oh God help me, please!

He ripped off my shirt and grabbed me around the throat as he entered me. He started with a slow short movement to open me to him. He had to push his way in; he pushed harder and harder till my body gave way and he was all the way inside. I felt the familiar wave of heat cover my body. It closed my eyes from the safety it spread over me. He tightened his grip around my throat, and with his other hand he took a pillow and covered my face. Panic rushed over me, my heart was pounding in my ears, I tried to reach up to push the pillow off me, but the restraints had me held down. I tried to scream, but what sound did come out was drowned by the pillow, so no one could possibly hear me.

I began thrashing my body around and trying to buck him off me. I felt him release the pillow and my throat; I heard him groan. He grabbed me around the waist and pulled my ass off the bed. He tilted my hips just a little and he smacked my ass. A whimper escaped out of my mouth. It felt so good, I knew he could kill me, but the pain was so good. He was moving faster now; he had found his rhythm he tilted my hips just a little more and found my spot. He grunted with satisfaction and said, "You will like this, it will hurt at first then it will bring you so hard that you will scream your pleasure for me, and when you do, I will release mine with you. You are mine, and I am yours." He started slamming himself into me harder and harder, then I felt him slide a finger into my ass, he copied his rhythm between both holes. He drove fast and hard, and deeper still. The orgasm hit me like none other. It tightened everything at once. I could feel the spasms coming harder and I grabbed my chains to have something to hold on to because it felt like I was falling. I screamed when the waves peaked, it hurt so very good! I screamed and pulled at my restraints, I pulled and I felt them give. I grabbed his back and scratched my pleasure into it. I felt his blood run across my fingers. He shoved one last time and released himself, that brought me screaming again. I could fill him spill inside, the warm feeling spread through me. I could feel the inner hunger starting to dissipate.

We lay there spent, we were drenched in sweat, and ecstasy. I giggled at the thought that only he could make me feel this way. I felt sad at the same time because someone was going to lose. But how could I walk away from this? How could I walk away from someone who made me feel this way? I didn't think that I could. Jeremy got up from the bed, and I felt him re-secure my restraints. Then all was quiet. The pillow was left on my face. I tried to yell at him to at least remove the pillow but just like that, he was gone.

I felt a hand rub my thigh. I knew this touch, but this wasn't Jeremy. But who was it? I couldn't see because of the damned pillow! My heart started to speed up again. I wanted to know who this was. I felt a mouth go over my breast, flicking my nipple with just the tip of the tongue. It arched my back and made me moan. The pleasure of the last orgasm was too fresh, and everything was still so sensitive.

A finger ran down my stomach and played with the outside of me. It drew a moan from me. I raised my hips asking for more. I could feel the heat building again. It was different this time though. I could tell the difference. I could tell this was Dayvan. I didn't know how I knew this, but I did.

He grabbed my waist and slammed himself inside of me. The pleasure of feeling him hit my bottom threw my head back and drew a screaming orgasm from me. I wanted more, and he obliged. He grabbed my hips and began working at me. He pounded against me like waves when the tides came in. He found no rhythm, he was sporadic. He did whatever he felt like doing now. It was fast then hard and the slow and soft, in between. He let go of my hips and grabbed my nipples and pinched them. A moan escaped from between my lips. I could feel the orgasm building and threatening to overtake me. "Yes, right there. Please harder. Oh God." my voice sounded foggy with pleasure.

He started pounding me, he bit my chest as he slammed himself inside of me. I screamed my way down the wave of pleasure that was taking me down. Then it peaked again and again until finally he pushed one last time and held in one place as he spilled himself inside of me. I felt his body go completely loose.

He let all of his weight fall on me. I knew it would be a minute before he would move. I could smell him. He smelled like Cedar and olives. What a weird combination, I thought to myself. But he smelled so good all at the same time. My Dayvan and I loved him; I could not lose either one of them. How was I going to do this to them?

Then it hit me. What had they just done? Why had they done this and if they are both here, who is at the other place? Had they given up on watching him?

Dayvan got up and all was quiet for a few minutes. I was just about to doze off when I felt two hands, one on each leg. Then a mouth on my breast. I moaned from the warm feeling it sent deep inside of me. I didn't care who this was. They felt so good. Then I could feel something slide across me. I knew immediately that this was Sarah. She had straddled me and was scissored on top of me. I felt her heat wash over me. She moaned as she rode me. She was so wet, and she slid against me as if she were made for me. I felt so complete at that moment. I could feel hands everywhere, I knew they were all here.

I started thinking, how were they all here and why were they all here? I could smell Dayvan with cedar and olives, I could smell Sarah, she smelled like strawberries and Jeremy smelled like musk and honeysuckles. They all smelled so good. The pleasure of the orgasm hit me out of nowhere. I arched my back as much as I could and pressed my hips upward feeling all of her that I could. She grabbed my leg and scratched her pleasure into it as her orgasm took her over the edge and washed her away. I felt her body spasm, and she laid down on top of me. I felt so energized, and calm. That sweet calmness that washes over you when you are home. I felt better, somehow all of this has healed some part of me.

The pillow moved and Sarah kissed me, Then Jeremy and then Dayvan. They were all here.

"What is going on? Why."

Jeremy cut me off mid-sentence. "Don't worry Serraid all is well. And now you are better too. Look" he pointed to my thighs and stomach. To my astonishment it looked as if nothing had ever happened to me.

"What the hell is going on? How did that just happen? I was all cut up earlier before you…." My voice trailed off as tears rolled down my cheeks. I was crying now too.

They all looked at me with sympathy. Dayvan answered and said, "Serraid as soon as we can, we will tell you everything but right now please just enjoy us. None of us are going anywhere, so don't worry. We are here and we all love you. We will all help you through this in our way. Jeremy showed me that he knows how to reach you now as I did long ago. I still know how to reach you, but in a different way and so does Sarah."

He smiled as he said this. I wondered if they were all on some kind of drug or something.

"I don't know what to say. I want to know what is going on right now. And will you guys please let me out of these damned chains? I want up, I'm not going to kill myself, I didn't try last night. I really didn't mean to cut that deep and I don't remember doing all the other ones. I swear it."

They all looked at me and then at each other. They nodded together and they started undoing my restraints. I rubbed my wrists and ankles. It felt good to be free again. I couldn't explain it, but I knew they had the best of me in mind when they did it. I wanted answers right then and I was about to ask when something flew through the front room window. The glass shattered all over the floor. We all rushed downstairs. I grabbed the gun that I had purchased at the pawn shop a few weeks ago.

When we all got downstairs, I saw a brick with a note attached to it. I grabbed it, opened it, and read it.

For now, this is over until our master has recovered from the fight. Tell your lover he is dead for what he did to Jargoan. He will see to it that you all pay for this treachery. Remember that some things are never forgotten or forgiven. Until then, enjoy your lives because they have just been declared shortened.

My hands started shaking and my breath was coming in short gasps as I read what this said. I turned and looked at Jeremy and Dayvan for an answer.

"What is going on? What the hell did you do and who is Jargoan?"

Jeremy said, "Well Jargoan is the man who was impersonating Dayvan. He is the man that hurt you and Sarah. Dayvan and I found him by himself last night after you hurt yourself and we decided that it would be best if this was all over. So, we cornered him in an alley, we beat him almost to death. His servants apparently missed him because they came with guns and attacked us. We fought them because we had decided either, he die or we do. There were several of his men, but we killed a few of them, but when Dayvan turned to finish Jargoan, he was gone. Someone had pulled him right out from under us. I'm sorry Serraid, I know now we must look over our shoulders again and I'm so sorry. We tried and we failed you." He lowered his head and his voice. I could hear the defeat in his voice, and it broke my heart.

"You did not fail, none of us did. You got your hands on him, and you almost killed him. That means we can do it again. Not all is lost, and we will catch him again. I promise." I looked at them and tried to hide the doubts I had about what I had just said.

I walked over to them and hugged all of them in one big group. I didn't want them to blame themselves for this. "I was the one that cut myself up and if anyone is to blame for this, I am. I take my responsibility. I'm sorry that I messed things up. I know that if I wouldn't have done that to myself that you guys would have been more on your toes last night and maybe this man would be dead." I began crying at the thought that I could have lost one or both last night because I couldn't control an old demon that raised his head.

We all realized that we were still without clothes. We all blushed and headed upstairs. I called first dibs on the shower. But we all ended up in there together. I needed a bigger shower if we were going to make a habit of this. We finished our shower and got out, got clean clothes on, and headed downstairs for something to eat.

I knew that we all needed to feel safe. That the loss of this battle was taking its toll on all of us. We were all blaming ourselves on some level. And for what it was worth we were all right on some level. But I wasn't going to point that out to them. I knew that I could handle the truth, but could they? Yep, that's me, always brutally honest with myself. I must be though, or everything loses focus in my mind.

We were one happy family, and I knew that when we found Jargoan again, we would most certainly kill him, before he could kill us; This I knew as a fact. As I finished that thought, my stomach lurched and I ran to the toilet with no time to spare.

"I must be coming down with something. I keep throwing up, maybe it's exhaustion or something to do with last night. Sarah, do you have something for an upset stomach?"

"Sure, let me go get something." she walked into her room and a couple of minutes later she came in with some Pepto bismuth. That stuff is nasty, but it's better than throwing up. I was about to take a big drink, when Dayvan and Jeremy came over. Dayvan took the bottle and told me they had something better for it. They had strange looks on their faces, but if they said they had something better, then I would listen because I hated being sick. I drank the tea they had given me, and it worked, I was better.

We sat down at the table, and I was starving even after getting sick. I knew that I needed to eat. Sarah said she would make lunch for all of us. I sat there with the two guys. I watched Jeremy move his head as if he were listening to something. Then he leaned over and sniffed my neck. He moaned as he did. He leaned back into his seat. I asked Sarah if lunch was almost ready because I thought Jeremy was going to eat me if not. She laughed and said it was almost done.

When I looked back at the guys, I caught Jeremy looking at Dayvan as if something were terribly wrong.

"What is it? Why are looking as if someone just killed your favorite pet?" I asked looking at both of them.

I heard Sarah drop a fork on the floor. "Ok, what the hell is going on here guys? Seriously you are freaking me out. Would someone please tell me what is going on? Sarah? Do you know what it is?"

"Sorry, I just lost my grip. I'm not sure what has come over me. I think all of the stress is starting to finally catch up with me." Sarah answered nervously.

"Serraid, there are many things that you must know, just not right now. There are some things that you are safer NOT knowing. Please believe us when we say that we are doing this to protect you. We know that you don't understand things right now, but I promise we will tell you very soon. Please just be patient with us." Jeremy said with a smile that didn't reach his eyes.

"I want to know! You can't keep keeping secrets from me, treating me like a child! I can protect myself if I know what I'm protecting myself from!" I slammed my fists down on the table. I could feel my anger getting the best of me, but I didn't care anymore. They would tell me what the hell was going on or I would, oh hell I didn't know what I'd do, but I'd do something! "Tell me right now! No more secrets, no more lies and shy looks! I'm sick of this shit! You guys are supposed to love me!"

Jeremy cut me off mid-sentence.

"It's my job to protect you at all costs! Damn it Serraid, you never listen to anything! You only want what you want and when you want it! Well guess what darling, it's not going to happen this time! I won't let you get the handle and screw things up again! I won't!" He was screaming at me.

I felt the tears well up, what the hell? Why am I crying? I was pissed but not crying pissed. I felt the heat rush through me and the pain struck again only this time it began in my stomach and spread outward like fingers. I dropped to the floor and screamed from the pain that was plunging me into darkness. I couldn't pass out! I wouldn't look like I was weak and in need of protection! Damn it!

"Serraid! Oh, my hell! Please, please darling, calm down. You must calm down; you must for their protection. Please baby, calm down." Sarah was rocking me and soothing me. She was stroking my hair softly and rocking me. The feeling of her skin helped to calm me, and I could feel the pain begin to wash away.

"Sarah" I said, with a soft cracked voice. I knew I was going to pass out, and there was absolutely nothing I could do about it. I allowed myself to fall into the blackness that surrounded me. I embraced the bliss of the cold cloud descending over me because with it came, peace, quiet and no pain.

I was standing there on the concrete frame of the old bunk house. I knew this forest; there was a man standing in the moonlight. He was handsome and there was something about him that drew me to him. He was the magnet, and I was the metal, I had to touch him. I walked over to him and ran my hand down his arm. He grabbed my hand, and I could feel the connection between us. I knew this was right, but there was something at the very back of my mind that warned me to be careful and walk away. I looked up at his face and into his eyes. He was so damn sexy, and he smelled of a sweet, sweet fragrance. It was enchanting, and it held me as if I were a child and it the blanket. He bent and kissed me; his lips were soft and plump and gentle on my lips. He tasted of oak, and he felt like suede. I wanted him with every fiber of my being. He whispered into my ear and asked, "Are you sure you want this?" I quivered at the sound of his voice and shakily said yes. He then grabbed me and laid me on the concrete pad and started kissing me. I placed my hands behind his neck pulling him closer and kissed him back. I moaned. He took off my clothes and removed his. He turned me on my hands and knees, and slid in. I was surprised at how ready I was with so little foreplay. He slid as deep as he could and he stopped. He waited a second, I became impatient and I began to work myself against him, over him. I found my rhythm; he stayed very still. I began to move faster and faster; I felt him swell inside ready and ripe for the harvest. He stopped me and flipped me over; he put his hand above my head and rammed himself as far as he could go. We danced together with our naked bodies, joined deeply and kissing. The wave hit us both at the same time. We both howled our pleasure to the moon. There was no one around to hear, so we could let loose and be as loud as we felt.

After we were finished, he held me a little bit, I remember telling him that I needed to head back home. I knew my mother would be super pissed, especially after she had followed me out looking for me. I was hoping that she would be asleep when I got back home.

We arrived back at my house, and I was sneaking back inside when all a sudden the light flipped on and…. I woke up.

Sarah was sitting beside me on the bed. She smiled at me when she realized that I had woken up. "What happened?"

"You passed out, you will be fine, you just need a little more rest. You are still weak from losing so much blood last night." She said with a heart wrenching sadness in her eyes.

"What is it Sarah? Is there something seriously wrong with me? Please tell me if there is."

"There is nothing seriously wrong with you Serraid. You are just weakened, and you need your rest. You also need to eat. I have fixed you something to eat. Now that you are awake, I will get it for you. I want you to try and eat as much as you can, ok?" She looked so worried.

"Ok, I am starving. I want to come and help you though. You shouldn't have to do everything by yourself."

No, you are to stay in bed until you have regained your strength. Don't look at me like that bitch, you heard me. You will stay in bed. It won't take you long girl I promise." She smiled at me.

She was the only one that could call me a bitch and get away with it, it's because she said it with love. I smiled at her and agreed to stay in bed. I was super tired, maybe

I hadn't realized how much blood I had really lost last night.

Sarah headed downstairs to get my food. I laid there wondering what the hell that dream was about. I knew that place and I knew that man, I just couldn't place how I knew them.

CHAPTER 11

Three days later I had recovered enough to get myself out of my bed. Jeremy, Dayvan and Sarah all agreed that until I was at top notch health, they would not upset me in any way. I started to notice how they all seemed to walk on glass around me; it was really beginning to piss me off. I hate it when people look at me like I am going to crumble at the littlest thing, or like I am weak. I drew a deep breath and decided to go out for a walk by my lonesome. I waited until they were busy and I crept out of the house. I felt like a child sneaking out of the house to go to party and hoping my parents didn't catch me. I knew it wouldn't take them long to realize I was gone so I tried to make it as far as possible, hoping they couldn't spot me. I just wanted to be alone.

I made it about six blocks away from my house when I began to get a sick feeling in my stomach. I sat down on a set of concrete steps; they led up to a house which had been empty for what appeared twenty years or better. I began to feel dizzy, I started thinking maybe this was not such a good idea. Although, the air felt great, and the room to breathe was amazing. I was enjoying the sun beating upon my skin. It made me feel alive, yes, I needed this. Determined not to allow this to defeat me, I bent over and placed my head between my knees and counted my breathing. I regained control of my head. I felt the dizziness go away and the sick feeling subsided. I knew it would be a few weeks before my body recovered from the loss of blood. These were all normal symptoms of anemia.

I was sitting there enjoying the outdoors, alone with only the birds singing on the power lines. The song they sang was relaxing. I wondered why I had never really paid attention to the birds before. Maybe I needed to slow down and pay attention to my surroundings more often. I had been so hell-bent on burying all my baggage, that I had not been enjoying the little things of life.

I heard the car before I saw it. I let out a deep breath because I knew I was going to get a big lecture for leaving the house alone, but damn it, I am an adult! Dayvan was driving, and Sarah was in the passenger seat, Jeremy was not with them. I felt relief at that. I didn't want to see him right now. I was getting pretty tired of him treating me like his child or something. I felt as if I was becoming more of his job (whatever that meant) than his lover and I was hating it.

The car stopped in front of me. I spared a look just in time to see Dayvan smile at me. I couldn't see anything funny about being tracked down like an animal, but hey maybe they knew something I didn't. He got out of the car, and the wind caught his hair. It waved as the invisible fingers of the wind pushed through it. I felt so much love well up inside of me at that moment, I began to cry. Ugh! Why was I crying so easily? I didn't like it.

"Hey, can I sit here with you for a moment? Don't worry, I'm not here to jump your case or anything. I just want to make sure you are ok and then we will leave and let you stay here for a while if this is what you need." Dayvan looked at me, knowing I was not happy. He was trying to give me some space and to make things more right than wrong. The love for him grew and welled up in my heart.

"Thank you Dayvan, yes you may sit here with me for a moment. Where's Jeremy?"

As soon as I asked and saw the hardening on his face, I knew I shouldn't have asked and wished I could take it back.

He answered my question with an underlying anger creeping into his voice, "He didn't come. I told him I didn't think you would want to see him for a little while. I knew he had upset you and I know you when you are pissed at someone." He reached up and gently pushed the hair out of my face and said, "I know you Serraid, I know so many things about you that you don't tell people. You keep pushing me away, and I keep trying to push back in. Sometimes I feel as if we are at war with each other. Then, Jeremy makes you so mad you almost. Well, he made you really mad and here you are asking where he is, it makes me wonder if I am enough for you anymore."

I placed my fingers across his lips to stop him, "I wasn't asking where he was because I wanted to see him, I was asking out of sarcasm, because I didn't want to see him and I'm surprised that he didn't come here just to take the chance to jump my ass again. Dayvan, I know you feel you are not enough for me, and honestly, I can't answer that right now. But I do know I love you and I don't want to be without you either. I don't know what to say but that."

He looked at my face and then into my eyes, he smiled, then he pulled me in and hugged me. "Just to hear you tell me that you love me again is worth it all. I never imagined I would hear you say those words to me again in this life. Hearing them means the world to me, it makes my heartbeat with purpose once more. You have always been my love, Serraid." He kissed my forehead. I knew at that moment Dayvan loved me.

Dayvan stood, he held out his hand for me. "I just want to sit here alone for a bit if you don't mind. I just need some breathing room."

"I understand, there are a lot of things happening and some of them you don't understand. I promise I will tell you as you need to know them. I'm sorry I am having to keep secrets from you. I never meant to have anything hid from you." He smiled at me, bent down, and kissed the top of my head. I could feel the heat building behind my eyes. I didn't know what to say to that, so I said nothing.

Dayvan turned, walked to the car, and drove away. I watched him and Sarah until I couldn't see them anymore then I started to cry. I hated being torn apart this way. I just didn't know what to do anymore. I didn't know how I was ever going to decide between two men who I loved. Jeremy's actions lately were making it easier to lean to Dayvan. That scared me too, because I still wasn't sure about who Dayvan was… Tears ran down my face, I tried wiping them away, but they were coming so fast I couldn't keep up with them. I sat there and cried until my eyes dried out. I knew I needed a release of emotions. I waited a few more minutes after I was done and decided to head back home. No since hiding, if Jeremy wanted a fight, he'd get one because I was sick and tired of him right now.

I walked slowly, trying to avoid the inevitable argument with Jeremy, and the closer I got to the house the faster my heartbeat. I thought about several things I wanted to say to him, and yet when I arrived at the house and saw him standing there on the porch in his tight jeans and button up shirt that was left open showing off his perfect figure underneath my thoughts froze. He was perfect to look at; he made my eyes scan every last inch of him. The rock-hard abs defined with ridges, and his shoulders rounded and toned, his hardened chin, damn it made me want to run over and throw myself into his arms. I wanted to be mad right now, not lustful…I didn't know how he did this to me…But looking at him, I felt things low grow tight.

As if he felt the surge of hormones from the porch, he looked over and spotted me. He smiled a sleek smile as if he knew something I wasn't aware of. His nostrils flared and he stood up straight. At first, I thought he was going to walk over to me, but I realized I was two steps from him. I stopped, wondering how I had reached him that fast. I didn't realize I had walked over to him. Was I losing time? Had I zoned out and just not realized I had begun walking again? No, that wasn't it. I felt as if the world was shifting out of place. Jeremy stepped over to me and caressed my face with his thumb. Just the slightest touch he made shivers go through me. I didn't want to be this way. I wanted to be mad, I wanted to scream at him and tell him everything that he did, what pissed me off and I was going to put him in his place damn it! Then he bent and kissed me, and all thought ceased except for taking him inside of me.

My legs grew warm, and my body grew tight as he kissed me passionately. He grabbed my neck and played with my hairline as he kissed me deeply. I felt all the strength leaving my body. Desire grew through me with each touch of his tongue. He was drinking me in and melting me. He tasted of caramel; I placed my hands around his neck and caressed his shoulders. I felt the chill run through him. He let out a small moan, then he backed away from me.

I stood there with my mouth swollen from him kissing me, wondering what just happened. I could not decipher the look upon Jeremy's face, he looked angry yet something else, I didn't understand.

"Serraid, I am sorry, I should not have kissed you like that right now. I know you are upset and it's the last thing you wanted to do." He looked saddened by the truth of it.

I tried to talk but no sound would come out, I cleared my throat and tried again, "On my walk here, I had planned on telling you where to shove it. Then I seen you standing there and I had to touch you. I wanted your touch and smell on me; I wanted to roll over you like a warm blanket." I couldn't believe I was telling him this when what I really wanted to do was yell at him. I was still mad at him.

"I know you do; I want you to just as bad as you want to. But you need to get all your anger out. Yell at me if you need to, scream at me, hit me, do whatever it is that you need to do to release all your anger out. I'm a big boy; I can handle it."

I stood there looking at him, wondering why he was willing to do this. I decided I was going to ask him. "Why are you doing this, Jeremy?" I asked cautiously.

His face went from being empty to filled with concern. "Serraid, you need to express your feelings more outward, don't hold them in. I know I have been an asshole lately, but I'm doing my job, I'm protecting the woman I love that is car…that is caring and going through a rough time."

I caught that he had almost said something which he did not want to say. "Why don't you just say what it was you were going to say. Why do you have to hide things from me? Do you think you are really protecting me?! Do you want to know what is making me mad? You hiding things from me and treating me like a child, like I can't handle whatever it is that you must tell me!" I drew in a deep breath, so I could say what I had to say next. "I'm sick and tired of all of you walking around like you are on glass, afraid that Poor little Serraid will break at the truth. You guys know me, you know I am a strong person. I don't like being in the dark and being followed around and told what to do and when to do it! Why can't you just fucking tell me?!"

I began to shake as the anger started peeking it's head up.

"Serraid, it's not because we feel you break against the truth, it's that we are truly trying to protect you. The less you know, the less danger you will be in for a while. We know we will eventually have to tell you everything, but for right now we have all decided that it's best to wait for a while. Maybe tell you little things here and there. I promise we are not trying to make this more difficult for you. We all love you."

I could see the truth in his eyes. They really were trying to protect me, but from what?

"Well, let me ask you this, who are you trying to protect me from?" I asked as I looked down at my hands that were folded in front of me.

"Ugh, I can't really tell you just yet. Partly because it's better you don't know right now. This situation is very delicate, Serraid."

My face flushed with the anger that suddenly washed over me. I was sick of him deciding what I needed to know and what I didn't need to know! "Either you tell me right now, or you can leave and not come back! I'm tired of you deciding what to tell me and what to tell me!" I glared at him as hard as I could.

"Serraid, please don't do this." his plead reaching his eyes. It hurt me to see the despair on his face.

I stood as straight as possible and said, "I mean it Jeremy, either you tell me or you can leave. I'm done with the silent treatments and the secrets! I'm so tired of being the only one who doesn't know what the hell is going on!"

It made me feel like shit to tell him this. I truly didn't want him to leave, my heart ached from the thought of him leaving, because I honestly thought that he would be that stubborn. Who are they to think they have the right to decide for me what I should and shouldn't know! What the fuck! This is the sort of things people do to the ones they love when they know they can't handle the truth. And honestly, I'm not that type of person. I have played every scenario through my head, and I hate that I have to jump to conclusions because someone else has decided that I can't handle the truth!

"If I answer your question, you might not be completely satisfied with the answer and you will be compelled to ask even more questions. But If I tell you the answer to this one, you cannot ask anymore. Do we have a deal?"

I stood there, mouth gaped open in disbelief. I could not believe Jeremy was trying to trick me into agreeing with this. I thought about my options for a minute. I didn't want him to leave, but I wanted the whole truth. I would have to take the deal for now, that way I would get some of what I needed to know and he wouldn't leave...

"Deal"

"We are partly trying to protect you from yourself." He shifted his weight as he said this. It appeared that he was preparing for me to hit him.

The anger shoved through me. How could he do this? I agreed with this and now he had taken advantage of that! "You arrogant, pompous asshole! How can you stand there and expect me to accept that as an answer?! I mean really. Did you really expect me to say, oh, ok that's fine, I'll take that answer.'? That's fine if you don't want to tell me! Fuck you, Jeremy!" I turned and began running down the sidewalk with tears running down my cheeks. I had trusted him, and this is what I received in return. I couldn't believe I had been that stupid. I ran faster, ignoring the pain that was beginning to run through me.

"Serraid, wait! Don't run away!" I heard Jeremy say as I ran away from him.

I ran even faster I pushed myself. I wanted to get away from the people who claimed to be my friends yet were lying to me. I didn't understand any of this. I was really beginning to feel I didn't know these people anymore. I began to feel warmth coming over me, I couldn't explain it, but it calmed me somehow. I slowed as I began to feel better somehow. I slowed even farther when I felt a familiar feeling of an energy slide over me. I knew this feeling, I slowly turned, and Jeremy was standing there looking at me with love and concern in his eyes. Seeing that look in his eyes made my heart patter to an uneven rhythm. He slowly licked his lips as he caught his breath.

"I'm sorry, Serraid, please don't go. I can't stand to see you hurt this way. I can't give you the answers you need right now, but I can give you this." as he spoke the last few words, he rushed over to me and wrapped his arms around my waist and picked me up. I wrapped my legs around him and he placed his lips on mine so hard they promised to bruise. I opened to him, I wanted to let him in. I wanted to feel him all through me. I opened my heart and my body. He rushed in, his tongue exploring my mouth with an urgency saying, he wouldn't wait. He ran his hands down my back and grabbed my ass and pulled me closer as a moan escaped his throat. I ate his moan, letting it fill the empty space inside me. I felt like eating caramel, and satiated a hunger I hadn't realized was there, I deepened the kiss and ran my tongue along his lips, tasting him begging him for more. He was hard and ready against his jeans, it felt as if the jeans would split any minute.

With a voice shaken with desire I said, "I want you right now, please, Jeremy." He turned down the next alley. He turned me facing the building and pulled my skirt up. I heard rather than saw him unbutton his pants. He leaned against me with his warm readiness. A chill ran from my head to my toes. I wanted him inside of me. "Give it!" I said in a begging tone. He pressed against my opening, I was tight and he had to push against me. He grabbed my hair and gently pulled my neck back and bit my shoulder. I could feel me getting more ready for his entry. He pushed against me, spreading me like water. The feeling of him pushing himself inside me made me cry out. My body ached with desire; my legs shook with it. Everything was alive throughout me, and I wanted more. He pushed one more time and he was completely inside, feeling him hit my bottom brought me. "Yes, please, harder." I moaned as he worked himself in and out, working me till I was ready for a rougher pace.

I felt myself give into his persuasion. As soon as I gave, he began moving faster and faster. He pushed harder and deeper. I could feel him hit the bottom of me each time he went inside, another orgasm took me, then another. I could feel him growing with each stroke and knew he was close, I reached around with my right hand and grabbed his hip and helped him move. I squeezed, and dug my nails into his skin, in return he pushed himself inside of me fast and hard, until at last, we both washed over the edge of our orgasms together. I screamed my pleasure into the wall, and he bit my shoulder moaning his pleasure into my skin. All thoughts of anger and unhappiness were lost to our pleasure. It felt so good, we were in our own little world where nothing or no one existed but us.

He let go of my shoulder and rubbed the hair away from my face. He kissed my cheek then turned my head and kissed my lips. I kissed him back; I wasn't mad anymore. It seemed that as long as he didn't touch me, I could be mad at him, but if he touched me, I couldn't think, I couldn't be mad at him. It was like he was a tranquilizer for me.

He moved so I could turn around and fix my clothes. I felt absolutely content. I looked over, Jeremy was staring at me and smiling.

"What are you smiling like that for?" I asked with a giggle.

"You are wonderful, and I love you. I don't want to fight anymore."

"I don't want to fight anymore either. I have come to a decision. I will wait for you to answer my questions. If you say you are all trying to protect me, then I will take your word for it. I don't want to be without you. I want you near me. I feel safe with you, and somehow, I feel complete with you. But I want you to know I feel that way with Dayvan as well. I have not made a choice, and I won't until we catch Jargoan, and he's dead. I don't know what I'm going to do, but you guys need to keep in mind that no matter which way I choose, someone is going to be hurt. I don't want to hurt either one of you, but it's inevitable."

"Serraid, let's not think about it right now. Let's just deal with today, today. Let's make it through this moment before we worry about making it through another one. I'm here and Dayvan is here too. Though I can't say I like him being around, he's tolerable. And I know you love him too. He loves you Serraid, as much as I hate saying it, but I know he does. I'm sorry you have to make a choice like this, I really am, but know this, you don't have to make a choice right now, so do not stress on it."

I stood there surprised and speechless at what Jeremy had just said. I could not believe he just said that about

Dayvan. What has gotten into him? "Thank you, Jeremy. I needed to know you understood. I know it is hard for you, but it's hard for me too." I kissed him deeply before he could say anything. I knew he loved me, and I knew it tore him apart inside to see someone else fighting for my love. Hell, it tore me apart knowing I was going to have to hurt someone. I didn't relish the idea of hurting someone.

We walked arm and arm back to the house. When we arrived, Sarah was crying on the front porch, Dayvan was standing there looking worried and mad at the same time.

"Hey guys what's going on?" I asked, fearing the answer.

"We got a delivery today." As Dayvan spoke, I felt my stomach sink to my feet.

"What was the delivery? Jeremy asked heading up the porch steps. I personally did not want to know the answer to that question.

"A small box arrived with a letter inside. The box contains what appears to be a human heart. And the letter is addressed to Serraid. We have not read the letter; we figure we would wait for you to return." Dayvan looked really tired and scared. I wanted to walk over and wrap my arms around him, but my legs did not want to move just yet. I really didn't want to read this letter but knew I had to.

"Give me the letter." I said reluctantly. It would be better to get this over with quickly, so we would know what we were dealing with.

"Serraid, I can read it for you. I know you are still not up to par." Jeremy said with concern in his voice.

"No, I will read it. I want to get this over with. Please Dayvan, just give me the damned letter." I was starting to feel fear and fatigue catching up with me.

Serraid,

You keep opposing me and THAT my dear is a mistake. I must say, I have not had this much fun chasing something since… very long ago. This is another present from Helga. You remember her, don't you babe? I thought maybe this would get your attention.

Your man caught me by surprise, he fights dirty. Next time, however, he will not get the drop on me. I plan on killing him Serraid, I want you to know this. Do not say I did not warn you.

You say you hate me, and I can't be trusted with anything. Well, I hate to rain on your parade sweetie, but have you met the ones whom you are living with? They are the ones to not be trusted!! They hide the truth from you every day! I know this because if you knew the truth you would act accordingly! Why not ask them what it is they are so afraid of you finding out, that makes them bury the truth about who you are and where you are from. Oh…. Poor thing, you really thought you knew, didn't you? Well, I'm here to bust your bubble, you are not who you think you are…Try to remember, really try to remember! You would be surprised at what is locked in your head Serraid.

I just wanted to give you some things to contemplate. I will mend my wounds because they are physical. You on the other hand when you find the truth may not be so well.

Until I'm mended enough to retrieve you…

Love, ~ J

I stood there shaking from anger, fear, and confusion. What did he mean by the truth about where I'm from and who I am? I was not expecting this kind of letter! I turned to Jeremy and said, "I know you said I couldn't ask more questions, but what the hell does this mean??" I slammed the letter to his chest hard enough to force the air out of him. "I mean it, Jeremy! This man knows more about me than I know about myself. How is this right?" I looked around to all three of them, "How can you say that you love me, and keep so many secrets about me? How is this fair? I'm sick of this shit! I'm going to go pack my shit and go stay somewhere where I know I can trust the people around me!" I stormed inside of the house, stomped up the stairs to my room, grabbed my suitcase, and started throwing clothes in it. I was not going to stay here another fucking minute with these people! If they would not tell me anything, then I would be better off somewhere else. I was not going to be trapped in this house a minute longer with people who were hiding shit about me from me! I was starting to get really angry. I felt an energy swirl around me, as this happened, I turned to see Dayvan standing in the doorway.

I let out a breath, "What do you want? And do not pretend you are concerned for me, because if you really did, you would tell me the truth!" I was tired and it showed in my voice.

"I was not going to tell you anything except I am sorry. I am not sorry for trying to protect you, but that it came this way. I really wanted you to find out the right way from me. But now there is no way that you can know." he looked worried as he spoke. After he was finished, he turned and walked down the stairs.

I stood there, anger filling me to the brim. I could feel my face burning and the pain shot through me like lightning. It doubled me over, and I screamed as it ripped through me. Fear gripped me! What was going on? Why was I hurting so bad?!

Jeremy and Sarah came rushing through the door so fast I could not take in how fast they were moving. They came and sat me down on the floor, leaning me against Sarah's chest with her legs wrapped around me, and Jeremy hugged me from the front! Immediately the pain began to subside. This brought another round of rage upon me; it bowed my back threatening to rip through my ribs! Jeremy whispered soothing words into my ear as Sarah kissed my shoulder. I was so angry, all I wanted was the truth! And still with all that had happened, they were going to keep it from me. Yet they thought they could calm me?! I was pissed, before I knew what happened I stood and threw Sarah and Jeremy away from me. Sarah landed against the wall hard enough that she knocked the picture off my wall, and Jeremy flew across the bed. My breath was rapid, and my chest felt as if someone had buried themselves into it, my hands felt as if they had been run over. My legs were shaking so badly I could hardly stand, yet I had enough strength to throw two grown people at the same time! What the hell is going on? Suddenly, I was bowed over and what sounded like a growl escaped my throat. My throat felt as if it were on fire, so dry! I heard Jeremy tell Sarah to get the Syringe and give me all of it. I felt a sharp pain in my leg, I turned to face Sarah, fear spread across her face, I lunged for her, she let out a high pitch scream as I grabbed her neck and began to squeeze. I thought to myself I was so angry, but I did not want to kill my friend. I squeezed harder, I seen her face go blue, I was killing her, I could hear her pulse slowing. I could smell the fear all over her. It smelled so good, I wanted to lick her face. Death and fear, and......food.

Panic set in at that thought! What was I doing?! What was going on?! That was the last conscious thought I had before darkness surrounded me and pulled me under its familiar blanket of comfort.

I woke with the feeling of cotton in my mouth, my head was pounding, and the light was killing my eyes. What the hell happened? I lay there trying to remember. I remembered the letter, getting angry and Oh god! "Sarah!!" I screamed out!

I looked around the room and there was no one there. Had I dreamt it? Please, let it be a bad dream... I yelled, "Sarah. Jeremy. Dayvan!! Anyone! Is anyone there?!" I listened for a response, a noise, something to let me know they were here. When I heard nothing, I tried again, "Please guys, I'm sorry, please answer me!" I was crying now. I felt the warm tears streaming down my face. I started to wipe them from my face when I realized I could not move my arms. I looked up and there were chains on my hands. I pulled at them, but they did not give. My heart started pounding in my chest! Fear was taking over. I looked around, realizing I was not in my home. Where was I? Oh God, did I kill them and Jargoan take me? I started pulling at the chains, desperately trying to break them. My feet were chained as well. I did not like this at all. I pulled once more at the chains, they did not budge. I began to scream, and cry from frustration.

I lay there crying for what felt like thirty minutes. I had come to terms with this being the way I was going to die. If he had me then I was certainly going to meet my death here. I thought of Sarah, I remember seeing her face turning blue by my hands. This made my tears start again. How could I have killed her? What was I thinking? I yanked at the damned chains again out of frustration! I discovered my body was sore all over. It felt as if I had been beaten. My stomach was flipping, probably from nerves. I had no way out of here; therefore, I was at his mercy. He won. I lost. As this realization settled over me, I began to drift off to sleep from exhaustion…

I woke to the smell of fried chicken. I opened my eyes and to my surprise Jeremy was standing there beside my bed.

"Where have you been?!" I yelled at him… "I woke up earlier and thought Jargoan had kidnapped me. I screamed for you and Sarah and Dayvan, but no one answered. Where are we?"

Jeremy looked concerned when he said, "We are somewhere safe. I am sorry you woke up before I returned. I should not have left you alone. I knew you would be hungry when you woke, so I went to get you some food."

"What do you mean, you should not have left me alone? Where is Sarah and Dayvan?" Fear began to shake through me.

"Sarah is resting, and Dayvan is out running errands for us." He scratched his head as if something were bothering him.

"Oh God! Did I hurt Sarah?! Is she all right?!" Fear tightening my chest and making my mouth taste of metal. I could feel my heart racing at this thought.

"She is fine. She was a little shaken up by your rage, but she will recover. You need to rest and take it easy. How do you feel? Serraid, I want you to close your eyes and concentrate on every part of your body and tell me how you feel and if anything hurts." he was looking a little pale.

I lay there and looked at him. Maybe it was the lighting making him look pale. Maybe not. I closed my eyes and started with my feet when I remembered the restraints. "Why am I chained down? Let me out of this right now!"

"I cannot do that. This is for your safety as well as ours. I am sorry Serraid, but we must keep you in them for a little while until I know it is safe for you." His face was twisted with concern.

"Why? What did I do that was so bad? Please, you cannot treat me like this! I am not a fucking animal! I thought you cared for me and wanted to show me the gentler side of love? What happened to that? Huh?!" I was yelling again and the anger threatened to take over. I knew I was being petty and throwing bullshit feelings back at him, but I did not care. I wanted out of these damned restraints, and I wanted out now!

"If you do not calm yourself, I will be forced to sedate you again, and that may not be the safest for the…. Oh, hell just calm down Serraid!"

I could not believe what I was hearing! Who the hell does he think he is to bark orders to me?! The anger washed over me like a well-known friend. I felt the pain rip through me just as Jeremy gave me a shot of something. A few seconds later I was dreaming…

I was laying on an old bed made of straw mattress. I was holding a newborn babe. I had just had her and she was perfect. Her skin was so soft, her eyes like a fine aged wine, her hair the color of the sun. She was amazing. Her little handheld my fingers as I cuddled her to my breast. The love that welled up inside of me was amazing.......I was so thankful for this little person. I looked up and Dayvan was standing there admiring his family. He smiled at us with loving eyes. He came and sat with us, gently rubbing her head with the tip of his thumb. He said, "We will call her Serraid. She is beautiful, and you did perfectly. I love you, Nali.." He bent and kissed my forehead. I felt so much love for him right then.

Then the dream was a few days later. I stood, looking out the window. I was watching Dayvan plowing the fields. He worked so hard to make sure we had what we needed. The kill from his last hunt was hanging on the poles outside, curing. It looked like he had already rubbed them with salt and herbs, they were almost ready to plant in the ground. I wrapped my scarf around my shoulders and walked outside to get some fresh air. I just needed the refreshing scent of it. I stood there watching Dayvan as he worked. I smiled at the thought of his warm body pressing against mine later. I needed him close. I had already finished bleeding from childbirth and was feeling much better. It was amazing. I didn't know how I had healed so fast, but I was favored I supposed.

"Well look who's decided to get some fresh air." I jumped at the sound of his voice. I had zoned off into nothing.

"Hey you, I just needed some breathing room in the air. How are you love? One day you won't have to work so hard for us. We will be rich." This was an ongoing joke with us. We pictured ourselves rich, with servants and butlers. Was it possible? Well, anything was possible but not likely.

"I understand, you have been working so hard with the new babe. How is my little love this morning?" He smiled as he asked about Serraid.

"She is sleeping. She's a ravenous little monster. She's going to drain me dry before a month is out." I giggled as I said this.

"She will slow down in a few days; they always do from what I'm told. The priest wants to come and see her and bless her. He wants to do this tomorrow, are you up for it my love?"

"Yes, I suppose I am. I want to get her blessed. I know she is a wonderful little creature, and she will grow to great things." The dream flashed forward to that evening.

It was dark out and I had just cleared the table from supper. I changed Serraid and fed her and laid her down for bed. I went to bed and laid with Dayvan. We talked about the day and plans each of us had. I dozed off listening to his heartbeat. I was woken by a crashing sound. "Dayvan! Wake up!" He jumped up, "What? What is it" When another sound came from the other room. Dayvan jumped up and grabbed his gun just as we heard Serraid cry, but her cries sounded muffled. I jumped up and ran into the room, what I saw was the worst thing I have ever experienced.

A wolf had come into the house through the window. It had Serraid in its mouth. I could see her bleeding. I rushed toward it, not caring about my safety. I had to get my baby away from this monster! "Let go of her!" I screamed at it, hitting it with the broom I had grabbed on my way over…I was hitting it with everything I had. It looked at me with its wolf eyes and growled. It bit down harder; I heard her little bones break under the pressure of its jaws. Her breathing and crying stopped; her little body went completely limp. I knew she was dead, but I was not going to let this animal take her away. I had not had her long enough to ever lose her! She was mine! Greif tore through me, my heart felt as if it was being ripped out of my chest. Tears began running down my face. I wouldn't let this thing have my child.

I broke the broom in half, and I drove the broken piece through its chest, aiming for the heart. I felt the heart give under the pressure of the wood. A whimper came from the wolf's mouth. It reached out and tried to claw me, but it dropped as soon as it lifted its paw away from the floor. As soon as I seen it falling, I reached out and grabbed Serraid from its mouth so her little body didn't hit the floor.

I knelt there on the floor, my knees sliding in the blood of the wolf, crying. I screamed at the top of my lungs as my heart broke. Life was gone out of her little body. "Mommy loves you little babe. Please don't be gone, please… "I didn't know what I was going to do without her. I had only had her for a few days, but she had captured me in every way. Her mouth would no longer coo or suckle, her hands would no longer hold my fingers, her eyes would never light up again. I heard something behind me, I snatched the other broken piece of the broom and spun around. Dayvan fell down beside me grabbing the wood out of my hand. He looked at our daughter, and I could see the grief take over his face. "No, no, no, please no…. I should have been able to save her. Nooo!!!" He screamed with his face toward the ceiling and his arms stretched out to each side. He howled and screamed his loss at the stars. I cried as I heard my mate grieving the loss of our precious daughter. My heart was broken; I was angry. I handed Serraid to Dayvan and stood up. I grabbed the other piece of the broom, walked over to the wolf, and started kicking it, screaming at it, "WHY? Why our house? Why our little babe? I hate you! Why, God why our little girl?" I could feel the grief taking over my voice as I screamed and kicked this wretched animal. When I screamed so much that my voice was dying, I began stabbing the animal over and over wanting to make its dead corpse feel the pain that was ripping my heart and stomach around my spine! I wanted to make it hurt like it made us hurt! That's when I saw the movement in its belly. I cut its stomach open to find the little pup still in its sac, dying from the death of its mother. My heart melted at the sight of this helpless creature dying for something its parent had done. I looked back at Serraid's lifeless body, this wolf deserved to die, but it's babe didn't. I grabbed the sac and tore it open and pulled it out, cut the cord, and wrapped it in the skirt of my petticoat. It snuggled down into the warmth and whimpered.

"What's that? Nali? What have you done?"

"I saved its pup. It was unborn, and I couldn't let it die because of the mother's wrongdoing." Tears rolled down my face, as I spoke, I could feel the anger and grief welling up inside of me again. I had lost my daughter, and this pup had lost its mother. She should have lost her pup! I doubled my fists and banged them on the floor of the cabin! I hit it over and over again until my hands were bloody and bruised. I looked up toward the ceiling and screamed, "WHY! Why did you have to do this to us?!!! Why us? What did we do to deserve this?!"

"Nali, please love, don't do this. God did not do this to us. This was not the work of the creator. This was the devil; he took her from us! Please do not blame God."

"Shut up! I don't want to hear you! I should have moved quicker! I should have had her with us, and this would never have happened. She never deserved this! I'm not worthy of her!" I grabbed the wood off of the floor, and went to shove it through my chest, I wouldn't allow myself to live any longer without her. I couldn't, a part of me was gone.

The pup stirred in my lap. The feeling of its small body reminded me of Serraid's little movement. My heart broke again. I thrust the wood toward my chest......

I woke up sweating, crying, and screaming! I was gasping for air. What was that dream all about?

"Serraid, are you alright?" Jeremy's voice was soothing.

"I just had a really bad dream; I need some water please." I remembered my hands being restrained. I looked up and to my surprise they were released. I moved my hands and got the blood flow back to them. I rubbed my wrists, they felt sore and bruised.

"Here, drink this. I knew you were having a nightmare because you fought against your restraints. I released you because I was afraid you would hurt yourself. Do you want to talk about what you dreamed about?"

He handed me a glass of water, and I took big drinks. The cold liquid felt like heaven to my dry irritated throat. I finished the rest of the water.

"Thank you, Jeremy. I am not sure what made me have that bad and real dream. I was me except I was called Nali. Dayvan was himself called by his name. We had a daughter, we named her Serraid, she was...." I could feel the tears welling up and my voice choked out. "She was killed by a wolf. I killed the wolf and cut its pup from its womb. I then went to kill myself when I woke up. The dream was so real Jeremy. I could have sworn I was there for real. There is something about the dream that feels so real."

Jeremy stood there, he had gone completely still with a worried look on his face. I could see the worry lines deepen with every thought that went through his mind. "Jeremy, what is it? Why do you look like you just seen a ghost?"

"Serraid, I have to go. I will be back and if possible, I will tell you all I know. Can you wait until then, please?"

"You promise to tell me everything when you return? How long will you be gone? I want the truth. I deserve the truth, Jeremy." I began to cry again.

Jeremy bent down and kissed my forehead and said, "Yes, I will tell you everything when I return. I must go away for a little while. Dayvan and Sarah will be here with you. You are not allowed outside right now. And you must remain calm no matter what happens. It is extremely important for you to remain calm. I should return in a month, sooner if I can accomplish my task. If for some reason I do not return tell Dayvan to tell you the truth. I will leave certain instructions with him while I am gone. I love you Serraid."

My heart clenched when I heard my name, it reminded me of the little babe I had once had and lost. Somehow, I knew she was mine. "I promise, I will wait for you. I love you Jeremy and please whatever it is that you will be doing, please be careful."

Dayvan walked into the room slowly. Jeremy looked at Dayvan and then they both looked at me. Jeremy told Dayvan that he needed to speak with him and then he would be going. I told them I needed something to eat. I felt as if I had not eaten in a year.

I looked at my stomach because it felt bruised, I was putting on some weight. I really needed to quit eating this way or I am going to get fat. I decided to take a shower while the guys were talking. I thought getting cleaned would make me feel a little better.

I sat up on the edge of the bed and let my head adjust to the new altitude. Then, I stood all the way up and headed for the shower. I could hear the guys talking by the door. I thought to myself I was going to miss Jeremy, yet at the same time I was looking forward to having some time with Dayvan. I wanted to ask him about this dream. Had we really had a little girl and lost her? I wanted answers. And without Jeremy around I would get them, because Dayvan was not as strong as Jeremy about hiding things from me. And if all else failed I could get it out of Sarah. She was my best friend. She would tell me if I asked her without the guys around. Or would she? I was not so sure I really knew them as well as I thought I did anymore.

CHAPTER 12

Later that night, Dayvan came in, he brought me dinner. I still felt as if I had been beaten up for days. My muscles were sore, and my skin still felt as if it had been burnt. I did not understand what was going on. While Dayvan was there watching me eat, I figured I would use this time to try to get some answers.

"Dayvan, I had a dream earlier today, before Jeremy left, that seemed so real I could swear it had happened. Did Jeremy tell you about it?"

Dayvan looked up at me with something gliding across his face, I could see his reluctance to answer the question. "He told me some of it." He said quietly.

"What exactly did he tell you about it?" I asked, pushing for whatever information he may have.

"He said you had a dream of having a baby that was killed. It is probably because of everything you have been through lately. It is your subconscious trying to put it in perspective." He said the last part just a little too quickly. I could see sweat beading across his forehead. He looked down to hide his face from me.

"Dayvan, I do not believe that. My dream was of me, you, and a baby. My name was Nali, and the baby's name was Serraid. Now, are you honestly going to expect me to believe it is just my subconscious?" I was starting to get a little upset.

Dayvan went completely still at the mention of Nali. I noticed it. I knew, seeing him react like that, this was not just a dream. I knew that name meant something to him. Now just to figure out what exactly. When he had been quiet for a minute without answering I asked, "Earth to Dayvan! Are you going to answer my question or just sit there and act like you do not understand the words coming out of my mouth?"

"Na…I mean Serraid I am sorry, Jeremy left me with specific orders. I am to tell you nothing until he comes back, or until you tell me to because he has not returned." A flush of color went across his cheeks as he spoke.

His answer upset me. "Dayvan, I never pictured you as a puppet, doing what others tell you to do all the time. How can you sit there and act as if everything is ok with lying to me? I just do not understand you guys. Especially you, Dayvan, you say you love me, yet you keep hiding things from me. How do you justify that?" The anger was starting to show in my voice.

"Serraid, I know you do not understand, but I swear that we are doing it for your own good. We are trying to protect you and the.... I mean we are just trying to protect you from things you do not know of yet. I promised you the other day I would tell you things as I could, and I meant it. I can tell you this. Your dream has a meaning. And I have not heard the name Nali in a very long time. If you keep digging into your own mind, you will remember things which you have forgotten, or that was taken from you for protection."

"But how will I know if it is just dreams or memories, Dayvan when I ask all you say is you can't tell me anything?! I'm tired of the games! I'm tired of being protected. I want to know what the hell is going on! If you won't tell me anything, then just leave. I'm tired and I have suddenly lost my appetite." It wasn't true, I still felt as if I was starving, but I was going to make him tell me what I wanted to know, one way or another even if I had to get him where it hurt. I knew he wanted to be close to me. I was just hoping that he wanted it enough that he would tell me what I wanted to know to stay there. If not, then I would need another strategy and would have to adjust my plans accordingly.

"I will tell you 'If' I can. I promise you. Your name is really Nali, not Serraid. I can tell you that. I know you probably have a thousand more questions now. But I cannot tell you the answers to those questions just yet." He looked tired. I could see the lines around his eyes. Sympathy ran through me. I knew I was not the easiest person to deal with.

"Ok, I'm not trying to make this more difficult than it already is. Just answer me this one question. Did we have a daughter named Serraid, that was killed by a wolf in our home? Please Dayvan, I need to know. It felt so real, and my heart still aches from the dream as if it had really happened." I could feel the tears swell up in my eyes and the vengeful anger coming.

Dayvan let out a long loud sigh and took my hands into his, a sad look crossed his face and eyes. "A long time ago, we had a daughter, I named her Serraid." Tears welled up in his eyes. "She was so perfect, and we loved her for the three days we had her. One night a hungry wolf came through our window and took her. It was cold that night and we had decided to keep Serraid in the living room with the fireplace so she would stay warmer. It's a decision that has torn me down for a very long time." He was crying now. Tear swelled up in my eyes again and spilled down my cheeks. I remembered the dream, and the grief I felt. It all came rushing back to me as if it was the same day.

"Did I try to kill myself?" I asked sniffling back the sorrow in my voice.

"You, you." he leaned over and hugged me tightly. He was sobbing, and I could not understand anything he was saying.

"Are you guys alright in here?" Sarah's voice cut through the grief like a warm knife in butter.

"Sarah!" I said, glad to see her. I let go of Dayvan and held my hand out to her. "I'm so sorry I attacked you. I love you and I never want to hurt you. I am truly sorry. Do you forgive me?"

She quickly walked over to me and took my hand and kissed it. "I forgive you Serraid. I know you did not mean to. I am fine, just look." She smiled a soft smile that did not quite reach her eyes.

I looked at her and there were no scars, cuts, or bruises. "Ok, I know you are ok. I am really sorry though. I do not know what I would have done if I would have hurt you, or worse if I had k."

Sarah cut me off with a kiss. She kissed me deeply and softly. Her lips were full against mine. I could feel myself awake. I touched her cheek with my hand and ran it across the back of her neck. I pulled her closer to me, exploring her mouth like a long-lost toy. She sat on the bed with me and ran her hand across my stomach, bringing goose bumps across my skin. She was perfect and I wanted her against me. I pulled off her shirt and unfastened her bra. I ran my hand up and down the bare skin of her back. I pulled her bra off completely and found her perfect nipples with my fingers. Sarah moaned as I played with them. I pinched her right nipple slightly making her back arch with the pleasure of it. I kissed her deeper, while sliding my hand down her waist. She was so damn sexy, her thin frame, perfect tits, and nice ass. She had the perfect spread from behind too. I found her, she was ready for me, wet, warm, and swollen. I slid my finger inside; I ate her moan as she released it in my mouth. I could feel her squeeze my finger; I slid another one inside of her. She was moving with my rhythm now. She was taking all that I could give her. I could feel her body responding, lubricating my slide.

Things went tight on me. I could feel my body wanting her. I pulled her up, so she was sitting on my shoulders, and I found her spot with my tongue. I flicked her button gently a couple of times and then rammed my fingers back inside while I licked her. She was moving, bucking, and moaning. I reached up with my free hand and played with her nipples. She went over the edge and gave me her pleasure, which I drank with pleasure of my own. I felt myself in a spasm. I realized that Dayvan had been licking me at the same time. I had not noticed until the orgasm took me. Sarah was leaned against his chest as he came up to slide inside of me. He played with her nipples while he entered me, I licked her again. The feeling of all three of us enjoying each other was too much. I could not stop it, the orgasm took me, making me squeeze Dayvan tight. He moaned and squeezed Sarah's nipples harder which made her orgasm take her. The sound of us all releasing together threw him over the edge. I felt him spill his warm seed inside of me.

We all three lay there, learning to breathe again, allowing our bodies to reground with the world. After a few minutes, I realized my strength was coming back. I was feeling much better; I felt as if I had slept for days. I thought it was odd how this seemed to happen every time we made love.

"I know this is probably not the time to ask questions, but why is it when we make love it seems to make me feel better? It happens every time, with you, Sarah, and Jeremy."

Dayvan was still trying to find his voice when Sarah said, "Because it's what we are, how we are made and the energy we share when we come together as one unit." She stated as if that answered everything.

"I'm confused, what do you me what we are, and how we are made?" My face must have looked as puzzled as I sounded because Dayvan laughed aloud. It was good to hear him laugh like that.

As he laughed, he said, "Oh, Nali, you seem to always find the most humorous way to state things. We are made to heal together, from each other. It is part of who we are. I promise I will tell you more soon. Please, do not press too much just yet, let's just enjoy this right now." He gave me a soft smile as he said it.

My heart softened. I knew they were both tensed up, not knowing if I would explode or accept what he had requested. I loved them both and I did not want to hurt them. I gave a soft smile letting them know I was going to accept this for now. I thought to myself, I would not take this too long, but for now for them I would hold my temper. Both Sarah and Dayvan let out a breath I had not realized they were holding. I knew right then, I had made the right choice.

About an hour later, Dayvan went to the store to get us something to eat. We were all starving from our session earlier. Sarah sat in the chair on the other side of my room. She was humming a tune to herself as she read the paper. She looked up and smiled as she noticed I was staring at her. I felt embarrassed for staring, but I could not help but admire her beauty. She seemed as if she had grown up ten years in the last month.

"Sarah, are you all right? It is just you seem to have matured so fast this last month. I am worried about you."

She stood up and walked over to me, placing a hand on my arm she said, "I am fine Serraid. It has been hard on all of us. I was always mature; I just like to have fun. Lately, we have had so many serious situations going on that I have not been able to be silly or funny much. I am sorry you are having to go through all of this, I wish I could make all of this go away for you."

"Oh, Sarah, you have nothing to be sorry for sweetie. I know you would take it all away and that is one of the many things I love you for. I am sorry my drama is spilling into your life. I do not want you to feel obligated to help, and I want you to know that you can leave anytime you want to. I will not blame you, and I will always love you no matter what." I smiled at her letting her know I meant it. I did love her, and I would not blame her if she did leave.

She looked at me, then bent down and kissed my head and said, "Darling, I could not leave you, ever. I have always been here, and I will always be here for you."

"What do you mean you have always been there? Did you know me when me and Dayvan lost Serraid?" I could feel the sorrow set on my chest from the memory of it.

"Yes, I did. I was there that night. I slept in barn that night so you and Dayvan could have a night alone. I have blamed myself for that night for a long time. If I would have stayed in the house, or if I had taken the babe with me, maybe." Tears started flowing down her face.

"Shhh…Don't cry Sarah, do not blame yourself either. It was not anyone's fault. None of us could have known a wolf would jump through the window. I have blamed myself too because if I had taken her to our room maybe it would not have happened. I am not sure why I had amnesia though. Why was everything locked up inside? Oh, hell shit is still locked up inside. The only memory I have is losing my baby. It feels like I am being punished or something."

"Nali, I know Jeremy will explain everything to you when he gets back. I would explain things to you if I knew it would help, but there are some things even I do not understand. I am afraid I would just confuse you even more." She touched my shoulder with sorrow on her face.

I took her hand in mine. "Explain Jeremy's, Dayvan's and your role in all this. Please, we can start there and then we can work through everything else."

She took a deep breath and let it out and then she said, "Jeremy is your carrier, Dayvan is your mate, and I am your helper. I know this does not mean anything to you. And you will have more answers. You will have to wait for Jeremy to answer the in-depth answers that you need."

"Jeremy told me once, that I am his mate. Why would he say that if Dayvan is my mate? And why are we using the word mate, I mean we are not animals we are humans." I was getting more and more confused and I felt angry at all the riddles. It seemed like they were answering my questions with riddles just to keep the truth from me. I never would have thought Sarah would have been this way to me. It hurt me, making me feel betrayed.

"I. I'm not sure why He would say that. See, I should not have said anything. Just forget I said it. Wait for Jeremy to show up and let him tell you everything you need to know." She started to look scared, like I was going to be mad at her.

I was getting mad at her, but then I realized I had asked her the questions. It was my fault she was feeling this way. I looked at her and let the sympathy show on my face. "Sarah, it is all right. I am sorry I asked you anything. I know that you are just trying to help. I am going to try to wait for Jeremy. But if I have any more questions I will ask Dayvan."

A look of relief crossed Sarah's face. I could see that she was more relaxed. I wanted her to be comfortable. I wanted her to be herself.

Dayvan returned with our food, and it smelled marvelous. He brought Bacon, eggs and Potatoes, Pancakes with strawberry jam and some orange juice.

"Thank you Dayvan. It smells delicious." I was already dipping some pancakes and eggs.

"You're welcome hun. I am glad to be able to take care of you again. I enjoy the time we have together." He smiled at me with his whole face.

"Hey, I have a question for you. Where did Jeremy go? What did he leave to take care of? I know you probably can't tell me, but I must ask."

"He went to find Jargoan. He said that he was going to find him while he was weak. He said he was going to capture him and bring him here so we can deal with him together." Dayvan must have seen the worry on my face because he said, "Do not worry Nali, Jeremy's good at what he does. He will be all right, I promise. He is strong and he is well trained. He will catch Jargoan and he will bring him here."

I sat there contemplating everything Dayvan had just said. Many questions came to my mind. There were so many answers that I needed, wanted, and would get. I chose to say nothing, because what I had to say was going to do none of us any good.

We finished our breakfast while we watched T.V. I got up and showered and put some clean clothes on. I walked into our living area and looked out a little window in the wall. There was nothing but trees and vines for miles that I could see. It seemed as if we were living in the woods. I hollered at Dayvan to come here.

When Dayvan came into the room I asked him, "Where are we? It looks as if we are in the woods, but where?"

"We are in a woodland area. I cannot tell you exactly where though. We do not want anyone to know. Sarah doesn't even know where we are. Only Jeremy and I Know exactly where. I am sorry Nali, I never wanted us to end up this way, me hiding things from you." He grabbed me from behind and gave me a big hug.

I leaned my head against his chest. I knew he meant the apology. It did not make it any easier to take though. I had to bite my tongue. I knew they were only doing this to protect me; what I wanted to know is why them? From whom? And why all the secrecy? I stood there enjoying the feeling of him against me. Knowing I was safe, I relaxed a little. I just wanted all of this to be over. Hopefully soon this will be over.

Later that evening, we decided to play some card games to help pass the time. There really was not much we could do. I hated being locked up inside, I wanted outside and get some air. I wanted to smell the fresh, crisp air with pine trees and oak leaves. I love the smell and the sound of the great outdoors. It made me wonder who had picked this place for us to hide out in.

"Dayvan, who picked this place for us to stay in?"

"Jeremy did, why, do you not like it? I thought you would like the touch of nature. You have always liked being in the wild."

"I love it, I was just wondering who picked it out. I guess I'm just feeling as if I do not know who anyone is, or who I am much anymore. I am second guessing myself and wondering who knows me better." I sighed heavily; I could feel the fatigue catching up with me. "I mean what is the point of giving me something I like, if I can't go out and enjoy it." I saw Sarah shift in her seat as if she were waiting for things to blow into a fight.

"We all know you very well, just different ways but we know you well none the less. I know this is all confusing. I wish we could help you. I can see you are tired; why don't you lay down and get some rest for a while?

I decided that He was right, I did need some rest. I headed toward my room. Once in my room, I closed the door and lay down to sleep. Maybe Jeremy would be back when I woke up, I doubted it, but I was hoping.

He stood outside of her door, with his head leaning against it. He was so in love with her, yet she was still out of his reach. He wanted to go into her and hold her the way he used to do. But one man had ripped all of that apart. Yes, Jargoan would pay for his iniquities. Jeremy would bring him to them, he knew. Jeremy was many things, but incompetent was not one of them. Jeremy would succeed, for he loves Nali too. He decided right then that he would kill Jeremy if it was necessary. His love was that deep for her, he would defy all their laws to have her back at his side. The question was, could she handle it? Would she still love him when she knew the truth of things?

He shook his head out of frustration, he could not think of such things right now. He would have her again, one way or another. If it came down to him making sure of it, they could work through it together. He heard something, he turned to see Sarah staring at him.

She walked up to him and placed her hand on his shoulder. Silently acknowledging his pain. She too knew how Dayvan loved Nali, but she also knew how Jeremy does too. She knew the pain Jeremy went through to admit to Nali, his love. When she accepted him, Jeremy was ecstatic. His eyes lit up, and face went all soft they way love makes you do. She feared what would happen if Nali could not choose. She did not blame her, for she knew the grief that Nali had faced. She also has seen that grief grow through all the years. Sarah just wanted Nali to be happy for a change, in fact, Sarah longed for the day when they could be done with all the jumping. I was so uncomfortable and frankly it had begun to be tiresome. Nali had delivered once; she could do it again. It was just a matter of timing and her friends keeping her calm.

Sarah thought about that for a moment. She decided that the best way to keep her calm was to tell her the truth of things. This way nothing would be a surprise, and it would let Nali know what she was fighting for this time. Now, she just had to figure out a way to tell her the truth without the guys finding out.

Dayvan grabbed Sarah's face and leaned it up toward him. He smiled at her and said, "Thank you, Sarah. You are an excellent friend. She is so lucky to have you, we all are."

Sarah, smiled back at him and quietly said, "It is nothing, really. I am loyal and I love you all. This is my life, and I would not trade it for anything. Do you really think that she will learn to calm herself? Do you really think the babe has a chance?"

Dayvan replied, "Yes, it has just as much chance as the last ones. This one is lucky though because it has all of us together to help its mommy. I just wish we knew if it were mine or if it were Jeremy's. It is hard to look at her and picture her with my child when I am not sure it is my child inside of her." He looked toward the ground.

"I know it is hard. Think of it this way, no matter who sired the child, it is all of ours. We are all friends, and we will stick together for twenty more centuries if that is what it takes." She placed her hand on his face and said, "You will have her back you know. Just be patient."

Dayvan looked into Sarah's eyes; he wanted to believe her, but the feeling in his stomach told him different. He said, "I see the way she looks at Jeremy. I'm afraid I am too late and have already lost her. The things that Jargoan did to her when he was pretending to be me have taken its toll. I can tell when she is trying to figure out if it was the real me or the fake me that did things to her. It tears me apart inside! I would never hurt her!"

"Hush Dayvan, before you wake her! You must calm yourself man, do not let yourself admit defeat just yet. You are a warrior, do not ever forget that. Now, get some sleep, I will take first watch. I will wake you when I am too tired to stand anymore. She will be yours, you just wait and see."

A smile crossed Dayvan's face, "Ok, I will try to rest. If anything, out of the ordinary happens, you get me right away! Do not hesitate or second guess yourself. Do not forget our safe words, we will need to use them more than ever right now." With that he turned and headed to his bedroom door.

Sarah stood there and wondered if Nali would ever forgive all of them for the lies and the dishonesty. Even though it was at her command, she may still not be too happy about it. Problem is, would she ever remember giving those orders? If not, they may all be dead, if she did then they all stood a chance. Sarah turned to head down the corridor to make her first round.

I woke up with a thirst that promised to be unquenchable. I decided I had slept enough for now. I got up and headed for the kitchen to get me some water. When I arrived in the kitchen, Sarah was sitting there looking out the window, while drinking hot chocolate. She appeared deep in thought.

"Hey you." I said trying not to frighten her too badly.

Sarah let out a shrill and almost spilled her hot chocolate, "Oh Nali, I did not hear you come in. You almost scared the life out of me!" She was wiping some of the chocolate off her shirt.

Walking toward her, I grabbed a towel off one of the kitchen chairs and handed it to her. "I am sorry Sarah, I did not mean to scare you. I woke up and I am so thirsty. It feels as if I have not had a drink in years."

"Well, that's normal for someone in your condition." She broke off realizing what she just said. "I mean, you know someone who's been under high levels of stress and so many injuries and anemia." She giggled shyly trying to busy herself with the towel while trying to look innocent.

"Sarah, look at me." I said touching her shoulder.

Sarah went completely still as if she was frozen in time. A look of fear went across her face, and her color went pale. She turned her face to me and smiled weakly. "Yes?"

"Come, let us sit and talk like old girlfriends; like we used to do before all this drama started. I miss it." I was trying to cover up the fact I had caught her in her words.

I wanted her to think I had missed it. This way she would open to my suggestions and maybe say something else without thinking.

"Yes, I miss it too. I will make some grilled cheese and hot chocolate. We can sit and eat a night snack and have some girl talk." She giggles, apparently pleased with herself for covering her slip of words up. She started getting everything ready for our snack.

I sat there at the kitchen table, and I watched Sarah float around the kitchen like an ant that was preparing for winter. I wondered to myself if she really thought I was going to let her little slip up pass with no recognition. I quietly giggled to myself because she did not seem to have a clue I had caught on. That pleased me very much. It is always easier to get information from someone when they are hiding something when they do not think that you are paying too close attention to things.

Sarah sat our food down at the table. My stomach grumbled as if I had not eaten all day. I felt like I could not get enough to eat lately. It seemed the more I ate, the more I wanted. She then went back to the counter and grabbed our mugs of hot chocolate. She sat mine down and then she sat in her chair. She was blowing on the top of her mug. I was not sure why we did this because it did not help cool it down any faster. I giggled at that.

"Thank you, Sarah, for the sandwiches and the hot chocolate. It all looks great as always." I grabbed one of the grilled cheese and tore it in half, while watching the cheese stretch between the pieces of bread. I am not sure why, but this was always my favorite part of eating these. I took a bite of my food, and it felt as if my mid-section lifted straight out in front of me, as if it were light as feathers. It startled me a little and a whimper escaped my throat.

"What is it, Nali? Are you all right?" Sarah was standing up and looked panicked.

"I am fine, it is just it…Well it felt like my stomach was lifting away from me for a second. It felt light as feathers, and I am not sure why. It felt so weird, but good at the same time." I was smiling at the memory of how it felt. "I have never felt anything like that before."

Sarah's face went completely white at my words. I stood up ready to catch her because I was concerned that she was going to pass out. "Sarah, are you all right? You look as if you have seen a ghost." I placed her back in her chair, "Here sit-down sweetie."

"I'm fine," she said with a shaky voice. "It's just it happened so soon, I wasn't prepared for this to happen so fast."

"Sarah, you are not making any sense. What are you talking about?" I could feel my heart beginning to speed up as the fear began to hit me.

"Nali, sit down, for we must talk. There are going to be some things I have to tell you, and you are not going to understand. There are some things I want to tell you that I have been ordered not to tell you, but I will tell you as I think you should know and will trust you to protect me when I do." She was clearly shaking and completely serious.

I sat down in my chair and began to eat my grilled cheese. I felt as if I were starving.

Sarah sat back in her chair and took a couple of deep breaths. Then she looked at me and said, "Nali, what you felt just then was an awakening. Every expecting mother has it. It is when the mother first feels the baby move. It is called many things, but our race calls it Awakening. Because at the time of the child's birth, your life awakens."

I sat there with my jaw on the floor. "Pregnant? But how? I mean I know how it happens, but shit…. I did not even know, I mean I have not even missed a cycle yet, and how did you know?" I was trying to think of what day it was, and when my next cycle was due. It was the 4th of March; my last cycle was on…." Shiiit!" I realized that my last cycle was on the 7th of January. I was almost two months past.

I stood up and started pacing. How could this happen? I knew time flew lately, but two months! My mind was racing over everything that had happened over the last few months. I mean it is no wonder I have had time lapses. Shit. Then it hit me, I could not be newly pregnant....

"Sarah, I am not pregnant, because if I were, I would be about four months along to feel the baby move. And I would only be about six to eight weeks along right now if I were. So, you see, I am not pregnant. You are mistaken." I could feel the calm resettling over me.

Sarah looked at me with a painful look on her face, she took my hand and said, "yes Nali, you are. Sit and I will explain and then if you still need proof, I will take you downstairs and show you on the ultrasound we have there."

I plopped down in my chair, why did we have an ultrasound machine here? Who has those just laying around the house? Why did they really have me here? The fear began to grip my chest again and I was beginning to have a hard time breathing. I put my head between my knees and took a couple of deep breaths.

Sarah came over and rubbed my back while I tried to recollect myself. I looked up and asked her, "Why is there an ultrasound machine here? And what are you guys planning to do with me? Am I a prisoner? Are you guys going to hurt me?" I could hear the panic setting into my voice. Apparently so did Sarah.

"Nali, calm down we are not the bad guys. We are here to help you and to make sure the baby is perfectly healthy and the delivery goes well. We are here to ensure the survival of both you and the babe." She gave me a long calming smile.

"I do not know what to believe anymore. Everything is happening so fast. I just do not know what to think anymore."

Sarah took my hand and lifted me out of the chair. She smiled a soft smile at me. "Grab your hot chocolate and come with me. I want to show you something."

I picked up my cup and grabbed the plate of grilled cheese because now my stomach was screaming with hunger. I followed Sarah down the stairs. We got to the red door, and she took out a key and unlocked the door. She opened the door and stepped to the side. She motioned for me to go through the door.

What I saw drew a gasp of surprise out of me. There was a complete delivery room complete with monitors, ultrasound, breakaway bed and a baby warmer, incubators and surgical instruments of all sorts.

"What is this place?" I asked allowing the surprise show through my tone.

"This is where we have planned for the baby to be born. It is sterile, safe and secure. It is stocked with everything we may possibly need for a healthy delivery for you and the babe."

I turned to face her because I could hear the fatigue in her voice. "Sarah, will you show me my baby? I want to see it.

She smiled and walked into the room; she closed and locked the door behind her. "Lay down on the bed and pull your pants down to your hips." She spoke as she moved the ultrasound closer to the bed.

I got on the bed and pulled my pants down to my hips like she said. She placed a washcloth around the top of my pants. Then she said, "This may be a little cold." as she sprayed some gel on my belly. It was then that I realized my belly had grown significantly in the last week. It looked as if I was about four months pregnant.

"Wow, I cannot believe how much weight I have put on. I need to go on a diet before I get fat."

Sarah giggled and said, "you do not need to go on a diet, Nali, this is normal for being pregnant. You are supposed to gain weight. Although, you do seem a little big for this term. But that could be because of the stress you have been through."

She placed this flat wand looking thing over my belly and spread the gel around. It felt wet, sticky, and nasty. It gave me goose bumps to feel its slickness sliding across my skin. She turned the monitor so I could see. And the screen looked like oil in water. I could not make out anything from it.

"What is that? I cannot see anything but smeared images."

Sarah giggled and said, "I haven't found your uterus yet. Be patient, you will see in a minute."

"How did you learn how to do all of this? I mean all this time I thought you were just this younger girl whom I'd met randomly. Just to find out that you are part of my life from long ago, which I still do not remember anything about."

"I learned this when it was invented. One of our people invented this machine to help our women to carry to term. It was a hard time for our people. No one seemed to be able to carry full-term children. I will explain it all in due time. Now let me concentrate."

She looked intently to the screen and suddenly said, "There you are, you little bugger." She pointed to the screen and said, "See this? This right here is your baby's head."

"It looks so weird. Like a little grape." It did look funny. There were no details, just the outline in black and white.

I was lost in the image of my child's head when I heard Sarah say, "Oh My, what is this?" She was silent, intently looking at the screen. I could see something, but I could not make out what it was.

"What? Is it ok? Please tell me what you are seeing because I cannot tell what you are seeing."

"Here is another one. You are having twins! You are having two babies, which is why your hunger and your temper is out of control."

"Wait! Did you just say I was having twins?! That is impossible! I mean…" my voice trailed off in thought. How could I take care of two babies?

"Can you tell me how far along I am and if they are girls or boys, if they are identical or not?"

Sarah looked at me and smiled. "I will tell you, just give me a sec." She dug a little deeper with her little wand thing. It felt as if she was trying to press it through my stomach. "Uh…Well…hello…." She said in a strange tone.

"What is it? What do you see? Please do not leave me in the dark…Please Sarah, just tell me."

"Well, see this? This is a little girl!" She sounded excited! "And this one is." She pressed the wand a little to the left and said, "a little boy. Oh, Nali! You have been blessed with a girl and a boy! I cannot tell if they will be identical or not yet, but I should be able to tell you that in a few more weeks. Oh, um…. wait, holy shiiiit!"

"What is it?" I asked in alarm, at the tone of her voice. Is there something wrong with the babes?"

"Well, no, but this is unprecedented, this has never happened before. Nali, you are having triplets! There are three babies!"

"Three?? How is this possible?" I started crying, this was all too much to take in. How could this be happening? My head felt like it was going to explode, my vision blurred, I could feel panic raising, how was I supposed to protect three children when I could not even protect one? "What am I going to do Sarah? How can I protect three of them when I let my little babe die?"

I laid there overwhelmed with the information I had just learned. I could see them on the screen, but somehow it seemed too impossible to be real. My mind wandered to the last few months, and I started to panic when I realized I had been with Dayvan and Jeremy! "Oh God! How could I have let this happen? How could I have been so irresponsible?" I was getting angry.

Sarah placed her hand on my shoulder and said, "This is a blessing, Nali! You have found favor! What is wrong?"

"I have been with more than one person. How will I tell them, and what will I tell them? I do not even know who the father is! What kind of mother am I?"

"We will do a DNA test on both of the men when the babies are born. The guys already know that you are pregnant. Jeremy heard the baby's heartbeat while we were still at the other house. He is the one who told us you were expecting. But he did not say anything about the second heartbeat though."

I started feeling dizzy. I needed something to drink. "Can you get me some water, please?"

"Sure, I will be right back." Sarah got up and headed toward the sink that was there. She took a little cup, filled it with water, and brought it to me.

I drank all of the water in the cup. I sat there still in disbelief. How could this happen to me? I didn't want children anytime soon. I wasn't ready to be a mother. "Sarah, how can I be a mother right now. I have some psychopath after me, wanting to kill me. How am I supposed to protect my children from him, I could not even protect myself?" I started crying, tears running down my face.

"Hush, dear. That is precisely why Jeremy went to capture Jargoan and bring him back here. You will be the one to deliver his punishment. Nothing will happen to you or your babies. We are doing everything we know to do to protect all four of you."

I felt the relief come over me. I heard a knock on the door. Sarah went over and asked for the safe word. Dayvan gave it. Sarah unlocked the door and let him in. He smiled at me. I returned the smile a second before the tears streamed down my face.

Dayvan rushed over to me and hugged me.

"Shhh. Nali, all is well. I know about the baby and I'm so happy for you right now. I know you are a great mother. I have seen you with children and you are wonderful."

"Babies, she is having triplets Dayvan." Sarah said.

Dayvan looked up in surprise. His mouth parted and then he closed it. He looked down at me, and tears filled his eyes. "Triplets, my love. Did you hear her?" he looked at Sarah and asked, "Boys? Girls?"

"Two are boys and the other is a girl! She has been blessed."

I drew in a deep breath because I had to tell him the truth. "Dayvan, I have to tell you this, I know that you know me and Jeremy have been together. These may very well be his children."

His eyes went sullen; I could see the anger flash across his face and then fear and then the tears streamed down his face. "I know this to be true. I know it is a chance. I hate the fact there could be any father but me. I am so sorry Nali for believing you were dead. I am sorry for not looking harder for you. I want these babies to be mine; I want you to be mine." He stopped and wiped the tears off of his face.

"I know you do Dayvan, and I am sorry I ever believed you were a cruel man. I should have known it was not you…" I remembered Jargoan raping me and fear tore through me. "Get away from me! Oh, God Sarah! These could be Jargoan's babies! He raped me remember!!! No, No No I will not have his children. Get them out! I do not want them! Take them out of me right now!" I felt as if I had just been invaded by something I never asked for. The joy I had just had, now was terror. What if they were his?

How could I love something that came from such evil? I could not, I knew I couldn't, I wouldn't allow his seed to grow, like a cancer inside of me. I felt like I was violated all over again. Disgust and I knew I was going to vomit.

"Nali, calm down! It is all right, they are not his children. Just calm down." Dayvan was stroking my head.

"How do you know they are not his?! There is no way to know that for sure! Quit lying to me!" I felt the pain rip through me, I felt as if I was being torn apart. "Sarah, help me! What is going on? The pain, make it stop!"

I felt a stick in my arm and a few seconds later I was falling into the black abyss of peacefulness that sleeping drugs give you.

CHAPTER 13

I started coming out of the sleep induced peace in time enough to hear Dayvan saying, "How do we know they are not his? What if they are his? Will they be evil as their father is evil?"

Sarah replied, "I do not think so. This could re-unite our clans together. Think about it, His clan could do no harm to Nali because she gave their family life! This could be the answer to the peace we have so desperately sought after!"

"Do NOT every say that! She will not have his children just so we can have peace with a clan that knows nothing but violence! How can this be happening? I was such a fool so long ago. But damnit! I loved her and she loved me. She did not want to be with them then. She still does not want to be with them. We must tell her who she is Sarah."

"Jeremy will not like it, not one bit. If we tell her the truth right now, he may have both of our heads. We must figure out a way to get her to remember on her own. There must be a way for her to remember." Sarah sounded too tired. Her voice was so strained.

I raised my head up so I could see where they were standing and said, "hey guys, what's going on?"

"Nali! How are you feeling honey? Are you hurting anywhere now?"

I thought about it for a minute and said, "No not anymore. Thank you, Sarah, for helping me earlier. I am sorry I got so angry. We will figure all of this out. I need to talk to Jeremy though. Is there any way of getting a hold of him?"

Dayvan shook his head no and said, "he left specific instructions for us not to try to contact him in any way because it may give up our location to Jargoan and Jeremy did not want to take any chance of that happening. He wants you protected at all costs, even if it risks his own life to do so."

"I cannot allow anyone else to die because of me! I need to talk to him, please!" I was feeling more and more that I was losing control of my own life. I could feel the anger building up in me again. My spine felt as if it was twisting in on itself, the pain wracked through me, and I let out a scream. Sarah came and tried calming me but all I could see was red! I wanted blood, anyone's, it did not matter who's it was. I stood up suddenly, throwing Sarah off me, and screaming, "this is my life, and I won't be told how to live it!" Then the pain was so horrible I fell to my knees, I could feel every muscle in my body tearing and starving for something, but I did not know what it was.

"Calm down, Nali!"

"DO NOT call me that! My name is Serraid!" I was screaming and could feel the power of authority in my own voice, and it half sounded like a growl. "I am tired of the games! I am tired of the lies and all the secrets! Call Jeremy NOW!"

"Ok, I will call him, just calm down, please!" Dayvan pleaded with me, but I was too far gone in this rage. I slammed my fist against his chest and screamed, "Quit telling me what to do!" Dayvan bear hugged me, and I immediately felt a little calmer, but this too seem to piss me off. How could he expect to be able to just calm me down with a hug? Who the fuck does he think he is? I was not thinking rationally, as the rage tore through me and my skin felt as if it was on fire. I needed to hurt something! I looked at him, and I bore into his eyes with mine, and I could feel him, his energy. I locked onto that and started to feed from it. I could feel him resisting and trying to break the connection, but he was not strong enough, like a mouse in a trap, he was mine.

"Serraid! Please let him go! You love him, please do not do this!"

My head snapped around to where Sarah was standing, I could hear Dayvan take a breath I did not know he couldn't take before. "You! You are supposed to be my best friend, my helper as you say. But what are you helping? What kind of friend stands there and lies in a friend's face? You are no better than the people trying to hurt me!"

Sarah looked shocked and hurt. I knew what I said was not true, but my anger was so strong now that there was no going back. I would have their heads for their treachery!

I tasted the medicine as it hit my vein before I even knew it was stuck in me. "Why? Why do you keep......." That is all I could get out before falling into the cold embrace of my truest friend, darkness. The cold, quiet, soothing darkness that was always there to embrace me, caress me with its cold touch, reaching into the deepest part of my soul, kissing me telling me it will all be all right.

There I was standing before a counsel made up of elders. My father being one of them. We were at war, and the only thing that could stop it was the wedding of two warring clans. My father had promised me to the Wraith clan, they were made of warriors, killers, pain bringers. I hated them, I did not want to marry into their clan, but like so many others, I, being a woman had no choice. I was after all the Succubus clan leader's daughter. I had no say in my life, except what my father told me to do. The incubus clan's leader was enraged, because his son wanted me as his bride, and oh how I loved him. He was handsome, kind, and I wanted a life with him. Dayvan was a good man. But Jargoan, he was horrible, and his entire clan was just like him. As Wraiths they only knew how to bring pain. They thrived on it. He was handsome, but that was a lie! His heart made him ugly! He only wanted me to control my clan; that's the only reason! I decided to make my own decisions.

I decided to sneak away with Dayvon, and we would hide and live our own lives together. We would become the leaders of our own clan one day and have a family. Children were rare for succubus' as we had a hard time carrying children, as our emotions made it virtually impossible. The incubus clans would help counter this by feeding off our emotions and taking them from us. Dayvon's second in command; Jeremy would sometimes come and help. Dayvon had confided in Jeremy about our plans of running away and had appointed him as my carrier, as he would help me carry the child to term. Then my best friend Sarah was going to be with us as a helper, some people call them slaves, because they serve us, but I loved Sarah and would never treat her like that.

On the night of the gathering, Me, Dayvan, Sarah and Jeremy all ran away together. We didn't think of the consequences of our actions because we were young. When the clans gathered and Jargoan's clan arrived, the girl they brought out was not me, but another girl from our clan. The wraith clan was furious as they thought my father had betrayed them. My father tried to explain that he didn't know of this treachery, and he would make sure that I was found and dragged back by the hair if needed. That's when Jargoan realized that Dayvon was also missing, Jargoan took that as an act of war. He killed my entire clan's men, keeping the women as trophies, enslaving them as baby makers! Word carried through the lands by the weeks end. When I heard about the slaughter, and that Jargoan was hunting us, my gut dropped. I cried and screamed. I wanted to go back but I was already with child, as me and Dayvan had been seeing each other for some time. We could not allow him to find us. We got on a ship and went as far as we could.

Jeremy stayed back to make sure that no one caught wind of what boat we got on.

Jargoan, was so furious! It was said that he would beat my mother every night while screaming "she was supposed to be mine!"

I woke up sweating! I knew this dream was real. I started screaming, I couldn't stop as I knew my selfishness cost my entire clan's life. The agony, the sheer pain that I felt in my heart knowing I caused all those deaths and the rape of my entire clan's women. I could not take it, I could not breathe. My shirt was too tight, I needed air, but I couldn't move my hands because they had been restrained yet again! "Get me the fuck out of these chains now! I will kill all of you!" The rage, and the pain ripping through me. I wanted to die. Then I felt it, a little push in my stomach, then another. I remembered that I was carrying babes, I calmed a little and apologized to them. I swear I could feel them, relax, like their energy calming me.

"Nali, I am right here. Please my love, please calm down and we will tell you what we can."

"I had another dream; I know that I caused the deaths of our clan's men and our clan's women to be enslaved." I told them about the dream. They paled as I told them, reliving what had happened. "Why did we do that? How could we do that? All I had to do was be his bride."

"He would have killed our babe, and you, just because another man sired it." Dayvan said.

"Our babe died anyways, so what good did it do? So many lives could have been spared if I had not been so selfish!" I cried as I spoke as I felt that I had caused a horrible war to become even worse.

"Nali, the war was raging before that, and he would have killed your father anyhow. He never intended to allow your father to live. He wanted all the clans. Some of the men and women from each clan made it out alive. And our clans remain today. That is why it is so important for you to have these babes. They will be the leaders of both of our clans by blood. Baby, don't you see how important they are?" He was laying his hand on my belly, which seemed to be getting bigger by the hour. About that time, one of the babies kicked, and he pulled his hand away in surprise. He looked at Sarah and asked if this should be happening so soon. Sarah seemed surprised and said that she had never heard of this happening before. But triplets were never heard of in any of the generations.

I could feel the hunger coming on again. "I need to eat something, I feel like I'm starving." Sarah went to get me some food. I took this time to speak with Dayvon and asked him, "why do you guys keep drugging me to keep me calm? Won't that hurt the babies?"

"No, it is safe for the babes. And if you get too angry you will feed off all the energy around you, including the babies. You could kill them and all of us Nali. This is why you must remain calm. You are a succubus; you can either feed off energy or give it."

Sarah came back into the room. "Here is some grilled cheese and hot ham sandwiches. You need to replenish your strength. We are going to tell you everything, and we will face Jeremy's wrath when he returns. He will be pissed because in telling you we risk everything. You must remain calm though. Each time you get angry enough to feed, it sends energy though our blood lines and can be traced. Do you understand?"

"Not really, but I promise to try to remain calm. If I start feeling like I am going to lose control I will have you stop. Agreed?"

"Agreed!" They both said at the same time.

"Nali, your dad promised you to Jargoan to save the clans, we were at war, and the Wraith clan was ruthless. They feed off pain and death; they thrive off it. When we lost our first child you were heartbroken. But when we lost our second you could not take it anymore. You tried to kill yourself. We stopped you, but you made us erase your memories and let you live a normal life as Serraid. You wanted, no, needed to forget the heart aches because you could not live with them anymore." Dayvan said with an empty look in his eyes. The pain clearly being relived all over again.

"How did our first child die?"

"That's not important right now."

"Yes, it is! I want to know."

Dayvan let out a long sigh, ran his hand through his hair, his lip trembled as he spoke, "I will tell you but please try to stay calm. We were young and learning. Promise?"

I knew I was not going to like what he had to say, I took a deep breath and tried to brace myself for what I was about to hear. "Yes, I promise."

"You were cooking dinner one night and I was tending to our fields. We had just landed here in America and were trying to make our way. Somehow one of the Wraith clansmen found us, and they attacked us, you tried hiding out of fear of them finding out about the baby. When they came there were three of them, and they almost killed me, you, out of rage came out to stop them. You began feeding from the energy around you, and you did not stop until they were all dead. You had to heal me as you also took almost all my energy as well. We did not know, Nali, we didn't know that you were also feeding from our unborn child as well. At least not until a couple of days later when you miscarried. You almost died. You didn't know, and you did not mean to." He grabbed my hand reliving that memory as if it were happening now.

As he spoke, I remembered that day. Tears started falling as I remembered killing my own child. My heart felt as if it stood still for a moment as it broke all over again. I was a horrible person; no wonder I have had such a horrible time. Karma was paying me back for everything I had done. My selfishness that cost countless lives, down to taking my own child's. I was not any better than Jargoan! I slammed my head down on the bed. I felt as if my insides were being ripped out of my spine. I was breaking and did not know how to handle this. When I could form words I asked, "How could any of you love me after what I have done?" I was disgusted with myself, and I was just now remembering. "Why would you agree to take those memories instead of making me face them? I did not deserve a way out of that! I deserve to die!" I was so mad at myself.

"Do not say that, Nali, you are powerful, and we were all young. You would never do these things on purpose!" Sarah looked at me with sadness in her eyes as she spoke. "You are like family; I have loved you since we were very young. You deserve happiness Nali, you deserve goodness. And It is time that we all heal and make this life better."

I looked at her with disbelief, how could she believe this? How could she look at me knowing that I betrayed our families, that I cost our families lives? How could anyone love someone so selfish that I ran away! Anger, pain, and sadness flooded me. Dayvan placed his hands on my belly, I could feel myself calm some.

"How do you do that?"

"What" Dayvan asked.

"Touch me and make me feel calmer" I said.

He answered, "Well as an incubus I can either give or take as well, and I can calm or make someone anxious. I can take life or give it and heal someone. Just the same as you or any of us."

I thought about that for a minute. Then I looked at Sarah and said, "since I asked you to take my memories can you give them back? Or unlock them somehow?"

"Well, I can, but it is better if you remember on your own, slowly, because that much pain all at once can be a dangerous thing. You have seen what you can do when you are angry or hurt. It is better to go slowly." Sarah said with concern and a knowing I could not understand.

"I understand." I did understand, but I felt like the only one that could not understand why I was allowed to forget. "Can you tell me why you agreed to take my memories, why you allowed me to forget and live a life without the pain?"

"I can answer that" Dayvan said. "When you lost Serraid, when the wolf came, you could not keep going. You tried to kill yourself. I stopped you, but you refused to eat, you refused to do anything. You were wasting away. Nothing we did helped. You were to heart broken."

I looked at Dayvan, he looked like he aged twenty years from just remembering that day. I reached out and tried to touch his hand, when I remembered that I was still restrained. "Can you please let me out of these?" Dayvan, released them and I sat up. I felt dizzy, and drained. I was starving. Sarah must have seen it because she came over and sat behind me and held me. I began to feel a little better.

"The babies are draining you as they grow." She reached out and touched my head, and I could feel a surge of energy go through me. I took a breath as it reached into the deepest part of me caressing my nerves like fine satin, playing them like an instrument looking for the right cord. I started crying as I could feel her love in that one touch.

"When you would not eat or drink or anything you asked us to let you die. We could not, we loved you too much. You begged us every day, and night to just let you die. You threw your energy into us, depleting your own.

We would replenish you every time you slept. Finally, one day you said that since we would not let you die, to just take away your memories. So that you could forget the pain. So, we all agreed to do that very thing. When we did, we took them all and allowed you to live the life you chose. We all stood back as watchers. As much as it hurt us to be without you, it was better than not having you at all." Dayvan was caressing my belly as he spoke. His eyes were empty, and tears were falling down his cheeks. The pain still being there.

"We made you believe your name was Serraid, as this was the one that broke your heart the most. We figured it would give you solace. You thrived in this new world, you were smart." Sarah said.

"I have these memories from when I was a child of people hating me and doing bad things to me. How is it that those are there? How is it that I remember parents that were not mine?"

Sarah looked at Dayvan, and they both paled a little. Dayvan finally spoke, "We do have an answer for that just yet." We do not know where those memories came from, kind of like my memory of the house fire that was not real."

"But I remember having those memories before seeing you as a therapist! How is that possible?" I was thinking back because this was making no sense at all. Was I going crazy?

"When we took your memories, we decided to just watch. We gave you a new identity and everything. Only we knew who you were. Or so we thought. When you came to see me for therapy, you began to tell me all these memories, I knew something was wrong, but did not know what. I still loved you, remember that. That is why I took up with you, and we ended up in a relationship. I could not walk away from you again. I see it as fate that you walked through my door. We all got jobs and did things where we could feed and thrive without being detected. He must have been watching us the entire relationship, and he chose the right time to take you from me and abuse you, for that is what he feeds upon, pain and fear."

"Wait, so you mean that even though we went through all the precautions that he still found us? And still manipulated everything to still get what he wanted? And that he kept the war going between our clans?" I could feel bile coming up my throat, as I thought about being with a monster like that, someone who I allowed to kill almost our entire clans; the man that killed my father and took my mother as a slave! I threw up, I could not stop it.

Dayvan and Sarah rubbed my back and held my hair as I threw up. They both spoke soothing words to me. I needed Jeremy…. "Where's Jeremy? I need him." I could see the irritation go over Dayvans face when I mentioned, Jeremy but I did not have time for his stupid jealousy right now.

"He is hunting Jargoan, he did call while you were asleep and said he was getting close. And that he should have him in a few days. Do not worry, he will be all right." Dayvan said with a coldness that irritated the fuck out of me.

"Tell me about Jeremy and why you are so angry with him over me? I understand jealousy but this is different." Sarah stilled as I asked this. Dayvan's face went red, and I could tell he was pissed. I didn't care; I was going to get answers for this. Because I loved both of them, and they both know it, and yet, here we are acting like fucking children!

Dayvan cleared his throat and said, "Jeremy was my second in command. He loved you as long as I did. But he knew that you loved me. He would never do anything to get in the way. When we took your memories, you found him at a club one night and you took him over. You took him to your place, he called me that night and begged me to get him, but I had not seen you and I was not going to risk your freedom. That was a mistake I wish I could take back every day. Because I thought Jeremy would be strong enough to walk away, especially after so many years had passed. But love knows no time. He could not tell you no, he loved you and you guys dated for a while. He fell head over heels in love, even more than he had been." Dayvans eyes were unfocused, he was clenching his jaw as he was thinking of what to say next.

I asked, "why don't I remember that? I do not remember dating him, in fact I do not remember anything but my childhood trauma, you being so kind and then you being horrible. And then college and working after I escaped. How is that possible?"

"We are not sure; we have been doing some research and have a theory but that is as far as we have gotten. I don't like going on theories, but as theories go, it is a compelling one." Dayvan said.

"What theory?" I asked him, hoping he would give an answer but afraid he would not.

"Since wraiths feed off pain, death, emotions we wondered if they could manipulate memories as well to create pain to feed from." Dayvon said softly.

I thought about that for a moment, if wraiths could really do that then would mean Jargoan had taken everything from me, my family, clan, child, memories, and the loves of my life! I could feel anger welling up inside of me again. Pain ripped through me as I felt the anger washing over me. I was screaming, all the pain, anger and hurt I could out.

Sarah placed her hands on my shoulders. "Nali, relax, just stay calm, remember the babies."

I tried to remember. I started calming down a little. "I need to take a break for a little bit guys. I need some time to process this. Is that, ok?"

"Yes of course." They both said.

I sat there thinking about everything that I was told. Trying to dig into my mind to remember. I felt the tears rolling down my cheeks. All of this and for what? What was gained by this? What was gained by my memories being taken except for a man to manipulate them even more. While I was crying, Dayvans phone rang. He stood to answer it. As he walked away, I looked at Sarah, she was crying as well. Remembering things that I am sure I could not yet.

"Sarah, did any of these actions do any good? Or was it all for nothing? I mean, it seems like Jargoan got what he wanted anyway. He hurt me, he hurt our families. What did I do?" I felt like I had let the entire world, all our people down because I was a selfish little brat that could not just do the one thing that needed to save our clans.

Sarah looked at me with a knowing, and she said, "Nali, you got to live, that was worth it. Yes, you still had pains, and heartbreak, but you are alive. We can still make a difference and bring peace to our clans."

"How can we bring peace to a clan that feeds off pain, death, anger and hurt? I do not see what good that clan is."

"It was not always this way. The wraith clan once thrived off love and kindness. But one day their leader was killed by their oldest son, because he was power hungry. He and his friends were always hurting people and feeding off the pain. When he controlled the clan, he brought pain to everyone and showed them how to feed off the pain. Their clansmen and women either fed off pain or they died. They had to comply to live. But now, we can show them a different way. We can show them they can still live off love. We take out Jargoan, he has no heirs, his line dies with him! You are the rightful leader of your clan; you can show them! Remember the pup you saved? The one from the wolf that killed your babe. Do you know what came of that pup? He lived and became the best protector of our lands. He grew up with love and learned to protect instead of kill. If your act of kindness can change the nature of an animal, think of what it can do to an entire clan? This is why he wanted to take all your love and turn it to pain. Because he knew you were the key to healing our clans!" She gave a weak smile when she spoke the last part.

Dayvan returned and said, "Jeremy was on his way back, and that I was to stay hidden no matter what." I nodded and asked when he would be here. I did not want this story session to end. He said, "tomorrow morning." I was anxious to see Jeremy; I had missed him. A part of me was afraid to show that because I did not want to hurt Dayvan, but I loved them both and either they were going to have to accept that, or they would both lose.

"So, I am the Succubus clan leader's daughter, and you are the Incubus clan leader's son. So, this makes Jeremy like your slave?" I was curious if they slaved people, or if they were friends like me and Sarah.

"Yes, to you and me. But Jeremy, his father adopted him, he was the son of another clan, his mother would never say who his father was. And now they are all dead, it is hard to say. All I know is that we grew up together, and he has always been there by my side as my second in command. He is my helper, your carrier. He was never to fall in love with you. His heart just did not get the memo." Dayvan seemed saddened. He looked like he was hurting.

I reached out and touched his face, turning him to face me. I kissed his lips and told him that I love him. Because I do, I love him, and I love Jeremy and I love Sarah. I loved all three of them the same. We were all going to have to talk about this and figure out what this meant for us. Because I could not picture my life without any of them in it.

We decided to rest and eat and then I fell asleep. I felt so drained. It was the first dreamless sleep I had in a while. When I woke, I heard a familiar voice, and I could not help but get excited. Just then, I felt his hand touch my face. A smile covered my face. I grabbed his hand without even opening my eyes. I brought him down and kissed his lips.

He moaned into my mouth, that is all it took, I opened my eyes and looked at him, I said, "I want to feel you inside of me, please Jeremy I need to feel you." I did not have to say anything else. Jeremy knelt down and kissed me hard enough to bruise my lips. He took off his clothes and climbed into bed with me. I slid my hand down his waist and found him hard and ready. I ran my hand down the length of him, and like always if felt like velvet. He twitched as I stroked him, I could feel myself getting wet just by touching him. He turned me over on my belly, and slapped my ass, I tilted it up, and said, "again." He slapped my ass harder. It made my pussy clinch as the pleasure built up inside me, I said, "again." He slapped me harder, and then rubbed it, he teased my opening with the head of cock and tried to push against him, but he moved back. I needed this, I needed to feel him. I asked with a raspy voice, "please." He slammed into me, every inch of him, and sat there allowing me to stretch for him. The instant pain of the quick invasion made my insides grow tight, and the warmth spread through me. I could feel my pleasure building, and he was not even moving yet. As if on cue, he began to move slowly in and out, moving to the very tip of himself then sliding all the way back inside. The feeling of him made me want to beg, I grabbed the sheets and pushed back into him, showing him, I needed more, harder. He read the writing in my movements; he grabbed my shoulders and started slamming into me. I started feeling my thighs getting warm, and my stomach tightening, my orgasm was working to the edge when he stopped, pulled out. I groaned at the emptiness left. He flipped me over, and slid back inside of me, looking me in the eyes, he said I love you Nali, I always have, and I want you to look at me, My lady when you cum for me. The love that I felt for him at that moment was unmeasurable. He looked into my soul and said cum for me right now, and just as he said it, I fell over the edge the orgasm coming on as if summoned by his words. I rode the waves just as he grabbed my lips with his and I could feel him spill his seed inside of me. I rode the second wave with him. Eating his pleasure is like a forbidden but tasteful fruit.

Just as we finished, I heard someone clear their throat and I could tell it was Dayvan by the irritation I heard in it. I opened my eyes and looked over at him, trying to tell him I love him just as much as I do Jeremy. I motioned for him to come to me. He walked over and I told him to stop. He looked at me with confusion, I said, "I want you to take off your clothes."

"Nali, I."

"Now!" I said.

He did as he was told. Then I motioned him all the way over and I took his hand and placed it on my breast, and the other inside me. He moaned when he felt how wet I was. He began moving his fingers in and out of me. I could feel the heat build inside of me; I moaned as the pleasure built. Jeremy moved over to the side and started sucking on the nipple that Dayvan was not playing with. A moan escaped my lips, I drew Dayvan down to kiss him, and he kissed me hard and deep, telling me with his actions just how much he wanted me. I moved him onto the bed; I climbed on top of him and slid him down my throat. I did not stop until he was completely in my mouth, there was nothing left of him I swallowed him whole. He moaned and I could taste him as his arousal grew. I moved my lips up and down his shaft, rolling my tongue around his head as I came up, looking him in the eyes, showing him how much I was enjoying him. I sat up and climbed on top and slid him inside of me. Jeremy moved behind me and as I started riding Dayvan, Jeremy started rubbing my clit. I began moving faster and I knew I was close. Dayvan began grabbing my hips, helping me. He squeezed harder and it threw me over and I rode my orgasm out on him. He was breathing heavily; I told him I love him and grunted and grabbed my throat and started thrusting inside of me until finally he reached his release. Jeremy also came on my back; we all enjoyed the pleasure of our orgasms together.

I never wanted this to end. This is how I wanted my life. With the men I love and the woman I love. Our family is whole, and open. I wish I could get my men to see this is when I am the happiest. Several minutes later we got up and showered. Sarah brought breakfast, she did not seem upset that we had sex without her. She knew that I needed this to bring the men together, because let's face it, it is not her they have the problem with.

After we ate breakfast, I decided that I would break the ice and start the conversations again. I was not sure if Sarah and Dayvan told Jeremy they had told me anything, but I was going to say now.

"Jeremy, did you find Jargoan?" I asked

"Yes, it was hard to find him, but I did. He is being detained now." Jeremy said with a satisfied look on his face.

"Where is he? Is he here?" I was anxious to face him and make him pay for everything he had done to our families.

"No, he is not here. I have my people getting him. They are waiting till he is alone and they are going to grab him and then call me. I want to make sure you are protected no matter what." He said with a satisfied look on his face.

"I want to talk to him when we have him. I need answers. I deserve answers!"

Jeremy looks around the room with a questioning look on his face. "What are you talking about? Answers for what he did to you. We can get those."

"No, I want answers for our families! I want to know what happened with my mother and the other women from our clans. I want to look him in the eyes when He realizes that it's the woman that escaped him that takes his life!" I could feel the venom in my words as I said them.

Jeremy looked pissed! Nostrils flared and he turned to Dayvan and Sarah and asked, "What did you two do?!

We had an agreement! We would not tell her anything until we knew it was safe!!!!"

Sarah spoke up, with her chin held up in defiance, "She needed to know. She was a danger to herself and to all of us but most of all to the triplets! She needed answers to keep her calm, she knew we were hiding things and that was making it all worse."

"Wait, what do you mean triplets? Like, there is three of them?" He looked like he was scared.

"Yes, as in there is three of them. Two boys and a girl." Sarah said with pride.

"This is unheard of; how is this possible? Twins are very rare, but triplets have never been documented in any of our clans. Are you sure there are three?" He was scratching his head as he was taking all this in.

"I'm not an idiot. I did go to school for this, and I know how to count. Yes, there are three and they are all three very healthy babes. They are draining her energy, but she is doing well. And she is handling the information that we are giving her very well." Sarah said with defiance in her voice.

"What have you told her so far?"

We filled him in on what I know. And I told him that I have more questions. I have so many more questions. But

I made sure he knew that I wanted to ask Jargoan questions as well. Jeremy said he did not want me anywhere near Jargoan while I was pregnant that it wasn't safe for anyone including the babies. I told him this is different, I could explain how I knew it, but I knew this was different. These babies were special, and I knew we had the strength to make it through anything.

Jeremy finally agreed that if he felt it was safe that he would allow me to ask Jargoan questions, but the first sign of anything being wrong. He would pull me away and I was not going to fight him at all. I agreed.

CHAPTER 14

The next day we were getting ready to eat lunch when Jeremy's phone rang and he jumped up, startling all of us.

"WHAT!! How did this happen?" Jeremy was yelling at his phone. We could not hear what was being said on the other end of the phone, but we could tell it was pissing Jeremy off. Jeremy screamed "FIND HIM!" and slammed his phone down on the table startling all of us. "FUCK!!!" he screamed.

"What's going on, Jeremy?" Sarah asked.

"They had him, they fucking had him, and his goons came out of nowhere and got the drop on my guys. Jargoan got away, he was wounded, but he got away! Damnit!!!" He screamed as he hit the wall with his fist. "How does he keep fucking getting away?!!! He growled.

I walked over and touched his shoulder and softly caressed it, allowing calming energy to shower through. "We will get him, I know we will, we must. He will mess up and when he does, we will snuff him out like a bad flame." I let my feelings sink into my words so he could feel them.

I felt one of the littles wiggle about that time. I giggled, taking Jeremy's hand and placing it on my belly, letting him feel the movement. His eyes lit up and a smile spread across his face for a moment. He looked at me, and said, "that is the coolest thing I have ever felt. Does it hurt?"

I giggled and said "no, it feels weird but doesn't hurt."

"Our babies need us to finish this up, so they never have to worry about paying for our fuck ups." He was so solemn when he said ours.

I nodded, "Yes our babies do need us to protect them." I looked right into his eyes, letting him know that these are his babies as much his as they are mine or Dayvans. "It doesn't matter which one of you are the father we will raise them as all of ours. We will be our own little clan."

A smile spread across his face. I could hear Dayvan groan behind us, I turned fast and said, " Listen we are all a family and we WILL raise these babies as all of ours, if you can't get on board with this then you can get the fuck out because I don't have time to keep stroking your ego every time you feel like you are entitled to something and no one else is!" I was so pissed that he was choosing now to make this a pissing contest. I was tired of the jealousy bullshit, and we were going to deal with this now. A house divided and all that.

"Dayvan, I love you! I also love Jeremy the same, and I love Sarah just the same. None of you are over the other, I love all three of you equally, none less! Why can't you understand that? Why can't you accept that?" I glared into his soul daring him to be honest with us all.

He looked at me for a moment with a shocked look on his face, and said, "Nali, I have loved you for centuries. I deserve to have you. All that we have been through, everything we have sacrificed. Don't you believe we deserve to be together?"

"You are not the only one that has loved me for centuries, Jeremy and Sarah have both loved me just as long, and we have all sacrificed. No, I haven't lost babies that were theirs by blood, but bond; we all felt those losses. How dare you think that you are the only one that felt those losses! How dare you feel like their emotions do not matter as much as yours!" We were fixing this shit today.

Jeremy looked between me and Dayvan with a look like he wanted to say something but didn't know if he should. I looked at him and asked if he had something to add.

Jeremy said, "Dayvan, I know that you have loved her for a long time, so have I. I have loved her since the first day I saw her playing around the well. I remember the smell of her hair, and the dirt on her face. So, I understand that you feel like you should have her. As a man, I feel possessive too, but she loves us both, and that is enough. If she wants all three of us, then why shouldn't she get what makes her happy? Why should our happiness surpass hers?"

With that I respected Jeremy a little more than I had already. I thought about what he said and added. "I know that My feelings do not surpass anyone else's either. We must all be in or all be out. I cannot choose between any of you, and I will not raise babies in a house that is torn with jealousy they can't put their own feelings aside for the children. The feelings that are allowed to overtake someone are the very feelings that drive the person. Just look at Jargoan; He wanted power, he wanted to rule over people and look at what it cost his clan. I'm not saying anyone here is like him at all, but the feelings we allow to rule us are the ones that we either build upon or ruin things." We were all quiet and I could tell that everyone was thinking about what I had just said.

After a few moments, Sarah spoke up and said, "Nali is right, I do not think anyone ever wakes up one day and says to themselves, 'I think I will be a horrible monster today.' They believe that their feelings and their beliefs are right and justified. They believe they can change the world."

We were all silent thinking about what she said. My stomach flipped because to believe there was anything good about Jargoan was too much. There could never be anything good to such an evil person. "No!" I said, shaking my head. "I cannot believe there is anything good to him or his evil followers! He thrives on death and apparently has for a long time. Just look at what he has done to us! Look at the fucking mess he has made of our lives and tell me you think there is anything good inside that fucking evil person!" I was crying by the end of my sentence. I missed my life, my job, my clients. "I just want to go back to the way things were, where I had a job, and was happy and finally healing from all his bullshit! He fucking took that from me; no, from us!" I sat down in the chair next to me.

Dayvan and Jeremy came and placed their hands on my shoulders in an attempt to calm me, but I could feel the furry beginning inside of me. I looked at Jeremy and asked if this furry was normal in a succubus pregnancy. He assured me he did not know as he had never found anything on triplets. That is when fear hits me again. "What if these are his? Could this be why I am feeling all this anger, hate and out of control?" I was sobbing because I did not want to think of these babies being his. I could not, I would not.

"The children are not like their sires, everything I have read it all really depends on the love they are showed. In any species it's the same Nali. Do not worry about those things right now it is not good for them." Jeremy spoke with truth. He had been researching this since finding out that I was pregnant, but triplets changed everything, because no one in our species had ever had triplets. Births were very rare, as the succubus would lose the babes before they knew they were pregnant, due to feeding off the energy, our bodies were made as a top predator. We could drain you dry, and you would never know what was happening. I too had been studying.

Sarah came and knelt in front of me, hugging me firmly. "It will all be ok; we are all together now. We are family. These babes will be so loved there will never be anything evil to them."

I tried to smile at her but couldn't quite make it reach my eyes. I knew she knew that it was forced, but I did not care.

Four months have passed, and nothing has happened except I have gotten as big as a whale. I have to have help getting up, and down out of a chair, and to turn over in bed. My belly is see through, and I can feel the babies more now. I can tell which one is kicking. The little girl is so strong. She is going to be a warrior. We have not heard anything on Jargoan and have not been able to locate him.

With winter coming and the babes as well, we are worried about more important things at the moment. I am starting to get worried because what happens if something goes wrong with the birth? Since we still have not been able to find anything in any archives about triplets. We have been keeping this a secret while researching, we do not want anyone to find out.

We were all sitting around the fire folding the baby clothes we had collected and blankets. I am nesting. I need everything to be perfect. My nerves are worse these days, the closer it gets.

While drinking hot chocolate and folding clothes there was a soft knock at the door. We all stopped what we were doing, because no one knew we were here, and no one ever came out this far into the Adirondack mountains, especially in the winter; that's why Jeremy chose this place. He had it built over 40 years ago for hiding just in case something was to happen.

The house has three stories, the basement which has a medical ward for delivery which extends into a tunnel that goes through the little mountain peak we were on, for escaping. Jeremy had added this when he found out about the babes. The main floor included the foyer, living room, dining room, kitchen.

The second story is where the bedrooms are, there is also a back set of stairs placed in the walls of each room to get to the basement, not that I could use those very quickly these days. There is a pond not far, and the trees are beautiful with the colors changing. The only way to find this place it to follow herd paths, which most people do not do anymore. I am too big to move out of the room before opening the door, so I just sit there with Sarah, and Dayvan on each side of me.

Jeremy looked out the peep hole in the door, and there were what appear two hikers and one was injured. "They don't feel like they are lying. I think she is really injured. But I do not know how they found this place. I really do not want to allow them inside.

Dayvan, you and Sarah help Nali up and Sarah you take her downstairs, Dayvan and I will go outside and see what this is about." The helped me up and Sarah and I made our way to the stairs. I did not want to leave the guys. I was worried, what if Jargoan had found us, what if this is a trap? "Please be careful, I love you both and I do not want to lose you. I need both of you. Do you hear me?" I said.

"We will be careful, now you go and hide and make sure the babies are safe in case this is trap." Dayvan said.

Sarah and I went downstairs and went into the safe room; this room is stocked with everything we needed to live for at least 15 days. And If I went into labor in here there were warmers and surgical tools and supplies in here just to be safe. Jeremy and Dayvan had really thought of everything.

I sat down in a chair. I was nervous because we could watch what is happening upstairs, but we are locked in here. There is no way anyone can make it through these walls. They were 5-foot reinforced concrete walls; the ventilation system was separate from the house and so was the water supply. We really were safe, but my guys were not, they were out there to deal with whatever may happen.

Sarah and I watched on the monitor as the guys opened the front door. The woman really did look injured. Her leg looked like it had been torn up by some kind of animal. The man also looked as if he had been attacked by something.

I felt like I was going to throw up as the memory of the wolf killing my baby flashed into my mind. I grabbed the trash can and released the contents of my stomach.

"Oh my god, are you ok Nali?" Sarah said with fear as she ran to me.

"Yes, I seen them and the memory of the day little Serraid died flashed through my head." I answered while taking the bottle of water she handed me.

"I cannot imagine, but I am here. And there is no wolf. Look, it is just two people. They do not look dangerous. The really do look injured."

I looked at the screen and all of a sudden Jeremy grabbed the guy by the collar and throat and lifted him off the ground against the wall, He was yelling in the guys face asking him how he found this place and who he worked for. I could tell by the look on the guy's face he had no idea what Jeremy was talking about.

I went for the safe room door, I needed to stop him, I needed to save this man, I was not sure why, but we needed to save him!

"Help me!" I screamed at Sarah as I tried to open the door.

"No, we can't go out there, it's not safe yet!" Sarah was scared I could taste it in the air.

"We need to save that man! I am not sure who he is but I know we need to save him! Go stop Jeremy, tell him not to hurt him! Please!" I tried to push as much urgency into my voice as I could. Sarah reluctantly listened after I promised to lock the door behind her.

I turned and watched the screen as Sarah ran up the stairs and yelled for Jeremy to stop. "Why? This man should never have been able to find this place! He is lying and I am going to kill him before he can alert anyone to where we are!"

Sarah answered, "Nali said NO! She said that we must save this man. She said that she does not know why but she knows in her heart we must save him! Please Jeremy, we can put them in the cells if you want, but please listen to Nali, I can tell she knows what she says." Her eyes were wide, and hands shaking.

Jeremy looked at her, and back at the man, he was scared too. He begged "please I don't know any of you, I just need help for my daughter. Please" Jeremy had a look on his face that I could tell even over the monitor that he was warring inside himself on what he should do. When finally, he said, "fine, we put them in the cells, we will treat their wounds and keep them separate. Am I understood?" He dropped the guy as he asked the question.

"Yes, we will do that, now let me help her, because she doesn't look like she is going to make it much longer without our help." Sarah said as she rushed over to the woman whose let looked really bad.

"Dayvan grab her and bring her to the surgical room! I am going to need to suture these wounds and fast!" Dayvan did as she asked.

I sat in the safe room trying to find some answer in my mind as to why we needed to save this man. Who was he? Why was he here? Why did I feel like I needed to save him, He felt familiar somehow. But I am sure I have never seen his face before.

Jeremy came into the safe room where I was still sitting. "Explain, now! Why would you risk everything for someone we do not even know? Why would you ask me to spare someone we do not know?"

"I don't know, I just felt the strong urge in my heart to save him. I am not sure why, I just know he is important somehow. He seems familiar in a way, but I know I have never seen him before." I explained with confusion sounding in my voice.

Jeremy came over to me and knelt, "He felt familiar to me as well, I thought it was someone working for Jargoan, and I wanted to kill him. The girl, though, is really hurt. He said they were attacked by a black bear. They camp up here off grid once a year as a father daughter thing, but never have had an issue with bears, or at least not like this before." He was rubbing my hand.

I looked at him and wished I could explain how I 'knew' what I knew but there were no ways to explain. I have had these feelings and premonitions before, and they are always right. "I know it may not make sense right now, but we will figure it out. Now, let's go meet our guests the proper way. Shall we?"

"Nali, I do not think that is a good idea. I do not want them to see you right now, not when it is so close to the due date, you could have those babies any day now." He was worried, I could tell be the waiver in his voice.

I reached up and touched his face, caressing it softly, "Jeremy, I know you are worried but there is something about this man. I need to speak with him, please."

Reluctantly, Jeremy stood up and helped me out of the chair I was sitting in. We went to the door when we heard a girl scream a blood curdling scream. Jeremy said, "Stay here! Nali, I mean it, shut the door, and do not open it unless we have our safe words." He kissed me and shut the door and was gone. I went to the monitors and tried finding out where the scream had come from. It was from the surgical room; the girl woke up and was in a fit of fear. Her eyes were wide, the whites showing like deer in headlights. She was fighting against her restraints and was screaming, seeing something that no one else could see. I knew that look, she was reliving a memory, a flash back she was stuck in it. I did the only thing I knew I had to do, I headed out the door to go help her. When I reached the surgical room, she was thrashing on the table, they had sedated her, but it was not working.

"Nali!! What are you doing here? I told you to stay put!" Jeremy screamed angrily.

"I know, but I saw her face, look at her Jeremy, she is scared! She is stuck in a memory. Something has happened to this poor girl, and she is stuck in it right now! She needs my help!" Sarah walked over with compassion on her face.

"Nali, I have tried to help her, I cannot even reach through the fear to help her right now. She is going to have to go through this on her own. You cannot risk the babies to help her, what if you." Her voice faded off as she looked like she was sorry before I could even speak.

"How dare you! How dare you mention that! I know my limits now, I know, ok! Fuck you Sarah for bringing that horrible day up!" She was talking about the day that I drained my baby's energy inside of me. I stood there in disbelief that she would mention that.

Tears started rolling down my face. The girl was still screaming, not ever faltering. I could hear her father down the hall, yelling asking what we were doing to his daughter. Everything was fucked.

"You know she did not mean it like that, Nali. She is just worried about you and the babies, is all. She would never intentionally hurt you like that." Dayvan said.

I knew he was right, in my heart I knew. But the pain was real, none the less.

"I know, but it hurts. I know what this girl is going through and I can help her. And yes, I can help her without hurting the babes. Please just let me help her" I whispered the last part.

He moved to the side and motioned me over to her. I reached her and she was thrashing against the restraints, eyes wide open but not seeing what was around her, no she was deep in this memory. Whatever triggered this was bad and deeply rooted. I walked around her feeling the energy around her trying to find a piece to pull at. That is when I felt it. A familiar energy. I gasped and pulled back, heart was racing and I was sweating. My hand trembled as I brought them to my lips to hide my fear.

"What is it, Nali?" Jeremy was there in an instant. He was worried. I could not blame him. I was scared too. What if I had made a horrible mistake? What if I had let the monster through the front door? I could not live through another loss, I just couldn't. I did not want to tell him what I felt because I was afraid, he would kill the girl. But I didn't want to hide anything either.

"Jeremy, it is the energy that is wound around this girl. Whatever memory she is stuck in right now deals with him." I could not hide the fear in my voice or my trembling hands and tearing eyes.

Jeremy pulled me away from her. "No!," I said. "She is innocent, what ever happened to her, happened at his hand. I have to help her." I walked over to her again. And I placed my hand upon her head. I suspected I could look into memories, after seeing a glimpse of hers the first time I touched her. So, I tried to look again with intention and what I seen there was horrible. Jargoan had her tied up in a cell, naked, cold, dark. He starved her, raped her for days. He fed off her pain. With every pain and every fear, he inflicted his wounds healed. I gasped and removed my hand as quickly as I placed it there.

"Oh. My. God! She…He…" I couldn't get the rest of my words out because I was crying too much. He had used her to heal. Jeremy had injured him so badly that he had to use someone to heal him and she was the unlucky contestant.

"What is going on Nali?" Sarah came and hugged me while I cried.

"He used her to heal. He held her captive for days in a cell, it was cold, dark, and wet. He had someone hurt her while he fed and healed off of her pain. She almost died, he used one of his slaves to save her and heal her and when she was healed, he began again he did this seven times until he was healed." I looked at Jeremy; He was pale because he knew exactly what caused this.

He sat down on the floor as his legs gave out on him, he held his head in his hands. "I did this, I made him do this to her. I'm a fucking piece of shit! How could I let him get away to do this to anyone?" He was crying now.

I looked over at him even though he could not see me through his hands, "Jeremy, you know this was not your fault. He chose to do this. He has slaves he could have used but he chose to use her instead. This is NOT your fault." I pushed all sincerity in my voice because I needed him to know this was not his fault. "Please look at me, love." He just shook his head; he was too deep in his own guilt.

"I cannot, I do not deserve anything, no amount of forgiveness could undo what has been done to her. Just look and listen to her, Nali! I did this! I did this to her when I didn't kill that bastard!"

"No, you didn't. Any more than I killed my babe because I did not kill the wolf that night." He looked up at the mention of that night. "You know you couldn't' have done anything that night, Nali, you know it." He said as he got up to come to me. "Yes, I know, and You know you couldn't have done anything different to stop this either." I looked right at him. He reached me and hugged me. "I don't deserve you; you know that?" he asked. "It is me that doesn't deserve you, Jeremy."

I went to the girl and placed my hand on her head and another on her heart. I reached that energy of that memory and I healed it. I took it and placed it somewhere out of her sight. She blinked as if seeing the room for the first time. "Please, please let me go, I won't tell anyone. Just please, I have a family that will miss me, they will come looking for me." She pleaded.

My heart ached for her; she still thought we were going to hurt her. I spoke softly and motioned for no one to move. "My name is Nali, and we are not going to hurt you. You were attacked by a bear while camping with your father, he is here too. Please calm down so we can finish suturing your leg. What is your name?" I looked at her softly. She looked at me in disbelief. "Stormy my...my name is Stormy."

"Nice to meet you, Stormy. Can you tell me your father's name?" I said gently so I would not spook her.

"His name is Jimmy. Is he ok? Did the bear kill him?"

"No, he is ok, he is down the hall in another room. Safe." I assured her. I pointed around the room and introduced everyone as I pointed at them. Her face paled when it landed on Jeremy.

"Oh God you! You he is going to kill you; he said your name so many times! He said he was going to kill you if he ever found you!" She was starting to get hysterical again. I touched her shoulder and urged her to calm down. I pressed a little calming energy into her.

"Stormy, I am going to help you heal a little. Can you relax for a bit?" I asked with a softness I did not even know I was capable of. She nodded. I began to press healing energy into her. I drew a little from everyone in the room to feed to her. Making sure not to touch the baby's energy.

All of a sudden, the babies started kicking hard. I was gasped because I thought I had hurt one of them. Then I felt it. A new energy leaving my body reaching out to Stormy, she calmed down and went to sleep, then just as quickly as it began it was over. "Huh, that's weird." I stated.

"What was that?" Sarah asked

"I am not sure, but I think one of the babes just calmed her and put her to sleep. I could feel the energy leave my body, but it was not mine." I looked down at my belly with wonder.

Jeremy, Dayvan and Sarah all came over and pressed their hands to my belly and as if to answer all three babies moved. They all gasped at the same time. I giggled because, well, it was funny to see three full grown warriors get startled by a couple of babies.

"How is this possible? You are sure we have looked everywhere for information on triplets?" I asked. Because there had to be a good explanation for all of this.

"Yes, we have looked everywhere we know of and found nothing. Let's talk to Jimmy and see if he knows anything about the time that Jargoan had Stormy." Jeremy said. He looked at me and Sarah, "You two stay here and take care of her, we are going to see what he knows. Until we know he is safe I do not want him anywhere near you and the babies. Got it?" I shook my head in agreement. Because this girl needs our help right now.

Me and Sarah worked on Stormie's leg cleaning it and suturing it as best as we could. This was a deep wound and would take a while to heal. It would take several sessions of our healing to help her, or she would be left with a horrible scar. We were cleaning up and putting supplies away when she woke up.

"Can I have some water please?" I took her over a glass of water and helped her dink it. "Where are we? Is my dad ok?" she was looking around out of fear mixed with curiosity.

"I will not tell you exactly where we are, but your dad is fine. He had some minor injuries. But mostly he is worried about you. The men are down the hall talking to him now."

The worry went across her face, and I could feel her energy shift. "How well do you know that Jeremy guy? I am asking because this man held me captive, he beat and raped me, starved me for weeks. And he kept talking about he was going to kill Jeremy. I know it is him because he would describe him when he was spitting his rage on me." She was crying then she looked up and said, "Wait, you said you name was Nali? Oh god he is going to find us all. He will kill us!" She was becoming hysterical again.

I tried to sound as calming as I could. "Stormy, no one is going to hurt you. I am so sorry you had the misfortune of meeting that monster. Jeremy is a good guy, he almost killed Jargoan, but Jargoan's goons got him away. He unfortunately used you to heal himself. I am so sorry you were caught in the middle of all of this. Does your dad know?"

"Yes, he was the one that rescued me. He killed four of this Jargoan's men when he did." She was still crying. I gave her a tissue to wipe her eyes. She sniffled and said, "then you are like us? We are, were, used to be of the Incubus clan. But the entire clan had to go into hiding from Jargoan. Which clan are, were you from?" She was starting to relax again.

"I am from the Succubus clan, so is Sarah. Jeremy and Dayvan are from the Incubus clan. I think you should talk to them."

"Are you sure that Jeremy is from the incubus clan?" she asked with sincerity in her voice.

"Why do you ask?"

"Because that man said he wouldn't allow Jeremy to take what is rightfully his!" She said with no feeling.

"He was talking about me. It is a very long story. One we will all have to talk about together. If that is ok with you to wait for the guys?" I asked her.

"Yes, I need some rest anyway. Thank you, Nali, for helping me heal. OH!" she exclaimed just noticing my belly. "Oh heavens! You are pregnant? How far along?"

"I am, and almost nine months now. I am due any day. So, you can see why we are being so cautious." I stated.

"Yes, you must be as there has not been a birth in any of the clans over one hundred years. Your baby will be the first new life we have to celebrate!"

"Did you say 100 years?" I asked her because surely that had been life born more recently.

"Yes, my dad helps all the clans, he has been working on fertility issues trying to figure out why none of the females can get pregnant. To this day he does not know. We have run tests, on the males and females and still have not found a reason as to why."

"Wait." Sarah said, "You mean no one has had babies, like not even mixed with humans?"

"None that we have found, and there is no physical reason for it that we have found. You can ask my dad about it. He has all of his research."

"Jeremy!" I yelled out the door. He came running, thinking something was wrong.

"Sorry, I did not mean to scare you, you need to know this. Her and her father are from the incubus clan. Her father has been doing research because there has not been a birth from any of the clans in one hundred years. Our babies will be the first ones. Maybe he can help us?"

Jeremy looked as confused as I felt. He scratched his head. Then he turned without saying a word and walked toward Jimmy.

I turned to go back into the room where Sarah and Stormy were. Sarah had undone Stormie's restraints. She was sitting there stretching. "Thank you, Nali. For everything." She hugged me as she said it. It startled me a little, then I relaxed into it. One of the babes decided to say hello by pressing against my stomach.

"OH!" she startled, "Oh my gosh, that felt so weird! Can I feel again?" I giggled at her innocence. "Yes, here let me see your hand" I placed it over the little girl, I could feel it was her, as if on cue she ran her little hand under Stormy's hand. I had to admit; it was pretty cool to share this with someone other than our little clan. I have felt so hidden I forgot how much I missed people.

"I'm going to go make supper, and then we can all talk around the table." Sarah said. With that she turned and headed for the kitchen, leaving me and stormy alone, Stormy enjoying the feel of the babes moving, and I will admit I was enjoying the contact.

CHAPTER 15

After about an hour of letting Stormy rest, and me just enjoying the babies moving, I was playing with the necklace that Sereena had given me. It felt like so long ago, I missed her smile and snarky remarks. I missed my life; but now I have a new life facing me. I am going to be a mom. Tears started to fill my eyes with the sadness of my old life and the joy of the new one I was facing.

"Dinners ready!" Sarah yelled down the stairs. Stormy came over and helped me get up, about the time my belly rumbled. I was starving.

"Stormy, how are you feeling? Are you up to going upstairs?"

"Yes, I think it will be good for us all to talk together." She said with a smile. When she noticed the necklace around my neck. "Oh my god! That is so beautiful, where did you get it!" She said as she rubbed the stone.

"I got this from a dear friend of mine, she is such a kind soul, you would love her. She's an older woman but she is snarky and funny." I said with a smile that lit my eyes and lit my face to the memory of my friend.

"It must be very old; it looks like an antique but it's very beautiful."

"Thank you" I said as we walked up to the stairs. "I think I am going to take the lift this time. I am not sure I can haul these babies up these stairs." It seemed so far away. "I'll meet you up there."

Once upstairs I could smell the food. She had made some honey siracha chicken and mashed potatoes and gravy and fried okra. Mmmm, my favorite. Since being pregnant I liked dipping my okra in chocolate ice cream. Don't judge. I am eating for three.

"That smells like heaven" I told Sarah as I kissed her on the forehead. I turned and went to sit down. The guys were not up here yet. "Have you heard anything from the guys since calling us for dinner?"

"Not yet, but I bet they will be up soon. Men cannot stay away from food." As if on cue, they came through the kitchen door. With Jimmy in tow.

"Sarah, Nali, this is Jimmy." Dayvan said while walking through the door.

"Dad!" Stormy jumped up and ran over and hugged him.

"Hey storm, are you ok? You were so hurt when I found this place." He was looking her over like a loving father. Watching it made my heart warm; this was going to be all of us in a few short months.

"I'm good dad, Nali and Sarah healed me almost completely and sutured what would not heal just yet. They did amazing dad." She was smiling with her entire face. I could tell by the look she loved her dad very much.

I wondered if this is how it would be with Jeremy and Dayvan, if they would accept not knowing who fathered the babies. And just being able to love them.

"Nali, are you all right? Why are you crying?" Jeremy came over to me.

"I was just thinking this is going to be us in a very short time with our babies. I was just hoping that you and Dayvan could love them the way he clearly loves his daughter." I had tears rolling down my face from the love I felt.

"We will all work this out together. But right now, we need food and information." He kissed the top of my head and sat next to me.

Jimmy and Stormy came and sat at the other end of the table and Sarah and Dayvan came and sat between them and us. We were all getting our food and settling in for the feast. We ate until we were all full. Which did not take much since these babies were taking up most of the room I had these days. I could tell they were getting cramped because they kept trying to stretch but there was no more room.

After dinner, the guys helped Sarah clean up, we all made our way into the living room and got comfortable. Jeremy and Dayvan sat on each side of me. I wanted Sarah near me but there just was not enough room.

"Jimmy was telling us about him and Stormy. They are also from the Incubus clan. But Jimmy is a historian by birth. He keeps all our history, our clans, the wars and so on." Jeremy looked at me when he said this.

"We know there was a war when Jargoan tried taking all the power from the clans." I said, not understanding where Jeremy was going with this.

"No, the war before Jargoan." Jeremy said. "I will let Jimmy tell you."

Jimmy cleared his throat. "I know this is going to seem really hard to believe but what I am about to tell you all is the truth. I have no reason to lie." He paused as if waiting for one of us to say something to stop him. When we just sat there looking at him, he continued.

"Hundreds of years ago, about eight hundred years ago now, there was only one clan. The succubus, incubus and wraiths, witches and historians all lived as one people. We all had our roles. The incubus and succubus had babies, and the wraiths helped them come into the world, the witches helped heal and protect us and our lands. They were our helpers. We all were one. We had each other's children. We loved freely. Then one day one of the wraiths was caught stealing a babe, she could not have any of her own, you see, so she tried to take one of the succubus babies. The father of the babe caught her and killed her, this did not go well with our council members, as you can imagine. The council was made up of incubus, succubus, wraith, one historian and a witch. This was to keep all the balances equal." Jimmy took a drink of his water before beginning again. "This woman's husband demanded that the man who killed his wife be killed as well, but the wife of the husband, the mother of the babe who was almost taken, demanded that he live as he was defending their baby. The dead woman's husband was furious. And demanded from the counsel a fair ruling, either the husband die, or they give him the baby that his wife wanted in place of his wife who was murdered. The council took three days to decide, because they could not produce an agreement on which was the most peaceful way to solve this. So, they said since they could not agree that the men would battle to the death, and which ever one lived would be the baby's father and the mother's husband. They felt this was a fair deal, the fates could decide who was worthy to live." Jimmy paused as if remembering like it was happening.

"What happened? Did they fight? Who won?" I asked. Wondering how this could start a war that would divide clans.

"Well, the men fought, and the father won, killing the man whose wife was caught trying to steal the babe. The council determined that fate had decided the original father was worthy of his babe. They thought this was the end of it. But the man's brother-in-law was furious, for he had now lost a sister and a brother-in-law over one babe. So, one night, he snuck in the babe's window and drained the energy out of the babe while it slept. He became the first deadly wraith. He fed on another taking their entire essence from them. He did this to the mother and the father leaving them all there for the village to find." He was now shivering remembering this day.

"Wait, so he killed them? Why? Why kill the babe when it was an innocent in all of that?" I asked horrified at the thought of someone doing this to a child, covering my own belly as if to protect my babies from what could have been.

"Yes, he killed them all. When the village found them the next day, they knew what had happened as the brother-in-law boasted about transcending to what he was meant to be. A live taker! He went around and told all the wraiths that they were brainwashed into believing they were live givers, when taking their lives was so much more rewarding. Such became his following. Many fled with him and began their own village, and soon we began to hear from the humans, of babies dying in their sleep, but we knew what was really happening. We decided it had to stop. The historians left and said they would not be part of this as they were only there to keep history as it is. The witches said they would not take lives. They were here to heal the lives and lands. So, they too went their own ways. That left the incubus and succubus and they soon became divided because they each thought their blood lines were more important than the other. And there you have the dividing of the clans." He took a drink of water and wiped the sweat off his brow.

"So, it all came down to who thought they should live? What happened how did we decide to try to reunite the clans? Why would my father ever bargain me away to someone like Jargoan?" I asked not understanding anything he just said.

"This war went on for centuries. When your mother and father met it was, let's say, not a 'normal' union. The succubus clan did not approve at first because of your mother's bloodline. She was from another high family, which were not necessarily seen as strong match. Your father fell in love with your mother, and he loved her with such passion, and she loved him all the same. They were a force to be reckoned with because your father was a direct descendant from the clan's leaders. You, Nali, are a true highborn. Making you more powerful and useful than anyone realized. Until Jargoan killed his father, that is."

I was having a hard time grasping all this information. It was beginning to make my head dizzy. "Is that why Jargoan wanted me so bad? He wanted to drain me so he could have power?"

"I cannot speak for him, only he knows his own mind and intentions. I do know that once he seen you, he became fearless, and reckless. He was always arguing with his parents telling them he must have you. No one understood what his obsession was. Then, one day we got word of him killing his father over an arranged marriage between him and an incubus woman to try to mend the clans. Jargoan's father was tired of the death. He remembered a time when they gave life, and he yearned for that day again. But Jargoan did not want any part of that; He only wanted power. So, he took it, by killing his father and his mother and his siblings. He made sure that he was the only one in line for his throne. No one stood a chance against him, and everyone was afraid to try. So, when he came to your father with a proposal of marriage to you to mend your clans, your mother was furious! She said she would die before she allowed that to happen, but your father begged her for this peace. Reluctantly after months of persuasion your mother agreed." He paused to breathe.

I took this time to ask, "so my mother did not want me to marry him, but my father was too much of a coward to fight? And I was just what, a piece on a chess board to placate the gods? I was used as a power play! They had to know about me and Dayvan, they had to know how I felt about him and him me." I was furious at the thought.

"Yes, they did know about you and Dayvan, but your dad was being forced unknowingly to anyone with the threat of death to his clan if he did not accept this offer. So, you see, he had no choice in his eyes. And when you left, well you know what happened." He said with sympathy in his voice.

"I killed them all. Why didn't my father tell me this? Maybe I would have made a different decision." I said between tears."

"He would have killed them anyways, Nali." Dayvan said as he rubbed his thumb over my hand.

"We do not know that Dayvan! We don't know that for sure. What if we caused the death of all our people and for what? Just to keep fucking hiding!" I was getting madder by the second.

"You must calm down, Nali. For the babies." Jeremy said. Trying to hold my hand.

But I jumped up and screamed at them, "Quit telling me what to fucking do like I'm a child." Then the realization hit me. And I looked at Jimmy, and asked, "How old am I?"

Jimmy looked at me like I should know and was confused by my question. "Is this a trick question?"

I looked dead in his eyes and said, "Tell me."

"Nali, you are 407 years old." You were two hundred years old when you and Dayvan ran away the first time." I turned and looked at Dayvan, he looked as pale as I felt. I then turned back to Jimmy.

"You said there has not been any babies born in a hundred years? Is that correct?" I was feeling very confused.

"Yes, that's correct." So, I had my babies after me and Dayvan left. You are telling me that was two hundred years ago?" The room was starting to spin.

Jeremy came up beside me and said "this cannot be right. We have not been gone for two hundred years. Jimmy, are you sure you are correct on your timeline?" he asked.

"No, you have only been gone 100 years because, there's a 100-year lapse where Nali wasn't accounted for until she was rescued from the camp." Jimmy said, looking confused. "Do you guys not remember?"

"It seems like we are all are having memory lapses of some sort and memory distortion." Jeremy stated.

"This would certainly explain why the confusion I see on all of your faces. Do you know caused it?"

Dayvon answered him saying, "well we have a theory about the wraiths being able to manipulate memories to bring the most painful ones, or to create them if not present, so they can feed from them."

Jimmy looked as if he was thinking of something. "You might be right. I do remember that there was a time when the wraiths would devour painful memories, to rid the person of the pain. So, it could be possible they figured out a way to create them as well."

The room was beginning to spin a little faster. "I need to sit down, I'm not feeling well." Jeremy turned me toward the couch. Everyone jumped up to come to my aid.

"We need to take a break guys. This is stressing her out too much." Sarah said.

Dayvan and Jeremy went to get me some water and a cold washcloth and some ginger tea. Stormy came over and draped a blanket over me. I was starting to feel a little better. Sarah and Jimmy were talking about something I could not hear.

The guys came back into the room when they got in the door. I felt a warm sensation as if I have peed my pants.

"Guys, I just peed my pants. I am so sorry. I don't know how that happened." I say very embarrassed. I could feel getting red from the embarrassment.

Sarah looks up and quickly walks up to me, yanks the blanket off my lap. Her face went pale and she looks up at Dayvan and Jeremy and says, "um, guys, she didn't pee herself, her water has broken."

CHAPTER 16

The room erupted in sheer panic as everyone was scrambling around figuring out what to do. Sarah shouted, "Stop! Everyone calm down! Dayvan, Jeremy you two carry Nali down to the medical room. Jimmy you and Stormy make sure all the windows and the doors are locked, then get some towels and come down to the medical room." She sounded like a drill sergeant barking orders.

The guys picked me up and I could feel water leaking out of me and it felt so nasty. The guys hurried as fast as they could while carrying a whale. I felt like someone had a tight belt around my waist and it was getting tighter. "Sarah, my stomach feels so tight, is this normal? Are the babies all right?"

"We will look at the ultrasound when we get downstairs to see which position they are all in. As long as the first one is head down, we should be fine to deliver the other two just fine." She said hastily.

I could feel my nerves kicking in, this was really happening, these babies are really coming. "It is too early! They are coming to soon." I was scared.

"These things happen especially when there are twins so with triplets it could certainly happen, we have everything we need here. Try not to worry." She said with as much of a reassuring smile as she could.

"Here, lay back here." Dayvan said as he and Jeremy laid me down on the bed. The pains were coming faster now, and they were getting stronger. I wanted to get my clothes off, they all felt too tight.

"I need to start and IV in case I need to give you fluids." She started helping me get my clothes off and she started an IV and hung a bag of fluids.

I felt like more water came out, and it grossed me out so much. I just wanted to be dry. "Can we dry me off please." I had a weird thing about getting wet.

Sarah takes the ultrasound machine and starts looking for the babies, and their positions. "Here Boy one is head down so we should be ok." She said with relief in her voice.

"Oh, I have not even picked out names yet! I am going to be a horrible mother! I was crying, how could I have not picked out names? What mother does that?" I was starting to panic. I felt as if I could not breathe, everything was happening so fast. Like the world shifted.

"You are going to be a great mother. We have had so many things happen, how could you think of names? Just relax love." Jeremy said.

"Fuck off!" I said as another pain struck me. It felt like my stomach had the worst Charlie horse ever. I was getting agitated. "I am sorry Jeremy, I did not mean it. I love you."

"I know you are hurting, if we could take this pain from you we would." Jeremy stated.

Him and Dayvan were on each side of me. I felt a little better. Stormy and Jimmy came into the room. "Here are the towels you wanted." Stormy said. She turned a little green as she said, "Ewe all the water, does it feel nasty."

She was trying to look around curiously which was pissing me off. This was not the time to be curious about anything. "Don't look at me!" I yelled.

Stormy said she was sorry and I could tell I had hurt her feelings.

"I am so sorry guys, I'm not sure what. Oh, FUCK ME that hurts so fucking bad! Is it supposed to hurt this bad?"

"Yes, it will get worse as the babes get closer to coming out." Sarah said.

"What? Worse? Oh fuck, I don't think I can do this! No, I am not doing this!" I yelled as I attempted to get up as another contraction hit me. I closed my legs and tried climbing off the table, not knowing where I was going. But The guys stopped me.

"I am so excited, I get to see history written here. I cannot remember triplets ever being born. You are truly special Nali." Jimmy said.

"FUCK OFF, Jimmy! This is NOT the fucking time to get excited! Do I look like a fucking history lesson? You can get out!" I screamed as the pain seemed to be getting worse.

"Nali, breathe in slow, count with me, One, two, three, four." Jeremy was counting.

I looked at him like he had two heads. Was he seriously trying to treat me like I was having a panic attack right now? Jeremy must have seen my thoughts on my face.

"Nali, it will help if you breathe. It will get oxygen to the babes and keep you from getting so nauseous. This is such a special time, Nali" he said with a calming smile.

I wondered how he did that, staying so calm during crises.

I screamed as the pain tore through my stomach; this was different from the other pains. This was stronger. I squeezed both of my guys' hands and tried to breathe. "I don't feel very fucking special right now!" I was hot, "is it hot in here?"

"It's the pain dear, just breathe." Sarah said. Stormy was helping her get things ready for when our little babies made their appearance.

I took slow deep breaths between the contractions; the guys were wiping the sweat and tears off my face. "Can I get some water?"

"No, but you can get some Ice chips that way you won't get sick." Sarah said.

The pains went on for what seemed like days, but Sarah reassured me that it had only been an hour and a half. Time was moving slowly; pain is a funny thing that way.

Another Pain tore through me and I felt a burning feeling down through my groins. "Sarah what is happening? I'm burning, oh God it hurts so bad, I feel like I need to push." I could feel a shift in the babies' energy, something was wrong. "Sarah! Something is wrong I can feel the baby, he is hurting!" I screamed. I still felt the need to push.

Sarah looked under the sheet and told me to place my feet in the stirrups, "That's because the first baby is crowning." Just as she said that there was a crash from upstairs. Jeremy and Dayvon look toward the stairs and down walks Jargoan.

My heart felt like it stopped, I was helpless, he was going to kill my babies, and I could do nothing to stop it. I started crying. And another pain tore through me. Jeremy and Dayvan ran to the door, and all of a sudden Jimmy is gone. Sarah and Stormy are talking to me trying to get me to breathe and not push.

Sarah says, "Baby one is crowning all the way, but the cord is wrapped around his neck, Nali, I need you to not push, I have to get the cord off his neck."

I could feel her touching and the pain was more than I ever had felt. I did not think I could take any more pain this was like having your lady bits mauled by a tiger. I could hear the men fighting, I looked over and they had Jargoan stopped outside the door. They were fighting to keep him from getting into the room. Jeremy was bleeding and I cried out as another pain tore through me.

Sarah then snapped at me, "Nali! Push now!" I grabbed my knees and pushed as hard as I could and it felt like jelly coming out of me. Next thing I hear is Dayvan being thrown through the door, falling still on the ground not moving. My heart drops! I cannot see him breathing.

"Dayvan! Answer me Dayvan please answer me!" I screamed. There was a long deep breath that left him just as the baby cried his first breath.

Tears streamed down my face, my heart felt like it was being ripped out of my chest. Dayvan was gone, the man I loved would not touch me every again. He would never say he loved me. He would never get to see the babies. He would not be around to help raise them.

I could not do this. I screamed out my anger! I was in so much pain, from having the babies and seeing one of the men I loved laying lifeless on the floor. So much pain that the sounds of baby were very distant.

"Nali, breathe, focus on the babies, don't look at him, remember the babies!" Sarah pled with me.

Then I remember Jeremy was still fighting. I could hear the fight, and it sounded awful. I did not want my babies to come into the world into violence. The first thing they were going to know was violence.

The sounds of the fight were too much, "I cannot do this Sarah, I can't. I do not want to. I just can't." I screamed.

"Yes, you can and you will Nali, you hear me? You have to for these babies. Do not give up. These babies need you! Now fucking straighten up! Sarah yelled with urgency.

Pain ripped through me again. Sarah handed the baby to Stormy, and she began cleaning it. I could hear his cries. He sounded so mad at the world. I could not blame him, look at what I had brought him into. I would be pissed too little man.

The pain was getting worse, it felt like this one was tearing me in two. Sarah told me to push with the contractions. This baby was a little higher so it would take a little longer to have him. She was pressing on my stomach with the contractions.

"What the fuck are you doing that for? It hurts so bad!" I screamed.

"It's to help move the babe down." Sarah replied.

As I lay there breathing and pushing through contractions, I could not take my eyes off my love, laying lifeless on the floor. I could not help but say prayers for Jeremy who was still fighting. I hated Jargoan more now than ever! I wanted him dead. I knew Jeremy would not let him get our babies.

Suddenly Jeremy and Jargoan crash through wall beside the door, both covered in blood, whose blood was whose, was impossible to tell. I screamed out of fear for Jeremy's life. Another contraction came and I pushed as Sarah had instructed. I could not think about anything but the fight that was happening right before my eyes. Jargoan hit Jeremy in the chest with his fist, and Jeremy hit him back in the face.

They threw blows wrapped with energy for power. It seemed as if Jargoan was feeding from the pain of the labor pains. He seemed to get stronger with every pain. He was hitting Jeremy over and over. Jeremy caught his arm and hit him in the ribs I could hear his air whoosh out. I thought Jeremy had knocked him out, but he swung and hit Jeremy right on the side of the head.

Suddenly, the pain disappeared and I could feel the second baby coming. I was not sure why the pain went away but I did not have time to think about that right now because this little one was coming and there was nothing stopping him.

Sarah says she can see his head and for me to keep pushing. I looked over and it looked like Jeremy was winning this battle. That allowed me to relax into the labor a little.

"One last push Nali!" Sarah said. I grabbed my knees and pushed, and I could feel him slide out of me. It felt different than the first. Suddenly, as soon as the second baby was born, all the pain rushed back in tenfold.

It was more that I could handle, and I threw up from the sudden return of it. I could hear the baby crying as Stormy cleaned it, he, too sounded pissed off.

"Is he ok?" I asked, "Are they both ok?" I needed to know.

"Yes, they are healthy baby boys, Nali, you are doing great. Just breathe." Sarah said.

Once the pain came back, this fueled Jargoan, no, almost gave him a huge boost of energy he grabbed Jeremy and slammed him against the wall, there was a sickening sound we all knew something was broken. He falls to the ground, not moving.

"JEREMY!!!" I screamed. I could feel my heart break again. Every part of my being felt like it was being shredded with grief. "No, no, no, this cannot be happening! Jeremy get up! Get the FUCK up!" but no matter how much I screamed he did not move.

Jargoan stood there breathing heavily from the battle.

Sarah told Stormy to help me deliver the third baby while she goes and fights to keep Jargoan away from me and the babies.

"No Sarah don't go!" But Jargoan was already halfway across the room and Sarah ran to meet him.

The pain ripped through me, and I was helpless as the pain gripped me. This one was different. Something was wrong. "Stormy, something is wrong. Oh fuck! This hurts so much!" I am not sure if it was because I had two babies already or if it was labor mixed with the grief, but I felt like my body was being ripped apart.

Stormy replied, "It's ok, this is normal, pain is normal in childbirth. Just breath."

I felt like the pain was going to kill me. My entire body was screaming with pain. I swear I could feel every cell of my body shredding apart. The pain was so bad. I felt like she was crowning. "I need to push! Please tell me she's crowning." I needed this to be over, I felt like I was going to die from the pain.

"She's crowning, just a few more pushes Nali, you can do this." Stormy says.

Each painful push felt like an eternity, the pain seemed never ending, there were no breaks between the contractions, the pain just never went away. Until suddenly relief as her head was born.

"don't push, I have to get the cord from around her neck." Stormy said. "Ok, now push!"

With one last push I felt her come all the way out but couldn't hear her breathing or crying.

"Is she breathing?" I waited for what seemed to be forever as I watched stormy work on her, rubbing her back, and giving her breaths. I cried out because I could not bear losing another person today. I watched in horror waiting to hear my little girl cry. Pleading to whatever God would hear me.

"Please Stormy, save my baby. Please!" I screamed.

I could hear Sarah fighting Jargoan, he was injured by the guys and Sarah was doing a decent job injuring him more. They were going blow for blow. She must have trained with the buys.

I looked at my baby to see if she was breathing yet, but Stormy was still working on her. She was so blue. I was crying and could barely see through the tears.

I heard Sarah scream the most horrible scream, I looked over and his hand was in her chest. He pulled back and held her heart in his hand. Just then the baby cried for the first time as Sarah took her final breath.

Seeing all my lovers dead around me, I feel something snap inside of me and suddenly I was a little girl sitting in a warm cottage, I had never seen before.

"Nali, hand me that flower there. Do you know what this is called?" My grandmother asked me.

"Lavender, it's my favorite." I smiled.

"You are right, and it is a good flower, Nali. Have you been practicing the rhyme I taught you?"

"Yes grandmother, I have but the words are so hard." I answered.

"Well Latin isn't supposed to be easy, little one." She says with a smile.

I want to make grandmother proud, so, I say the rhyme for her.

"Sine me celare quod in sanguine meo est ut me protegas donec tempus opportunum advenerit." I said proudly, holding my chin high.

Grandmother said, "Very good little one,

Now when the time is right little one, repeat with me.

Permitte Mihi Ut Tempore Necessitatis Mear Recuperem quod olim clausum erat."

I heard the words come out of my mouth without realizing I was speaking. Suddenly, the necklace that Sereena gave me starts glowing and my head feels like it is splitting in two, as memories come rushing back with the force of a thousand waves.

I feel this energy welling inside of me as I remember how to use my powers. I see Jargoan approaching where I was. I know I must kill him. I take every ounce of painful memories Jargoan has inflicted upon me and my family and force it into his mind and his body.

I see him stumble and I know I must push more, so I dig deeper, and take the pain and suffering of every clan member and shove it into him. This overwhelms him, his eyes go blank, I watch as his mind shatters. Suddenly his appearance changes, and it's like I am staring at a male version of myself mixed with a version of Jargoan. I was confused for a second, then I glimpsed his eyes and a memory rushes back of me holding a baby boy, with those eyes. It is now I realize, I have not killed Jargoan, but as this man's heart stops, I realize it is our son.

I watch his body fall to the floor; The pain intensifies as the memories rush back. The room sways as I have almost drained all my energy and I, too, am falling to the ground. As if underwater, I can hear what sounds like

Stormy calling out to me, screaming my name. As a figure all too familiar walks in the room.

"Jargoan" I whispered. "Why? Why do you do these things? How could you let your, our son come in your place?"

He looked at me unsympathetically and said, "Children are replaceable, what is another malleable mind I can mold" as he reaches for one of the babies.

I lifted my hand out trying to get to the babe, and to stop him. He laughs as he looks at my broken body and walks out the door.

Silence filled the room and my dearest friend returned and wrapped me with its cold dark fingers. I gave into the abyss of darkness and silence because that is all I could do.